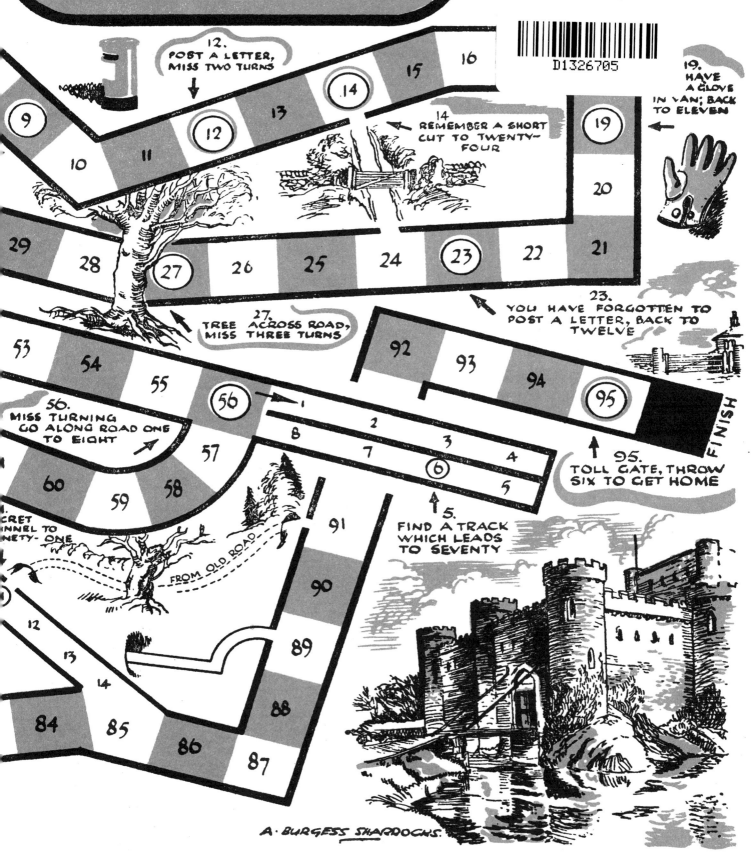

THE WAY TO THE CASTLE
a 'SECRET SEVEN' GAME

D1326705

12. POST A LETTER, MISS TWO TURNS

14 REMEMBER A SHORT CUT TO TWENTY-FOUR

19. HAVE A GLOVE IN VAN; BACK TO ELEVEN

23. YOU HAVE FORGOTTEN TO POST A LETTER, BACK TO TWELVE

27. TREE ACROSS ROAD, MISS THREE TURNS

56. MISS TURNING GO ALONG ROAD ONE TO EIGHT

SECRET TUNNEL TO NINETY-ONE

FROM OLD ROAD

5. FIND A TRACK WHICH LEADS TO SEVENTY

95. TOLL GATE, THROW SIX TO GET HOME

FINISH

A. BURGESS SHARROCKS.

Enid Blyton's

ADVENTURE TREASURY

Enid Blyton's

ADVENTURE TREASURY

COMPILED BY

MARY CADOGAN
&
NORMAN WRIGHT

Hodder
Children's
Books

First published in Great Britain in 1999
by Hodder Children's Books

10 9 8 7 6 5 4 3 2 1

For further information on Enid Blyton, please contact www.blyton.com

A Catalogue record for this book is available from the British Library

ISBN 0 340 76513 5

Printed and bound in Italy by Rotolito Lombarda

Hodder Children's Books
a division of Hodder Headline
338 Euston Road
London NW1 3BH

CONTENTS

Foreword
Introduction

THE SECRET CAVE (1929) ···1
THE HIDEY-HOLE (1932) ···10
THE SECRET ISLAND (1938) – an extract ·····················17
THE TREASURE HUNTERS (1940) – an extract ·············29
THE SECRET OF SPIGGY HOLES (1940) – an extract ·····47
FIVE ON A TREASURE ISLAND (1942) – an extract ········65
THE SECRET OF CLIFF CASTLE (1943) – an extract ······77
SMUGGLER BEN (1943) ···86
FIVE GO ADVENTURING AGAIN (1943) – an extract ····138
THE ISLAND OF ADVENTURE (1944) – an extract ········150
THE MYSTERY OF THE SECRET ROOM (1945) – an extract ·····161
A NIGHT ON THUNDER ROCK (1947) ························177
SMUGGLERS' CAVE (1947) ··186
THE VALLEY OF ADVENTURE (1947) – an extract ········194
NUMBER SIXTY-TWO (1947) ···206
THE CASE OF THE FIVE DOGS (1947) ···························214
FIVE GO OFF TO CAMP (1948) – an extract ·················223
THE RILLOBY FAIR MYSTERY (1950) – an extract ·········229
OFF WITH THE ADVENTUROUS FOUR AGAIN (1951) ·····240
SECRET SEVEN ON THE TRAIL (1952) – an extract ········262
THE RUBADUB MYSTERY (1952) – an extract ···············272
FIVE GO DOWN TO THE SEA (1953) – an extract ··········285
GOOD WORK, SECRET SEVEN (1954) – an extract ·········304
THE ADVENTURE OF THE SECRET NECKLACE (1954) – an extract·317
SECRET SEVEN WIN THROUGH (1955) – an extract ·······326
JUST A SPOT OF BOTHER! (1957) ··································338
THE FIVE FIND-OUTERS AND
DOG TACKLE THE MYSTERY SNEAK THIEF (1962) ·········354
A HAPPY ENDING – a poem ··367
AFTERWORD – a poem ···368

A Memoir of Enid Blyton ···370

FOREWORD

BY
HELEN CRESSWELL

You don't know how lucky you are. You are about to enter the magical world of Enid Blyton, and have adventures beyond your wildest dreams. (Would the grown-ups *you* know let you go exploring caves, or spend nights under the stars on a secet island?)

At your age I devoured every Enid Blyton story I could lay my hands on. They took me into worlds that were light-years away from my own dull suburban life, where the only excitement was a game of hopscotch on the quiet, tree-lined streets, or perhaps a trip to the park. There was no chance for me of adventures among lashing seas, lighthouses, castles and dungeons, with hidden treasure, secret tunnels, camp-fires and midnight feasts. I envied those daring Famous Five, who were allowed by their grown-ups to go wherever they pleased to foil kidnappers, blackmailers, smugglers, desperate men with guns. And I envy you, now, because you have all that excitement to come. All you have to do is carry on reading.

Every writer is born from a reader, but I as a writer owe something special to Enid Blyton. When I was a child I read the *Beano* and *Dandy* (and *Hotspur* and *Wizard*) and every week I also had *Sunny Stories*. It was here that I met *The Faraway Tree* and *The Wishing Chair*. It was also, and this is the important bit, where I met Enid Blyton herself.

At the front of each issue of *Sunny Stories* was a letter from her, with her address at the top: Green Hedges. In it she told us about her life, her pets, her children Gillian and Imogen. I seemed to know them so well that they were almost part of my family.

What is more, this letter made me realise for the first time the amazing fact that writers were real people, that they were actually alive, and led real lives. Up to then I had thought all writers – Hans Christian Andersen, Arthur Ransome, Thomas Hardy – were some fabulous, other-worldly beings – something I could never myself be (though it was what I had always secretly dreamed of.)

That weekly letter from the pen of Enid Blyton seemed to say to me personally, "Dear Helen, here I sit at my desk writing stories and, one day, if you want to, that is what you can do, too."

And so I did. Though I'm afraid my stories have never been read by so many millions of children.

Carry on reading. You don't know how lucky you are...

INTRODUCTION

We feel sure that you will enjoy reading the stories in *The Enid Blyton Adventure Treasury* as much as we have enjoyed choosing them.

Enid Blyton always enjoyed writing stories and in 1926 began contributing all the stories for a little magazine entitled *Sunny Stories*. At first these were mainly fairy and animal tales but gradually she began to include a sprinkling of adventure stories. In 1937, when her first long adventure story, *The Secret Island*, was serialised in *Sunny Stories*, it was so popular with readers that they immediately demanded another tale featuring the same characters. Soon afterwards she created other characters and series for her adventure- and mystery-loving readers. These became so popular that she continued to write about them until her death in 1968.

All the familiar adventure and mystery series are represented in this Treasury: *The Famous Five, Secret Seven, Adventure* series, Barney books, *Secret* series, *Mystery* series, *The Adventurous Four* and the *Five Find-Outers*. We have chosen stories and extracts spanning almost the whole of Enid Blyton's writing life, and the adventures appear here in the order in which they were originally written. You will meet again many of your favourite characters from these series, such as George and Julian; Fatty and Bets; Lucy-Ann and Philip; Colin and Barbara; Mike, Nora and Peggy, and others too. Not forgetting some of Blyton's popular animal characters — dogs like Timmy, Buster and Scamp; Miranda the mischievous monkey, and Kiki, whose vivid phrases will stay in your memory. You will also meet some of the 'baddies' the children have to tackle: kidnappers, smugglers — even foreign agents!

As well as stories and characters which will be familiar, you will be meeting new friends and making intriguing discoveries.

We have included many of the splendid illustrations that were drawn for the stories when they were first published, and we know that these will increase your enjoyment of reading these adventures.

The colourful centre sections of the Treasury give you a taste of some of the exciting covers used over the years, as well as some of the games and puzzles based on your favourite characters.

But remember that it is also an adventure to *read*. If it is too cold or wet for you to have a real adventure out of doors, you can, through the pages of this book, let your imagination take you into Blyton's golden sunshiny world where you can join your heroes and heroines as they camp on tree-clad islands, explore secret passages or search for buried treasure. You may be on moors or mountains, lakes or islands, but the weather will be fine, the sea just right for swimming, and ice-creams will be at hand!

So now, without any more words from us, it is time for you to turn the page and enter Enid Blyton's world of adventure stories, where excitement and mystery await you...

MARY CADOGAN and NORMAN WRIGHT

THE SECRET CAVE

∽ ILLUSTRATED BY ∽
PAT HARRISON

*This is a very early Enid Blyton adventure story,
first published in 1929. It tells of the adventure
three children have while exploring an overgrown garden.*

The adventure of the secret cave really began on the day when we all went out on the cliff to fly our new kite. I am Roger, and Joan and William are my sister and brother. William's the eldest, and Joan and I are twins. We live in a house near the sea, but it is very lonely because there is no other house anywhere near us, except the big house on the cliff, and that is empty. We often wished it was full of children so that we could play with them,

but as it wasn't we had to be content to play by ourselves.

Mummy and Daddy were going away for a month on a sea-trip, and they were leaving that very day. We were all feeling very sad about it, because home is a funny sort of place without Mummy. But it was holiday time, and our governess had gone, so there was only old Sarah to look after us, and we thought we'd have quite a good time really.

Mummy gave us a glorious new kite just as she said goodbye, and told us to go and fly it as soon as they had gone; then we shouldn't feel so bad about everything. So when the car had disappeared down the hill, we took our new kite and went out on the windy cliff.

William soon got it up in the air, and it flew like a bird. But suddenly the wind dropped and the kite gave a great dip downwards. William pulled hard at it, but it wasn't any good. Down and down it went, and at last disappeared behind some trees.

"Bother!" we said. "Let's go and look for it."

We raced over the cliff till we came to the clump of stunted trees behind which our kite had gone. Then we found that the string disappeared over the high wall that surrounded the big house on the cliff.

"The kite must have fallen in the garden," said William. "What shall we do?"

"Go and knock at the front door and ask for it," said Joan. "There might be a caretaker there."

So we ran round to the front gate and went up the long drive. We soon came to the front door. It was a big wooden one with a large knocker. William knocked hard and we heard the sound go echoing through the house.

Nobody came, so we each of us knocked in turn, very loudly indeed. After we had waited for about five minutes without anyone opening the door, we decided that the house must be quite empty, without a caretaker or anyone at all.

"Well, how are we to get our kite?" I asked.

"The only thing to do is to climb over the wall," said William. "We can't ask anyone's permission because there isn't anyone to ask. Come on. We can't lose our lovely kite."

So we ran down the drive again and made our way to the back of the garden wall, which stood high above our heads. William managed to climb up it first, and then jumped down on the other side.

"Come on, you others," he called. "It's all right. Oh, wait a minute, though. I've got an idea. Stand away from the wall, both of you. I've found a box here, and I'm going to throw it over. You can stand on it, and then you will easily be able to climb up the wall."

William threw over the box. Then we stood on it and just managed to reach the top. We jumped down, and there we all were in the deserted garden of the house on the cliff.

It was a very wild place, for no one had bothered about it for years.

Everything was overgrown, and the paths were covered with green moss that was like velvet to walk on. I don't know why, but we felt at first as if we ought to talk in whispers.

"Where's our kite?" said Joan. "Look, William, there's the string. Let's follow it and we shall soon find the kite."

So we followed the string, and it led us over a stretch of long grass that had once been a big lawn, down a thick shrubbery, and past some greenhouses whose glass was all broken.

"There it is!" William said, and he pointed to where a little shed stood hidden away in a dark corner. We all looked at it, and, sure enough, there was the kite perched up on the roof. It didn't take us long to pull it down, but we found that one of the sticks that ran across it was broken, so we couldn't fly it any more that day. We were sorry about that, and wondered what we should do for the rest of the morning.

"Why can't we stay here and explore the garden?" asked Joan. "We shouldn't do any harm, and it would be great fun."

"All right, we will," said William, who always decides everything because he is the eldest.

So we began exploring, and it really was fun. Then it suddenly began to rain, and as none of us had our mackintoshes with us we got wet.

"We must shelter somewhere," said William. "Sarah will be very cross if we go home soaked through."

"Well, what about that little shed, where we found the kite?" I asked. "That would do nicely."

So we raced to the shed, but the door was locked, so we couldn't get in.

"How about a window?" cried Joan. "Here's one with the latch broken. Push it, William. Oh, good, it's open and we can climb in. What an adventure we're having!"

We all climbed in. I went to the door, and what do you think? The key was inside!

"Well, if that isn't a curious thing," said William, looking at it. "If you lock a door from the inside you usually lock yourself in too. But there's nobody here. It's a mystery!"

But we soon forgot about the key in our excitement over the shed. It really was a lovely little place. There was a funny old chair with a crooked leg that William felt sure he could mend if he had his tools. There was a battered old table

3

in one corner, and two small stools, one with a leg off. Along one side of the shed was a shelf, which was very dusty and dirty.

"I say! Wouldn't this shed make a perfectly lovely little house for us to play in on rainy days?" said William suddenly. "We could clean it up and mend the stool and chair."

"Oh, William, do let's!" said Joan, clapping her hands in delight. "I've got some pretty orange stuff Mummy gave me, and I can make it into little curtains for the two windows. We can bring a pail and a scrubbing-brush and clean the whole place up beautifully."

"And we can use the shelf for storing things on," I said. "We can bring apples and biscuits here, and some of our books to read. Oh, what fun! But we must keep it a secret, or perhaps Sarah would stop us."

"Well, we mustn't do any harm anywhere," said William. "After all, it isn't our shed, but I'm sure if the man who owns it, whoever he is, knew that we were going to clean it up and make it nice, he would only be too glad to let us. Now, the rain's stopped – we must run home or we shall be late for dinner."

We took our broken kite and raced home. We didn't need to climb over the wall again, because we found a dear little door in the wall with the key inside. So we opened the door, slipped out, locked it again, and William took the key away in his pocket in case tramps found it.

We were so excited at dinner-time that Sarah got cross with us and threatened to send us to bed half an hour earlier if we didn't eat our food properly. At last dinner was over and we ran out into our own garden to decide what we should take to the house on the cliff.

"Let's borrow the gardener's barrow," said William. "We can put heaps of things in that and wheel it easily."

So we got the barrow and piled the things into it. Joan found the orange stuff and put that in, and popped her work-basket in too. I found a very old carpet that nobody used in the attic, and I put that in. William took his tools, and we went and asked Cook if she could give us anything to eat.

She was very nice, and gave us three slices of cake, a bottle of lemonade, and a bag of raisins. Then we had a great stroke of luck, because the gardener told us we could pick the apples off one of the trees and keep them for ourselves.

You can guess we had soon picked about fifty or sixty and put them into a basket. That went into the barrow too, and then it really was almost as much as we could manage to wheel it along.

"We can easily come back for our books and anything else we can think of," said William. So off we went, all helping to push. At last we came to the little door in the wall and William unlocked it. We went through the garden until we came to our dear little shed.

"Oh, we ought to have brought something to clean it up with," said Joan. "Never mind, William. Empty these things out on to a newspaper in the corner, and we'll go back for a pail and a scrubbing-brush and soap."

Back we went, and at last after two or three more journeys we really had got everything we could think of that day. Then we had a lovely time cleaning up the shed. The floor was laid with big white flagstones, and they looked lovely when we had scrubbed them clean. We washed the shelf and all the bits of furniture too, and soon the shed looked fine.

That was all we had time to do that day, but early the next morning we were back again, as you can guess. Joan made the little curtains and tied them back with a piece of old hair-ribbon. They did look nice. William and I mended the stool and the chair and arranged the things we had brought.

Cook had given us half a jar of strawberry jam and a pot of honey, and we had bought some biscuits and nuts. Our books went up on the shelf, and the apples stood in a corner in their basket.

"Well, it really looks quite homey," said Joan, jumping round the shed joyfully. "What fun we shall have here. Don't my little curtains look nice, and isn't the carpet fine? Our feet would have been very cold on those bare flagstones."

Well, I can't tell you how we enjoyed our time in that little shed. Every day that it rained we went there, and as it was a very wet summer we spent most of our time there. We ate our biscuits and apples, read our books and did puzzles, and Sarah thought we were as good as gold, though she didn't know at all where we went every day. She thought we were down by the sea, I think.

But the most exciting part of our adventure hadn't come yet. I must tell you about it now.

We had been using the shed for about three weeks when William lost a sixpence. It rolled on to the floor and disappeared. We turned back the carpet to look for it.

"There's a flagstone here that seems rather loose," said William. "Perhaps the sixpence has gone down the crack."

"It *is* loose!" said Joan. "Why, I can almost lift it!"

"I believe we *could* lift it," said William. We slipped a thin iron bar in one of the cracks, and then suddenly the stone rose up! It came quite easily, and stood upright, balanced on one side.

And where it had been was a big black hole, with stone steps leading downwards!

What do you think of that? We were all so astonished that we simply kneeled there and stared and stared.

"Why, it's a secret passage!" said William at last. "What about exploring it?"

"Do you think it's safe?" asked Joan.

"Oh, I should think so," said William. "We can take our torches with us. This passage explains the key left inside the door. Someone must have gone to this shed, locked it from the inside, and then gone down the passage somewhere. It must lead out to some place or other. Oh, what an adventure!"

We got our torches from the shelf, and then, with William leading, we all climbed down the steps. They soon ended and we found ourselves in a narrow passage that led downwards fairly steeply.

"Do you know, I believe this passage leads to the sea-shore," said William suddenly. "I think it is going right through the cliff, and will come out to one of those rocky caves we have sometimes seen from a boat."

And we found that William was right. For the passage, always sloping downwards, suddenly opened out into a small dark cave. William couldn't see at first whether or not there was any way out of it besides the way we had come, and then he suddenly found it! It was just a small opening, low down at one end, so small that a man would have found it

6

quite difficult to squeeze through.

We squeezed through easily enough, of course, and then we found ourselves in a very big wide cave, lit by daylight. The thunder of breaking waves seemed very near, and as we made our way to the big opening where the daylight streamed through we saw the rough sea just outside it.

"You were right, William," I said. "That passage from our shed led right through the cliff down to this cave that is open to the sea. Look! When we stand on this ledge the waves almost reach our feet. I shouldn't be surprised if in very rough weather the sea washes right into the cave."

"I don't think so," said William, turning round to look. "You see, the floor slopes upwards fairly steeply. Oh my! Just look there!"

We turned to see what he was exclaiming at, and what do you think? The floor of the cave was strewn with boxes of all sizes and shapes!

"Why, perhaps it's a smugglers' cave!" we cried. We rushed to the boxes, but all except two were locked fast. In the two unlocked ones were many clothes – very old-fashioned ones they were, too.

"Well, this is a find!" said William. "I say, what about dressing up in these clothes and giving Sarah a surprise?"

We thought that would be lovely, so we quickly turned out the clothes and found some to fit us. Joan had a lovely frock right down to her ankles, and I had a funny little tunic sort of suit, and so did William. We put them on in the little shed because it was lighter there.

"Now, are we all ready?" said William. "Well, come along then. We'll give Sarah the surprise of her life, and then we'll take her and the gardener to see our wonderful find."

We danced through the door of the shed – and oh, my gracious goodness, didn't we get a shock?

Two gentlemen were walking up the moss-grown path by the shed! They saw us just at the same moment as we saw them, and we all stopped quite still and stared at one another.

One of the gentlemen looked as if he simply couldn't believe his eyes. He took off his glasses and cleaned them, and then he put them on again. But we were still there, and at last he spoke to us.

"Am I dreaming – or am I back in the days of long ago?" he said. "Are you children of nowadays, or little long-ago ghosts?"

"We're quite real," said William. "We're only dressed up."

"Well, that's a relief," said the man. "But what are you doing here? This garden belongs to my house."

"Oh, are you the man who owns the house?" asked William.

"Yes," he answered, "and this gentleman is perhaps going to buy it from me. I'm too poor to keep it as it should be kept, you see. But you still haven't told me what you are doing here."

Well, of course, we had to confess everything then. We told him how we had found the dear little shed by accident, and made it a sort of a home. And then we told him of our great find that afternoon.

"What!" he cried. "Do you really mean to say you've found the secret passage to the cave? Why, it's been lost for years and years, and no one knew the secret. I lived here when I was a boy, but I never found it either, though I looked everywhere."

Of course we had to show him the way down to the cave, and when he saw the boxes lying there he turned so pale that Joan asked him if he was going to faint.

"No," he said. "But I'm going to tell you a little story, and you will understand then why I feel rather peculiar."

And this is the story he told us.

"Many, many years ago," he began, "my family lived in France. There came a time when they were unjustly accused as traitors, and were forced to fly from the country. They packed up all their belongings and put them on board a ship to be brought to this country, where they had a house. This was the house. It had a secret passage from the shed to the sea, and the idea was to land at night with their belongings and go up through the passage unseen. They meant to live in the house until the trouble had blown over and they could go about here in safety, or return to France."

"And did they?" asked William.

"No. Just as all the luggage had been safely put on board and the family were saying goodbye to their friends on shore, some men came galloping up and took them prisoners. The ship hurriedly put off without them and sailed safely to this place. The luggage was dumped down in this cave and the ship went back towards France. But, so the story goes, a storm came, and the whole crew were drowned. As for the family, some died in prison, and none of them ever came back to this house except one. He had been a small boy at the time and had no idea where the secret passage was and, though he searched everywhere, he could not find it. So he gave it up and decided that all the family belongings were lost for ever."

"And are these what he was looking for?" I asked.

"They are," said the man. "And, thanks to you, they are found again. Well, well, what an excitement! Now perhaps I shan't have to sell my own house. I might even be able to come and live here again with my family."

"Have you got any children?" asked William.

"Yes, six," said the man.

Well, we all gave a shout at that! Fancy having six children near to play with, when you've never had any at all! It seemed too good to be true.

But it *was* true! Mr Carnot, for that was the man's name, found that the boxes *did* contain all his old family treasures and, by selling some, he had more than enough money to live at his old home once again with his family. I can tell you it was a most exciting day when they all arrived.

Daddy and Mummy could hardly believe all we had to tell them when they came home, but when Mr Carnot took them into our shed and down the passage to the cave, they soon knew it was true.

And now we have heaps of playmates. They are Billy, Anne, Marjorie, Jeanne, Laurence, and the baby. We often use the secret passage and sometimes we even row to the cave in a boat, just like the sailors did all those many years ago.

THE HIDEY-HOLE

~ ILLUSTRATED BY ~

CHRISTINA S. REED

*Two children search for hidden treasure in the hope
of saving their family home from being sold.*

Brian and Peggy lived in a very old house. It was called Old Priory and
their grandfather had lived there and his father before him. Daddy had
often told them about his grandfather, their great-grandfather; who had
lived there when he was as small as Brian and Peggy.

Great-grandfather's picture hung on the wall, and Daddy often said that Brian
was very like him.

"He used to be like you, Brian, always collecting things!" said Daddy,
laughing. "You collect butterflies, flowers and lots of other things, and your great-
grandfather collected things too. All those old swords on the wall there are part of
his collection — and those funny old mugs in that cabinet."

Brian and Peggy loved their old house. It had funny little up-and-down steps
from one room to another, the windows were all shapes, round, square or oblong,
and the fireplaces were enormous.

And then one day Daddy said they would have to sell Old Priory and move
to a smaller house!

"Oh, Daddy, why?" cried Brian and Peggy in dismay.

"Well, dears, times are very hard," said Daddy with a sigh. "I can't make
enough money to keep up this big old house. It is always needing something doing
to it. Soon you will both have to go to good schools and I must save up for that."

"Couldn't you wait for a few years till I grow up and earn money?" asked
Brian. "Then *I* could help to pay for the house, Daddy."

"I'm afraid I can't," said Daddy, smiling. "No, unless something unexpected
happens we must sell the house this autumn, Brian."

Mummy was just as sad as the children. She loved the funny old house
and lovely garden — but it wasn't a bit of use, they couldn't afford to live there
much longer.

Brian and Peggy made the most of that last summer. They couldn't bear to think that soon they would be living in another house, a new house with no exciting old corners, no old attics where cobwebs stretched over forgotten chests, and no lovely garden round it with the trees that their great-great-grandfather had planted – for *he* had lived there too!

Daddy bought a small house in a little town nearby. The children hated the look of it after their own friendly home. Peggy cried about it when she was in bed at night.

"I feel as if all my roots are being pulled up," she said to Brian. "We're like plants who have lived in one place all our lives and are being pulled up to be planted somewhere else."

"Well, lots of people do the same," said Brian. "Cheer up, Peggy. You'll soon have forgotten Old Priory when you've settled down in the new house."

"I never, never shall forget it!" said Peggy, fiercely. "And you won't either. You're only saying all this to comfort me – but you feel just the same as I do, inside yourself!"

"Yes, I do," said Brian. "Oh, I do wish something would happen so that Daddy needn't move after all!"

The weeks went by and Mother began to pack things into boxes. Brian and Peggy had to help and they were very sad.

"Mummy," Peggy said one day, "I suppose there aren't any secret rooms or secret cupboards in this house, are there?"

"I don't think so, darling," said Mummy. "Why?"

"Well, if there were, and we found them, we might find some treasure inside," said Peggy. "You know, Mummy – boxes of gold, or diamond necklaces, or things like that!"

Mummy laughed. "Oh, no, darling," she said. "We shan't find any treasure like that."

"If we did, and it was worth a lot of money, Daddy could keep Old Priory and we needn't move," said Peggy.

"Things like that only happen in books," said Mummy. "They never happen in real life."

Peggy and Brian ran off to get some more things for Mummy to pack. Brian had been thinking of what Peggy had said.

"You know, Pegs," he said, "that's quite a good idea of yours, about secret cupboards and things. This *is* a very old house, and I'm sure that somewhere or other there must be hidey-holes. And if there *are*, there would certainly be treasure in them, because that's what they were used for."

"Well, Brian, shall we hunt for secret hidey-holes every single day till we have to move?" cried Peggy. "We might find something!"

"Yes, let's," said Brian. So they began that very afternoon. How they hunted! First they went to the big attics and looked there. They pressed the wall all around to see if there were any secret doors. They hunted along the floor to see if there were hidden trap-doors. They peeped into the cupboards there to see if there was any chance of secret holes inside.

But not a thing could they find! They searched until it was dark, and at last had to give up.

"Well, I'm sure there are no hidey-holes in the attics," said Brian, sighing. "We've hunted everywhere. Aren't we dirty, Peggy? We want hot baths!"

"Tomorrow we'll try the other rooms," said Peggy, hopefully. "If only we *could* find something!"

Day after day the two children hunted here, there and everywhere. Mummy couldn't *think* how it was that they made themselves so dirty.

Soon September came, and Brian and Peggy were quite in despair, for that was the month they were to leave Old Priory and move into the little new house.

"We've hunted everywhere!" said Brian.

"All except the nursery," said Peggy. "But we know that so well that it's impossible to find anything new there."

"Still, we might as well try it," said Brian. "Then we shall have searched every corner of the house!"

So they tried the nursery. They even took up the carpet and looked underneath it. They felt round all the cupboards. They pressed all the oak panels that ran round the walls – but nothing happened at all.

"I suppose there's nothing by the window-seat?" said Peggy.

All round one big bay window ran a wooden seat, and underneath the seat was a cupboard where the children kept their oldest toys. The new ones they kept in the toy-cupboard on the opposite side of the fireplace.

"We might as well look," said Brian. So they opened the door of the cupboard under the seat. They pulled out all their toys and felt round the cupboard.

"Peggy," said Brian, suddenly, "doesn't it seem to you that this end part of the cupboard near the fireplace isn't as big as it ought to be? It seems too short to me."

Peggy popped her head in and looked.

"Yes," she said. "It doesn't look quite right somehow. Let's get a torch."

So they got a torch, and had a good look at the cupboard. It seemed to be much smaller at the fireplace end than at the other end, and Peggy couldn't make out why.

"There must be some reason," she said, getting excited. "Let's feel about and see if we can find some catch or knob."

But they couldn't. The wood was quite flat. There was nothing to get hold of at all.

And then suddenly something happened! Peggy threw an old wooden brick into the end of the cupboard and with a grating sound the top part slid open and the surprised children saw a dark hole beyond!

"Brian! Look! That brick must have hit a catch or something, and part of the cupboard end has slid back. Oh, Brian, we've found a secret place at last!"

Brian went red with excitement. He held the torch near the hole, but could not see anything in it.

"I'll have to get right into the cupboard and put my arm into the hole," he said. "I can't reach it from here."

So he crawled into the cupboard and got as far up the narrow end as he could. Then he felt round the hole, and discovered that the sliding piece ran in a groove behind the next piece of wood, leaving a square hole about a foot high. He put his hand into the hole - and there was something there!

"I've found something!" he cried excitedly to Peggy.

"Oh, what is it?" she begged. "Tell me, quick!"

"The hidey-hole isn't very big," said Brian, feeling all round it. "There are two things here - something that feels like a box, and something that feels like a book. I'll get them out in half a minute!"

"Wait! I'll get Mummy and Daddy!" cried Peggy, trembling with joy. "They must share in this!"

She sped off to get them, and very soon came back with them behind her.

"What have you found, Brian?" asked Daddy. "Hand them out and let's see!"

Brian crawled out of the cupboard and put something down on the floor. Everyone looked to see what he had found. There was a square wooden box with H. H. L. stamped on it, and an old book.

They opened the box — and Peggy could have cried with disappointment, for all it contained was — what do you think? Why, just a collection of sea-shells!

"Oh, Mummy, it's only shells!" said Peggy, blinking away the tears. "And I *did* think it would be treasure."

"And the book is only a silly collection of old stamps," said Brian, in disgust, opening it. "And it's not even filled - there are only about twelve pages with stamps on."

"Half a minute, Brian - let me have a look," said Daddy, in a peculiar voice, and he took the book from Brian. He looked closely at the stamps, turning over each page. Then he looked up and his face was quite red and his eyes were shining.

"Well, children, I don't know — but I believe some of these old stamps are worth a great deal of money! They must have been collected when your great-grandfather was a boy. He probably started this little collection and put it away with the shells in that secret hidey-hole of his - and then didn't bother about them any more. You know I told you he always loved collecting things!"

"Oh, Daddy! Do you really think the stamps are worth a lot of money?" cried Brian, eagerly.

"I'm not going to say for certain until I've taken the book up to London and

14

shown it to a man who knows all about stamps," said Daddy. "But I think I know enough about stamps to see that these are very valuable ones - very rare indeed!"

Oh, what excitement there was in Old Priory! How they laughed and talked! Daddy and Mummy each crawled into the window-seat cupboard to look at the hidey-hole, which was quite empty now.

"It must have been my grandfather's little secret place," said Daddy. "Fancy you two finding it!"

"Well, we hunted just everywhere!" said Peggy. "That was the last place we thought of!"

The next day Daddy took the book of stamps up to London and when he came back he hadn't got it with him.

"Good news!" he cried. "All the stamps are worth money, and five of them are worth heaps and heaps of money! Thousands of pounds! What do you think of that?"

"Oh, Daddy! Can we stay on at Old Priory?" asked the children, both together.

"I think so," said Daddy. "I've left the stamps with a stamp expert, and he will

tell me what they sell for in a few days' time. We must wait for that."

Very soon the news came – the stamps had been sold for a small fortune, and Daddy needn't sell their own home, nor even think of it! What a wonderful piece of good luck it was!

"Three cheers for great-grandfather!" cried Brian, standing in front of the old picture, and waving his hand round his head. "Hip hip hurrah!"

And Peggy believes she saw the old man in the picture give a smile!

THE SECRET ISLAND

AN EXTRACT

❧ ILLUSTRATED BY ❧

E. H. DAVIE

After their parents disappear while on a flight to Australia, Mike, Peggy and Nora go to live in the country with their cruel aunt and uncle. The children make friends with Jack, who is badly treated by his Uncle Henry. The four decide to run away and live on a small island at one end of an isolated lake. They make a house of willow canes and settle down to life on the island...

CHAPTER XII
THE CAVES IN THE HILLSIDE

The days slipped past, and the children grew used to their happy, carefree life on the island. Jack and Mike went off in the boat one night and fetched the old milking-pail from Aunt Harriet's farm, and a load of vegetables from the garden. The plums were ripening, too, and the boys brought back as many as would fill the milking-pail! How pleased the girls were to see them!

Now it was easy to milk Daisy the cow for they had a proper pail. Peggy cleaned it well before they used it, for it was dusty and dirty. When Jack or Mike had milked Daisy they stood the pail of milk in the middle of the little spring that gushed out from the hillside and ran down to the lake below. The icy-cold water kept the milk cool, and it did not turn sour, even on the hottest day.

Jack got out the packets of seeds he had brought from his grandfather's farm, and showed them to the others. "Look," he said, "here are lettuce seeds, and radish seeds, and mustard and cress, and runner beans! It's late to plant the beans, but in the good soil on this island I daresay they will grow quickly and we shall be able to have a crop later in the year."

"The mustard and cress and radishes will grow very quickly!" said Peggy. "What fun! The lettuces won't be very long, either, in this hot weather, if we keep them well watered."

"Where shall we plant them?" asked Mike.

"Well, we'd better plant them in little patches in different corners of the island," said Jack. "If we dig out a big patch and have a sort of vegetable garden, and anyone comes here to look for us, they will see our garden and know someone is here! But if we just plant out tiny patches, we can easily throw heather over them if we see anyone coming."

"Jack's always full of good ideas," said Nora. "I'll help to dig and plant, Jack."

"We'll all do it," said Jack. So together they hunted for good places, and dug up the ground there, and planted their precious seeds. It was Peggy's job to water them each day and see that no weeds choked the seeds when they grew.

"We're getting on!" said Nora happily. "Milk and cream each day, eggs each day, wild raspberries when we want them, and lettuces, mustard and cress, and radishes soon ready to be pulled!"

Jack planted the beans in little bare places at the foot of a brambly hedge. He said they would be able to grow up the brambles, and probably wouldn't be noticed if anyone came. The bean seedlings were carefully watched and nursed until they were strong and tall, and had begun to twist themselves round any stem near. Then Peggy left them to themselves, only watering them when they needed it.

It was sometimes difficult to remember which day it was. Jack had kept a count as best he could, and sometimes on Sundays the children could hear a church bell ringing if the wind was in the right direction.

"We ought to try and keep Sunday a day of rest and peace," said Mike. "We can't go to church, but we could make the day a good sort of day, if you know what I mean."

So they kept Sunday quietly, and the little island always seemed an extra peaceful day then. They hardly ever knew what the other days were — whether it was Tuesday or Thursday or Wednesday! But Jack always told them when it was Sunday, and it was the one day they really knew. Nora said it had a different feel, and certainly the island seemed to know it was Sunday, and was a dreamier, quieter place then.

One day Jack said they must explore the caves in the hillside.

"If anyone does come here to look for us, and it's quite likely," he said, "we must really have all our plans made as to what to do, and know exactly where to hide. People who are really looking for us won't just sit about on that beach as the trippers did, you know – they will hunt all over the island."

"Well, let's go and explore the caves today," said Mike. "I'll get the lantern."

So, with the lantern swinging in his hand, and a box of matches ready in his pocket to light it, Jack led the way to the caves. The children had found three openings into the hillside – one where the hens had been put, another larger one, and a third very tiny one through which they could hardly crawl.

"We'll go in through the biggest entrance," said Jack. He lit the lantern, and went into the dark cave. It seemed strange to leave the hot July sunshine. Nora shivered. She thought the caves were rather strange. But she didn't say anything, only kept very close to Mike.

Jack swung the lantern round and lit up all the corners. It was a large cave – but not of much use for hiding in, for every corner could be easily seen. Big cobwebs hung here and there, and there was a musty smell of bats.

Mike went all round the walls, peeping and prying – and right at the very back of the cave he discovered a curious thing. The wall was split from about six feet downwards, and a big crack, about two feet across, yawned there. At first it seemed as if the crack simply showed rock behind it – but it didn't. There was a narrow, winding passage there, half hidden by a jutting-out piece of rock.

"Look here!" cried Mike, in excitement. "Here's a passage right in the very rock of the hillside itself. Come on, Jack, bring your lantern here. I wonder if it goes very far back."

Jack lifted up his lantern and the others saw the curious half-hidden passage, the entrance to which was by the crack in the wall. Jack went through the crack and walked a little way down the passage.

"Come on!" he cried. "It's all right! The air smells fresh here, and the passage seems to lead to somewhere."

The children crowded after him in excitement. What an adventure this was!

The passage wound here and there, and sometimes the children had to step over rocks and piles of fallen earth. Tree-roots stretched over their heads now and again. The passage was sometimes very narrow, but quite passable. And at last it ended – and Jack found that it led to an even larger cave right in the very middle of the hill itself! He lifted his lantern and looked round. The air smelled fresh and sweet. Why was that?

"Look!" cried Nora, pointing upwards. "I can see daylight!"

Sure enough, a long way up, a spot of bright daylight came through into the dark cave. Jack was puzzled. "I think some rabbits must have burrowed into the hill, and come out unexpectedly into this cave," he said. "And their hole is where we can see that spot of daylight. Well – the fresh air comes in, anyhow!"

From the big cave a low passage led to another cave on the right. This passage was so low that the children had to crawl through it – and to their surprise they found that this second cave led out to the hillside itself, and was no other than the cave into which it was so hard to crawl because of the small entrance.

"Well, we are getting on," said Jack. "We have discovered that the big cave we knew leads by a passage to an even bigger one – and from that big one we can get into this smaller one, which has an opening on to the hillside – and that opening is too small for any grown-up to get into!"

"What about the cave we put the hens into?" asked Nora.

"That must be just a little separate cave by itself," said Jack. "We'll go and see."

So they squeezed themselves out of the tiny entrance of the last cave, and went to the hen-cave. But this was quite ordinary – just a little low, rounded cave smelling strongly of bats.

They came out and sat on the hillside in the bright sunshine. It was lovely to sit there in the warmth after the cold, dark caves.

"Now listen," said Jack thoughtfully. "Those caves are going to be jolly useful to us this summer if anyone comes to get us. We could get Daisy into that big inner cave quite well, for one thing."

"Oh, Jack! She'd never squeeze through that narrow, winding passage," said Peggy.

"Oh yes, she would," said Jack. "She'd come with me all right – and what's more, Daisy is going to practise going in and out there, so that if the time comes when she has really got to hide for a few hours, she won't mind. It wouldn't be any good putting her into that cave, and then having her moo fit to lift off the top of the hill!"

Everyone laughed. Mike nodded his head. "Quite right," he said. "Daisy will have to practise! I suppose the hens can go there quite well, too?"

"Easily," said Jack. "And so can we!"

"The only things we can't take into the cave are our boat and our house," said Mike.

"The boat would never be found under those brambles by the water," said Jack. "And I doubt if anyone would ever find Willow House either, for we have built it in the very middle of that thicket, and it is all we can do to squeeze through to it! Grown-ups could never get through. Why, we shall soon have to climb a tree and drop down to Willow House if the bushes and trees round it grow any more thickly!"

"I almost wish someone *would* come!" said Peggy. "It would be so exciting to hide away!"

"A bit *too* exciting!" said Jack. "Remember, there's a lot to be done as soon as we see anyone coming!"

"Hadn't we better plan it all out now?" said Mike. "Then we shall each know what to do."

"Yes," said Jack. "Well, I'll manage Daisy the cow, and go straight off to fetch her. Mike, you manage the hens and get them into a sack, and take them straight up to the cave. Peggy, you stamp out the fire and scatter the hot sticks. Also you must put out the empty cigarette packet, the tin, and the cardboard carton that the trippers left, so that it will look as if trippers have been here, and nobody will think it's funny to find the remains of a fire, or any other odd thing."

"And what shall I do?" asked Nora.

"You must go to the spring and take the pail of milk from there to the cave," said Jack. "Before you do that scatter heather over our patches of growing seeds.

And Peggy, you might make certain the cave-cupboard is hidden by a curtain of bracken or something."

"Ay, ay, Captain!" said Peggy. "Now we've all got our duties to do – but you've got the hardest, Jack! I wouldn't like to hide Daisy away down that narrow passage! What will you do if she gets stuck?"

"She won't get stuck," said Jack. "She's not as fat as all that! By the way, we'd better put a cup or two in the cave, and some heather, in case we have to hide up for a good many hours. We can drink milk then, and have somewhere soft to lie on."

"We'd better keep a candle or two in the entrance," said Peggy. "I don't feel like sitting in the dark there."

"I'll tell you what we'll do," said Jack thoughtfully. "We won't go in and out of that big inner cave by the narrow passage leading from the outer cave. We'll go in and out by that tiny cave we can hardly squeeze in by. It leads to the inner cave, as we found out. If we keep using the other cave and the passage to go in, we are sure to leave marks, and give ourselves away. I'll have to take Daisy that way, but that can't be helped."

"Those caves will be cosy to live in in the wintertime," said Peggy. "We could live in the outer one, and store our things in the inner one. We should be quite protected from bad weather."

"How lucky we are!" said Nora. "A nice house made of trees for the summer – and a cosy cave-home for the winter!"

"Winter's a long way off yet," said Jack. "I say! – I'm hungry! What about frying some eggs, Peggy, and sending Mike to get some raspberries?"

"Come on!" shouted Peggy, and raced off down the hillside, glad to leave behind the dark, gloomy caves.

CHAPTER XIII
THE SUMMER GOES BY

o one came to interfere with the children. They lived together on the island, playing, working, eating, drinking, bathing – doing just as they liked, and yet having to do certain duties in order to keep their farmyard going properly.

Sometimes Jack and Mike went off in the boat at night to get something they needed from either Jack's farm or Aunt Harriet's. Mike managed to get into his aunt's house one night and get some of his and the girls' clothes – two or three dresses for the girls, and a coat and shorts for himself. Clothes were rather a difficulty, for they got dirty and ragged on the island, and as the girls had none to change into, it was difficult to keep their dresses clean and mended.

Jack got a good deal of fruit and a regular amount of potatoes and turnips from his grandfather's farm, which still had not been sold. There was always enough to eat, for there were eggs, rabbits, and fish, and Daisy gave them more than enough milk to drink.

Their seeds grew quickly. It was a proud day when Peggy was able to cut the first batch of mustard and cress and the first lettuce and mix it up into a salad to eat with hard-boiled eggs! The radishes, too, tasted very good, and were so hot that even Jack's eyes watered when he ate them! Things grew amazingly well and quickly on the island.

The runner beans were now well up to the top of the bramble bushes, and Jack nipped the tips off, so that they would flower well below.

"We don't want to have to make a ladder to climb up and pick the beans," he said. "My word, there are going to be plenty – look at all the scarlet flowers!"

"They smell nice!" said Nora, sniffing them.

"The beans will taste nicer!" said Jack.

The weather was hot and fine, for it was a wonderful summer. The children all slept out of doors in their "green bedroom", as they called it, tucked in the shelter of the big gorse bushes. They had to renew their beds of heather and bracken every week, for they became flattened with the weight of their bodies and were uncomfortable. But these jobs were very pleasant, and the children loved them.

"How brown we are!" said Mike one day, as they sat round the fire on the beach, eating radishes, and potatoes cooked in their jackets. They all looked at one another.

"We're as brown as berries," said Nora.

"What berries?" said Mike. "I don't know any brown berries. Most of them are red!"

"Well, we're as brown as oak-apples!" said Nora. They certainly were. Legs, arms, faces, necks, knees – just as dark as gypsies! The children were fat, too, for although their food was a peculiar mixture, they had a great deal of creamy milk.

Although life was peaceful on the island, it had its excitements. Each week Jack solemnly led poor Daisy to the cave and made her squeeze through the narrow passage into the cave beyond. The first time she made a terrible fuss. She mooed and bellowed, she struggled and even kicked — but Jack was firm and kind and led her inside. There, in the inner cave, he gave her a juicy turnip, fresh-pulled from his grandfather's farm the night before. Daisy was pleased. She chewed it all up, and was quite good when she was led back through the passage once more.

The second time she made a fuss again, but did not kick, nor did she bellow quite so loudly. The third time she seemed quite pleased to go, because she knew by now that a fine turnip awaited her in the cave. The fourth time she even went into the cave by herself and made her way solemnly to the passage at the far end.

"It's an awfully tight squeeze," said Mike, from the back. "If Daisy grows any fatter she won't be able to get through, Jack."

"We won't meet our troubles half-way," said Jack cheerfully. "The main thing is, Daisy likes going into the cave now, and won't make a fuss if ever the time comes when she has to be put there in a hurry."

July passed into August. The weather was thundery and hot. Two or three thunderstorms came along, and the children slept in Willow House for a few nights. Jack suggested sleeping in the cave, but they all voted it would be too hot and stuffy. So they settled down in Willow House, and felt glad of the thick green roof above them, and the stout, heather-stuffed walls.

The wild raspberries ripened by the hundred. Wild strawberries began to appear in the shady parts of the island – not tiny ones, such as the children had often found round about the farm, but big, sweet, juicy ones, even nicer than garden ones. They tasted most delicious with cream. The blackberries grew ripe on the bushes that rambled all over the place, and the children's mouths were always stained with them, for they picked them as they went about their various jobs.

Jack picked them on his way to milk Daisy, and so did Mike. Peggy picked them as she went to get water from the spring. Nora picked them as she went to feed the hens.

Nuts were ripening, too, but were not yet ready. Jack looked at the heavy clusters on the hazel-trees and longed for them to be ripe. He went to have a look at the beans. They were ready to be picked! The runners grew up the brambles, and the long green pods were mixed up with the blackberry flowers and berries.

"Beans for dinner today!" shouted Jack. He went to fetch one of the many baskets that Peggy knew how to weave from willow twigs, and soon had it full of the juicy green beans.

Another time Jack remembered the mushrooms that used to grow in the field at the end of his grandfather's farm. He and Mike set off in the boat one early morning at the end of August to see if they could find some.

It was a heavenly morning. Mike wished they had brought the girls, too, but it would not do to take a crowd. Someone might see them. It was just sunrise. The sun rose up in the east and the whole sky was golden. A little yellowhammer sang loudly on a nearby hedge, "Little bit of bread and no cheese!" A crowd of young sparrows chirruped madly in the trees. Dew was heavy on the grass, and the boys' bare feet were dripping wet. They were soaked to the knees, but they didn't mind. The early sun was warm, and all the world was blue and gold and green.

"Mushrooms!" said Jack, in delight, pointing to where two or three grew. "Look – fresh new ones, only grown up last night. Come on! Fill the sack!"

There were scores in the field. Jack picked the smaller ones, for he knew the bigger ones did not taste so nice and might have maggots in them. In half-an-hour their sack was full and they slipped away through the sunny fields to where they had moored their boat.

"What a breakfast we'll have!" grinned Jack. And they did! Fried mushrooms and fried eggs, wild strawberries and cream! The girls had gone out strawberry hunting whilst the boys had gone to look for mushrooms.

Nora learned to swim well. She and Peggy had to practise every day in the lake till Jack said they were as good as he and Mike were. They were soon like fish

in the water, and tumbled and splashed about each day with yells and shrieks. Jack was clever at swimming under water and would disappear suddenly and come up just beside one of the others, clutching hard at their legs! What fun they had!

Then there came a spell of bad weather — just a few days. The island seemed very different then, with the sun gone, a soft rain-mist driving over it, soaking everything, and the lake-water as cold as ice.

Nora didn't like it. She didn't like feeding the hens in the rain. She asked Peggy to do it for her. But Jack heard her and was cross.

"You're not to be a fair-weather person," he told her. "It's all very well to go about happily when the sun is shining and do your jobs with a smile — but just you be the same when we get bad weather!"

"Ay, ay, Captain!" said Nora, who was learning not to be such a baby as she had been. And after that she went cheerfully out to feed the hens, even though the rain trickled down her neck and ran in a cold stream down her brown back.

They were rather bored when they had to keep indoors in Willow House when it rained. They had read all their books and papers by that time, and although it was fun to play games for a while, they couldn't do it all day long. Peggy didn't mind — she always had plenty of mending to do.

She showed the boys and Nora how to weave baskets. They needed a great many, for the baskets did not last very long, and there were always raspberries, strawberries, or blackberries to pick. Mike, Jack, and Nora thought it was fun to weave all kinds and shapes of baskets, and soon they had a fine selection of them ready for sunny weather.

Then the sun came back again and the children lay about in it and basked in the hot rays to get themselves warm once more. The hens fluffed out their wet feathers and clucked happily. Daisy came out from under the tree which gave her shelter, and gave soft moos of pleasure. The world was full of colour again and the children shouted for joy.

The beans, radishes, lettuces, and mustard and cress grew enormously in the rain. Jack and Mike picked a good crop, and everyone said that never had anything tasted so delicious before as the rain-swollen lettuces, so crisp, juicy, and sweet.

All sorts of little things happened. The hole in the boat grew so big that one day, when Mike went to fetch the boat from its hiding-place, it had disappeared! It had sunk into the water! Then Jack and Mike had to use all their brains and all their strength to get it up again and to mend it so that it would not leak quite so badly.

The corn for the hens came to an end, and Jack had to go and see if he could find some more. There was none at his grandfather's farm, so he went to Mike's farm – and there he found some in a shed, but was nearly bitten by a new dog that had been bought for the farm. The dog bit a hole in his trousers, and Peggy had to spend a whole morning mending them.

Another time there was a great alarm, because Nora said she had heard the splashing of oars. Jack rushed off to get Daisy, and Mike bundled the hens into a sack – but, as nothing more seemed to happen, Peggy ran to the top of the hill and looked down the lake.

No boat was in sight – only four big white swans, quarrelling among themselves, and splashing the water with their feet and wings!

"It's all right, boys!" she shouted. "It's only the swans! It isn't a boat!"

So Daisy was left in peace and the hens were emptied out of the sack again. Nora was teased, and made up her mind that she would make quite certain it was a boat next time she gave the alarm!

One day Jack slipped down the hillside when he was reaching for raspberries and twisted his ankle. Mike had to help him back to the camp on the beach. Jack was very pale, for it was a bad twist.

Peggy ran to get some clean rags and soaked them in the cold spring water. She bound them tightly round Jack's foot and ankle.

"You mustn't use it for a while," she said. "You must keep quiet. Mike will do your jobs."

So Jack had to lie about quietly for a day or two, and he found this very strange. But he was a sensible boy, and he knew that it was the quickest way to get better. Soon he found that he could hop about quite well with a stout hazel stick Mike cut for him from the hedges – and after a week or so his foot was quite all right.

Another time poor Peggy overbalanced and fell into a gorse bush below her on the hill. She was dreadfully scratched, but she didn't even cry. She went to the lake and washed her scratches and cuts, and then got the supper ready. Jack said he was very proud of her. "Anybody else would have yelled the place down!" he said, looking at the scratches all over her arms and legs.

"It's nothing much," said Peggy, boiling some milk. "I'm lucky not to have broken my leg or something!"

So, with these little adventures, joys, and sorrows, the summer passed by. No one came to the island, and gradually the children forgot their fears of being found, and thought no more of it.

THE TREASURE HUNTERS

AN EXTRACT

∼ ILLUSTRATED BY ∼
JOYCE DAVIES

*John, Susan and Jeffery are staying with their grandparents
at Greylings Manor. They are very sad as the Manor, which has
been in their family for centuries, is about to be sold as the
family can no longer afford its upkeep. They decide that they
will use their last stay at the Manor to look for the lost
Greylings treasure. While searching in the woods, they come
upon a building that is completely overgrown with weeds and
brambles. They borrow an axe from the gardener and go back
to find out exactly what it is they have discovered...*

CHAPTER IV
THE LITTLE SECRET HOUSE

Jeffery went to the overgrown clump and began to chop away at the ivy stems. Some of them were very thick. He chopped hard above the steps where Rags had found a rabbit-hole.

He hadn't chopped for long before he gave a shout. "Yes! Look – there *is* a house of some sort under all this ivy. I'm chopping by the door. Come and pull away the stems for me."

Susan and John went to help Jeffery. He had chopped so hard that he was very hot, and his face was wet. He took out his handkerchief and mopped his forehead.

Susan and John began to tear away the broken stems of ivy. They were more careful with the blackberry sprays, because they were prickly. The honeysuckle came away more easily, for its stems were thin and brittle.

"Yes!" said Susan, excited. "There *is* a door behind here. Oh, Jeffery! Fancy there being a little secret house hidden under all this ivy and creeper – a house forgotten long ago and never used except by the rabbits."

Jeffery laughed. He took up his axe again. "Well, the rabbits must be getting a shock now," he said. "Stand away, you two. I don't want to chop your heads off!"

"Let *me* have a turn!" begged Susan, who was simply longing to chop too. But Jeffery shook his head firmly.

"Certainly not, Susan," he said. "You know quite well that we promised Tipps I would be the only one to chop. I'm the oldest and the biggest, and I know how to use an axe. Goodness knows what *you* might do, Susan, if you began chopping!"

Jeffery chopped hard. Some of the ivy stems were as thick as the trunks of small trees. The roots that these stems had put out held firmly to the door underneath – but once Jeffery had chopped the stems in half, it was easy to pull away the brown roots that clung everywhere.

"Jeffery, we've made quite a hole already!" said Susan, dancing about in excitement. "Oh, Jeffery, hurry! Soon there will be enough room for us to creep through."

"Well, I'm hurrying as much as I can," said Jeffery. "But it's jolly hard work."

Crash! Crash! The axe cut through one stem after another, and at last there was a hole big enough for anyone to crawl through, about the middle of the doorway.

Jeffery twisted a handkerchief round his hand and bent back some of the more prickly sprays that the others couldn't manage.

He poked the axe in through the hole. There was a wooden door behind. "I can see the handle!" said Jeffery, in excitement.

He slipped his hand along the door and tried the handle. It would not even turn!

"It won't move," said Jeffery.

"Let *me* try," said John. "My wrist is very strong – perhaps I can turn the handle."

But none of them could. It was stiff with the rust of many, many years, and would not move. The three children were terribly disappointed.

"Let's see if we can find a window and chop the ivy away from that," said John. "We could get in through a window."

So they tried to find a window – but the creeping ivy and brambles were so thick that it was quite impossible to guess where a window might be.

Scratched and pricked all over their arms and legs, the children looked at one another and wondered what to do.

"There *must* be some way we can get in!" said John.

"Yes – there *is*!" cried Susan. "I know what to do!"

"What?" asked the boys.

"Chop down the door, of course!" shouted Susan, in excitement. "Can't you chop a big enough hole in the door for us to squeeze through, Jeffery?"

"But do you think we *ought* to do that?" said Jeffery. "I mean – after all, it's a door, and it isn't right to chop holes in doors."

"It can't matter with *this* door," said John, eager to try Susan's idea. "It must be nearly falling to pieces as it is! Go on, Jeffery – chop a hole in it! We'll never get in if you don't. I simply can't wait any longer!"

Jeffery didn't want to wait either. He lifted the axe and chopped at the door with it. The wood was quite rotten and gave way easily. The axe went through it at once. A few strokes, and there was a large hole in the door, through which the children could easily squeeze!

"Good!" said Jeffery, panting. "I say – doesn't it look dark inside there?"

"I guess it's full of spiders and earwigs!" said Susan, staring at the dark hole in the door. "It's a good thing we none of us mind them. Who's going in first?"

Nobody seemed quite so keen on going in after all! It really did look dark and mysterious through the hole in the door. It smelled a bit funny too.

"I believe I've got a candle-end somewhere in my pocket!" said Jeffery suddenly. He always carried a strange collection of things about with him. "You never know when any of them may come in useful," he would say, when the others teased him about them. He felt in first one pocket and then another – and then brought out a candle-end – about two inches of red candle.

"I've got some matches somewhere too," he said.

"Oh, do hurry, Jeffery!" said Susan, always the impatient one. "I want to see inside this strange, secret little house. Fancy finding a house all hidden and covered with creeper, that nobody has been inside for years and years and years!"

Jeffery found his matches, and lit the candle-end. He held the candle inside the hole in the door. The three children pressed round it to see inside the strange woodland house.

It did indeed look very mysterious. It was full of dark shadows. It looked small, high and round. A bench ran round it, and there was a small fireplace or hearth at the back. A table was against the wall at one side, with something on it. The children could not see what it was.

"Let's go in!" whispered Susan.

"What are you whispering for?" whispered back John.

"I don't know – but it seems funny to talk out loud now!" said Susan, still in a whisper.

Jeffery squeezed in through the hole first. He said "Oh! What's that!" and quickly climbed out again.

"What do you mean? What's the matter?" asked John, half-frightened.

"Something touched my face," said Jeffery. "I didn't like it!"

"It was a spider's web, you silly!" said Susan. She laughed, and the sound seemed to make things bright and ordinary again. "You baby, Jeffery! Fancy being frightened of a spider's web!"

"Well, it didn't feel nice touching my cheek like that," said Jeffery. "You go in first, Susan, if you think a spider's web is so funny! Take the candle!"

So Susan climbed in through the hole in the door, brushing aside the hanging spiders' webs with her hand. She held the candle up and looked round the strange little house.

It had had two windows, but both these were blocked up with ivy and other creepers. The bench round the wall was thick with the dust of many, many years. So was the table. Susan held the candle up and looked to see what was on the table.

"Jeffery, the people who were here last drank out of these glasses!" she said.

"There are two here — all dirty and dusty. Oh, isn't it strange to come here and find glasses still on the table!"

By this time the two boys had crept into the little house too, and were staring round in excitement.

"Those glasses are like the very old ones that Granny keeps in the cupboard in the drawing-room!" said Jeffery, picking one up. "She won't use them because she says they are old and rare — how pleased she will be to have two more!"

"Look at the fireplace," said Susan, holding the candle to it. "There are the remains of a fire there. What fun it must have been to come to this house on a cold day, light a fire, and sit here in the middle of the wood, with that lovely pool gleaming below!"

"Yes, mustn't it," said Jeffery. "I'd like it myself! I'd love a little secret house like this. The squirrels would come to it — and the robins. The rabbits would peep inside, and perhaps a hedgehog would walk in, and sniff around."

"That does sound lovely," said Susan, delighted. "Poor little house — hidden away and forgotten all these years. Let's make it ours!"

"Oh, yes!" cried the boys, thrilled with the idea.

"We'll clear away the ivy from the windows, and let the light through," said Susan, busy planning as she loved to do. "We'll bring a brush and sweep the dust away. We'll clean up the whole house — and we'll make a fire here one day, and boil a kettle for tea!"

"What fun!" shouted Jeffery, and he jumped for joy. A long spider's thread caught his ear, and he rubbed it away. "I'd like to clear away these clinging cobwebs," he said. "I really don't like them!"

"Let's go home again now," said Susan. "The candle won't last any more. It's running down on my fingers now and the wax is very hot. We'll bring candles here when we come, and keep them on the mantelpiece. Let's take the two old glasses with us."

Off they went back home, carrying the two glasses carefully. They whistled to Rags, who had been chasing rabbits the whole of the time, and then made their way through the dim wood. What an exciting day they had had!

CHAPTER V
THE HOUSE GETS A SPRING-CLEAN

Granny and Granpa were thrilled to hear about the secret house in the woods, but Granny was not at all pleased to hear of the axe.

"You are not allowed to use such dangerous things," she said to Jeffery. "Tipps is foolish to let you have an axe. You must not use that again, Jeffery."

"All right, Granny," said Jeffery. "But I am really very careful, you know, and after all, I shall soon be twelve!"

"Look, Granny, here are the glasses," said Susan — and she put them on the table. She had carefully washed them, and polished them with a clean cloth. They shone beautifully. Granny gave a cry of delight and picked them up.

"Look, Thomas!" she said to Granpa. "Two of those beautiful, heavy old glasses that we have in my cupboard over there. How lovely! These are rare, now, children, and I am delighted to have them. They are over a hundred years old!"

She put them proudly in her glass-fronted cupboard in the corner of the drawing-room. They were fat glasses, short and very heavy — the children wished they could use them each day for their lemonade but Granny wouldn't hear of it!

"Granny, we are going to make that little secret house our very own," said Jeffery. "We are going to clean it up, and keep a few books and things there. We shall clean up the steps that lead down to the pond — and then, when it is all ready, you must come and have tea with us there!"

"We can boil a kettle on the little hearth," said Susan, jumping round like a grasshopper. "We can make a fire! There's a table there too, and a bench round the wall. Oh, it really is a most exciting little house!"

"Well, I can't see why you shouldn't make it your own house if you want to," said Granny. "Greylings Wood is ours, and the house was ours too – so you can have it for a playhouse, if you like."

For the next few days the children spent all their time in the wood, going to and from their new house, carrying brooms and pans and cloths! Jane the housemaid was quite cross at the disappearance of so many of her cleaning things, and the children had to promise to bring them all back safely when they had finished with them.

Susan took charge of the cleaning as she was the girl. They all went to the house the next day, and climbed in through the door again. This time they had plenty of candles and two candlesticks. They put two candles into the stands and stood them on the little mantelpiece. They lit the house up well.

"You two boys had better see what you can do about the windows," said Susan. "It would be a good thing to let some light and air into the house. It still smells old and musty."

"We mustn't have the axe this time," said Jeffery, staring at the windows. "But I could borrow Tipps' little saw, and saw through the ivy-stems. It wouldn't take long."

So Jeffery ran back to Greylings and borrowed the saw. He and John took it in turns to saw the thick stems, and soon they were able to pull the ivy and brambles away from the window, and to let in air and light.

There was no glass in the windows – they were simply round holes in the rather thick wall. Whilst the boys were clearing the two windows Susan got busy with the cleaning. She tied a handkerchief round her hair and put on an old overall. The house was dustier than anywhere she had ever seen!

Rags was thrilled with the house. He jumped in and out of the hole in the door a dozen times in an hour, and trotted all round the house, sniffing everywhere. He would have liked to live there always, surrounded by rabbits!

Susan removed all the cobwebs first. They hung down from the roof, they stretched here and there, and were grey with dust. They were soon down! Big spiders scuttled away. A robin hopped in at the hole in the door, and flew to the mantelpiece. He carolled a tiny song as if to say, "I'll help with the spiders!" But he didn't. He flew out again, and sat on a branch outside, watching the children with his bright black eyes.

Susan swept down the walls with her broom. She swept the mantelpiece, the bench, and table. When she had got all the dust on to the floor, she began to sweep that into her pan.

The dust made the children sneeze. They blew their noses, and then settled down to their work again. It was fun.

"Get me some water from the pool, John, will you?" asked Susan, when she had swept up all the dust she could find. "I want to do a little scrubbing now!"

"I'll help you," said John, who liked to scrub.

"Well, I've got two scrubbing brushes here, so you can have one," said Susan happily. It was lovely having a secret house like this, making it their very own.

John fetched a pail of water from the pond. The children had found that there was a complete flight of overgrown steps leading down from the little house to the pool. Jeffery was determined to clean them and uncover them all as soon as he had finished the windows.

There was a lot to do, but the children enjoyed every minute. The sun was very hot in the garden of Greylings, but here in the wood, it was cool and green. The children had brought lemonade with them, and they drank it when they felt too hot.

Susan scrubbed the floor, the bench, and the table. The floor was of brightly-coloured tiles, set in a pattern, and at some time had had a rug over it, for Susan found threads of it still left.

"I say! What a lovely floor!" said Jeffery, looking in from one of the window-holes. "It looks beautiful now! Who would have thought there was a floor like that!"

It took the children three days to get the little house really nice. At the end of that time it was lovely!

Jeffery had managed to get the door to open now, and had cleared away all the creepers over the doorway, so that light came in there as well as in at the windows. Tipps' saw was not so quick at clearing ivy as the axe, but that couldn't be helped.

John had cleared the steps that led down to the pool. He had torn away the creeping roots that hid them, and had cleared them of earth and moss. They were of white marble and shone beautifully. John *was* proud of them.

Susan had made the house look really lovely. Everything was clean there now. The brightly-coloured tiles shone on the floor. The table and bench were quite clean, and the fireplace was cleared too, and was neatly laid ready for a fire, with paper, twigs, and old wood that the boys had found outside.

They begged an old rug from Granny for the floor. They brought along a little vase which they filled with flowers for the middle of the table. Susan even brought an old clock that she had found in a cupboard. It had belonged to Granpa, and one of its legs was broken. It had not been worth mending and had been put away in a cupboard.

John mended its leg. Susan wound it up and it went. So to the secret house it was carried, and there it stood on the mantelpiece, ticking away cheerfully!

"I always think a clock makes a house feel cosy and lived-in," said Susan happily. "Doesn't it all look nice? Let's have tea here tomorrow! We won't ask Granny and Granpa yet. We'll wait till we're sure the fire goes all right, and the chimney doesn't smoke. We'll try tomorrow!"

Rags was *most* interested in the house. He ran in and out, and Susan did wish he could be taught to wipe his feet. He seemed to take a delight in running in the muddiest places he could find, and then walking over the clean floor of the little house!

The next day the children brought along the things for tea at the house. Susan carried a kettle of water to boil for tea. The boys brought a picnic basket full of food. Inside there were unbreakable cups and plates which Granny had given them to keep in their house.

"Isn't this fun!" said Susan, as she put a pretty little cloth on the table. "Jeffery, do let *me* light the fire, please, to boil the kettle! After all, I did lay it ready."

Everybody wanted to light the fire, but Susan was allowed to do it. She kneeled down and put a lighted match to the paper. It flared up at once. The twigs began to crackle. The wood soon caught fire, and a lovely glow filled the hearth.

But it wasn't so lovely after a little while. Smoke began to pour out from the fireplace, and filled the little house. The children coughed.

"Oh dear! It's smoking!" said Susan. "What a nuisance! Do you suppose we ought to have swept the chimney?"

"Well, I shouldn't have thought the fire was used often enough to make the chimney really sooty," said Jeffery.

Susan poked the lighted wood to the back of the fireplace, hoping that the smoke would soon go up the chimney. But it didn't. It went pouring out into the room. Soon the children's eyes began to smart, and they choked with the stinging smoke.

"Wood smoke is always horrid," said Jeffery, going outside to wipe his streaming eyes. "This won't do, Susan. We'll have to put out the fire. We can't boil water for tea today. We'll have to do that when we've put the chimney right."

"I expect it's stuffed up with ivy stems and leaves," said John. He kicked the fire out, and soon only a few wisps of smoke rose from the hearth.

But it was impossible to have tea in the smoky house. Susan was very disappointed about it. She took the tea outside, and they sat on the steps, looking down to the little pond, and ate their egg sandwiches, ginger cake, and chocolate

biscuits there. They drank the water out of the kettle, pouring it into their cups.

"This is really a lovely place!" said Susan. "Look how the sun comes slanting through the trees just there, and lights up the pond. What a lot of waterlilies there are out today!"

"There's a red squirrel watching us," said John in a low voice. "Don't move. He's in that hazel tree over there."

The children watched the big-eyed creature. He sat on the branch, his bushy tail curled up behind him. Then with a light bound he leaped to the ground and scampered up the steps to them. Rags saw him and would have pounced on him, but Jeffery had him by the collar.

Susan held out a bit of chocolate biscuit. The squirrel took it in a tiny paw and then bounded into the trees, carrying it in his mouth.

"He likes chocolate!" said Susan. "Oh, isn't he sweet! I'd like to tell him to live in our little house when we are not there. He can be our caretaker!"

As the shadows began to grow longer, one or two rabbits came slipping out of their holes. They sat not far off, washing their big ears, bending them down as they cleaned them. The children watched, keeping quite still. Rags whined, and longed to chase them, but they would not let him.

"We *are* lucky to have a little house all to ourselves in the wood," said John. "All the animals and birds will soon be tame for us, and we can feed them and make friends with them!"

The robin was already very tame. It took crumbs from Susan's hand, and did not seem at all afraid. A big freckled thrush sat nearby and eyed the children warily, turning its head first to one side and then another.

"It looks at us first out of one eye and then out of the other!" said Jeffery, with a laugh. He threw the thrush a bit of bread – but the robin flew down and got it before the thrush stirred from the branch.

"I could stay here all evening," said Susan. "But I'd really like to see what's the matter with that chimney, Jeffery. I'd like to put it right before Granny and Granpa come to tea!"

"Well, we'll have a look at it now," said Jeffery, getting up. The squirrel bounded up a tree as he moved, and the rabbits shot into their holes, showing white bobtails. Rags raced after them at once, and began to scrape earth into the air in a great shower!

"Have you got the brush here that you had yesterday, Susan?" said Jeffery. "The one with a long handle, I mean. I could put that up the chimney to see if there is anything stopping it up."

"Yes, there it is," said Susan. "In the corner."

Jeffery took it. He went to the fireplace and kneeled down beside it. "I expect there is a bird's nest or something stopping it up," he said. "It is a very short chimney, and it should be quite easy to clear."

He put the broom up – and at once a shower of twigs and moss and leaves came down. It all fell into the fireplace. "A bird's nest," said Jeffery. He pushed the brush up as high as he could. Another shower of twigs and moss came down.

"Go outside and see if the brush is sticking out of the chimney," said Jeffery to John. John went out and looked. He came back.

"Yes," he said. "I can just see it. The chimney should be clear now."

"Right," said Jeffery. He pulled the brush down – but the end of it stuck against something in the chimney. Jeffery tugged hard, but the brush-end would not come.

"Blow!" he said. "What's the matter with it?" He put his head up the chimney and felt about with his hand. To his surprise he found something sticking out halfway across the chimney. This was what the brush had caught on. Jeffery felt round it. It felt like a box or something. He grew excited.

"I say!" he called. "There's a sort of opening in the side of this chimney – a kind of hidey-hole, I should think! And there's something been stuffed into it – something too big for the hole – so that it sticks out half across the chimney!"

"Oh, Jeffery! Get it down, quick, get it down!" shouted John and Susan.

"I'll try," said Jeffery. "It seems to have stuck. No – here it comes!"

CHAPTER VI
A MOST EXCITING DISCOVERY

He had tugged so hard at the box that it had moved from its place. He slid it out from the hole. It was heavy and Jeffery could not hold it in one hand. The box slid down the chimney and landed in the back of the fireplace with a crash.

"Gracious!" said Susan. "What a funny old box!"

"Isn't it exciting!" said John, almost beside himself with joy. "Is it the treasure?"

"Of course not!" said Jeffery. "The box is too small to hold the treasure! But it may hold something exciting, all the same."

It was an iron box, with a stiff clasp in front. On the top of the box was a raised letter – G.

"G for Greylings," said Susan, tracing the letter with her finger. "This is an old Greylings box. Open it Jeffery, quickly! Whatever can be inside it?"

It was not easy to open. The years had made the clasp very stiff, and Jeffery had to get a knife from the picnic basket to force it open.

"Shake it, John, and see it if rattles," said Susan eagerly. "Perhaps it might have a few old brooches inside."

John shook it – but it did not rattle.

"It sounds empty!" he said. "Oh dear – I do hope it isn't!"

Jeffery took the box from John, and began to work at the stiff fastening. It suddenly gave way, and Jeffery opened the lid. The three children peered inside in excitement.

"There's nothing inside it at all!" said Jeffery in the greatest disappointment. "Look – it's empty!"

So it was. Nothing was to be seen except the sides and bottom of the box itself.

John was puzzled. "But Jeffery," he said, "why should anyone want to hide a box in a secret chimney-hole, if there was nothing in it?"

"How should *I* know?" said Jeffery gloomily. "It must have been hidden there over a hundred years ago. Perhaps more. A silly joke, perhaps."

"It couldn't have been a joke," said Susan, taking the box from Jeffery. "Nobody sticks things up chimneys for a joke! Do you suppose there *was* something in the box – and somebody found it and put the box back again after taking out the things inside?"

"Well, that's an idea," said Jeffery. "But how disappointing for us!"

Then Susan made a discovery. "Look, Jeffery," she said, holding up the box. "Doesn't it seem to you as if the box ought to be bigger inside than it is?"

"Whatever do you mean?" asked the boys.

"Well," said Susan, "if you look at the outside of the box it seems quite big – but if you look *inside*, it doesn't look *big enough!*"

"You mean – there might be a secret bottom to it!" cried Jeffery, and he snatched the box from Susan. He examined it very carefully – and then he nodded. "Yes – there *is* a false bottom to it. You're right, Susan. How clever of you!"

"How can we open the secret part?" cried John, going red with excitement.

"I don't know," said Jeffery, busy pressing and tapping to see if he could open it. "My goodness! Suppose there is something really thrilling here after all!"

Susan and John could hardly keep their hands off the box as Jeffery tried to open the bottom part. It was no good – he couldn't do it.

He gave it to John, and John tried. Then Susan had a try. But no matter what they did they couldn't open the bottom of the box.

"It's some clever little trick, I'm sure," said Jeffery, in despair. "Oh, I *do* wish we could find it."

Susan grew impatient. She turned the box upside down and banged it with her fist. It slipped from her knee and fell on to the floor.

"Susan, be careful!" cried Jeffery – and then he stopped, and stared at the box. It had fallen upside down, and as Jeffery stared, he saw that the bottom of the box had slid crooked! Somehow or other in its fall, the secret spring had been touched, and the bottom was now loose!

Jeffery grabbed the box. He pressed on the bottom of it, as he held it upside down. The bottom slid away neatly, and the three children saw a small narrow space inside, hidden between the false bottom and the real one.

And this time there was something inside! Yes, there really was!

It wasn't brooches or anything like that – it was a sheet of thick parchment-like paper, doubled over. Just that and nothing more.

"A bit of paper," said Jeffery, taking it out very carefully. It fell in two as he touched it, breaking at the fold. It was very, very old.

"What does it say?" asked Susan, bending over to see it.

"It's a map," said John. "What a funny old map!"

"So it is," said Jeffery. "But what's it a map *of*?"

"Goodness knows!" said Susan. "And what's this one word on the map – just here? It's such old, old printing that I can't even read it!"

"What's that first letter?" said Jeffery, trying to make it out. "It's a J, I think. J – and that's an R, I believe. J – R – there's no word beginning with Jr."

"J – R – is that an E?" wondered Susan. "It's a funny one! And the next letter is certainly an A. Jrea – worse than ever!"

"And then comes an F," said Jeffery. "Jr – eaf – it must be some foreign language!"

"There are some more letters after that," said John. "I give it up! But I know what we'll do – we'll ask someone who can read old writing, and see if they can tell us what the word is. Perhaps if we know what the word is, we should know what the map means."

"Gracious! Look at the time!" said Susan. "Granny will be wondering whatever has happened to us! We'd better pack up and go home."

So they packed up their things, and, leaving the kettle behind for another day, they went to Greylings, carrying the old box with them. What a find they had had!

When they got to Greylings, they found a car in the drive. "It's the same one that came the other day," said Jeffery, looking at it. "It belongs to those people who want to buy the house."

"Well, Granny and Granpa will be busy with them, then," said Susan. "We'd better go into the study and wait till the visitors have gone."

So into the study they went – and, of course, they got out the strange map, pieced it together once more – and tried to find out what the word said.

"If only we could find out!" sighed Susan. And then a voice behind her said, "And what do you want to find out, little girl?"

The children looked round. They saw that Granny had brought a gentleman into the room – the man who wanted to buy the house. She was showing him the study once more, and the children had not heard the door open.

Jeffery did not want to say anything about the map. He tried to take it off

the table – but as it was in half, he only managed to get one piece before the man leaned over the table to look.

"I want to know what that word says," said Susan, in her clear voice. "We've been puzzling and puzzling over it. It's an old map we found today, hidden in this old iron box, up the chimney of our secret house in the woods."

Granny looked surprised. So did the man. He bent over the piece of parchment at once. "Where's the word?" he said. "Ah – well, let me see. That first letter is a T."

"T! We thought it was a J," said Susan.

"T – R – E – A – S —" read the man.

"S!" said Susan scornfully. "That's not S, it's F."

"In the old days the letter S was written like an F," said the man. Then he jumped, because Jeffery gave a shout. He didn't mean to shout, but he couldn't help it. If the first letter was a T – and the fifth was an S – then he knew what the word was!

But he didn't say it. He tried to take the paper out of the man's hand – but the man held on to it. "Wait, wait," he said, "I haven't finished. T-R-E-A-S-U-R-E. The word is 'treasure'! How very interesting!"

The three children's faces went red with excitement and joy. So it's a map showing where the treasure was hidden! thought Jeffery to himself. We can puzzle it out – and perhaps find the treasure for Granny!

"May I take this old piece of paper to a friend of mine who is extremely clever at puzzling out old papers?" said the gentleman suddenly, turning politely to Granny. "I could perhaps find out a good deal more for you, Mrs Greyling, and it might be most interesting."

"Well – it's kind of you," said Granny, not knowing quite what to do. "But I'd rather like to keep the paper and show it to my husband."

"Very well," said the man, "I'll take it with me now, show it to my friend at once, and send it back to you tonight, with a note telling you what he says about it."

But Jeffery did not want the precious paper to go out of his sight. "Please, it's mine," he said. "I want it. We found it ourselves."

"Of course, of course, my dear boy," said the man, smiling at Jeffery. "I quite understand your feelings. I will only keep the paper an hour. My friend is staying at a hotel nearby, and will tell me at once his opinion of it – whether it is genuinely old or not – and if it contains anything of importance to you. Your grandmother has been so kind to me that I would like to do her this little service, if I may."

Poor Granny could do nothing but smile and thank him. She did indeed think it was kind of him, but she was sorry because she guessed that the children wanted to show her their find and talk about it as soon as the man had gone. But as she hoped he would buy Greylings, she did not like to offend him.

"Take it, by all means," said Granny politely. "It would be kind of you to find out exactly what the paper means – if it *does* mean anything!"

The man patted Jeffery on the shoulder. The boy was angry, and looked it. What right had this man to go off with their precious paper?

He went almost at once, carrying the parchment carefully in his hand.

The children clustered together as soon as Granny took the man out of the room to his car.

"What did you want to go and tell our secret to a stranger for, you stupid, silly girl?" said Jeffery to Susan. "Now see what you've done! He's guessed it's something to do with the long-lost Greylings Treasure – and he's got the map. At least – he's only got half of it, thank goodness! I was quick enough to get the other half, and hide it behind my back before he saw it. So he won't be able to tell much from his half!"

"That was quick of you, Jeffery," said John. "But really, Susan is an idiot to go and blurt out our secret like that."

"I'm sorry," said Susan, looking ready to cry. "I didn't think. I really felt so excited."

"Well, Susan, if that's a map showing where the treasure was hidden, we don't want strangers going after it and finding it," said Jeffery. "I should have thought you would have been sharp enough to keep your tongue quiet."

"Don't grumble at me so, Jeffery," said Susan, who hated her big brother to think she was silly. "I'm very, very sorry, really I am."

"Well, don't say a word another time," said Jeffery. "We must just wait and see what happens now – I hope the man brings back our paper all right."

THE SECRET OF SPIGGY HOLES

AN EXTRACT

~ ILLUSTRATED BY ~

E. H. DAVIE

*Mike, Nora and Peggy, who shared their adventures on
the secret island with farm-boy Jack, have been reunited with their
parents, who have adopted Jack. During the summer
holidays they go to stay at Spiggy Holes, a sleepy seaside village
not far from the secret island. While there, they discover that young
Prince Paul of Baronia is being held prisoner by
Mr Diaz and Luiz, two followers of his uncle, who wants
to take Paul's father's crown when he dies. The children
rescue Prince Paul and decide to take him to the secret
island where they hope he will be safe from his enemies...*

CHAPTER XIX
OFF TO THE SECRET ISLAND

George rowed the boat silently over the calm sea towards the little
fishing village of Longrigg. Jack helped him, and the children sat
quietly in the boat until George said it was safe to talk.

"No one can hear you now," he said. "So talk away!"

And then what a noise there was as Mike told the others all that had
happened when he was a prisoner with Paul. And Paul joined in excitedly, telling
how he had been captured in his own father's palace and taken away to Cornwall
over sea and land in ships, aeroplanes, and cars. Poor Paul! He was really very glad

to be with friends once more, for although he had not been very badly treated by Mr Diaz and Luiz, he had been kept a close prisoner for some time.

Soon the moon came up and flooded the sea with its silvery light. The children could see one another's faces as they talked, and every time the oars were lifted from the water silvery drops fell off the blades.

"There's Longrigg!" said George, as they went round a cliff that jutted out into the sea. Everybody looked. The children had been to Longrigg before with George in his boat, but it looked different now in the moonlight — a huddle of silvery houses set in a cove between the cliffs.

"It's like an enchanted village," said Nora dreamily. "And I guess our secret island will look enchanted too, tonight, when we get there. Oh, I do feel so very excited when I think that we're really going there again!"

The children began to talk of their adventure on the secret island the year before — how they had kept their own cow there and their own hens. How they had built their own house of willows, and had found caves in the hillside to live in during the winter. Paul listened, and longed to see the wonderful island!

They landed at Longrigg. George took them through the deserted village street to his brother's garage, a tiny place at the top of the street. A man was there waiting for them.

"Hallo, Jim," said George. "Here are the passengers for your trip. And mind, Jim, not a word to anyone about this. I'll explain everything to you when you come to see me tomorrow. Till then, say nothing to anybody."

"Right, George," said Jim, who seemed very like his brother as he stood there, sturdy and straight in his dark overalls.

"Goodbye, George, and thanks for all your help," said Jack, getting into the car with the others. "Have we got the food? Oh yes — it's in the back. Good!"

"Goodbye," said George. "I'm going back to Peep-Hole now in case Miss Dimity wants a bit of help. Stay on your secret island till you hear from us. You'll all be quite safe there!"

The car started up and Jim set off up the cliff-road. The children waved to George, and then the car turned a bend and was out of sight. They were on their way to Lake Wildwater — on their way to the island!

It was about forty miles away, and the car purred softly through the moonlit night. Paul was very sleepy and went sound asleep beside Peggy — but the others were too excited to sleep.

Jack watched the country flash by — five miles gone, ten, twenty, thirty, forty!

They were almost there. Jim was to drive to where the children's aunt and uncle had once lived, and then leave them. They could find their way then to the lake, and get their boat, which was always ready.

"Here we are," said Jim. The car stopped. Jim got out. "I'll give you a hand with the food down to the boat," he said. So the six of them carried the food to where the boat was locked up in a small boat-house. Captain Arnold, the children's father, had built them a little house for their boat in case they wished to visit their secret island at any time. Mike had the key on his key-ring. He got it out and unlocked the boat-house. There lay the boat, dreaming of the water. The moon shone into the boat-house, and Jack was able to see quite well, as he undid the rope and pushed the boat from the house.

The food was put in. Everyone but Jim got into the boat. Jim said goodbye and good luck and strode back over the fields to his waiting car. The five children were alone!

Jack and Mike took the oars. Paul was wide awake now and was full of excitement, longing to see this wonderful secret island that he had heard so much about.

"It won't be long now," said Nora, her eyes shining happily in the moonlight. The oars made a pleasant splashing sound in the silvery waters, and the boat glided along smoothly.

On and on they went — and then, rounding a corner of the wooded bank of the lake, they came suddenly in sight of their island!

"Look! There it is, Paul!" cried Peggy. Paul looked. He saw a small island floating on the moonlit lake, with trees growing down to the water's edge. It had a hill in the middle of it, and it looked a most beautiful and enchanting place.

"Our secret island," said Nora softly, her eyes full of happy tears, for she had loved their island with all her heart, and had spent many, many happy days there along with the others the year before.

For a while the two boys leaned on their oars and looked silently at their island, remembering their adventures there. Then they rowed quickly again, longing to land on the little beach they knew so well.

"There's our beach, with its silvery sand all glittering in the moonlight!" cried Nora. The boat slid towards it and grounded softly in the sand. Jack leaped out and pulled the boat in. One by one the children got out and stood on the little sloping beach.

"Welcome to our island, Paul," said Peggy, putting her arm round the excited boy. "This is our very own. Our father bought it for us after our adventures here last year – but we didn't think we'd visit it this summer! We left it last Christmas, when we were living in the hill-caves. They were so cosy!"

"Come along up the hill and find the caves," said Jack. "We are all awfully tired, and we ought to get some sleep. We'll get the rugs and things out of the cave, and heat some cocoa and have a meal. Then I vote we make our beds on the heather, as we used to do. It's very hot tonight, and we shall be quite warm enough."

"Hurrah!" said Mike in delight. "Give me a hand with this box of food, Jack. The girls can bring the other things, if Paul will help them."

"Of course I will," said Paul, who really felt as if he was living in a peculiar dream! They all made their way up the beach, through a thicket of bushes and trees, and up a hillside where the bracken was almost as tall as they were. The moon shone down still from a perfectly clear sky, and except that the colours were not there, everything was as clear as in daylight.

"Here's our cave!" said Jack in delight. "The heather and bracken are so thick in front of it that I could hardly see it. Mike, have you got your torch handy? We shall need to go into our inner store-cave to get a few things tonight."

Mike fished in his pocket for his torch. He gave it to Jack. "Thanks," said Jack. "Peggy, come with me into the store-cave, will you, and we'll get out the rugs. Mike, will you and Nora choose a place for a fire and make one? We'll have to have some cocoa or something. I'm so hungry and thirsty that I could eat grass!"

"Right, Captain!" said Nora, feeling very happy indeed. It was wonderful to be on the island like this – able to sleep in the heather and have a camp-fire. She and Mike and Paul hunted about for twigs and wood, and found a nice open place near the cave for the fire.

Peggy and Jack went to the back of the cave, found the passage that led into the inner cave, and crept through to the big store-cave beyond that lay in the heart of the hillside.

"Everything's here just as we left it!" said Peggy, pleased, as Jack shone his torch around. "Oh, there's the kettle, Jack — and I want a saucepan, too, for the soup tonight and eggs tomorrow morning. Dimmy put some into the box. Look, there's the rabbit-skin rug we made last year — and the old blankets and rugs too. Bring those Jack, we'll need them tonight."

Jack piled the rugs in his arms. Peggy took the kettle and the saucepan. They went back to the outer cave, and then looked for the others outside. Mike had got a good fire going. Paul was sitting beside it in delight. He had never seen a camp-fire before.

"Nora, get the cocoa tin, a bag of sugar, and the tinned milk," said Peggy. "Mike, go to the spring and fill this kettle with water, will you? I'll boil water for the cocoa and we'll add milk and sugar afterwards."

Mike went off with the kettle to the cold spring that gushed out from the hillside and ran down it in a little stream. He soon filled it and came back. "What are we going to have to eat?" he asked hungrily.

"Soup out of a tin, bread, biscuits, and cocoa," said Peggy.

"Oooooh!" said everyone in delight.

Mike opened the tin, glad that Dimmy had remembered to put in a tin-opener! He poured the rich tomato soup into the saucepan, and then set it on the fire firmly. "Shall I make another fire to boil the kettle?" he asked.

"Oh no," said Peggy. "The soup will soon be ready, and we've got to cut the bread, and get out the biscuits. You do that, Nora. Where's the biscuit tin, Mike?"

The soup cooked in the saucepan. Peggy sent Jack for cups and dishes and bowls and spoons from the inner cave. The kettle was put on to boil. Peggy cleverly poured the soup from the saucepan into the dishes and handed a plateful to everyone. Hunks of bread were given out too. The kettle sang on the fire, and the smoke rose in the moonlight and floated away in the clear air.

"This is simply perfect," said Mike, tasting his tomato soup and putting big pieces of bread into it. "I wish this meal could last for ever."

"You'd get pretty tired of tomato soup if it did!" said Jack. Everyone laughed. Peggy made the cocoa and handed round big cups of it, with tinned milk and sugar, and a handful of biscuits for everyone.

How they enjoyed that meal by the camp-fire! Mike said he wished they needn't go to sleep – but they were all so terribly sleepy that it was no good wishing that!

"I shall fall asleep sitting here soon," said Nora, rubbing her eyes. "What a nice supper that was! Come on, everyone, let's make our beds in the heather and wash the supper things tomorrow."

So they spread the rugs out in the soft heather and lay down just as they were in their clothes – and in two seconds they were all fast asleep on the secret island, lost in happy dreams of all they were going to do the next day!

CHAPTER XX
PEACE ON THE ISLAND

All night long the five children slept soundly on their rugs in the heather. The three boys were in the shelter of a big gorse bush, and the two girls cuddled together beside a great blackberry bush. The heather was thick and soft and as springy as any bed.

The sun rose up and the sky became golden. The birds twittered and two yellowhammers told everyone that they wanted a "little bit of bread and no cheese!" The rabbits who had played about near the sleeping children shot off to their holes. A rambling hedgehog sniffed at Mike, and then went away too.

Jack awoke first. He was lying on his back, and he was very much astonished when he opened his eyes and looked straight up into the blue sky. He had expected to see the ceiling of his bedroom at Peep-Hole — and he saw sky and tiny white feathery clouds, very high up.

Then he remembered. Of course — they were on the dear old secret island! He lay there on his back looking up happily at the sky, waiting for the others to wake. Then he sat up. Far below him were the calm, blue waters of the lake. It was a perfect day — sunny, warm, and calm. Jack looked at his watch, and stared in surprise — for it was half-past nine!

"Half-past nine!" said Jack in amazement. "How we have slept! I wish the others would wake up — I'm jolly hungry."

He got up cautiously and slipped his few clothes off. He ran down to bathe in the lake. The water was delicious. He dried himself in the hot sun and dressed again. He went to the spring and filled the kettle for breakfast. Then he busied himself in making a fire.

Mike awoke next, and then Peggy and Nora together. Paul still slept on. The girls were full of joy to find themselves on the secret island, and they flew down to bathe in the lake with Mike. When Paul awoke they asked him if he too would like to have a swim, but he shook his head.

"I can't swim," he said. "And I don't want to bathe in the lake. I just want to stay here with Jack."

They got breakfast. Nora ran down to the lake to wash the supper things. Jack fetched more wood for the fire, which was burning well. Peggy cut big slices of bread and butter, and popped some eggs into the saucepan to boil. "Two eggs for everyone," she said. "I know quite well you'll all be able to eat heaps and heaps! Nora, find the salt, will you? I'll boil the eggs hard, and we can nibble them and dip them in the salt."

"Let's have some of these ripe plums too," said Mike, uncovering the basket. "They won't last very long in this hot weather. And where are the biscuits, Peggy? Surely we didn't finish them all last night."

"Of course not," said Peggy, fishing them out from under a bush and taking off the lid. "I hid them there because I know what you boys are like with biscuits!"

They sat round in the heather, eating their hard-boiled eggs, thick slices of bread and butter, ripe plums, and biscuits, drinking cocoa that Peggy had made for them.

"I don't know why, but we always seem to have most delicious meals on our secret island," said Mike. "They always taste nicer here than they do anywhere else."

"Paul, don't you want your second egg?" asked Peggy, seeing that Paul had not eaten it. He shook his head.

"I am not used to your English breakfasts," he said. "At home, in my own country, we simply have a roll of bread and some coffee. But I would like to eat my egg later in the morning, Peggy. It is so nice. I have never had a hard-boiled egg before."

Paul began to talk of his own land. He was a nice boy, with beautiful manners that struck the others as rather comic sometimes. He would keep bowing to Peggy and Nora whenever he spoke to them. He had learned English from his governess, and spoke it just as well as the other children did.

He told them about his father and mother. He cried when he spoke of his mother, who did not know where he was. Peggy and Nora felt very sorry for the little prince. They comforted him, and told him that soon his troubles would be over.

"You are so lucky not to have to be princes or princesses," he told the children. "You can have a jolly time and do as you like – but I can't. You will never be kidnapped or taken prisoner – but maybe it will happen to me again sometime or other. There are many people who do not want me to be king when my father dies."

"Do you want to be?" asked Jack.

"Not at all," said Paul. "I would like best of all to live with you four children, and be an ordinary boy. But I am unlucky enough to have been born a prince and I must do my duty."

"Well, stop worrying about things for a little while," said Peggy. "Enjoy your few days here on our secret island. It will be a real holiday for you. Jack will teach you to swim, and Mike will teach you how to make a camp-fire. You never know when things like that will be useful to you."

The children all felt rather lazy after their late night. Peggy and Nora washed up the breakfast things, and Peggy planned the lunch. The children had eaten all the ripe plums and Peggy wondered if she should open a large tin of fruit. She would cook some potatoes and peas too, and they could have some of the meat off the cold joint they had brought.

"What about picking some wild raspberries, as we used to do last year?" asked Nora eagerly. "Don't you remember the raspberry canes on one part of the island, Peggy? – they were simply red with delicious raspberries!"

"We'll go and see if there are any still ripe," said Peggy. "But first let's see if Willow House is still in the little wood beyond the beach."

The children had built a fine little house of willow branches the summer before, which had sheltered them well on wet or cold days and nights. They all went running down the hill to see if Willow House was still standing.

They squeezed through the thick trees until they came to the spot where Willow House was – and it stood there, green and cool, inviting them to go inside.

"But the whole of Willow House is growing!" cried Peggy. "Every branch has put out leaves – and look at these twigs shooting up from the roof! It's a house that's alive!"

She was right. Every willow stick they had used to build their house had shot out buds and leaves and twigs – and the house was, as Peggy said, quite alive. Inside the house long twigs hung down like green curtains.

"Dear little Willow House," said Peggy softly. "What fun we had here! And how we loved making it – weaving the willow twigs in and out to make the walls – and you made the door, Jack. And do you remember how we stuffed up the cracks with heather and bracken?"

The others remembered quite well. They told Paul all about it and he at once wanted to stop and build another house.

"No, we don't need one," said Jack. "We can sleep out-of-doors now – and if rain comes we'll just sleep in the cave."

Paul ran in and out of Willow House. He thought it was the nicest place in the world. "I wish I had a house of my own like this," he said. "Mike, Jack, will you come back to my country with me and teach me how to build a willow house?"

The boys laughed. "Come along and see if we can find some ripe raspberries," said Mike. "You'll like those, Paul."

They all went to the part of the island where the raspberries grew. There were still plenty on the canes, though they were getting over now.

Peggy and Nora had brought baskets. Soon they had the baskets half-full, and their mouths were stained with pink. As many went into their mouths as into the baskets!

"It's one o'clock," said Mike, looking at his watch. "Good gracious! How the morning has gone!"

"We'll go back and have lunch," said Peggy. So back they all went in the hot sun, feeling as hungry as hunters, although they had eaten so many raspberries!

They had a lovely lunch — cold mutton, peas, potatoes, raspberries, and tinned milk. Mike brought them icy-cold water from the spring, and they drank it thirstily, sending Paul for some more when it was finished. Paul wanted to do jobs too, and Peggy thought it was a good idea to let him. The sun had caught his pale little face that morning and he was quite brown.

"What shall we do this afternoon?" asked Paul.

"I feel sleepy," said Peggy, yawning. "Let's have a nice snooze on the heather — then we could have a bathe before tea, and a jolly good meal afterwards."

It was a lovely lazy day they had, and they thoroughly enjoyed it after all the alarms and adventures of the last week or two. Jack began to teach Paul to swim, but he was not very good at learning, though he tried hard enough!

They had tea, and then they went boating on the lake in the cool of the evening. "We might try a bit of fishing tomorrow," said Jack. "It would be fun to have fried fish again, Peggy, just as we did last year."

"Do you suppose we are quite, quite safe here?" asked Paul anxiously, looking over the waters of the lake as they rowed about.

"Of course!" said Jack. "You needn't worry, Paul. Nobody will come to look for you here."

"If Mr Diaz knew about your secret island he might come here to seek me," said Paul. "Hadn't we better keep a watch in case he does?"

"Oh no," said Jack. "There's no need to do that, Paul. Nobody would ever find us here, I tell you."

"Where did you used to watch, when you were here last year and were afraid of people coming to look for you?" asked Paul.

"There's a stone up on the top of the hill where we used to sit, among the heather," said Jack. "You get a good view all up and down the lake from there."

"Then tomorrow I will sit and watch there," said Paul at once. "You do not know Mr Diaz as well as I do, and I think he is clever enough to follow us, and to take me prisoner again. If I see him coming in a boat, there will be time to hide away in the caves, won't there?"

"Oh yes," said Jack. "But he won't come. Nobody will guess you are here with us."

But Paul was nervous – and when the next day came he ran off by himself.

"Where's he gone?" asked Jack.

"Oh, up to the hill-top to watch for his enemies!" said Nora, with a laugh. "He won't see anything, I'm sure of that!"

But Prince Paul *did* see something that very afternoon!

CHAPTER XXI
THE ENEMY FIND THE ISLAND

Prince Paul was sitting on top of the little hill that rose in the middle of the island. He was quite sure that his enemies would try to find him, and would think of coming to the children's secret island.

He sat there for two or three hours, watching the lake around the island. It was very calm and blue. Paul yawned. It was rather boring sitting there by himself – but the other children wouldn't come, for they said there was no fear of enemies coming so soon.

Paul saw Mike and Jack far below at the edge of the water. They were getting out the boat to go and fish. The girls came running down to join them. They had already asked Paul to come, but he wouldn't. He was really afraid of water, and it was all that the others could do to get him in to bathe.

Paul stood up and waved to the others. They waved back. They didn't like leaving him alone, but really they couldn't go and sit up there for hours. Besides, Peggy had said that if they caught some fish she would fry it for supper, and that really sounded rather delicious!

"We shan't be long, Paul!" shouted Mike. "We shall only be round the south end of the island, which is a good fishing-place. Yell to us if you want us."

"Right!" shouted back Paul, and he waved again. He really thought it was strange the way the four children seemed to like the water so much – they were always bathing and paddling and boating! But Paul liked them immensely, especially Mike, who had been a great help to him when he had been a prisoner in the tower.

He watched the boat leave the little beach and row round to the other side of the island. The boat looked very small from where he stood, and the children looked like dolls! But he could hear their voices very clearly. They were getting their fishing-lines ready.

Paul half wished he was with them, they all sounded so jolly. He watched them for some time, and then he turned round and gazed down the blue waters of the lake on the other side of the island.

And he saw a boat there! Yes – a boat that was being rowed by two men! Paul stood and watched, his heart beating fast. Who were the two men? Could they be Mr Diaz and Luiz? He hated them both and was afraid of them. Had they come to find him again?

He turned to the opposite side of the lake and yelled to the four children in the boat there.

"Jack! Mike! There's a boat coming up the lake!"

"What?" shouted Jack.

Paul yelled again, even more loudly. "I said, there's a boat coming up the lake!"

The four children looked at one another in dismay and surprise. "Surely Mr Diaz can't have found out where we are," said Mike. "Though he's quite clever enough to guess, if he knows we are the children who ran away to a secret island last year!"

"What shall we do, Jack?" asked Nora.

"We haven't time to do anything much," said Jack anxiously. "I think it wouldn't be safe to go and hide on the island – those men will search it thoroughly, caves and all. We'd better get Paul down here, and row off to the mainland in the boat. We could hide in the trees there for a bit."

"Good idea, Jack," said Mike. He stood up in the boat and yelled to Paul, who was anxiously waiting for his orders.

"Come on down here, Paul. We'll go off in the boat. Hurry up!"

Paul waved his hand and disappeared. When he appeared at the edge of the water, the others saw that he was carrying something. He had a loaf of bread, a packet of biscuits, and two tins of fruit!

"I say! You've got brains to think of those!" said Jack, pleased. "Good for you, Paul!"

Paul went red with pleasure. He thought the four children were wonderful, and he was very proud to be praised by Captain Jack!

"I just had time to push all our things into a bush," said Paul. "And I grabbed these to bring, because I guessed we might have to stop away for some hours."

"Good lad," said Jack. "Come on in. We haven't any time to lose. Tell us about the boat. How far away was it?"

As Jack and Mike rowed their boat away from the island, away to the

mainland, Paul told them all he had seen, which wasn't very much. "I couldn't see who the men were, but they *looked* as if they might be Mr Diaz and Luiz," he said. "Oh, Jack — I don't want to be caught and kept a prisoner again. It is so lovely being with you."

"Don't you worry," said Jack, pulling hard at the oars. "We'll look after you all right, if we have to stuff you down a rabbit-hole and pile bracken over it to hide you!"

That made them all laugh, and Paul felt better. The boys were pulling across to the mainland swiftly, hoping to reach it before the other boat could possibly catch any sight of them. The island was between them and the strange boat, but it might happen that the two men rowed round it and would then see the children's boat.

They reached the mainland safely. Jack chose a very wooded part, and rowed the boat in right under some overhanging trees, where it could not possibly be seen. Then he and the others got out.

"I'd better climb a high tree and see if I can possibly see what's going on on the island opposite us," said Jack.

"I'll climb one too," said Mike. "I'd like to watch as well. Come on, Paul, would you like to climb one too?"

"No, thank you," said Paul, who didn't like climbing trees any more than he liked bathing.

"Well, you stay behind and look after the girls," said Jack. Paul was pleased with that. It made him feel important.

But the girls didn't want much looking after! They wanted to climb trees too! However, they busied themselves in looking for a clear space to picnic in. Jack's tree was a very high one. He could see the island quite well from it. He suddenly saw the boat coming round one side of the island, and he knew who the two men were!

"Yes – it's our dear friend Mr Diaz and his sleepy helper Luiz," thought Jack to himself. "They must have missed seeing the little beach where we usually land, and they've come round to the other side of the island. Well, that means we can keep a jolly good watch on them!"

Mike and Jack watched the boat from their perches up in the trees. The two men landed and pulled the boat on to the shore. They stood and talked for a while and then they separated and went off round the island.

"I'm afraid they won't find us!" Jack called softly to Mike, who was at the top of a tree nearby. "And unless they find the things we brought with us, that Paul so cleverly stuffed into a bush, they may not even think we've *been* to the island!"

"It was a good idea of yours to come across to the mainland, Jack," answered Mike. "We're safe enough here. We could even make our way through the woods and walk to the nearest town, if we had to!"

"Look! There's one of the men at the top of the hill," said Jack. Mike looked. The hill was not near enough to see if the man was Mr Diaz or Luiz, but it was certainly one of them. He was shading his eyes and looking all down the waters of the lake.

"Good thing our boat's hidden!" said Mike. "I wonder how long they're going to hunt round the island! I don't want to spend the night in these woods – there's no heather here and the ground looks very damp."

The boys watched for two hours and then they began to feel very hungry.

Mike left Jack on watch and climbed down to the girls, who had been picking a crowd of wild strawberries, small and very sweet. Paul was with them, and he ran to Mike and rained questions on him about the men in the boat.

Mike told him all he had seen. "But what I really came down for was to say we'd better have something to eat," he said. "I'll clean the fish we've caught, Peggy, and light you a small fire. You can cook them, then, on some hot stones, and we'll have a meal."

He cleaned the fish they had caught, and made a fire. "I hope the men on the island don't think our smoke is anything to do with *us!*" he said.

They had a lunch of cooked fish, bread, biscuits, and wild strawberries. Then Mike went up his tree again to watch, and Jack came down and had his share of the meal. It was really rather fun. The children enjoyed their lunch, and wished there was more of it!

"But we must keep the two tins of fruit, and the rest of the bread and biscuits for later on in the day," said Peggy, putting them safely aside under a bush. "Thank goodness Paul had the brains to bring what he could! We'd only have had the fish to eat if he hadn't!"

Jack and Mike took it in turns to watch from a tree the rest of the day. They saw no more signs of the two men on the island, but they knew that they had not left, because their boat was still there.

When it began to get dark, and the boys could no longer see clearly from their perches in the trees, Jack wondered what was the best thing to do.

He climbed down and talked to the others. "We'd better have another meal," he said, "and finish the rest of the food. I'm afraid we shall have to spend the night here."

"We could sleep in the boat," said Nora. "That would be more comfortable than the damp ground here. There are two old rugs in the boat too. And Peggy and I have explored a bit and found where a great mass of bracken grows. We could collect it before it's quite dark, and use that for bedding in the boat! It will be fairly soft for us."

"Good," said Jack. "Show us where the bracken is, Nora, and Paul, Mike, and I will carry armfuls to the boat. Peggy, will you get a meal?"

"Right," said Peggy. It was dark to get a meal under the trees, but the little girl did the best she could. She opened the tins of fruit – Paul had even been sensible enough to snatch up the tin-opener! She cut the rest of the bread into slices, and put two biscuits for everyone. That was all there was.

The boys and Nora came back with armfuls of bracken. They set it in the boat. Then they went back to where Peggy was waiting. Jack had his torch in his pocket, so they were able to see what they were eating. They shared the fruit in the tins, ate their bread and biscuits, and drank the fruit juice, for they were very thirsty.

"And now to bed," said Jack. "Bed in a boat! What peculiar adventures we have! But all the same, it's great fun!"

CHAPTER XXII
MIKE'S MARVELLOUS IDEA

The children made their way to where the boat was tied to a tree. It was now piled with sweet-smelling bracken. Jack had taken up the seats, so that the whole of the boat was a bed. The two girls got in and cuddled down, and then the three boys settled themselves too. It was a bit of a squeeze, but nobody minded. They wrapped the two old rugs round them and talked quietly.

The lake-water lapped gently against the boat, saying "lip-lip-lip" all the time. It was a pleasant sound to hear. An owl hooted in a trembling voice not far off. "Ooooooooo! Oo-oo-oo-oo!"

Paul sat up in a fright. "Who's that?" he said.

Mike pulled him down. "It's only a bird called an owl, silly!" he said. "Don't sit up suddenly like that, Paul, you pull the rug off us."

Paul lay down again and cuddled up to the other two boys. He was glad that the noise was only made by a bird.

The moon came up soon, and shone down through the black branches of the trees above. The water of the lake turned to silver. "Lip-lip-lip" it said all the time against the boat. Nora listened to it and fell asleep. Peggy lay on her back and looked at a star that shone through the trees, and suddenly fell asleep too. Paul was soon asleep, but Mike and Jack talked quietly for some time.

They couldn't imagine what Mr Diaz and Luiz were going to do next. If they stayed long on the island the children couldn't go back there – and as they had no food, this was serious. On the other hand, if they tried to make their way through the thick woods nearby, they might get quite lost.

"If only we could make Mr Diaz and Luiz prisoners, just as they made you and Paul, it would be grand," said Jack. "Then we could do what we liked."

Mike lay silent for a moment – then he made such a peculiar noise that he really frightened Jack.

"Mike! What's up?" said Jack in alarm. "Are you ill?"

"No," said Mike in a very excited voice. "It was only that I suddenly got such a marvellous idea I wanted to shout – and I only just stopped the shout in time. That was the funny noise you heard – me stopping the shout. But oh, Jack, I've really got the most *wonderful* idea!"

"What is it?" asked Jack in surprise.

"Well, it was you saying that you wished we could make Mr Diaz and Luiz prisoners that really gave me the idea," said Mike. "I know how we could! If we could only get their boat away from the island tonight, they wouldn't be able to leave – and they'd be prisoners there!"

"Mike! That's a most *marvellous* idea!" said Jack. "It solves all our difficulties. You really are a clever chap! Once they are prisoners on the island, we can row to the village at the end of the lake, get a car, and go back to Peep-Hole in safety!"

"Yes," said Mike, trembling with excitement. "How shall we do it, Jack?"

"Wait a minute," said Jack, frowning in the moonlight. "I've just thought of something. Suppose Mr Diaz and Luiz can swim? They could easily swim across to the mainland and escape that way."

"But they *can't* swim," said Mike. "I heard Luiz tell Mr Diaz he couldn't, and Mr Diaz said he couldn't either. It was when I was a prisoner up in the tower – they often used to come and sit with us there, and they talked to one another. So if neither of them can swim they really *would* be prisoners!"

Jack was so delighted that he wanted to sing and dance. He carefully took off his share of the rug and put it over the sleeping Paul.

"We needn't wake Paul or the girls," he said. "We will undress, Mike, then slip into the water over the edge of the boat, and swim to the island. You can swim as far as that, can't you?"

"Easily," said Mike. "Then we'll undo their boat get into it and row off! Oh, Jack, this is the most exciting thing we've ever done! I wonder if they'll see us!"

"I don't expect so," said Jack. "They'll be asleep in our cave, I expect!"

The boys undressed without waking the girls or Paul. They slid into the water over the side of the boat and swam off in the moonlit lake, only their two dark heads showing on the calm, silvery surface.

It was rather farther to the island than they expected. Mike was tired when they reached the men's boat, but Jack, who was a marvellous swimmer, was quite fresh. He got in and pulled Mike in too. He undid the rope that tied the boat to a tree.

Then he pushed off, the oars making a splashing noise in the silence of the night. No sooner had they gone a little way out on the lake than a shout came from the island, and Luiz stood up. He had been asleep on some heather, and had awakened to hear the sound of oars.

"Hey! That's our boat you've got! Bring it back at once!"

"We'll bring it back some day!" yelled back Jack in delight.

"You just bring it back now, at once!" yelled Luiz, suddenly realising that he and Mr Diaz would not be able to leave the island at all without a boat. "You wicked boys!"

"Goodbye, dear friends," shouted Jack, seeing Mr Diaz suddenly appearing down the hill. He had been sleeping in the cave and had awakened at the noise of shouting. "See you some day soon!"

∾

FIVE ON A TREASURE ISLAND

AN EXTRACT

ᕦ ILLUSTRATED BY ᕤ

EILEEN SOPER

*This extract is from the very first Famous Five book.
Georgina, who likes to be called George, is an only child who
spends most of her time with her dog, Timmy. She likes
nothing better than to row her boat and explore the small, rocky
island that belongs to her. When her cousins, Julian, Dick and
Anne, come to stay, she finds it difficult to get on with them, but
eventually they become good friends and George promises to take
them to explore Kirrin Island the very next fine day...*

CHAPTER VI
A VISIT TO THE ISLAND

The three children looked eagerly at the weather the next day when they
got up. The sun was shining, and everything seemed splendid.

"Isn't it a marvellous day?" said Anne to George, as they dressed.
"I'm so looking forward to going to the island."

"Well, honestly, I think really we oughtn't to go," said George, unexpectedly.

"Oh, but why?" cried Anne, in dismay.

"I think there's going to be a storm or something," said George, looking out
to the south-west.

"But, George, why do you say that?" said Anne, impatiently. "Look at the sun
— and there's hardly a cloud in the sky!"

"The wind is wrong," said George. "And can't you see the little white tops to the waves out there by my island? That's always a bad sign."

"Oh George – it will be the biggest disappointment of our lives if we don't go today," said Anne, who couldn't bear any disappointment, big or small. "And besides," she added artfully, "if we hang about the house, afraid of a storm, we shan't be able to have dear old Tim with us."

"Yes, that's true," said George. "All right – we'll go. But mind – if a storm does come, you're not to be a baby. You're to try and enjoy it and not be frightened."

"Well, I don't much like storms," began Anne, but stopped when she saw George's scornful look. They went down to breakfast, and George asked her mother if they could take their lunch as they had planned.

"Yes," said her mother. "You and Anne can help to make the sandwiches. You boys can go into the garden and pick some ripe plums to take with you. Julian, you can go down to the village when you've done that and buy some bottles of lemonade or ginger-beer, whichever you like."

"Ginger-pop for me, thanks!" said Julian, and everyone else said the same. They all felt very happy. It would be marvellous to visit the strange little island. George felt happy because she would be with Tim all day.

They set off at last, the food in two kit-bags. The first thing they did was to fetch Tim. He was tied up in the fisher-boy's back yard. The boy himself was there, and grinned at George.

" 'Morning, Master George," he said. It seemed so odd to the other children to hear Georgina called "Master George"! "Tim's been barking his head off for you. I guess he knew you were coming for him today."

"Of course he did," said George, untying him. He at once went completely mad, and tore round and round the children, his tail down and his ears flat.

"He'd win any race if only he was a greyhound," said Julian, admiringly. "You can hardly see him for dust. Tim! Hey, Tim! Come and say 'Good morning'."

Tim leaped up and licked Julian's left ear as he passed on his whirlwind way. Then he sobered down and ran lovingly by George as they all made their way to the beach. He licked George's bare legs every now and again, and she pulled at his ears gently.

They got into the boat, and George pushed off. The fisher-boy waved to them. "You won't be very long, will you?" he called. "There's a storm blowing up. Bad one it'll be, too."

"I know," shouted back George. "But maybe we'll get back before it begins. It's pretty far off yet."

George rowed all the way to the island. Tim stood at each end of the boat in turn, barking when the waves reared up at him. The children watched the island coming closer and closer. It looked even more exciting than it had the other day.

"George, where are you going to land?" asked Julian. "I simply can't imagine how you know your way in and out of these awful rocks. I'm afraid every moment we'll bump into them!"

"I'm going to land at the little cove I told you about the other day," said George. "There's only one way to it, but I know it very well. It's hidden away on the east side of the island."

The girl cleverly worked her boat in and out of the rocks, and suddenly, as it rounded a low wall of sharp rocks, the children saw the cove she had spoken of. It was like a natural little harbour, and was a smooth inlet of water running up to a stretch of sand, sheltered between high rocks. The boat slid into the inlet, and at once stopped rocking, for here the water was like glass, and had hardly a wrinkle.

"I say – this is fine!" said Julian, his eyes shining with delight. George looked at him and her eyes shone too, as bright as the sea itself. It was the first time she had ever taken anyone to her precious island, and she was enjoying it.

They landed on the smooth yellow sand. "We're really on the island!" said Anne, and she capered about, Tim joining her and looking as mad as she did. The others laughed. George pulled the boat high up on the sand.

"Why so far up?" said Julian, helping her. "The tide's almost in, isn't it? Surely it won't come as high as this."

"I told you I thought a storm was coming," said George. "If one does, the waves simply tear up this inlet, and we don't want to lose our boat, do we?"

"Let's explore the island, let's explore the island!" yelled Anne, who was now at the top of the little natural harbour, climbing up the rocks there. "Oh do come on!"

They all followed her. It really was a most exciting place. Rabbits were everywhere! They scuttled about as the children appeared, but did not go into their holes.

"Aren't they awfully tame?" said Julian, in surprise.

"Well, nobody ever comes here but me," said George, "and I don't frighten them. Tim! Tim, if you go after the rabbits, I'll spank you."

Tim turned big sorrowful eyes on to George. He and George agreed about every single thing except rabbits. To Tim rabbits were made for one thing – to chase! He never could understand why George wouldn't let him do this. But he held himself in and walked solemnly by the children, his eyes watching the lolloping rabbits longingly.

"I believe they would almost eat out of my hand," said Julian.

But George shook her head.

"No, I've tried that with them," she said. "They won't. Look at those baby ones. Aren't they lovely?"

"Woof!" said Tim, agreeing, and he took a few steps towards them. George made a warning noise in her throat, and Tim walked back, his tail down.

"There's the castle!" said Julian. "Shall we explore that now? I do want to."

"Yes, we will," said George. "Look – that is where the entrance used to be – through that big broken archway."

The children gazed at the enormous old archway, now half-broken down. Behind it were ruined stone steps leading towards the centre of the castle.

"It had strong walls all round it, with two towers," said George. "One tower is almost gone, as you can see, but the other is not so bad. The jackdaws build in that every year. They've almost filled it up with their sticks!"

As they came near to the better tower of the two the jackdaws circled round them with loud cries of "Chack, chack, chack!" Tim leaped into the air as if he thought he could get them, but they only called mockingly to him.

"This is the centre of the castle," said George, as they entered through a ruined doorway into what looked like a great yard; whose stone floor was now overgrown with grass and other weeds. "Here is where the people used to live. You can see where the rooms were — look, there's one almost whole there. Go through that little door and you'll see it."

They trooped through a doorway and found themselves in a dark, stone-walled, stone-roofed room, with a space at one end where a fireplace must have been. Two slit-like windows lit the room. It felt very strange and mysterious.

"What a pity it's all broken down," said Julian, wandering out again. "That room seems to be the only one quite whole. There are some others here — but all of them seem to have either no roof, or one or other of the walls gone. That room is the only liveable one. Was there an upstairs to the castle, George?"

"Of course," said George. "But the steps that led up are gone. Look! You can see part of an upstairs room there, by the jackdaw tower. You can't get up to it, though, because I've tried. I nearly broke my neck trying to get up. The stones crumble away so."

"Were there any dungeons?" asked Dick.

"I don't know," said George. "I expect so. But nobody could find them now — everywhere is so overgrown."

It was indeed overgrown. Big blackberry bushes grew here and there, and a few gorse bushes forced their way into gaps and corners. The coarse green grass sprang everywhere, and pink thrift grew its cushions in holes and crannies.

"Well, I think it's a perfectly lovely place," said Anne. "Perfectly and absolutely lovely!"

"Do you really?" said George, pleased. "I'm so glad. Look! We're right on the other side of the island now, facing the sea. Do you see those rocks, with those peculiar big birds sitting there?"

The children looked. They saw some rocks sticking up, with great black shining birds sitting on them in odd positions.

"They are cormorants," said George. "They've caught plenty of fish for their dinner, and they're sitting there digesting it. Hallo — they're all flying away.

I wonder why!"

She soon knew – for, from the south-west there suddenly came an ominous rumble.

"Thunder!" said George. "That's the storm. It's coming sooner than I thought!"

CHAPTER VI
WHAT THE STORM DID

The four children stared out to sea. They had all been so interested in exploring the exciting old castle that not one of them had noticed the sudden change in the weather.

Another rumble came. It sounded like a big dog growling in the sky. Tim heard it and growled back, sounding like a small roll of thunder himself.

"My goodness, we're in for it now," said George, half-alarmed. "We can't get back in time, that's certain. It's blowing up at top speed. Did ever you see such a change in the sky!"

The sky had been blue when they started. Now it was overcast, and the clouds seemed to hang very low indeed. They scudded along as if someone was chasing them – and the wind howled round in such a mournful way that Anne felt quite frightened.

"It's beginning to rain," said Julian, feeling an enormous drop spatter on his outstretched hand. "We had better shelter, hadn't we, George? We shall get wet through."

"Yes, we will in a minute," said George. "I say, just look at these big waves coming! My word, it really is going to be a storm. Golly – what a flash of lightning!"

The waves were certainly beginning to run very high indeed. It was strange to see what a change had come over them. They swelled up, turned over as soon as they came to rocks, and then rushed up the beach of the island with a great roar.

"I think we'd better pull our boat up higher still," said George suddenly. "It's going to be a very bad storm indeed. Sometimes these sudden summer storms are worse than a winter one."

She and Julian ran to the other side of the island where they had left the boat. It was a good thing they went, for great waves were already racing right up to it. The two children pulled the boat up almost to the top of the low cliff and George tied it to a stout gorse bush growing there.

By now the rain was simply pelting down, and George and Julian were soaked. "I hope the others have been sensible enough to shelter in that room that has a roof and walls," said George.

They were there all right, looking rather cold and scared. It was very dark there, for the only light came through the two slits of windows and the small doorway.

"Could we light a fire to make things a bit more cheerful?" said Julian, looking round. "I wonder where we can find some nice dry sticks."

Almost as if they were answering the question a small crowd of jackdaws cried out wildly as they circled in the storm. "Chack, chack, chack!"

"Of course! There are plenty of sticks on the ground below the tower!" cried Julian. "You know — where the jackdaws nest. They've dropped lots of sticks there."

He dashed out into the rain and ran to the tower. He picked up an armful of sticks and ran back.

"Good," said George. "We'll be able to make a nice fire with those. Anyone got any paper to start it — or matches?"

"I've got some matches," said Julian. "But nobody's got paper."

"Yes," said Anne, suddenly. "The sandwiches are wrapped in paper. Let's undo them, and then we can use the paper for the fire."

"Good idea," said George. So they undid the sandwiches, and put them neatly on a broken stone, rubbing it clean first. Then they built up a fire, with the paper underneath and the sticks arranged criss-cross on top.

It was fun when they lit the paper. It flared up and the sticks at once caught fire, for they were very old and dry. Soon there was a fine crackling fire going and the little ruined room was lit by dancing flames. It was very dark outside now, for the clouds hung almost low enough to touch the top of the castle tower! And how they raced by! The wind sent them off to the north-east, roaring behind them with a noise like the sea itself.

"I've never, never heard the sea making such an awful noise," said Anne. "Never! It really sounds as if it's shouting at the top of its voice."

What with the howling of the wind and the crashing of the great waves all round the little island, the children could hardly hear themselves speak! They had to shout at one another.

"Let's have our lunch!" yelled Dick, who was feeling terribly hungry as usual. "We can't do anything much whilst this storm lasts."

"Yes, let's," said Anne, looking longingly at the ham sandwiches. "It will be fun to have a picnic round the fire in this dark old room. I wonder how long ago other people had a meal here. I wish I could see them."

"Well, I don't," said Dick, looking round half-scared as if he expected to see the old-time people walk in to share their picnic. "It's quite a strange enough day without wanting things like that to happen."

They all felt better when they were eating the sandwiches and drinking the ginger-beer. The fire flared up as more and more sticks caught, and gave out quite a pleasant warmth, for now that the wind had got up so strongly, the day had become cold.

"We'll take it in turn to fetch sticks," said George. But Anne didn't want to go alone. She was trying her best not to show that she was afraid of the storm — but it was more than she could do to go out of the cosy room into the rain and thunder by herself.

Tim didn't seem to like the storm much either. He sat close by George, his ears cocked, and growled whenever the thunder rumbled. The children fed him with tit-bits and he ate them eagerly, for he was hungry too.

All the children had four biscuits each. "I think I shall give all mine to Tim," said George. "I didn't bring him any of his own biscuits, and he does seem so hungry."

"No, don't do that," said Julian. "We'll each give him a biscuit – that will be four for him – and we'll still have three left each. That will be plenty for us."

"You are really nice," said George. "Tim, don't you think they are nice?"

Tim did. He licked everyone and made them laugh. Then he rolled over on his back and let Julian tickle him underneath.

The children fed the fire and finished their picnic. When it came to Julian's turn to get more sticks, he disappeared out of the room into the storm. He stood and looked around, the rain wetting his bare head.

The storm seemed to be right overhead now. The lightning flashed and the thunder crashed at the same moment. Julian was not a bit afraid of storms, but he couldn't help feeling rather overawed at this one. It was so magnificent. The lightning tore the sky in half almost every minute, and the thunder crashed so loudly that it sounded almost as if mountains were falling down all around!

The sea's voice could be heard as soon as the thunder stopped – and that was magnificent to hear too. The spray flew so high into the air that it wetted Julian as he stood in the centre of the ruined castle.

I really must see what the waves are like, thought the boy. If the spray flies right over me here, they must be simply enormous!

He made his way out of the castle and climbed up on to part of the ruined wall that had once run all round the castle. He stood up there, looking out to the open sea. And what a sight met his eyes!

The waves were like great walls of grey-green! They dashed over the rocks that lay all around the island, and spray flew from them, gleaming white in the stormy sky. They rolled up to the island and dashed themselves against it with such terrific force that Julian could feel the wall beneath his feet tremble with the shock.

The boy looked out to sea, marvelling at the really great sight he saw. for half a moment he wondered if the sea might come right over the island itself! Then he knew that couldn't happen, for it would have happened before. He stared at the great waves coming in – and then he saw something rather odd.

There was something else out on the sea by the rocks, besides the waves – something dark, something big, something that seemed to lurch out of the waves and settle down again. What could it be?

"It can't be a ship," said Julian to himself, his heart beginning to beat fast as he strained his eyes to see through the rain and the spray. "And yet it looks more like a ship than anything else. I hope it isn't a ship. There wouldn't be anyone saved from it on this dreadful day!"

He stood and watched for a while. The dark shape heaved into sight again and then sank away once more. Julian decided to go and tell the others. He ran back to the firelit room.

"George! Dick! There's something strange out on the rocks beyond the island!" he shouted, at the top of his voice. "It looks like a ship — and yet it can't possibly be. Come and see!"

The others stared at him in surprise, and jumped to their feet. George hurriedly flung some more sticks on the fire to keep it going, and then she and the others quickly followed Julian out into the rain.

The storm seemed to be passing over a little now. The rain was not pelting down quite so hard. The thunder was rolling a little further off, and the lightning did not flash so often. Julian led the way to the wall on which he had climbed to watch the sea.

Everyone climbed up to gaze out to sea. They saw a great, tumbled, heaving mass of grey-green water, with waves rearing up everywhere. Their tops broke over the rocks and they rushed up to the island as if they would gobble it whole. Anne slipped her arm through Julian's. She felt rather small and scared.

"You're all right, Anne," said Julian, loudly. "Now just watch – you'll see something strange in a minute."

They all watched. At first they saw nothing, for the waves reared up so high that they hid everything a little way out. Then suddenly George saw what Julian meant.

"Gracious!" she shouted, "it is a ship! Yes, it is! Is it being wrecked? It's a big ship – not a sailing-boat, or fishing-smack!"

"Oh, is anyone in it!" wailed Anne.

The four children watched and Tim began to bark as he saw the strange dark shape lurching here and there in the enormous waves. The sea was bringing the ship nearer in to shore.

"It will be dashed on to those rocks," said Julian, suddenly. "Look – there it goes!"

As he spoke there came a tremendous crashing, splintering sound, and the dark shape of the ship settled down on to the sharp teeth of the dangerous rocks on the south-west side of the island. It stayed there, shifting only slightly as the big waves ran under it and lifted it a little.

"She's stuck there," said Julian. "She won't move now. The sea will soon be going down a bit, and then the ship will find herself held by those rocks."

As he spoke, a ray of pale sunshine came wavering out between a gap in the thinning clouds. It was gone almost at once. "Good!" said Dick, looking upwards. "The sun will be out again soon. We can warm ourselves then and get dry – and maybe we can find out what that poor ship is. Oh Julian – I do so hope there was nobody in it. I hope they've all taken to boats and got safely to land."

The clouds thinned out a little more. The wind stopped roaring and dropped to a steady breeze. The sun shone out again for a longer time, and the children felt its welcome warmth. They all stared at the ship on the rocks. The sun shone on it and lit it up.

"There's something odd about it somehow," said Julian, slowly. "Something awfully odd. I've never seen a ship quite like it."

George was staring at it with a strange look in her eyes. She turned to face the three children, and they were astonished to see the bright gleam in her blue eyes. The girl looked almost too excited to speak.

"What is it?" asked Julian, catching hold of her hand.

"Julian — oh Julian — it's my wreck!" she cried, in a high, excited voice. "Don't you see what's happened! The storm has lifted the ship up from the bottom of the sea, and has lodged it on those rocks. It's my wreck!"

The others saw at once that she was right. It was the old wrecked ship! No wonder it looked odd. No wonder it looked so old and dark and such a strange shape. It was the wreck, lifted high out of its sleeping-place and put on the rocks nearby.

"George! We shall be able to row out and get into the wreck now!" shouted Julian. "We shall be able to explore it from end to end. We may find the boxes of gold. Oh, *George!*"

THE SECRET OF CLIFF CASTLE

AN EXTRACT

~ ILLUSTRATED BY ~
GEORGE BROOK

*Peter and Pam are staying with their cousin, Brock, in a
remote part of the country. From their window they can see
deserted Cliff Castle and decide to go and explore it...*

CHAPTER III
CLIFF CASTLE

Now that the children were right up to the castle, it looked enormous!
It rose up in front of them, square and sturdy, a tower at each end.
Its small, slit-like windows had no glass in. The great front door was
studded with big nails that had gone rusty. There was a large
knocker, which the children longed to use – but which, of course, they dared not
touch!

"What a lot of steps go up to the front door!" said Peter, standing at the top
of the flight, and looking down it. "It must have cost an awful lot of money to
build this place. The walls look as thick as can be – made of solid stone!"

"Let's go all the way round the castle and see what we can see," said Pam.

So they went down the great flight of steps again, and began to make their
way round the towering walls of the strange castle. It was difficult, because
creepers, bushes and weeds grew high up the walls. Tall nettles stood in great
patches, and the children had to make their way round them after Pam was badly
stung on her bare legs.

"We'll find some dock leaves to help the stings," said Peter, and he found a patch of dark green dock leaves. He picked some and Pam pressed the cool leaves against her burning skin.

"That's better," she said. "Gracious, I shan't go near nettles again today!"

They went on their way round the great grey walls. The slit-like windows were placed at regular intervals. The children gazed up at them.

"You know, in the olden days, they had those funny narrow windows so that archers could shoot their arrows out without being hit themselves," said Brock, rather learnedly. "I can't imagine why the old man should have built windows like that for himself, long after the time of bows and arrows had gone! It must make the rooms inside awfully dark."

"I wish we could see them, don't you?" said Pam excitedly. "Just imagine how strange they would look after all these years when nobody has been here — cobwebs all over the place — dust everywhere. Oooh — it would be awfully strange."

They could not go all round the castle, because, when they came to the side that faced due west, the hill fell away so steeply that it was impossible to go any further. The walls of the castle were built almost sheer with the hillside, and there was a very big drop down to the bottom of the hills below.

"Isn't it strange?" said Brock, peering over the edge of the steep cliff. "I shouldn't care to fall down there!"

"Let's have our lunch now," said Peter, all at once feeling terribly hungry. "It's almost time. We can find a nice place out of the hot sun and sit down, can't we?"

"Rather!" said Brock, feeling hungry too. "Look — what about that shady bit over there, facing the castle? We can look at the castle whilst we're eating."

They sat down in the shady spot, and undid all they had to eat. It had seemed a lot when Brock's mother had packed it up — but it didn't seem nearly so much when three hungry children began to eat it. They unscrewed the tops of the lemonade bottles, and drank eagerly. Except that the lemonade tasted a little warm, it was delicious.

Pam finished her lunch first, because she did not want so much as the boys, and gave some of hers to them to finish up. She lay back against a tree and looked up at the silent grey castle.

She looked at the strange narrow windows and began to count them. When she came to the second row, she spoke out loud:

"Look, Peter; look, Brock — there's a window in the second row upwards that is bigger than the others. I wonder why."

The boys looked up. Peter screwed up his eyes to see why the window should be bigger.

"I don't think it's meant to be bigger," he said at last. "I think the weather has sort of eaten it away. It looks to me as if the bottom part of it has crumbled away. Perhaps a pipe comes out just there, and has leaked down the window and made the stone and brickwork rotten."

"Do you see the tree that grows up to that window?" said Brock, in sudden excitement. "I believe we could climb it and look in at that window! I wonder what we should see if we did!"

Peter and Pam stared at him, and then at the tree that grew up to the window. What fun it would be if they really could climb it and have a peep inside the castle!

"Well, let's see if we can peep inside any of the lower windows first," said Peter. "I don't think Aunt Hetty would be awfully pleased with us if we climbed trees in these clothes. We really want old clothes for that."

"Oh, bother our clothes!" said Brock, his red face shining with excitement. "I vote we climb up! But we'll have a peep in at one of the lower windows first. Peter, you come and give me a leg-up."

It wasn't long before Peter was bending down, heaving Brock up to the narrow window-sill to see inside the slit-like window. Brock peered through, but could see nothing at all.

"It's so dark inside," he said. "It wouldn't be so bad if the sun wasn't so brilliant today — but my eyes just simply can't see a thing inside the darkness of the castle."

"Well, we'll climb the tree then!" cried Pam, running to it. She loved climbing trees as much as the boys did.

"Wait a bit, Pam," cried Brock. "Peter and I will go up first, and give you a hand. You're only a girl, you know."

It always made Pam cross to be told she was only a girl. "I'm as strong as you are, anyway!" she cried, and looked about for an easy way to climb.

But Brock was up the tree before either of the others. He was a country boy, used to climbing, and he saw at once the best way to go up. He was soon lost to sight among the greenery.

His voice came down to them: "Go up the way I did. It's not difficult."

Peter followed him, and then Pam. Pam had to have a hand from Peter every now and again, and she was glad of it. They were soon all of them up on a high

branch beside Brock. He grinned at them.

"Good climbing!" he said. "Now, look — see this branch? It reaches right to that window. It's pretty strong, and I think it will bear us all. But we'd better go one at a time, in case it doesn't."

"You go first, then," said Peter. Brock edged his way along the branch, working carefully with his arms and legs. The bough bent beneath his weight and swung down below the window-sill. Brock came back.

"No good," he said. "We'll try the next branch. That looks a good deal stronger — and although it grows right above the window at its tip, our weight will bend it down till it rests almost on the window-sill, I should think."

They all climbed a little higher. Then Brock worked his way along the next branch. As he said, his weight bent it gradually down, and by the time he was at the end of it, its tip rested on the sill itself. Part of it even went right through the window-opening into the castle.

"Fine!" said Brock. He put one leg across the stone window-sill, and peered into the slit. He could see nothing but darkness. But certainly the weather had worn away the stone around that window, for the opening was almost big enough to take Brock's stout body!

"I believe I could get right inside!" he called to the others. He stood upright on the sill and tried to work his way in. It was a very tight fit, for Brock was not thin! He had to squeeze himself in till he almost burst.

He found that the wall was very thick — about a yard thick, before he had got right through the window. Then he jumped down to the floor inside and called out through the slit:

"Come on! It's not very difficult! We'll be able to explore the castle from top to bottom, if you can get through!"

CHAPTER IV
INSIDE THE CASTLE

Pam felt a little nervous about going right into the castle, but she couldn't hold back if the boys thought it was all right. So she followed Peter when he squeezed himself through the slit in the stone walls, and held his hand tightly when he gave it to her to help her to jump down into the darkness. Two slit-like windows lit the room they were in. It seemed as dark as night to the children when they first looked round — but their eyes soon grew accustomed to it, and they began to see quite well. Shafts of bright sunlight lit up the room in two places — the rest seemed rather dark.

They stared round, and then Pam cried out in disappointment:

"Oh — the room is empty! It's just like a prison cell! There's absolutely nothing here!"

She was right. There was nothing to see at all, except for bare walls, bare floor, and bare ceiling. At the far side was a closed door, big and strong. It had an iron handle. Brock went over to it.

"Well, we may be unlucky in this room, finding nothing to see," he said, "but maybe there will be plenty to see somewhere else! Let's open this door and explore!"

He pulled at the door by the great iron handle. It opened! Outside was a dark passage. Brock felt in his pockets, remembering that he had a torch somewhere. He found it, and switched it on.

The passage led from a narrow stone stairway, and seemed to wind round a corner. "Come on," said Brock. "This way! We'll open a few doors and see what there is to be seen."

He opened a door nearby. But again there was nothing to be seen but bareness. He shut the door, and the noise echoed through the stone castle in a very strange way. It sounded as though dozens of doors were being shut, one after another. Pam shivered.

"Oooh!" she said. "It's not nice to make a noise in this place. Even a little sound echoes round like thunder."

No room just there had anything in it at all. It was most disappointing. Brock then led the way to the stone staircase. It wound downwards in the heart of the castle, and as it came towards the bottom, grew a little wider.

It ended in a vast room with an enormous fireplace at one end. "This must be the kitchen," said Pam, in surprise. "And I suppose those stairs we came down were the back stairs. There must be a bigger flight somewhere else. I did think they were very narrow stairs for such a huge castle."

The kitchen was furnished. There was a big wooden table, and around it were set stout wooden chairs. Pots and pans hung around the stove. There was an iron pot hanging over what had once been a fire. Brock peered into it. There was an evil-smelling, dark liquid in it.

"Something made by witches!" he said, in a deep, mournful voice that made Pam jump. Brock laughed. "It's all right," he said. "It's only some soup, or something gone bad after all these years!"

The kitchen was dark and dirty, and there was not much to be seen there. The children went out of it and came into a great hall from which four doors led off. Brock opened one.

And then, indeed, there was something to be seen! The big room beyond the door was furnished most magnificently! Great couches, carved chairs, cabinets, tables — all these stood about the room just as they had been left! But how mournful they looked, for they were adorned with great spiders' webs, and when the children walked into the room, clouds of fine grey dust flew up from their feet.

Sunlight came in long golden shafts through four of the slit-like windows, and divided the room into quarters. It made the whole room even strager than it might have been, for the brilliance of the sunlight lay in sharp contrast to the blackness of the shadows in the far corners.

"Oooh! What an enormous spider!" said Pam, with a shudder, as a great eight-legged spider ran out from under a table. The boys didn't mind spiders. They didn't even mind walking into the cobwebs that hung here and there from the enormous chandeliers that had once held dozens of candles to light the room. But Pam couldn't bear the strange, light touch of the webs on her hair, and longed to get out into the sunshine again.

"Isn't it odd, to have left everything just like this?" said Brock wonderingly. "Look at those curtains. They must once have been simply gorgeous — but now they are all faded and dusty."

He touched one – and it fell to pieces in his hand. It was almost as if someone had breathed on it and made it melt!

"The brocade on the furniture is all rotten, too," said Pam, as she felt it. It shredded away under her fingers. "Everything is moth-eaten. What a horrid, sad place this feels. I don't like it. Let's get away."

"No – we'll explore first," said Peter. "Don't be a spoilsport, Pam. Come with us. You'll be quite all right."

Pam didn't want to be a spoilsport, so she followed the boys rather unwillingly as they went out of the room and into the next.

The same things were found there – furniture and curtains, rotten and decayed. A musty smell hung over everything. It was most unpleasant. Pam began to feel sick.

"I hate this smell," she said. "and I hate walking into these horrid webs. I can't seem to see them – and it's horrid to get them all round my head."

"Let's go upstairs again," said Brock. "And this time we'll go up by the main stairway – look, that great flight of steps over there – not by the little narrow back staircase we came down."

They mounted the enormous stone steps, and came to some big rooms furnished as bedrooms. Up they went again and came to more rooms. Leading out of one of them was a tiny staircase all on its own. It wound up into one of the stone towers that stood at the end of the castle.

"Let's go up this staircase!" cried Peter. "We shall get a marvellous view over the countryside!"

So up they went and came to the open door of a strange, square little room that seemed to be cut right out of the heart of the tower. A tiny slit on each side lit it. A stone bench ran round the walls, but otherwise there was nothing in the room.

"What a wonderful view!" cried Pam, peering out of one of the slits. She saw the whole of the countryside to the east lying smiling in the hot August sun. It looked marvellous.

"I can see our house!" cried Brock. "Over there, beyond the farm. Oh, how tiny it looks! And how small the cows and horses look, too. Like animals on a toy farm."

So they did. It was fun to peer out and see everything from so high up. But soon the children grew tired of it and thought they would go downstairs again.

So down they went, and then paused on the first floor where they had first squeezed in through the window. But somehow they couldn't find the room they had climbed inside! It was strange. They opened door after door, but no, there wasn't a tree outside a window.

"I've lost my bearings," said Peter at last. "I've no idea where that room was. Well, if we don't want to stay here all night we've got to get out somehow! I vote we go right downstairs into the hall, then make our way to the kitchen, and up that back stairway again. We know the room was somewhere near the top of that."

So down they went, into the hall, into the kitchen, and then towards the back stairway.

But just near the stairway was a small door, very low, set in the wall. The children stared at it. They hadn't noticed it before.

"Perhaps we could open this and get out by it," said Peter. "It would save us all that big climb down the tree. I tried the front door to see if we could get out by that, but it was much too heavy. The bolts had all rusted into the door, and I couldn't even turn the handle. Let's try this funny little door."

"It's so low we'll have to bend down to get out

of it!" said Brock with a laugh. They went to the little door and looked at it. It was latched on the inside, but not bolted or locked, though the key stood in the door. Peter lifted the latch.

After a push, the door opened a little way, and then stuck fast. The two boys together pushed hard. It opened just a little further, and sunshine came through.

Peter put his head round the edge. "There's a great patch of nettles and a gorse bush preventing it from opening," he said. "Got a knife, Brock? I believe if I hacked away at this gorse bush a bit I could make the door open enough to let us out!"

Brock passed him a fierce-looking knife. Peter hacked at the bush, and cut off the pieces that were stopping the door from opening.

"Cut away the nettles, too," begged Pam. "My legs still sting from that other patch we went into."

Peter did his best. Then he and Brock were able to push the door open just enough to let them squeeze through one by one. They were all rather glad to be standing out in the bright sunshine again, after the dim, musty darkness of the silent castle.

"I say — if we just push this door to, and leave it like that, not locked or bolted, we shall be able to get in whenever we want to!" said Peter. "We might find it rather fun to come and play smugglers or something here. We could pile weeds against the door so that nobody else would notice it."

"Good idea!" said Brock. So they shut the door gently, then forced the gorse bush back against it, and pulled pieces from a nearby hedge to throw against the door to hide it.

Pam got stung again by the nettles, and almost cried with the pain. Peter had to hunt for dock leaves again!

"Cheer up!" he said. "What do a few nettle-stings matter? We've had quite an adventure this afternoon! We'll come back here again soon and have a fine time."

Pam wasn't sure she wanted to. But she didn't say so! The boys talked eagerly about the afternoon's excitement on the way home — and by the time they reached the house, Pam had begun to think that nettle-stings or no nettle-stings, it had all been simply marvellous!

❧

SMUGGLER BEN

ILLUSTRATED BY
G. W. BACKHOUSE

*Enid Blyton wrote this story during the Second World War.
It is an exciting adventure about a group of children who
discover an old smugglers' tunnel.*

CHAPTER I
THE COTTAGE BY THE SEA

Three children got out of a bus and looked round them in excitement. Their mother smiled to see their glowing faces.

"Well, here we are!" she said. "How do you like it?"

"Is this the cottage we're going to live in for four weeks?" said Alec, going up to the little white gate. "Mother! It's perfect!"

The two girls, Hilary and Frances, looked at the small square cottage, and agreed with their brother. Red roses climbed all over the cottage even to the chimneys. The thatched roof came down low over the ground-floor windows, and in the thatch itself other little windows jutted out.

"I wonder which is our bedroom," said Hilary, looking up at the roof. "I hope that one is — because it will look out over the sea."

"Well, let's come in

During the 1950s, Eileen Soper, the artist responsible for illustrating the Famous Five books, painted at least twenty scenes used for a series of Famous Five jigsaw puzzles. The two illustrated here were titled 'Five Have a Wonderful Time' and 'Five on Holiday'.

Two Secret Seven jigsaw puzzles produced by Bestime during the 1950s.
The artwork was by Bruno Kay.

'Find Out' was a Pepys card game first produced in 1958.
It was based on the Five Find-Outers books.

The Secret Seven card game below features all of the characters.
Can you spot the card showing Enid Blyton talking to the Seven?

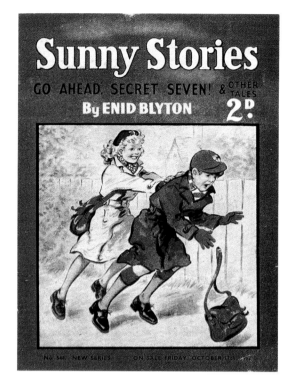

In 1948 the magazine *Sunny Stories* serialised 'Five Go Off To Camp'. Eileen Soper painted this picture of the Five especially for the cover of the first episode.

This Secret Seven cover was painted for the cover of *Sunny Stories* in 1952 when the magazine serialised 'Go Ahead Secret Seven'.

'The Rilloby Fair Mystery' was the second of the 'Barney' books. This splendid jacket was painted for the book by Gilbert Dunlop who illustrated the entire series.

and see," said Mother. "Help with the suitcases, Alec. I hope the heavy luggage has already arrived."

They opened the white gate of Sea Cottage and went up the little stone path. It was set with orange marigolds at each side, and hundreds of the bright red-gold flowers looked up at the children as they passed.

The cottage was very small inside. The front door opened straight on to the little sitting-room. Beyond was a tiny dark kitchen. To the left was another room, whose walls were covered with bookshelves lined with books. The children stared at them in surprise.

"What a lot of books!" said Alec. "Do they belong to the person who let you the house, Mother? Was he a very learned person? These books look awfully dull."

"The man who owns this house is someone who is interested in olden times," said Mother, "so most of these books are about long-ago days, I expect. They belong to Professor Rondel. He said that you might dip into any of the books if you liked, on condition that you put them back very carefully in the right place."

"Well, I don't think *I* shall want to do any dipping into these books!" said Hilary.

"No – dipping in the sea will suit *you* better!" laughed Frances. "Mother, let's see our bedrooms now."

They went upstairs. There were three bedrooms, one very tiny indeed. Two were at the front and one was at the back. A small one and a large one were at the front, and a much bigger one behind.

"I shall have this big one," said Mother. "Then if Daddy comes down there will be plenty of room for him, too. Alec, you can have the tiny room overlooking the sea. And you two girls can have the one next to it."

"That overlooks the sea, too!" said Hilary joyfully. "But, Mother – wouldn't *you* like a room that looks out over the sea? Yours won't."

"I shall see the sea out of this little side window," said Mother, going to it. "And anyway, I shall get a wonderful view of the moors at the back. You know how I love them, especially now when the heather is out."

The children gazed out at the moors ablaze with purple heather. It was really a lovely spot.

"Blue sea in front and purple heather behind," said Alec. "What can anyone want better than that?"

"Well – tea for one thing," said Frances. "I'm most terribly hungry. Mother, could we have something to eat before we do anything?"

"If you like," said Mother. "We can do the unpacking afterwards. Alec, there is a tiny village down the road there, with about two shops and a few fishermen's cottages. Go with the girls and see if you can buy something for tea."

They clattered down the narrow wooden stairway and ran out of the front door and down the path between the marigolds. They went down the sandy road, where blue chicory blossomed by the wayside and red poppies danced.

"Isn't it heavenly!" cried Hilary. "We're at the seaside — and the holidays are just beginning. We've never been to such a lovely little place before. It's much, much nicer than the big places we've been to. I don't want bands and piers and steamers and things. I only want the yellow sands, and big rocky cliffs, and water as blue as this."

"I vote we go down to the beach after tea, when we've helped Mother to unpack," said Alec. "The tide will be going out then. It comes right up to the cliffs now. Look at it splashing high up the rocks!"

The children peered over the edge of the cliff and saw the white spray flying high. It was lovely to watch. The gulls soared above their heads, making laughing cries as they went.

"I would love to be a gull for a little while," said Frances longingly. "Just think how glorious it would be to glide along on the wind like that for ages and ages. Sometimes I dream I'm doing that."

"So do I," said Hilary. "It's a lovely feeling. Well, come on. It's no good standing here when we're getting things for tea. I'm awfully hungry."

"You always are," said Alec. "I never knew such a girl. All right — come on, Frances. We can do all the exploring we want to after tea."

They ran off. Sand got into their shoes, but they liked it. It was all part of the seaside, and there wasn't anything at the sea that they didn't like. They felt very happy.

They came to the village — though really it could hardly be called a village. There were two shops. One was a tiny baker's, which was also the little post office. The other was a general store that sold everything from pokers to strings of sausages. It was a most fascinating shop.

"It even sells foreign stamps," said Alec, looking at some packets in the window. "And look — that's a fine boat. I might buy that if I've got enough money."

Hilary went to the baker's. She bought a large crusty loaf, a big cake and some currant buns. She asked for their butter and jam at the other store. The little old lady who served her smiled at the children.

"So you've come to Sea Cottage, have you?" she said, "Well, I hope you have a good holiday. And mind you come along to see me every day, for I sell sweets, chocolates and ice-creams, as well as all the other things you see."

"Oooh!" said Hilary. "Well, we'll certainly come and see you then!"

They had a look at the other little cottages in the village. Fishing-nets were drying outside most of them, and one or two of them were being mended. A boy of about Alec's age was mending one. He stared at the children as they passed. They didn't know whether to smile or not.

"He looks a bit fierce, doesn't he?" said Hilary. They looked back at the boy. He did look rather fierce. He was very, very dark, and his face and hands were burned almost black. He wore an old blue jersey and long trousers, rather ragged, which he had tied up at the ankles. He was barefooted, but beside him were big sea-boots.

"I don't think I like him much," said Frances. "He looks rather rough."

"Well, he won't bother us much," said Alec. "He's only a fisher-boy. Anyway, if he starts to be rough, I shall be rough, too — and he won't like that!"

"You wouldn't be nearly as strong as that fisher-boy," said Hilary.

"Yes, I would!" said Alec at once.

"No, you wouldn't," said Hilary. "I bet he's got muscles like iron!"

"Shut up, you two," said Frances. "Don't quarrel on our very first day here."

"All right," said Alec. "It's too lovely a day to quarrel. Come on — let's get back home. I want my tea."

They sat in the garden to have their tea. Mother had brought out a table and stools, and the four of them sat there happily, eating big crusty slices of bread and butter and jam, watching the white tops of the blue waves as they swept up the shore.

"The beach looks a bit dangerous for bathing," said Mother. "I'm glad you are all good swimmers. Alec, you must see that you find out what times are best for bathing. Don't let the girls go in if it's dangerous."

"We can just wear bathing-costumes, Mother, can't we?" said Alec. "And go barefoot?"

"Well, you won't want to go barefoot on those rocky cliffs, surely!" said Mother. "You can do as you like. But just be sensible, that's all."

"We'll help you to unpack now," said Hilary, getting up.

"Gracious, Hilary – you don't mean to say you've had enough tea yet?" said Alec, pretending to be surprised. "You've only had seven pieces of bread and jam, three pieces of cake and two currant buns!"

Hilary pulled Alec's hair hard and he yelled. Then they all went indoors. Mother said she would clear away the tea when they had gone down to the beach.

"I know you're longing to do that," she said, with a smile. "But you must just come and unpack a few things with me. You girls can carry the things to the bedrooms and arrange them neatly in the chests-of-drawers there. Alec can undo everything."

In half-an-hour all the unpacking was done and the children were free to go down to the beach. The tide was now out quite a long way and there was plenty of golden sand to run on.

"Come on!" said Alec impatiently. "Let's go. We won't change into bathing-things now, it will waste time. We'll go as we are!"

So off they sped, down the marigold path, through the white gate, and into the sandy lane. A small path led across the grassy cliff-top to where steep steps had been cut in the cliff itself in order that people might get up and down.

"Down we go!" said Alec. "My word – doesn't the sea look grand! I've never seen it so blue in my life!"

CHAPTER 11
A HORRID BOY – AND A DISAPPOINTMENT

They reached the beach. It was wet from the tide and gleamed brightly as they walked on it. Their feet made little prints on it that faded almost as soon as they were made. Gleaming shells lay here and there, as pink as sunset.

The sound of the sea boomed in their ears as they ran over the sands. They felt joyous and happy. There was something wonderful about the seaside. It was all so new and fresh and clean, and the noise the sea made was lovely. The crying of the gulls went with it, and the children felt as if they would almost burst with joy.

There were big rocks sticking up everywhere, and around them were deep and shallow pools. The children loved paddling in them because they were so warm. They ran down to the edge of the sea and let the white edges of the waves curl over their toes. It was all lovely.

"The fishing-boats are out," said Alec, shading his eyes as he saw the boats setting out on the tide, their white sails gleaming in the sun. "And listen — is that a motor boat?"

It was. One came shooting by at a great pace, and then another. They came from the big seaside town not far off where many trippers went. The children watched them fly past, the white spray flying into the air.

"That looks good fun," said Alec. "I hope we manage to get a boat to go rowing and fishing in, don't you, girls? An ordinary boat, I mean. Perhaps Mother would see if there's one to be had here. Maybe one of the fishermen would let us hire one for ourselves."

They wandered along by the sea, exploring all the rock pools, picking up shells and splashing in the edge of the water. They saw nobody at all until they rounded a rocky corner of the beach and came to a small cove, well hidden between two jutting-out arms of the cliff.

They heard the sound of whistling, and stopped. Sitting beside a small boat, doing something to it, was the fisher-boy they had seen before tea.

He now had on his sea-boots, a red fisherman's cap with a tassel hanging down, and a bright red scarf tied round his trousers.

"That's the same boy we saw before," said Alec.

The boy heard the sound of voices on the breeze and looked up. He scowled, and his dark face looked savage. He stood up and looked threateningly towards the three children.

"Well, he looks fiercer than ever," said Hilary at last. "What's the matter with him, I wonder? He doesn't look at all pleased to see us."

"Let's go on and take no notice of him," said Alec. "He's no right to glare at us like that. We're doing no harm!"

So the three children walked into the hidden cove, not looking at the fisher-boy at all. But as soon as they had taken three or four steps, the boy shouted at them loudly.

"Hey, you there! Keep out of this cove!"

The children stopped. "Why should we?" said Alec.

"Because it belongs to me," said the boy. "You keep out of this. It's been my cove for years, and no one's come here. I won't have you trippers coming into it and spoiling it."

"We're *not* trippers! cried Hilary indignantly. "We're staying at Sea Cottage for a whole month."

"Well, you're trippers for a month then instead of for a day!" said the boy sulkily. "Clear off, I tell you! This is my own place here. I don't want anyone else in it. If you come here I'll set on you and beat you off."

The boy really looked so fierce that the children felt quite frightened. Then

out of his belt he took a gleaming knife. That settled things for the two girls. They weren't going to have any quarrel with a savage boy who held such a sharp knife.

But Alec was furious. "How dare you threaten us with a knife!" he shouted. "You're a coward. I haven't a knife or I'd fight you."

"Alec! Come away!" begged Frances, clutching hold of her brother. "Do come away. I think that boy's mad. He looks it anyway."

The boy stood watching them, feeling the sharp edge of his knife with his thumb. His sullen face looked as black as thunder.

Frances and Hilary dragged Alec off round the rocky corner. He struggled with them to get free, and they tore his flannel shirt.

"Now look what you've done!" he cried angrily. "Let me go!"

"Alec, it's seven o'clock already and Mother said we were to be back by then," said Hilary, looking at her watch. "Let's go back. We can settle with that horrid boy another day."

Alec shook himself free and set off home with the girls rather sulkily. He felt that the evening had been spoilt. It had all been so lovely – and now that nasty boy had spoilt everything.

The girls told their mother about the boy, and she was astonished. "Well, he certainly does sound rather mad," she said. "For goodness sake don't start quarrelling with him. Leave him alone."

"But, Mother, if he won't let us go into the little coves, it's not fair," said Hilary.

Mother laughed. "Don't worry about that!" she said. "There will be plenty of times when he's busy elsewhere, and the places you want to go to will be empty. Sometimes the people who live in a place do resent others coming to stay in it for a while."

"Mother, could we have a boat, do you think?" asked Alec. "It would be such fun."

"I'll go and see about one for you tomorrow," said Mother. "Now it's time you all went to bed. Hilary is yawning so widely that I can almost count her teeth!"

They were all tired. They fell into bed and went to sleep at once, although Hilary badly wanted to lie awake for a time and listen to the lovely noise the sea made outside her window. But she simply couldn't keep her eyes open, and in about half a minute she was as sound asleep as the other two.

It was lovely to wake up in the morning and remember everything. Frances woke first and sat up. She saw the blue sea shining in the distance and she gave Hilary a sharp dig.

"Hilary! Wake up! We're at the seaside!"

Hilary woke with a jump. She sat up, too, and gazed out to the sea, over which white gulls were soaring. She felt so happy that she could hardly speak. Then Alec appeared at the door in his bathing-trunks. He had nothing else on at all, and his face was excited.

"I'm going for a dip," he said in a low voice. "Are you coming? Don't wake Mother. It's early."

The girls almost fell out of bed in their excitement. They pulled on bathing-suits, and then crept out of the cottage with Alec.

It was about half-past six. The world looked clean and new. "Just as if it has been freshly washed," said Hilary, sniffing the sharp, salt breeze. "Look at those pink clouds over there! And did you ever see such a clear blue as the sea is this morning. Ooooh – it's cold!"

It was cold. The children ran into the water a little way and then stopped and shivered. Alec plunged right under and came up, shaking the drops from his hair. "Come on!" he yelled. "It's gorgeous once you're in!"

The girls were soon right under, and the three of them spent twenty minutes swimming out and back, diving under the water and catching each other's legs, then floating happily on their backs, looking up into the clear morning sky.

"Time to come out," said Alec at last. "Come on. Race you up the cliff!"

But they had to go slowly up the cliff, for the steps really were very steep. They burst into the cottage to find Mother up and bustling round to get breakfast ready.

"Well, you certainly are early birds!" she said. "Go and put on dry bathing-costumes and your cardigans and then come and help me."

At half-past seven they were all having breakfast. Afterwards Mother said she would tidy round the house and then do the shopping. The girls and Alec must make their own beds, just as they did at home.

"When we are down in the village I'll make inquiries about a boat for you," promised Mother, when at last the beds were made, the kitchen and sitting-room tidied and set in order. "Now, are we ready? Bring that big basket, Alec. I shall want that."

"Mother, we must buy spades," said Alec. "That sand would be gorgeous to dig in."

"Gracious! Aren't you too big to dig?" said Mother. The children laughed.

"Mother, you're not too big either! Don't you remember how you helped us to dig that simply enormous castle last year, with the big moat round it? It had steps all the way up it and was simply lovely."

They set off joyously, Alec swinging the basket. They did a lot of shopping at the little general store, and the little old lady beamed at them.

"Do you know where I can arrange about hiring a boat for my children?"

Mother asked her.

"Well," said the old lady, whose name was Mrs Polsett, "I really don't know. We use all our boats hereabouts, you know. You could ask Samuel. He lives in the cottage over yonder. He's got a small boat as well as a fishing-boat. Maybe he'd let the children have it."

So Mother went across to where Samuel was sitting mending a great fishing-net. He was an old man with bright blue eyes and a wrinkled face like a shrivelled brown apple. He touched his forehead when Mother spoke to him.

"Have you a boat I could hire for my children?" Mother asked.

Samuel shook his head. "No, ma'am," he said. "I have got one, it's true – but I'm not hiring it out any more. Some boys had it last year, and they lost the oars and made a great hole in the bottom. I lost more money on that there boat than I made."

"Well, I'm sure my three children would be very careful indeed," said Mother, seeing the disappointed faces around her. "Won't you lend it to them for a week and see how they get on? I will pay you well."

"No, thank you kindly, ma'am," said Samuel firmly.

"Is there anyone else who has a boat to spare?" said Alec, feeling rather desperate, for he had really set his heart on a boat.

"No one that I know of," said Samuel. "Some of us lost our small boats in a big storm this year, when the sea came right over the cliffs, the waves were so big. Maybe I'll take the children out in my fishing-boat if they're well behaved."

"Thank you," said Hilary. But they all looked very disappointed, because going out in somebody else's boat wasn't a bit the same as having their own.

"We'll just go back to old Mrs Polsett's shop and see if she knows of anyone else with a boat," said Mother. So back they went.

But the old lady shook her head.

"The only other person who has a boat – and it's not much of a boat, all patched and mended," she said, "– is Smuggler Ben."

"Smuggler Ben!" said Alec. "Is there a smuggler here? Where does he live?"

"Oh, he's not a real smuggler!" said Mrs Polsett, with a laugh. "He's my grandson. But he's just mad on tales of the old-time smugglers, and he likes to pretend he's one. There were smugglers' caves here, you know, somewhere about the beach. I dare say Ben knows them. Nobody else does now."

The children felt terribly excited. Smugglers – and caves! And who was Smuggler Ben? They felt that they would very much like to know him. And he had a boat, too. He would be a fine person to know!

"Is Smuggler Ben grown up?" asked Alec.

"Bless you, no!" said Mrs Polsett. "He's much the same age as you. Look — there he goes — down the street there!"

The children turned to look. And as soon as they saw the boy, their hearts sank.

"It's the nasty boy with the knife!" said Hilary sadly. "*He* won't lend us his boat."

"Don't you worry about his knife," said old Mrs Polsett. "It's all pretence with him. He's just play-acting most of the time. He always wishes he could have been a smuggler, and he's forever pretending he is one. There's no harm in him. He's a good boy for work — and when he wants to play, well, let him play as he likes, I say! He doesn't get into mischief like most boys do. He goes off exploring the cliffs, and rows in his boat half the time. But he does keep himself to himself. Shall I ask him if he'll lend you his boat sometimes?"

"No, thank you," said Alec politely. He was sure the boy would refuse rudely, and Alec wasn't going to give him the chance to do that.

They walked back to Sea Cottage. They felt sad about the boat — but their spirits rose as they saw their bathing-costumes lying on the grass, bone-dry.

"What about another swim before lunch?" cried Alec. "Come on, Mother. You must come, too!"

So down to the sea they all went again, and by the squeals, shrieks and shouts, four people had a really wonderful time!

CHAPTER III
HILARY HAS AN ADVENTURE

One evening, after tea, Frances and Alec wanted to go for a long walk. "Coming, Hilary?" they said. Hilary shook her head.

"No," she said. "I'm a bit tired with all my swimming today. I'll take a book and go and sit on the cliff-top till you come back."

So Alec went off with Frances, and Hilary took her book and went to find a nice place to sit. She could see miles and miles of restless blue sea from the cliff. It was really marvellous. She walked on the cliff-edge towards the east, found a big gorse bush and sat down beside it for shelter. She opened her book.

When she looked up, something nearby caught her eye. It looked like a little-worn path going straight to the cliff-edge. "A rabbit path, I suppose," said Hilary to herself. "But fancy the rabbits going right over the steep cliff-edge like that! I suppose there must be a hole there that they pop into."

She got up to look – and to her great surprise saw what looked like a narrow, rocky path going down the cliff-side, very steep indeed! In a sandy ledge a little way down was the print of a bare foot.

Well, someone has plainly gone down this steep path! thought Hilary. I wonder who it was. I wonder where it leads to. I've a good mind to find out!

She began to go down the path. It really was very steep and rather dangerous. At one extremely dangerous part someone had driven in iron bars and stretched a piece of strong rope from bar to bar. Hilary was glad to get hold of it, for her feet were sliding down by themselves and she was afraid she was going to fall.

When she was about three-quarters of the way down she heard the sound of someone whistling very quietly. She stopped and tried to peer down to see who was on the beach.

Why, this path leads down to that little cove we saw the other day! she thought excitedly. The one where the rude boy was. Oh, I hope he isn't there now!

He was! He was sitting on his upturned boat, whittling at something with his sharp knife. Hilary turned rather pale when she saw the knife. It was all very well for old Mrs Polsett to say that her grandson was only play-acting – but Hilary was sure that Ben really felt himself to be somebody fierce – and he might act like that, too.

As she stood and watched him, unseen, she saw the sharp knife slip. The boy gave a cry of pain and clutched his left hand. He had cut it very badly indeed. Blood began to drip on to the sand.

The boy felt in his pocket for something to bind up his hand. But he could find nothing. He pressed the cut together, but it went on bleeding. Hilary was tender-hearted and she couldn't bear to see the boy's face all screwed up in pain, and do nothing about it.

She forgot to be afraid of him. She went down the last piece of cliff and jumped down on the sand. The boy heard her and turned, his face one big scowl. Hilary ran up to him.

She had a big clean handkerchief in her pocket, and she took this out. "I'll tie up your hand for you," she said. "I say – what an *awful* cut! I should howl like anything if I did that to myself."

The boy scowled at her again. "What are you doing here?" he said. "Where are the others?"

"I'm alone," said Hilary. "I found that funny steep path and came down it to see where it led to. And I saw you cut your hand. Give it to me. Come on, Ben — hold it out and let me tie it up. You might bleed to death if you go on like this."

The boy held out his cut hand. "How do you know my name is Ben?" he said, in a surly voice.

"Never mind how I know!" said Hilary. "You're Smuggler Ben! What a marvellous name! Don't you wish you really *were* a smuggler? I do! I'm just reading a book about smuggling and it's terribly exciting."

"What book?" asked the boy.

Hilary bound up his hand well, and then showed him the book. "It's all about hidden caves and smugglers coming in at night and things like that," she said. "I'll lend it to you if you like."

The boy stared at her. He couldn't help liking this little girl with her straight eyes and clear, kind little voice. His hand felt much more comfortable now, too. He was grateful to her. He took the book and looked through the pages.

"I'd like to read it after you," he said, more graciously. "I can't get enough books. Do you really like smuggling and that kind of thing?"

"Of course," said Hilary. "I like anything adventurous like that. Is it true that there are smugglers' caves along this coast somewhere?"

The boy stopped before he answered. "If I tell you, will you keep it a secret?" he said at last.

"Well — I could tell the others, couldn't I?" said Hilary. "We all share everything, you know, Alec and Frances and I."

"No, I don't want you to tell anyone," said the boy. "It's my own secret. I wouldn't mind sharing it with you, because you've helped me, and you like smuggling, too. But I don't want the others to know."

"Then don't tell me," said Hilary, disappointed. "You see, it would be mean of me to keep an exciting thing like that from the others. I just couldn't do it. You'd know how I feel if you had brothers and sisters. You just have to share exciting things."

"I haven't got any brothers or sisters," said the boy. "I wish I had. I always play alone. There aren't any boys of my age in our village – only girls, and I don't like girls. They're silly."

"Oh well, if you think that, I'll go," said Hilary offended. She turned to go, but the boy caught her arm.

"No, don't go. I didn't mean that you were silly. I don't think you are. I think you're sensible. Let me tell you one of my secrets."

"Not unless I can share it with the others," said Hilary. "I'm simply longing to know – but I don't want to leave the others out of it."

"Are they as sensible as you are?" asked Ben.

"Of course," said Hilary. "As a matter of fact, Frances, my sister, is nicer than I am. I'm always losing my temper and she doesn't. You can trust us, Ben, really you can."

"Well," said Ben slowly, "I'll let you all into my secret then. I'll show you something that will make you stare! Come here tomorrow, down that little path. I'll be here, and just see if I don't astonish you."

Hilary's eyes shone. She felt excited. She caught hold of Ben's arm and looked at him eagerly.

"You're a sport!" she said. "I like you, Smuggler Ben. Let's all be smugglers, shall we?"

Ben smiled for the first time. His brown face changed completely, and his dark eyes twinkled. "All right," he said. "We'll all be. That would be more fun than playing alone, if I can trust you all not to say a word to any grown-up. They might interfere. And now I'll tell you one little secret – and you can tell the others if you like. I know where the old smugglers' caves are!"

"Ben!" cried Hilary, her eyes shining with excitement. "Do you really? I wondered if you did. Oh, I say, isn't that simply marvellous! Will you show us them tomorrow? Oh, do say you will."

"You wait and see," said Ben. He turned his boat the right way up and dragged it down the beach.

"Where are you going?" called Hilary.

"Back home in my boat," said Ben. "I've got to go out fishing with my uncle tonight. Would you like to come back in my boat with me? It'll save you climbing up that steep path."

"Oh, I'd love to!" said Hilary joyfully. "You know, Ben, we tried and tried to hire a boat of our own, but we couldn't. We were so terribly disappointed. Can I get in? You push her out."

Ben pushed the boat out on to the waves and then got in himself. But when he took the oars he found that his cut hand was far too painful to handle the left oar. He bit his lip and went a little pale under his brown.

"What's the matter?" said Hilary. "Oh, it's your hand. Well, let me take the oars. I can row. Yes, I can, Ben! You'll only make your cut bleed again."

Ben gave up his seat and the girl took the oars. She rowed very well indeed, and the oars cut cleanly into the water. The boat flew along over the waves.

"You don't row badly for a girl," said Ben.

"Well, we live near a river at home," said Hilary, "and we are often out in our uncle's boat. We can all row. So you can guess how disappointed we were when we found that we couldn't get a boat here for ourselves."

Ben was silent for a little while. Then he spoke again. "Well – I don't mind lending you my boat sometimes, if you like. When I'm out fishing, you can have it – but don't you dare to spoil it in any way. I know it's only an old boat, but I love it."

Hilary stopped rowing and looked at Ben in delight. "I say, you really are a brick!" she said. "Do you mean it?"

"I always mean what I say," said Ben gruffly. "You lend me your books – and I'll lend you my boat."

Hilary rowed all round the cliffs until she came to the beach she knew. She rowed inshore and the two got out. She and Ben pulled the boat right up the beach and turned it upside down.

"I must go now," said Ben. "My uncle's waiting for me. See you tomorrow."

He went off, and Hilary turned to go home. At the top of the beach she saw Frances and Alec staring at her in amazement.

"Hilary! Were you with that awful boy in his boat?" cried Frances. "However did you dare?"

"He isn't awful after all," said Hilary. "He's quite nice. He's got wonderful secrets – simply wonderful. And he says we can use his boat when he doesn't want it!"

The other two stared open-mouthed. They simply couldn't believe all this.

Why, that boy had threatened them with a knife – he couldn't possibly be nice enough to lend them his boat.

"I'll tell you all about it," said Hilary, as they set off up the cliff-path. "You see, I found a little secret way down to that cove we saw – and Ben was there." She told them the whole story and they listened in silence.

"Things always happen to you, Hilary," said Frances, rather enviously. "Well, I must say this is all very exciting. I can hardly wait till tomorrow. Do you really think Smuggler Ben will show us those caves? I wonder where they are? I hope they aren't miles away!"

"Well, we'll see," said Hilary happily. They went home hungry to their supper – and in bed that night each of them dreamed of caves and smugglers and all kinds of exciting things. This holiday promised to be more thrilling than they had imagined!

CHAPTER IV
AN EXCITING EVENING

The children told their mother about Ben. She was amused.

"So the fierce little boy has turned out to be quite ordinary after all!" she said. "Well, I must say I'm glad. I didn't very much like to think of a little savage rushing about the shore armed with a sharp knife. I think it's very nice of him to lend you his boat. You had better bring him in to a meal, and then I can see him for myself."

"Oh, thanks, Mother," said Hilary. "I say – do you think we could get ourselves some fishermen's hats, like Ben wears – and have you got a bright-coloured scarf or sash that you could lend us, Mother? Or three, if you've got them. We're going to play smugglers, and it would be fun to dress up a bit. Ben does. He looks awfully grand in his tasselled hat and sash and big boots."

"Hilary, you don't seriously think I am going to hand you out all my precious scarves, do you?" said Mother. "I'll give you some money to go and buy three cheap hats and scarves with, if you like – and you can all wear your wellingtons if you want big boots. But I draw the line at getting you sharp knives like Ben. Look how even he cut himself today!"

The children were delighted to think they could buy something they could dress up in. The next morning they set off to Mrs Polsett's and asked to see fishermen's hats. She had a few and brought them out. "I knitted them myself," she said. "Here's a red one with a yellow tassel. That would suit you fine, Miss Hilary." So it did. Hilary pulled it on and swung the tasselled end over her left ear just as she had seen Ben do.

Frances chose a blue one with a red tassel and Alec chose a green one with a brown tassel. Then they bought some very cheap scarves to tie round their waists. They went back home, pulled on their wellingtons, and put on their hats and sashes. They looked grand.

"Just like the old-time smugglers must have looked!" said Alec, who had an idea that smugglers were half pirates and half smugglers. "We look a bit silly in bathing-suits though. We'd better put on our grey jerseys over our suits. That will look better."

When the afternoon came they made their way along the top of the cliff, all dressed up. Alec had a knife, too. True it was only a pocket-knife. Still, he felt very fierce when he opened the blade and danced about, shouting.

Hilary showed them where the little narrow path ran down the steep cliff.

"Goodness," said Alec, peering over the edge. "What a terrifying way down! I feel half-afraid of falling. I'm sure I can never get down those steep bits."

"There's a rope tied there," said Hilary, going down first. "Come on. Ben will be waiting. I saw his boat out on the water as we came along the cliff."

They all went down the path, slowly for fear of falling. When they jumped down the last rocky step into the little cove, they saw Ben there waiting for them, sitting on his little boat. He was dressed just as they were, except that his boots were real sea-boots, and he wore trousers tucked well down into them. He didn't move as they came up, nor did he smile.

"Hallo, Ben!" said Hilary. "I've brought my brother and sister as you said I could. This is Alec, and this is Frances. I've told them what you said. We're all terribly excited."

"Did you tell them it's all a deep secret?" said Ben, looking at Hilary. "They won't give it away?"

"Of course we won't," said Alec indignantly. "That would spoil all the fun. I say — can we call you Smuggler Ben? It sounds fine."

Ben looked pleased. "Yes, you can," he said. "And remember, I'm the captain. You've got to obey my orders."

"Oh," said Alec, not liking this idea quite so much. "Well — all right. Lead on. Show us your secret."

"You know, don't you, that there really were smugglers here in the old days?" said Ben. "They came up the coast quietly on dark nights, bringing in all kinds of goods. Folk here knew they came, but they were afraid of them. They used to take the goods to the old caves here, and hide them there till they could get rid of them overland."

"And do you really know where the caves are?" said Alec eagerly. "My word, Smuggler Ben – you're a wonder!"

Smuggler Ben smiled and his brown face changed at once. "Come on," he said. "I'll show you something that will surprise you!"

He led the way up the beach to the cliffs at the back. "Now," he said, "the entrance to the old caves is somewhere in this little cove. Before I show you, see if you can find it!"

"In this cove!" cried Hilary. "Oh, I guess we shall soon find it then!"

The three children began to hunt carefully along the rocky cliff. They ran into narrow caves and out again. They came to a big cave, went into that and came out again. It seemed nothing but a large cave, narrowing at the back. There were no more caves after that one, and the children turned in disappointment to Ben.

"You don't mean that these little caves and that one big one are the old smuggling caves, do you?" said Hilary. "Because they are just like heaps of other caves we have seen at the seaside."

"No, I don't mean that," said Ben. "Now you come with me and I'll show you something exciting."

He led them into the big cave. He took them to the right of it and then jumped up to a rocky

ledge which was just about shoulder high. In half a moment he had completely disappeared! Hilary felt about on the ledge and called to him in bewilderment.

"Ben! Smuggler Ben! Where have you gone?"

There was no answer. The three children stared up at the ledge. Alec jumped up to it. He felt all along it, up and down and sideways. He simply couldn't imagine where Ben had gone to!

There was a low laugh behind them. The children turned in surprise – and there was Ben, standing at the entrance to the big cave, laughing all over his brown face at their surprise.

"Ben! What happened? Where did you disappear to? And how did you get back to the entrance without us seeing you?" cried Hilary. "It's like magic. Do tell us. Quick!"

"Well, I'll show you," said Ben. "I found it out quite by accident. One day I came into this cave and fell asleep. When I woke up, the tide was high and was already coming into the cave. I was trapped. I couldn't possibly get out, because I knew I'd be dashed to pieces against the rocks outside. The sea was so stormy."

"So you climbed up on to this ledge!" cried Hilary.

"Yes, I did," said Ben. "It was the only thing to do. I just hoped and hoped the sea wouldn't fill the cave up completely, or I knew I'd be drowned. Well, I crouched there for ages, the sea getting higher and higher up till it reached that ledge."

"Gracious!" said Frances, shivering. "You must have been afraid."

"I was, rather," said Ben. "Well, I rolled right to the back of the ledge, and put up my hand to catch hold of any bit of jutting-out rock that I could – and instead of knocking against rock, my hand went into space!"

"What do you mean?" said Alec, in astonishment.

"Come and see," said Ben, and he took a torch out of his pocket. All the children climbed on to the ledge, and squeezed together there, watching the beam of Ben's torch. He directed it upwards – and then, to their amazement, they saw a perfectly round hole going upwards right at the far corner of the rocky ledge. It didn't look very big.

"See that?" said Ben. "Well, when I felt my hand going up that hole I slid over to this corner and put my arm right up the hole. And this is what I found."

He shone his torch up the rounded hole in the rock. The three children peered up, one after another.

Driven into the rock were great thick nails, one above the other. "See those?" said Ben. "Well, I reckon they were put there by some old-time smuggler."

"Did you get up the hole?" asked Alec.

"You bet I did!" said Ben. "And pretty quick, too, for the sea was washing inches above the ledge by that time and I was soaked through. I squeezed myself up, got my feet on those nails – they're sort of steps up, you see – and climbed up the hole by feeling for the nails with my feet."

"Where does the hole lead to?" asked Frances, in excitement.

"You'd better come and see," said Ben, with a sudden grin. The children asked nothing better than that, and at once Alec put his head up the hole. It was not such a tight fit as he expected. He was easily able to climb up. There were about twenty nails for foothold and then they stopped. There was another ledge to climb out on. The boy dragged himself there, and looked down.

"Can't see a thing!" he called. "Come on up, Smuggler Ben, and bring your torch."

"I'll give Hilary my torch," said Ben. "She can shine it for you up there when she's up, and shine it down for us to climb up by, too. Go on, Hilary."

So Hilary went up next with the torch – and when she shone it around her at the top, she and Alec gave a shout of astonishment.

They were on a ledge near the ceiling of a most enormous cave. It looked almost as big as a church to the children. The floor was of rock, not of sand. Strange lights shone in the walls. They came from the twinkling bits of metal in the rocks.

"Frances! Hurry," cried Hilary. "It's marvellous here."

Soon all four children were standing on the ledge, looking down into the great cave. In it, on the floor, were many boxes of all kinds – small, big, square, oblong. Bits of rope were scattered about, too, and an old broken lantern lay in a corner.

"*Real* smugglers have been here!" said Hilary, in a whisper.

"What are you whispering for?" said Alec, with a laugh. "Afraid they will hear you?"

"No – but it all seems so mysterious," said Hilary. "Let's get down to the floor of the cave. How do we get there?"

"Jump," said Ben.

So they jumped. They ran to the boxes and opened the lids.

"No good," said Ben. "I've done that long ago. They're quite empty. I often come to play smugglers here when I'm by myself. Isn't it a fine place?"

"Simply marvellous!" said Alec. "Let's all come here and play tomorrow. We can bring candles and something to eat and drink. It would be gorgeous."

"Oooh, yes," said Hilary. So they planned everything in excitement, and then climbed back to the ledge, and down through the hole into the first cave. Out they went into the sunshine. Ben smiled as much as the rest.

"It's fun to share my secret with you," he told the others half shyly. "It will be grand to play smugglers all together, instead of just by myself. I'll bring some sandwiches tomorrow, and some plums. You bring anything you can, too. It shall be our own secret smugglers' cave — and we're the smugglers!"

CHAPTER V
YET ANOTHER SECRET

The next day the four children met together in the big cave. They felt very thrilled as they climbed up the hole and then jumped down into the smugglers' cave. They had brought candles and food with them, and Alec had bottles of home-made lemonade on his back in a leather bag.

They played smugglers to their hearts' content. Ben ordered them about, and called them "My men", and everyone enjoyed the game thoroughly. At last Alec sat down on a big box and said he was tired of playing.

"I'd like something to eat," he said. "Let's use this big box for a table."

They set the things out on the table. And then Hilary looked in a puzzled way at the box.

"What's up?" asked Alec, seeing her look.

"Well, I'm just wondering something," said Hilary. "How in the world did the smugglers get this big box up the small round hole to this cave? After all, that hole only just takes us comfortably — surely this box would never have got through it."

Frances and Alec stared at the box. They felt puzzled, too. It was quite certain that no one could have carried such a big box through the hole. They looked at Ben.

"Have you ever thought of that?" Alec asked him.

"Plenty of times," said Ben. "And, what's more, I know the answer!"

"Tell us!" begged Hilary. "Is there another way into this cave?"

Smuggler Ben nodded. "Yes," he said. "I'll show it to you if you like. I just wanted to see if any of my three men were clever enough to think of such a thing. Come on — I'll show you the other way in. Didn't you wonder yesterday how it was that I came back into the other cave after I'd disappeared up the hole?"

He stood up and the others rose, too, all excited. Ben went to the back of the cave. It seemed to the children as if the wall there was quite continuous — but it wasn't. There was a fold in it — and in the fold was a passage! It was wide, but low, and the children had to crouch down almost double to get into it. But almost immediately it rose high and they could stand. Smuggler Ben switched on his torch, and the children saw that the passage was quite short and led into yet another cave. This was small and ran right down to the rocky side of the cliff very steeply, more like a wide passage than a cave.

The children went down the long cave and came to a rocky inlet of water. "When the tide comes in, it sweeps right through this cave," said Ben, "and I reckon that this is where the smugglers brought in their goods – by boat. The boat would be guided into this watery passage at high tide, and beached at the far end, where the tide didn't reach. Then the things could easily be taken into the big cave. The smugglers left a way of escape for themselves down the hole we climbed through from the first cave – you know, where the nails are driven into the rock."

"This gets more and more exciting!" said Alec. "Anything more, Ben? Don't keep it from us. Tell us everything!"

"Well, there is one thing more," said Ben, "but it just beats me. Maybe the four of us together could do something about it though. Come along and I'll show you."

He led them back to the little passage between the big cave and the one they were in. He climbed up the wall a little way, and then disappeared. The others followed him.

There was another passage leading off into the darkness there, back into the cliff. Ben shone his torch down it as the others crowded on his heels.

"This is a passage that goes right back into the cliff itself," said Ben. "It isn't made in the rock, though – it's made in the rather sandy soil."

"Let's go up it!" cried Alec excitedly.

"We can't," said Ben, and he shone his torch before him. "The passage walls have fallen in just along there – look!"

So they had. The passage ended in a heap of stones, soil and sand. It was completely blocked up.

"Can't we clear it?" cried Alec.

"Well, we might, as there are so many of us," said Ben. "I didn't feel like tackling it all by myself, I must say. For one thing I didn't know how far back the passage was blocked. It might have fallen in for a long way."

"I wonder where it leads to," said Alec. "It seems to go straight back. I say – isn't this thrilling!"

"We'll come and dig it out tomorrow," said Hilary, her eyes dancing. "We'll bring our spades – and a sack or something to put the stones and soil in. Then we can drag it away and empty it."

"Golly! That *will* be fun," said Alec. "Captain, what are your orders?"

"Be here tomorrow after tea," said Smuggler Ben, laughing. "I'll bring my uncle's big spade. That's a powerful one – it will soon dig away the soil."

So the next day the children crowded into the cave with spades and sacks. They used the ordinary way in, climbing up the hole by the nails and jumping into the cave from the high ledge. Then they made their way into the low passage, and climbed up where the roof rose high, till they came to the blocked-up passage. They went on by the light of their torches and came to the big fall of stones and soil.

"Now, men, to work!" said Smuggler Ben, and the gang set to work with a will. The boys shovelled away the soil and stones, and the girls filled the sacks. Then the boys dragged them down the passage, let them fall to the opening between the two caves, climbed down, dragged the sacks into the large cave and emptied them into a corner. Then back they went again to do some more digging.

"What's the time?" said Alec at last. "I feel as if we've been working for hours. We mustn't forget that high tide is at half-past seven. We've got to get out before then."

Hilary looked at her watch. "It's all right," she said. "It's only half-past six. We've plenty of time."

"Gracious! Hasn't the time gone slowly!" said Frances in surprise. "Come on – we can do a lot more!"

They went on working, and after a time Ben began to feel rather uncomfortable. "Hilary, what's the time now?" he said. "I'm sure it must be getting near high tide."

Hilary glanced at her watch again. "It's half-past six," she said, in surprise.

"But you said that before!" cried Ben. "Has your watch stopped?"

It had! Hilary held it to her ear and cried out in dismay. "Yes! It's stopped. Oh, blow! I wonder what the right time is."

"Quick! We'd better go and see how the tide is," said Ben, and he dropped his spade and rushed to the entrance of the blocked-up passage. He dropped down and went into the big cave, and then climbed up to the ledge, and then down by the nail-studded hole on to the ledge in the first cave.

But even as he climbed down to the ledge, he felt the wash of water over his foot. "Golly! The tide's almost in!" he yelled. "We're caught! We can't get out!"

He climbed back and stood in the big cave with the others. They looked at him, half-frightened.

"Don't be scared," said Smuggler Ben. "It only means we'll have to wait a few hours till the tide goes down. I hope your mother won't worry."

"She's out tonight," said Alec. "She won't know. Does the water come in here, Ben?"

"Of course not," said Ben. "This cave is too high up. Well — let's sit down, have some chocolate and a rest, and then we might as well get on with our job."

They lolled about for half an hour and then went back to the blocked-up passage to dig again. They all wondered how far back the passage had fallen in. They did hope that their work wouldn't be too long.

"If it's fallen in too much we'll have to give it up," said Smuggler Ben, the tassel of his cap falling over his face as he dug. "That's really why I didn't start on the job by myself. I felt it might have fallen in for miles."

Time went on. The boys went to see if the tide was falling, but it was still very high. It was getting dark outside. The boys stood at the end of the long, narrow cave, up which the sea now rushed deeply. And as they stood there, they heard a strange noise coming nearer and nearer.

"Whatever's that?" said Alec, in astonishment.

"It sounds like a motor boat," said Ben.

"It can't be," said Alec.

But it was. A small motor boat suddenly loomed out of the darkness and worked itself very carefully up the narrow passage and into the long cave, which was now full of deep water! The boys were at first too startled to move. They heard men and women talking in low voices.

"Is this the place?"

"Yes — step out just there. Wait till the wave goes back. That's it — now step out."

Ben clutched hold of Alec's arm and pulled him silently away, back into the entrance between the caves. Up they went in the blocked passage. The girls called out to them: "What's the tide like?"

"Sh!" said Smuggler Ben, so fiercely that the girls were quite frightened.

They stared at Ben with big eyes. The boy told them in a whisper what he and Alec had seen.

"Something's going on," he said mysteriously. "I don't know what. But it makes me suspicious when strange motor boats come to our coasts late at night like this and run into a little-known cave. After all, our country is at war — they may be up to no good, these people. They may be enemies!"

All the children felt a shivery feeling down their backs when Ben said this. Hilary felt that it was just a bit *too* exciting. "What do you mean?" she whispered.

"I don't exactly know," said Ben. "All I know for certain is that it's plain somebody else knows of these caves and plans to use them for something. I don't know what. And it's up to us to find out!"

"Oooh! I wish we could!" said Hilary at once. "What are we going to do now? Wait here?"

"Alec and I will go down to the beginning of this passage," said Ben. "Maybe the people don't know about it. We'll see if we can hear what they say."

So they crept down to the beginning of the passage and leaned over to listen. Three or four people had now gone into the big cave, but to Ben's great disappointment they were talking in a strange language, and he could not understand a word.

Then came something he did understand! One of the women spoke in English. "We will bring them on Thursday night," she said. "When the tide is full."

Another man answered. Then the people went back to their motor boat, and the boys soon heard the whirring of the engine as it made its way carefully out of the long, narrow cave.

"They're using that cave rather like a boat-house," said Ben. "Golly, I wonder how they knew about it. And what are they bringing in on Thursday night?"

"Smuggled goods, do you think?" said Alec, hot with excitement. "People always smuggle things in wartime. Mother said so. They're smugglers, Ben — smugglers of nowadays! And they're using the old smugglers' caves again. I say — isn't this awfully exciting?"

"Yes, it is," said Smuggler Ben. "We'd better come here on Thursday night, Alec. We'll have to see what happens. We simply must. Can you slip away about midnight, do you think?"

"Of course!" said Alec. "You bet! And the girls, too! We'll all be here! And we'll watch to see exactly what happens. Fancy spying on real smugglers, Ben. What a thrill!"

CHAPTER VI
A STRANGE DISCOVERY

Mother was in by the time the children got back home, and she was very worried indeed about them.

"Mother, it's all right," said Alec, going over to her. "We just got caught by the tide, that's all, playing in caves. But we were quite safe. We just waited till the tide went down."

"Now listen, Alec," said Mother, "this just won't do. I shall forbid you to play in those caves if you get caught another time, and worry me like this. I imagined you all drowning or something."

"We're awfully sorry, Mother," said Hilary, putting her arms round her. "Really, we wouldn't have worried you for anything. Look — my watch stopped at half-past six, and that put us all wrong about the tide."

"Very well," said Mother. "I'll forgive you this time — but I warn you, if you worry me again like this, you won't be allowed to set foot in a single cave!"

This was a most alarming threat. It would be too dreadful if they couldn't go on Thursday night. They all went up to bed, making up their minds that they wouldn't give their mother any cause for alarm at all during the next few days.

The next day it poured with rain, which was very disappointing. Alec ran down to the village to see what Ben was doing. The two boys talked excitedly about what had happened the night before.

"Mother says will you come and spend the day with us?" said Alec. "Do come. You'll like Mother, she's a dear."

"I'd like to come," said Ben. "But will your mother think I look all right like this? I haven't got any other clothes except my Sunday trousers."

"Of course you look all right," said Alec. "Come on. Let's go now. This rain isn't very funny — it's trickling down my neck already."

The two boys went back to Sea Cottage. The girls welcomed them, and Mother shook hands with Ben very politely.

"I'm glad you can come for the day," she said. "You'd better go up to the girls' bedroom and play there. I want the sitting-room to do some writing in this morning."

So they all went up to the bedroom above, and sat down to talk. "It's nice of Mother to send us up here," said Hilary. "We can talk in peace. What are our plans for Thursday, Captain?"

"Well, I don't quite know," said Ben slowly. "You see, we've got to be there at midnight, haven't we? – but we simply must be there a good time before that, because of the tide. You see, we can't get into either cave if the tide is up. We'd be dashed to pieces. You've no idea how big the waves are when they come sweeping into that little cove."

The children stared at Smuggler Ben in dismay. None of them had thought of that.

"What time would we have to be there?" asked Alec.

"We'd have to be there about half-past nine, as far as I can reckon," said Ben. "Can you leave by that time? What would your mother say?"

"Mother wouldn't let us, I'm sure of that," said Hilary, in disappointment. "She was so dreadfully worried about us last night. I'm quite sure if we told her what we wanted to do, she would say 'No' at once."

"She isn't in bed by that time, then?" said Ben.

The children shook their heads. All four were puzzled and disappointed. They couldn't think how to get over the difficulty. There was no way out of the cottage except through the sitting-room door – and Mother would be in the room, writing or reading, at the time they wanted to go out.

"What about getting out of the window?" said Alec, going over to look. But that was quite impossible, too. It was too far to jump, and, anyway, Mother would be sure to hear any noise they made.

"It looks as if I'll have to go alone," said Ben gloomily. "It's funny – I used to like doing everything all by myself, you know – but now I don't like it at all. I want to be with my three men!"

"Oh, Ben – it would be awful thinking of you down in those caves, finding out what was happening – and us in our bed, wanting and longing to be with you!" cried Hilary.

"Well, I simply don't know what else to do," said Ben. "If you can't come, you can't. And certainly I wouldn't let you come after your mother had gone to bed, because by that time the tide would be up, and you'd simply be washed away as soon as you put foot on the beach. No – I'll go alone – and I'll come and tell you what's happened the next morning."

The children felt terribly disappointed and gloomy. "Let's go downstairs into that little study place that's lined with books," said Hilary at last. "I looked into one of the books the other day, and it seemed to be all about this district in the old days. Maybe we might find some bits about smugglers."

Ben brightened up at once. "That would be fine," he said. "I know Professor Rondel was supposed to have a heap of books about this district. He was a funny man — never talked to anyone. I didn't like him."

The children went downstairs. Mother called out to them: "Where are you going?"

"Into the book-room," said Hilary, opening the sitting-room door. "We may, mayn't we?"

"Yes, but be sure to take care of any book you use, and put it back into its right place," said Mother. They promised this and then went into the little study.

"My word! What hundreds of books!" said Ben, in amazement. The walls were lined with them, almost from floor to ceiling. The boy ran his eyes along the shelves. He picked out a book and looked at it.

"Here's a book about the moors behind here," he said. "And maps, too. Look — I've been along here — and crossed that stream just there."

The children looked. "We ought to go for some walks with you over those lovely moors, Ben," said Alec. "I'd like that."

Hilary took down one or two books and looked through them, too, trying to find something exciting to read. She found nothing and put them back. Frances showed her a book on the top shelf.

"Look," she said, "do you think that would be any good? It's called *Old-Time Smugglers' Haunts.*"

"It might be interesting," said Hilary, and stood on a chair to get the book. It

was big and old and smelled musty. The girl jumped down with it and opened it on the table. The first picture she saw made her cry out.

"Oh, look — here's an old picture of this village! Here are the cliffs — and there are the old, old houses that the fishermen still live in!"

She was quite right. Underneath the picture was written: "A little-known smugglers' haunt. See page 66."

They turned to page sixty-six, and found printed there an account of the caves in the little cove on the beach. "The best-known smuggler of those days was a dark, fiery man named Smuggler Ben," said the book. The children exclaimed in surprise and looked at Ben.

"How funny!" they cried. "Did you know that, Ben?"

"No," said Ben. "My name is really Benjamin, of course, but everyone calls me Ben. I'm dark, too. I wonder if Smuggler Ben was an ancestor of mine — you know, some sort of relation a hundred or more years ago?"

"Quite likely," said Alec. "I wish we could find a picture of him to see if he's like you."

But they couldn't. They turned over the pages of the book and gave it up. But before they shut it Ben took hold of it. He had an idea. "I just wonder if by chance there's a mention of that blocked-up passage," he said. "It would be fun to know where it comes out, wouldn't it?"

He looked carefully through the book. He came again to page sixty-six, and looked at it closely. "Someone has written a note in the margin of this page," he said, holding it up to the light. "It's written in pencil, very faintly. I can hardly make it out."

The children did make it out at last. "For more information, see page 87 of *Days of Smugglers*," the note said. The children looked at one another.

"That would be a book," said Alec, moving to the shelves. "Let's see who can find it first."

Hilary found it. She was always the sharpest of the three. It was a small book, bound in black, and the print was rather faded. She turned to page eighty-seven. The book was all about the district they were staying in, and on page eighty-seven was a description of the old caves. And then came something that excited the children very much.

"Read it out, Ben, read it out!" cried Alec. "It's important!"

So Ben read it out. "From a well-hidden opening between two old smugglers' caves is a curious passage, partly natural, partly man-made, probably by the smugglers themselves. This runs steadily upwards through the cliffs, and eventually stops not far from a little stream. A well-hidden hole leads upwards on to the moor. This was probably the way the smugglers used when they took their goods from the caves, over the country."

The children stared at one another, trembling with excitement. "So that's where the passage goes to!" said Alec. "My word – if only we could find the other end! Ben, have you any idea at all where it ends?"

"None at all," said Ben. "But it wouldn't be very difficult to find out! We know whereabouts the beginning of the passage are – and if we follow a more or less straight line inland till we come to a stream on the moors, we might be able to spot the hole!"

"I say! Let's go now, at once, this very minute!" cried Hilary, shouting in her excitement.

"Shut up, silly," said Alec. "Do you want to tell everyone our secrets? It's almost lunch-time. We can't go now. But I vote we go immediately afterwards!"

"Professor Rondel must have known all about those caves," said Ben thoughtfully. "I suppose he couldn't have anything to do with the people we overheard last night? No – that's too far-fetched. But the whole thing is very strange. I do hope we shall be able to find the entrance to the other end of that secret passage."

Mother called the children at that moment. "Lunch!" she cried. "Come along, bookworms, and have a little something to eat."

They were all hungry. They went to wash and make themselves tidy, and then sat down and ate a most enormous meal. Ben liked the children's mother very much. She talked and laughed, and he didn't feel a bit shy of her.

"You know, Alec and the girls really thought you were going after them with that knife of yours," she said.

Ben went red. "I did feel rather fierce that day," he said. "But it's awful when people come and spoil your secret places, isn't it? Now I'm glad they came, because they're the first friends I've ever had. We're having a fine time."

Mother looked out of the window as the children finished up the last of the jam tarts.

"It's clearing up," she said. "I think you all ought to go out. It will be very wet underfoot, but you can put on your wellingtons. Why don't you go out on the moors for a change?"

"Oh yes, we will!" cried all four children at once. Mother was rather astonished.

"Well, you don't usually welcome any suggestion of walking in the wet," she said. "I believe you've got some sort of secret plan!"

But nobody told her what it was!

CHAPTER VII
GOOD HUNTING

After lunch the children put on their boots and macs. They pulled on their sou'westers, and said goodbye to their mother, and set off.

"Now for a good old hunt," said Ben. "First let's go to the cliff that juts over my little cove. Then we'll try to make out where the passage begins underground and set off from that spot."

It wasn't long before they were over the cove. The wind whipped their faces, and overhead the clouds scudded by. Ben went to about the middle of the cliff over the cove and stood there.

"I should say that the blocked-up passage runs roughly under here," he said. "Now, let's think. Does it run quite straight from where it begins? It curves a bit, doesn't it?"

"Yes, but it soon curved back again to the blocked-up part," said Alec eagerly. "So you can count it about straight to there. Let's walk in a straight line from here till we think we've come over the blocked-up bit."

They walked over the cliff inland, foot-deep in purple heather. Then Ben stopped. "I reckon we must just about be over the blocked-up bit," he said. "Now listen – we've got to look for a stream. There are four of us. We'll all part company and go off in different directions to look for the stream. Give a yell if you find one."

The four of them parted and wandered off over the moor. The wind was drying the heather fast, and it was quite pleasant to walk there.

Soon Alec gave a yell. "There's a kind of stream here! It runs along for a little way and then disappears into a sort of little gully. I expect it makes its way down through the cliff somewhere and springs out into the sea. Would this be the stream, do you think?"

Everyone ran to where Alec stood. Ben looked down at the little brown rivulet. It was certainly very small.

"It's been bigger once upon a time," he said, pointing to where the bed was dry and wide. "Maybe this is the one. There doesn't seem to be another, anyway."

"We'll hunt about around here for an opening of some sort," said Alec, his face red with excitement.

They all hunted about, and it was Hilary who found it – quite by accident!

She was walking over the heather, her eyes glancing round for any hole, when her foot went right through into space! She had trodden on what she thought was good solid ground, over which heather grew — but almost at once she sank on one knee as her foot went through some sort of hole!

"I say! My foot's gone through a hole here," she yelled. "Is it the one? It went right through it. I nearly sprained my ankle."

The others came up. Ben pulled Hilary up and then parted the heather to see. Certainly a big hole was there — and certainly it seemed to go down a good way.

"I believe it's a rabbit hole!" said Alec.

"No, it isn't," said Ben, scraping round the edge of the hole with his knife, to make it bigger. "There are lots of these holes on the moors. Some of them lead down to underground channels. They're filled up whenever they're found because they're dangerous to walkers. The heather has practically filled this one up itself — but if we all tug away bits we'll soon enlarge the hole."

The children tugged away at armfuls of heather and soon got the tough roots out. The sides of the hole fell away as they took out the heather. Ben switched his torch on when it was fairly large. There seemed to be quite a big drop down.

"We'd better slide down a rope," he said.

"We haven't got one," said Alec.

"I've got one round my waist," said Ben, and undid a piece of strong rope from under his red belt. A stout gorse bush stood not far off, and Ben wound it round the strong stem at the bottom, pricking himself badly but not seeming to feel it at all.

"I'll go down," he said. He took hold of the rope and lay down on the heather. Then he put his legs into the hole and let himself go, holding tightly to the rope. He slid into the hole, and went a good way down.

"See anything?" yelled Alec.

"Yes. There *is* an underground channel here of some sort!" came Ben's voice, rather muffled. "I believe we're on to the right one. Wait a minute. I'm going to kick away a bit with my feet, and get some of the loose soil away."

After a bit Ben's voice came again, full of excitement.

"Come on down! There's a kind of underground channel, worn away by water. I reckon a stream must have run here at some time."

One by one the excited children slipped down the rope. They found what Ben had said — a kind of underground channel or tunnel plainly made by water of some kind in far-off days. Ben had his torch and the others had theirs. They switched them on.

Ben led the way. It was a
curious path to take. Sometimes
the roof was so low that the children
had to crouch down, and once they had
to go on hands and knees. Ben showed
them the marks of tools in places where
rocks jutted into the channel.

"Those marks were made by the
smugglers, I reckon," he said. "They
found this way and made it into a usable
passage. They must have found it
difficult getting some of their goods
along here."

"I expect they unpacked those
boxes we saw and carried the goods on
their backs in bags or sacks," said
Frances, seeing the picture clearly in her
mind. "Ooooh — isn't it strange to
think that heaps of smugglers have
gone up this dark passage carrying
smuggled goods years and years ago!"

They went on for a good way and
then suddenly came to an impassable bit where the roof had fallen in. They
stopped.

"Well, here we are," said Ben, "we've come to the blocked-up part once more.
Now the thing is — how far along is it blocked up — just a few yards, easy to clear
— or a quarter of a mile?"

"I don't see how we can tell," said Alec. The four children stood and looked
at the fallen stones and soil. It was most annoying to think they could get no
farther.

"I know!" said Hilary suddenly. "I know! One of us could go in at the other
end of the passage and yell. Then, if we can hear anything, we shall know the
blockage isn't stretching very far!"

"Good idea, Hilary," said Ben, pleased. "Yes, that really is a good idea. I'd
better be the one to go because I can go quickly. It'll take me a little time, so you

must be patient. I shall yell loudly when I get up to the blocked bit, and then I shall knock on some stones with my spade. We did leave the spades there, didn't we?"

"We did," said Alec. "I say – this is getting awfully exciting, isn't it?"

Ben squeezed past the others and made his way up the channel. He climbed up the rope and sped off over the heather to the cliff-side. Down the narrow path he went, and jumped down into the cove.

Meanwhile, the others had sat down in the tunnel, to wait patiently for any noise they might hear.

"It will be terribly disappointing if we don't hear anything," said Frances. They waited and waited. It seemed ages to them.

And then suddenly they heard something! It was Ben's voice, rather muffled and faint, but still quite unmistakable: "Hallooooooooo! Hallooooooooo!"

Then came the sharp noise of a spade on rock: Crack! Crack! Crack!

"Hallooooooooo!" yelled back all three children, wildly excited. "Hallooooooooo!"

"COME – AND – JOIN – ME!" yelled Ben's voice. "COME – AND – JOIN – ME!"

"COMING, COMING, COMING!" shouted Alec, Hilary and Frances, and all three scrambled back up to the entrance of the hole, swarming up the rope like monkeys.

They tore over the heather back to the cliff-side and almost fell down the steep path. Down into the cove on the sand – in the big cave – up on to the ledge – up the nail-studded hole – out on the ledge in the enormous cave – down to the rocky floor – over to the passage between the two caves – up the wall – and into the blocked-up passage where Ben was impatiently waiting for them.

"You *have* been quick," he cried. "I say – I could hear your voices quite well. The blocked piece can't stretch very far. Isn't that good? Do you feel able to tackle it hard now? If so, I believe we might clear it."

"I could tackle anything!" said Alec, taking off his mac. "I could tackle the cliff itself!"

Everyone laughed. They were all pleased and excited, and felt able to do anything, no matter how hard it was.

"What's the time?" suddenly said Alec, when they had worked hard for a time, loosening the soil and filling the sacks. "Mother's expecting us in to tea, you know."

"It's a quarter-past four already," said Hilary, in dismay. "We must stop. But we'll come back after tea."

They sped off to their tea, and Mother had to cut another big plateful of bread and butter because they finished up every bit. Then off they went again, back to their exciting task.

"I say, I say, I say!" suddenly cried Alec, making everyone jump. "I've just thought of something marvellous."

"What?" asked everyone curiously.

"Well – if we can get this passage clear, we can come down it on Thursday night, from outside," said Alec. "We don't need to bother about the tides or anything. We can slip out at half-past eleven, go to the entrance on the moor and come down here and see what's happening!"

"Golly! I never thought of that!" cried Hilary.

Ben grinned. "That's fine," he said. "Yes – you can easily do that. You needn't disturb your mother at all. I think I'd better be here earlier, though, in case those people change their plans and come before they say. Though I don't think they will, because if they come in by motor boat, they'll need high tide to get their boat into the long cave."

The children went on working at the passage. Suddenly Ben gave a shout of joy.

"We're through! My spade went right through into nothing just then! Where's my torch?"

He shone it in front of him, and the children saw that he had spoken the truth. The light of the torch shone beyond into the other side of the passage! There was only a small heap of fallen earth to manage now.

"I think we'll finish this," said Alec, though he knew the girls were tired out. "I can't leave that little bit till tomorrow! You girls can sit down and have a rest. Ben and I can tackle this last bit. It will be easy."

It was. Before another half-hour had gone by, the passage was quite clear, and the children were able to walk up and down it from end to end. They felt pleased with themselves.

"Now we'll have to wait till Thursday," sighed Alec. "Gosh, what a long time it is – a whole day and a night and then another whole day. I simply can't wait!"

But they had to. They met Ben the next day and planned everything. They could hardly go to sleep on Wednesday night, and when Thursday dawned they were all awake as early as the sun.

"Thursday at last!" whispered Hilary. "My goodness – I wonder what's going to happen tonight?"

CHAPTER VIII
THURSDAY EVENING

The day seemed very long indeed to the children — but they had a lovely surprise in the afternoon. Their father arrived, and with him he brought their Uncle Ned. Mother rushed to the gate to meet them as soon as she saw them, and the children shouted for joy.

"Oh, what fun! Are you going to stay long? Daddy, will you swim with us this afternoon? I say, you should see our smugglers' things! How long are you going to stay? Is Uncle Ned staying, too?"

Uncle Ned said he could stay a day or two, and Daddy said he would stay for a whole week.

"Where's Uncle Ned going to sleep?" asked Alec. "In my room?"

In the ordinary way the boy would have been very pleased at the idea of his uncle sleeping in the same room with him — but tonight a grown-up might perhaps spoil things.

"Ned will have to sleep on the sofa in the sitting-room," said Mother. "I don't expect he will mind. He's had worse places to sleep in this war!"

Both Daddy and Uncle Ned were in the army. It was lucky they had leave just when the children were on holiday. They could share a bit of it, too! All the children were delighted.

"I say — how are we going to slip out at half-past eleven tonight if Uncle Ned is sleeping in the sitting-room?" said Hilary, when they were alone. "We shall have to be jolly careful not to wake him!"

"Well, there's nothing for it but to creep through to the door," said Alec. "And if he does wake, we'll have to beg him not to tell tales of us."

The night came at last. The children went to bed as usual, but not one of them could go to sleep. They lay waiting for the time to pass — and it passed so slowly that once or twice Hilary thought her watch must have stopped. But it hadn't.

At last half-past eleven came — the time when they had arranged to leave, to go to meet Ben in the passage above the caves. Very quietly the children dressed. They all wore shorts, jerseys, their smugglers' hats, sashes and rubber shoes. They stole down the stairs very softly. Not a stair creaked, not a child coughed.

The door of the sitting-room was a little open. Alec pushed it a little farther and put his head in. The room was dark. On the sofa Uncle Ned was lying, his regular breathing telling the children that he was asleep.

"He's asleep," whispered Alec, in a low voice. "I'll go across first and open the door. Then you two step across quietly to me. I'll shut the door after us."

The boy went across the room to the door. He opened it softly. He had already oiled it that day, by Ben's orders, and it made no sound. A streak of moonlight came in.

Silently the three children passed out and Alec shut the door. Just as they were going through the door, their uncle woke. He opened his eyes – and to his very great amazement saw the figures of the three children going quietly out of the open door. Then it shut.

Uncle Ned sat up with a jerk. Could he be dreaming? He opened the door and looked out. No – he wasn't dreaming. There were the three figures hurrying along to the moor in the moonlight. Uncle Ned was more astonished than he had ever been in his life before.

Now what in the world do these kids think they are doing? he wondered. Little monkeys – slipping out like this just before midnight. What are they up to? I'll go after them and see. Maybe they'll let me join in their prank, whatever it is. Anyway, Alec oughtn't to take his two sisters out at this time of night!

Uncle Ned pulled on a mackintosh over his pyjamas and set out down the lane after the children. They had no idea he was some way behind them. They were thrilled because they thought they had got out so easily without being heard!

They got to the hole in the heather and by the light of their torches slid down the rope. Uncle Ned was more and more amazed as he saw one child after another slide down and disappear completely. He didn't know any hole was there, of course. He found it after a time and decided to go down it himself.

Meanwhile, the children were halfway down the passage. There they met Ben, and whispered in excitement to him. "We got out without being seen – though our uncle was sleeping on the sofa near the door! Ben, have you seen or heard anything yet?"

123

"Not a thing," said Ben. "But they should be here soon, because it's almost midnight and the tide is full."

They all went down to the end of the passage, and jumped down to stand at the end of the long, narrow cave. This was now full of water, and the tide rushed up it continually.

"Easy enough to float any motor boat right in," said Ben. "I wonder what they're bringing."

"Listen!" said Hilary suddenly. "I'm sure I can hear something."

They all listened, but the wind and the waves made such a noise just then that it was impossible to hear anything. Then they heard something quite clearly.

"It's the chug-chug-chug of that motor boat again," whispered Alec, a shiver going down his back. He wasn't frightened, but it was all so exciting he couldn't help trembling. The girls were the same. Their knees shook a little. Only Ben was quite still and fearless.

"Now don't switch your torches on by mistake, for goodness sake," whispered Ben, as the chugging noise came nearer. "We'll stay here till we see the boat coming into the long channel of this cave – then we'll hop up into the passage and listen hard."

The motor boat came nearer and nearer. Then as it nosed gently into the long cave with its deep inlet of water, the engine was shut off.

"Now we must go," said Ben, and the four children turned. They climbed up into the passage above the caves and stood there, listening.

People got out of the motor boat, which was apparently tied up to some rock. Torches were switched on. Ben, who was leaning over the hole from the passage, counted three people going into the big cave – two men and a woman. One of the men seemed somehow familiar to him, but he was gone too quickly for Ben to take a second look.

"Well, here we are," said a voice from the enormous cave below. "I will leave you food and drink here, and you will wait here till it is safe to go inland. You have maps to show you how to go. You know what to do. Do it well. Come back here and the motor boat will fetch you a week from now."

The children listening above could not make out at all what was happening. Who were the people? And what were the two of them to do? Alec pressed hard by Ben to listen better. His foot touched a pebble and set it rolling down into the space between the caves. Before he could stop himself he gave a low cry of annoyance. There was instant silence in the cave. Then the first voice spoke again

very sharply: "What was that? Did you hear anything?"

A wave roared up the narrow cave nearby and made a great noise. Whilst the splashing was going on Ben whispered to Alec: "Move back up the passage, quick! You idiot, they heard you! They'll be looking for us in a minute!"

The children hurried back along the passage as quietly as they could, their hearts beating painfully. And halfway along it they bumped into somebody!

Hilary screamed. Frances almost fainted with fright. Then the somebody took their arms and said:

"Now what in the world are you kids doing here at this time of night?"

"Uncle Ned, oh, Uncle Ned!" said Hilary, in a faint voice. "Oh, it's marvellous to have a grown-up just at this very minute to help us! Uncle Ned, something very strange is going on. Tell him, Alec."

Alec told his astonished uncle very quickly all that had happened. He listened without a word, and then spoke in a sharp, stern voice that the children had never heard before.

"They're spies! They've come over from the coast of Ireland. It's just opposite here, you know. Goodness knows what they're going to do — some dirty work, I expect. We've got to stop them. Now let me think. How can we get them? Can they get away from the caves except by motor boat?"

"Only up this passage, until the tide goes down," said Ben. "Sir – listen to me. I could slip down the hole and cast off the motor boat by myself. I know how to start it up. I believe I could do it. Then you could hold this passage, couldn't you, and send Alec and the girls back to get their father? You'd have to get somebody to keep guard outside the cave as soon as the tide goes down, in case they try to escape round the cliffs."

"Leave that to me," said Uncle Ned grimly. "Can you really get away in that motor boat? If you can, you'll take their only means of escape. Well, go and try. Good luck to you. You're a brave lad!"

Ben winked at the others, who were staring at him open-mouthed. Then he slipped along down the passage again until he came to the opening. He stood there listening before he let himself down into the space between the caves. It was plain that the people there had come to the conclusion that the noise they had heard was nothing to worry about, for they were talking together. There was the clink of glasses as the body dropped down quietly to the floor below the passage.

"They're wishing each other good luck!" said the boy to himself, with a grin. He went to the motor boat, which was gently bobbing up and down as waves ran under it up the inlet of water in the cave. He climbed quietly in. He felt about for the rope that was tide round a rock, and slipped it loose. The next wave took the boat down with it, and as soon as he dared, Ben started up the engine to take her out of the deep channel in the cave.

He was lucky in getting the boat out fairly quickly. As soon as the engine started up, there came a shout from the cave, and Ben knew that the two men there had run to see what was happening. He ducked in case there was any shooting. He guessed that the men would be desperate when they saw their boat going.

He got the boat clear, and swung her out on the water that filled the cove. The boy knew the coast almost blindfold, and soon the little motor boat was chug-chug-chugging across the open sea towards the beach where a little jetty ran out, and where Ben could tie her up. He was filled with glee. It was marvellous to think he had beaten those men – and that woman, too, whoever she was. Spies! Well – now they knew what British boys and girls could do!

He wondered what the others were doing. He felt certain that Alec and the girls were even now speeding up the passage, climbing out through the heather and racing back home to wake their father.

And that is exactly what they were doing! They had left their uncle in the passage – no one could escape by that passage, even if they knew of it.

"Tell your father what you have told me, and tell him Ben has taken the boat away," he said. "I want men to guard the outer entrance of the caves as soon as the tide goes down. I'll remain here to guard this way of escape. Ask him to bring my army revolver. Go quickly!"

CHAPTER IX
THINGS MOVE QUICKLY

Alec and the two girls left their uncle and stumbled up the dark passage, lighting their way by their small torches. All three were trembling with excitement. It seemed suddenly a very serious thing that was happening. Spies! Who would have thought of that?

"Somehow I only thought of smugglers," said Alec out loud, making the girls jump, for his voice went echoing strangely around them.

"Well, they *are* kind of smugglers, I suppose," said Hilary. "Smugglers that smuggle spies across, instead of other goods. Fancy! We never thought we were going to get mixed up in anything like this when we first saw those caves."

They went on up the passage. Soon they came to the place where the roof fell very low indeed, and down they went on their hands and knees to crawl through the low tunnel.

"I don't like that bit much," said Frances, when they were through it. "I shall dream about that! Come on — we can stand upright again now. Whatever do you suppose Daddy and Mother will say?"

"I can't imagine," said Alec. "All I know is that it's a very lucky thing for us that Daddy and Uncle happened to be here now. Golly — didn't I jump when we bumped into Uncle Ned in this passage! My heart nearly leaped out of my body!"

"I screamed," said Hilary, rather ashamed of herself. "But honestly I simply couldn't help it. It was awful to bump into somebody strange like that in the darkness. But wasn't I glad when I heard Uncle Ned's voice!"

"Here we are at last," said Alec, as they came to where the rope hung down the hole. "I'll go up first and then give you two girls a hand. Give me a heave, Hilary."

Hilary heaved him up and he climbed the rope quickly, hand over hand, glad that he had been so good at gym at school. You never knew when things would come in useful!

He lay down on the heather and helped the girls up. They stood out on the moor in the moonlight, getting back their breath, for it wasn't easy to haul themselves up the rope.

"Now come on," said Hilary. "We haven't any time to lose. I shouldn't be surprised if those spies know about the passage and make up their minds to try it. We don't want to leave Uncle Ned too long. After all, it's three against one."

They tore over the heather, and came to the sandy lane where Sea Cottage shone in the moonlight. They went in at the open door and made their way to their parents' bedroom. Alec hammered on the door, and then went in.

His father and mother were sitting up in astonishment. They switched on the light and stared at the three children, all fully dressed as they were.

"What's the meaning of this?" asked their father. But before he could say a

word more the three children began to pour out their story. At first their parents could not make out what they were talking about, and their mother made the girls stop talking so that Alec could tell the tale.

"But this is unbelievable!" said their father, dressing as quickly as possible. "Simply unbelievable! Is Ned really down a secret passage, holding three spies at bay? And Ben has gone off with their motor boat? Am I dreaming?"

"No, Daddy, you're not," said Alec. "It's all quite true. We kept everything a secret till tonight, because secrets are such fun. We didn't know that anything serious was up till tonight, really. Are you going to get help?"

"I certainly am," said Daddy. He went to the telephone downstairs and was soon on to the nearest military camp. He spoke to a most surprised commanding officer, who listened in growing amazement.

"So you must send a few men over as quickly as possible," said Daddy. "The children say there are three men in the caves – or rather, two men and one woman – but there may be more, of course – and more may arrive. We can't tell.

Hurry, won't you?"

He put down the receiver of the telephone and turned to look at the waiting children. "Now let me see," he said thoughtfully. "I shall want one of you to take me to where Ned is — and I must leave someone behind to guide the soldiers down to the cove. They must be there to guard the entrance to the caves, so that if the spies try to escape by the beach, they will find they can't. Alec, you had better come with me. Frances and Hilary, you can go with Mother and the soldiers, when they come, and show them the way down the cliff and the entrance to the caves. Come along, Alec."

The two set off. Alec talked hard all the way, for there was a great deal to tell. His father listened in growing astonishment. Really, you never knew what children were doing half the time!

"I suppose your mother thought you were playing harmless games of smugglers," he said, "and all the time you were on the track of dangerous spies! Well, well, well!"

"We didn't really know they were spies till tonight," said Alec honestly. "It was all a game at first. Look, Daddy — here's the hole. We have to slide down this rope."

"This really is a weird adventure," said his father, and down the rope he went. Alec followed him. Soon they were standing beside Uncle Ned, who was still in the passage, standing guard.

"There's been a lot of excited talking," he said in a low voice to his brother, "and I think they've been trying to find a way out. But the tide is still very high, and they daren't walk out on the sand yet. If they don't know of this passage, they won't try it, of course — but we'd better stay here in case they do. When are the soldiers coming?"

"At once," said Daddy. "I've left the two girls behind to guide them down to the cove. Then they will hide, and guard the entrance to the caves — that is as soon as the tide goes down enough."

"Do the spies know you're here, Uncle Ned?" asked Alec, in a low voice.

"No," said his uncle. "They think someone has gone off with their motor boat, but that's all they know. What about creeping down to the end of the passage to see if we can overhear anything? They might drop a few secrets!"

The three of them crept down to the end of the passage, and leaned out over the hole that led down to the space between the two caves. They could hear the waves still washing up the narrow channel in the long cave.

The two men and the women were talking angrily. "Who could have known we were here? Someone has given the game away! No one but ourselves and the other three knew what we were planning to do."

"Is there no other way out?" said a man's impatient voice, very deep and foreign. "Rondel, you know all these caves and passages — or so you said. How did the old smugglers get their goods away? There must have been a land path they used."

"There was," said the other man. "There is a passage above this cave that leads on to the moors. But as far as I know it is completely blocked up."

"As far as you know!" said the other man, in a scornful voice. "Haven't you found out? What do you suppose you are paid for, Rondel? Aren't you paid for letting us know any well-hidden caves on this coast? Where is this passage? Do you know?"

"Yes, I know," said Rondel. "It's above this one, and the entrance to it is just between this cave and the one we used for the motor boat. We have to climb up a little way. I've never been up it myself, because I heard it was blocked up by a roof-fall years ago. But we can try it and see."

"We'd better get back up the passage a bit," whispered Alec's father. "If they come up here, we may have trouble. Get up to that bit where the big rock juts out and the passage goes round it. We can get behind that and give them a scare. They'll shoot if they see us. I don't want to shoot them if I can help it, for I've a feeling they will be more useful alive than dead!"

Very silently the three went back up the passage to where a rock jutted out and the way went round it. They crouched down behind the rock and waited, their torches switched off. Alec heard their breathing and it sounded very loud. But they had to breathe! He wondered if Daddy and Uncle Ned could hear his heart beating, because it seemed to make a very loud thump just then!

Meanwhile, the three spies were trying to find the entrance to the passage. Rondel had a powerful torch, and he soon found the hole that led to the ledge where the secret passage began.

"Here it is!" he said. "Look — we can easily get up there. I'll go first."

Alec heard a scrambling noise as the man climbed up. Then he pulled up the other two. They all switched on their torches and the dark passage was lit up brightly.

"It seems quite clear," said the other man. "I should think we could escape this way. You go ahead, Rondel. We'll follow. I can't see any sign of it being blocked up, I must say! This is a bit of luck."

They went on up the passage talking. They went slowly, and Alec and the others could hear their footsteps and voices coming gradually nearer. Alec's heart beat painfully and he kept swallowing something in his throat. The excitement was almost too much for him to bear.

The three spies came almost up to the jutting-out rock. And then they got the shock of their lives! Alec's father spoke in a loud, stern voice that made Alec jump.

"Halt! Come another step, and we'll shoot!"

The spies halted at once in a panic. They switched off their torches.

"Who's there?" came Rondel's voice.

Nobody answered. The spies talked together in low voices and decided to go back the way they had come. They were not risking going round that rock! They didn't know how many people were there. It was plain that somebody knew of their plans and meant to capture them.

Alec heard the three making their way quietly back down the passage.

"Daddy! I expect they think the tide will soon be going down and they hope to make their escape by way of the beach," whispered Alec. "I hope the soldiers will be there in time."

"Don't you worry about that!" said his father. "As soon as the tide washes off the beach, it will be full of soldiers."

"I wish I could be there," said Alec longingly. "I don't expect the spies will come up here again."

"Well, you can go and see what's happening if you like," said Daddy. "You uncle and I will stay here – but you can see if the soldiers have arrived and if the girls are taking them down to the cove."

Alec was delighted. More excitement for him, after all! He went up the passage and swarmed up the rope out of the entrance-hole. He sped over the moor to the cottage.

But no one was there. It was quite empty. I suppose the soldiers have arrived and Mother and the girls have taken them to the cove, thought Alec. Yes – there are big wheel-marks in the road – a lorry has been here. Oh – there it is, in the shade of those trees over there. I'd better hurry or I'll miss the fun!

Off he dashed to the cliff-edge, and down the narrow, steep path. Where were the others? Waiting in silence down on the beach? Alec nearly fell down the steep path trying to hurry! What an exciting night!

CHAPTER X
THE END OF IT ALL

J ust as Alec was scrambling down the steep cliff, he heard the sound of a low voice from the top. "Is that you, Alec?"

Alec stopped. It was Ben's voice. "Ben!" he whispered in excitement. "Come on down. You're just in time. How did you get here?"

Ben scrambled down beside him. "I thought it was you," he said. "I saw you going over the edge of the cliff as I came up the lane. What's happened?"

Alec told him. Ben listened in excitement.

"So they know there's someone in the secret passage," he said. "They'll just have to try to escape by the beach then! Well, they'll be overpowered there, no doubt about that. I tied up the motor boat by the jetty, Alec. It's a real beauty — small but very powerful. It's got a lovely engine. Then I raced back to see if I could be in at the end."

"Well, you're just in time," said Alec. "I'm going to hop down on to the beach now and see where the others are."

"Be careful," Ben warned him. "The soldiers won't know it's you, and may take a pot-shot at you."

That scared Alec. He stopped before he jumped down on to the sand.

"Well, I think maybe we'd better stay here then," he said. "We can see anything that happens from here, can't we? Look, the tide is going down nicely now. Where do you suppose the others are, Ben?"

"I should think they are somewhere on the rocks that run round the cove," said Ben, looking carefully round. "Look, Alec — there's something shining just over there — see? I guess that's a gun. We can't see the man holding it — but the moonlight just picks out a shiny bit of his gun."

"I hope the girls and Mother are safe," said Alec.

"You may be sure they are," said Ben. "I wonder what the three spies are doing now. I guess they are waiting till the tide is low enough for them to come out."

At that very moment Rondel was looking out of the big cave to see if it was safe to try and escape over the beach. He was not going to try to go up the cliff-path, for he felt sure there would be someone at the top. Their only hope lay in slipping round the corner of the cove and making their way up the cliff some way off. Rondel knew the coast by heart, and if he only had the chance he felt certain he could take the others to safety.

The tide was going down rapidly. The sand was very wet and shone in the moonlight. Now and again a big wave swept up the beach, but the power behind it was gone. It could not dash anyone against the rocks now. Rondel turned to his two companions and spoke to them in a low voice.

"Now's our chance. We shall have to try the beach whilst our enemies think the tide is still high. Take hold of Gretel's hand, Otto, in case a wave comes. Follow me. Keep as close to the cliff as possible in case there is a watcher above."

The three of them came silently out of the big cave. Its entrance lay in darkness and they looked like deep black shadows as they moved quietly to the left of the cave. They made their way round the rocks, stopping as a big wave came splashing up the smooth sand. It swept round their feet, but no higher. Then it ran back down the sand again to the sea, and the three moved on once more.

Then a voice rang out in the moonlight: "We have you covered! There is no escape this way! Hands up!"

Rondel had his revolver in his hand in a moment and guns glinted in the hands of the others, too. But they did not know where their enemies were. The rocks lay in black shadows, and no one could be seen.

"There are men all round this cove," said the voice. "You cannot escape. Put your hands up and surrender. Throw your revolvers down, please."

Rondel spoke to the others in a savage voice. He was in a fierce rage, for all his plans were ruined. It seemed as if he were urging the others to fight. But they were wiser than Rondel. The other man threw his revolver down on the sand and put his hands above his head. The woman did the same. They glinted there like large silver shells.

"Hands up, you!" commanded a voice. Rondel shouted something angry in a foreign language and then threw his gun savagely at the nearest rocks. It hit them and the trigger was struck. The revolver went off with a loud explosion that echoed round and round the little cove and made everyone, Rondel as well, jump violently.

"Stand where you are," said a voice. And out from the shadow of the rocks came a soldier in the uniform of an officer. He walked up to the three spies and had a look at them. He felt them all over to see if there were any more weapons hidden about them. There were none.

He called to his men. "Come and take them."

Four men stepped out from the rocks around the cove. Alec and Ben leaped down on to the sand. Mother and the two girls came out from their hiding-place in a small cave. Ben ran up to the spies. He peered into the face of one of the men.

"I know who this is!" he cried. "It's Professor Rondel, who lived in Sea Cottage. I've seen him hundreds of times! He didn't have many friends — only two or three men who came to see him sometimes."

"Oh," said the officer, staring with interest at Ben. "Well, we'll be very pleased to know who the two or three men were. You'll be very useful to us, my boy. Now then — quick march! Up the cliff we go and into the lorry! The sooner we get these three into a safe place the better."

Alec's father and uncle appeared at that moment. They had heard the sound of the shot when Rondel's revolver struck the rock and went off, and they had come to see what was happening. Alec ran to them and told them.

"Good work!" said Daddy. "Three spies caught — and maybe the others they work with, too, if Ben can point them out. Good old Smuggler Ben!"

The three spies were put into the lorry and the driver climbed up behind the wheel. The officer saluted and took his place. Then the lorry rumbled off into the moonlit night. The four children watched it go, their eyes shining.

"This is the most thrilling night I've ever had in my life," said Alec, with a sigh. "I don't suppose I'll ever have a more exciting one, however long I live. Golly, my heart did beat fast when we were hiding in the cave. It hurt me."

"Same here," said Hilary. "Oh, Daddy — you didn't guess what you were in for, did you, when you came down yesterday?"

"I certainly didn't," said Daddy, putting his arm round the two girls and pushing them towards the house. "Come along – you'll all be tired out. It must be nearly dawn!"

"Back to Professor Rondel's own house!" said Alec. "Isn't it funny! He got all his information from his books – and we found some of it there, too. We'll show you if you like, Daddy."

"Not tonight," said Daddy firmly. "Tonight – or rather this morning, for it's morning now – you are going to bed, and to sleep. No more excitement, please! You will have plenty again tomorrow, for you'll have to go over to the police and to the military camp to tell all you know."

Well, that was an exciting piece of news, too. The children went indoors, Ben with them, for Mother said he had better sleep with Alec for the rest of the night.

Soon all four children were in their beds, feeling certain that they would never, never be able to go to sleep for one moment.

But it wasn't more than two minutes before they were all sound asleep, as Mother saw when she peeped into the two bedrooms. She went to join Daddy and Uncle Ned.

"Well, I'd simply no idea what the children were doing," she told them. "I was very angry with them one night when they came home late because they were caught by the tide when they were exploring those caves. They kept their secret well."

"They're good kids," said Daddy, with a yawn. "Well, let's go to sleep, too. Ned, I hope you'll be able to drop off on the sofa again."

"I could drop off on the kitchen stove, I'm so tired!" said Ned.

Soon the whole household slept soundly, and did not wake even when the sun came slanting in at the windows. They were all tired out.

They had a late breakfast, and the children chattered nineteen to the dozen as they ate porridge and bacon and eggs. It all seemed amazingly wonderful to them now that it was over. They couldn't help feeling rather proud of themselves.

"I must go," said Ben, when he had finished an enormous breakfast. "My uncle is expecting me to go out fishing with him this morning. He'll be angry because I'm late."

But before Ben could go, a messenger on a motor bike arrived, asking for the four children to go over to the police station at once. The police wanted to know the names of the men with whom Professor Rondel had made friends. This was very important, because unless they knew the names at once, the men might hear of Rondel's capture and fly out of the country.

So off went the four children, and spent a most exciting time telling and retelling their story from the very beginning. The inspector of the police listened carefully, and when everything had been told, and notes taken, he leaned back and looked at the children, his eyes twinkling.

"Well, we have reason to be very grateful to you four smugglers," he said. "We shall probably catch the whole nest of spies operating in this part of the country. We suspected it – but we had no idea who the ringleader was. It was Rondel, of course. He was bringing men and women across from Ireland – spies, of course – and taking them about the country either to get information useful to the enemy, or to wreck valuable buildings. He was using the old smugglers' caves to hide his friends in. We shall comb the whole coast now."

"Can we help you?" asked Ben eagerly. "I know most of the caves, sir. And we can show you Rondel's books, where all the old caves are described. He's got dozens of them."

"Good!" said the inspector. "Well, that's all for today. You will hear from us later. There will be a little reward given to you for services to your country!"

The children filed out, talking excitedly. A little reward! What could it be?

"Sometimes children are given watches as a reward," said Alec, thinking of a newspaper report he had read. "We might get a watch each."

"I hope we don't," said Hilary, "because I've already got one – though it doesn't keep very good time."

But the reward wasn't watches. It was something much bigger than that. Can you possibly guess what it was?

It was the little motor boat belonging to the spies! When the children heard the news, they could hardly believe their ears. But it was quite true. There lay the little motor boat, tied up to the jetty, and on board was a police officer with instructions to hand it over to the four children.

"Oh – thank you!" said Alec, hardly able to speak. "Thank you very much. Oh, Ben – oh, Ben – isn't it marvellous!"

It *was* marvellous! It was a beautiful little boat with a magnificent engine. It was called *Otto*.

"That won't do," said Hilary, looking at the name. "We'll have that painted out at once. What shall we call our boat? It must be a very good name – something that will remind us of our adventure!"

"I know – I know!" yelled Alec. "We'll call it *Smuggler Ben*, of course – and good old Ben shall be the captain, and we'll be his crew."

So *Smuggler Ben* the boat was called, and everyone agreed that it was a really good name. The children have a wonderful time in it. You should see them chug-chug-chugging over the sea at top speed, the spray flying high in the air! Aren't they lucky!

FIVE GO ADVENTURING AGAIN

AN EXTRACT

~ ILLUSTRATED BY ~
EILEEN SOPER

It is the Christmas holidays and George, Julian, Anne and Dick are having extra lessons from a tutor named Mr Roland. Because Mr Roland doesn't like Timmy the dog, Uncle Quentin makes George keep him in an outdoor kennel. The Five visit Kirrin Farmhouse and discover an old parchment that gives directions for finding the "Secret Way". After searching for clues, they discover that an entrance to the Secret Way is hidden in Uncle Quentin's study. One night some of Uncle Quentin's important papers are stolen. The Five believe that two artists staying at Kirrin Farmhouse may be responsible. With thick snow making it impossible for anyone in the district to leave their homes, the Five decide to explore the Secret Way in the hope that it leads to the farm...

CHAPTER XIV
THE SECRET WAY AT LAST!

The four children crept downstairs through the dark and silent night. Nobody made a sound at all. They made their way to the study. George softly closed the door and then switched on the light.

The children stared at the eight panels over the mantelpiece. Yes —

138

there were exactly eight, four in one row and four in the row above. Julian spread the linen roll out on the table, and the children pored over it.

"The cross is in the middle of the second panel in the top row," said Julian in a low voice. "I'll try pressing it. Watch, all of you!"

He went to the fireplace. The others followed him, their hearts beating fast with excitement. Julian stood on tiptoe and began to press hard in the middle of the second panel. Nothing happened.

"Press harder! Tap it!" said Dick.

"I daren't make too much noise," said Julian, feeling all over the panel to see if there was any roughness that might tell of a hidden spring or lever.

Suddenly, under his hands, the panel slid silently back, just as the one had done at Kirrin Farmhouse in the hall! The children stared at the space behind, thrilled.

"It's not big enough to get into," said George. "It can't be the entrance to the Secret Way."

Julian got out his torch from his dressing-gown pocket. He put it inside the

opening, and gave a low exclamation.

"There's a sort of handle here — with strong wire or something attached to it. I'll pull it and see what happens."

He pulled — but he was not strong enough to move the handle that seemed to be embedded in the wall. Dick put his hand in and the two boys then pulled together.

"It's moving — it's giving way a bit," panted Julian. "Go on, Dick, pull hard!"

The handle suddenly came away from the wall,

and behind it came thick wire, rusty and old. At the same time a curious grating noise came from below the hearthrug in front of the fireplace, and Anne almost fell.

"Julian! Something is moving under the rug!" she said, frightened. "I felt it. Under the rug, quick!"

The handle could not be pulled out any farther. The boys let go, and looked down. To the right of the fireplace, under the rug, something had moved. There was no doubt of that. The rug sagged down instead of being flat and straight.

"A stone has moved in the floor," said Julian, his voice shaking with excitement. "This handle works a lever, which is attached to this wire. Quick – pull up the rug, and roll back the carpet."

With trembling hands the children pulled back the rug and the carpet – and then stood staring at a very strange thing. A big flat stone laid in the floor had slipped downwards, pulled in some manner by the wire attached to the handle hidden behind the panel! There was now a black space where the stone had been.

"Look at that!" said George, in a thrilling whisper. "The entrance to the Secret Way!"

"It's here after all!" said Julian.

"Let's go down!" said Dick.

"No!" said Anne, shivering at the thought of disappearing into the black hole.

Julian flashed his torch into the black space. The stone had slid down and then sideways. Below was a space just big enough to take a man, bending down.

"I expect there's a passage or something leading from here, under the house, and out," said Julian. "Golly, I wonder where it leads to?"

"We simply must find out," said George.

"Not now," said Dick. "It's dark and cold. I don't fancy going along the

Secret Way at midnight. I don't mind just hopping down to see what it's like — but don't let's go along any passage till tomorrow."

"Uncle Quentin will be working here tomorrow," said Julian.

"He said he was going to sweep the snow away from the front door in the morning," said George. "We could slip into the study then. It's Saturday. There may be no lessons."

"All right," said Julian, who badly wanted to explore everything then and there. "But for goodness' sake let's have a look and see if there *is* a passage down there. At present all we can see is a hole!"

"I'll help you down," said Dick.

So he gave his brother a hand and Julian dropped lightly down into the black space, holding his torch. He gave a loud exclamation. "It's the entrance to the Secret Way all right! There's a passage leading from here under the house — awfully low and narrow — but I can see it's a passage. I do wonder where it leads to!" He shivered. It was cold and damp down there. "Give me a hand up, Dick," he said. He was soon out of the hole and in the warm study again.

The children looked at one another in the greatest joy and excitement. This *was* an Adventure, a real Adventure. It was a pity they couldn't go on with it now.

"We'll try and take Timmy with us tomorrow," said George. "Oh, I say — how are we going to shut the entrance up?"

"We can't leave the rug and carpet sagging over that hole," said Dick. "Nor can we leave the panel open."

"We'll see if we can get the stone back," said Julian. He stood on tiptoe and felt about inside the panel. His hand closed on a kind of knob, set deep in a stone. He pulled it, and at once the handle slid back, pulled by the wire. At the same time the sunk stone glided to the surface of the floor again, making a slight grating sound as it did so.

"Well, it's like magic!" said Dick. "It really is! Fancy the mechanism working so smoothly after years of not being used. This is the most exciting thing I've ever seen!"

There was a noise in the bedroom above. The children stood still and listened.

"It's Mr Roland!" whispered Dick. "He's heard us. Quick, slip upstairs before he comes down."

They switched out the light and opened the study door softly. Up the stairs they fled, as quietly as church mice, their hearts thumping so loudly that it seemed as if everyone in the house must hear the beat.

The girls got safely to their rooms and Dick was able to slip into his. But Julian was seen by Mr Roland as he came out of his room with a torch.

"What are you doing, Julian!" asked the tutor, in surprise. "Did you hear a noise downstairs? I thought I did."

"Yes – I heard quite a lot of noise downstairs," said Julian, truthfully. "But perhaps it's snow falling off the roof, landing with a plop in the ground, sir. Do you think that's it?"

"I don't know," said the tutor doubtfully. "We'll go down and see."

They went down, but of course there was nothing to be seen. Julian was glad they had been able to shut the panel and make the stone come back to its proper place again. Mr Roland was the very last person he wanted to tell his secret to.

They went upstairs and Julian slipped into his room. "Is it all right?" whispered Dick.

"Yes," said Julian. "Don't let's talk. Mr Roland's awake, and I don't want him to suspect anything."

The boys fell asleep. When they awoke in the morning, there was a completely white world outside. Snow covered everything and covered it deeply. Timothy's kennel could not be seen! But there were footmarks round about it.

George gave a squeal when she saw how deep the snow was. "Poor Timothy! I'm going to get him in. I don't care what anyone says! I won't let him be buried in the snow!"

She dressed and tore downstairs. She went out to the kennel, floundering knee deep in the snow. But there was no Timmy there!

A loud bark from the kitchen made her jump. Joanna the cook knocked on the kitchen window. "It's all right! I couldn't bear the dog out there in the snow, so I fetched him in, poor thing. Your mother says I can have him in the kitchen but you're not to come and see him."

"Oh, good – Timmy's in the warmth!" said George, gladly. She yelled to Joanna, "Thanks awfully! You *are* kind!"

She went indoors and told the others. They were very glad. "And *I've* got a bit of news for *you*," said Dick. "Mr Roland is in bed with a bad cold, so there are to be no lessons today. Cheers!"

"Golly, that *is* good news," said George, cheering up tremendously. "Timmy in the warm kitchen and Mr Roland kept in bed. I do feel pleased!"

"We shall be able to explore the Secret Way safely now," said Julian. "Aunt

Fanny is going to do something in the kitchen this morning with Joanna, and Uncle is going to tackle the snow. I vote we say we'll do lessons by ourselves in the sitting-room, and then, when everything is safe, we'll explore the Secret Way!"

"But why must we do lessons?" asked George in dismay.

"Because if we don't, silly, we'll have to help your father dig away the snow," said Julian.

So, to his uncle's surprise, Julian suggested that the four children should do lessons by themselves in the sitting-room.

"Well, I thought you'd like to come and help dig away the snow," said Uncle Quentin. "But perhaps you had better get on with your work."

The children sat themselves down as good as gold in the sitting-room, their books before them. They heard Mr Roland coughing in his room. They heard their aunt go into the kitchen and talk to Joanna.

They heard Timmy scratching at the kitchen door – then paws pattering down the passage – then a big, inquiring nose came round the door, and there was old Timmy, looking anxiously for his beloved mistress!

"Timmy!" squealed George, and ran to him. She flung her arms round his neck and hugged him.

"You act as if you hadn't seen Tim for a year," said Julian.

"It seems like a year," said George. "I say, there's my father digging away like mad. Can't we go to the study now? We ought to be safe for a good while."

They left the sitting-room and went to the study. Julian was soon pulling the handle behind the secret panel. George had already turned back the rug and the carpet. The stone slid downward and sideways. The Secret Way was open!

"Come on!" said Julian. "Hurry!"

He jumped down into the hole. Dick followed, then Anne, then George.

Julian pushed them all into the narrow, low passage. Then he looked up. Perhaps he had better pull the carpet and rug over the hole, in case anyone came into the room and looked around. It took him a few seconds to do it. Then he bent down and joined the others in the passage. They were going to explore the Secret Way at last!

CHAPTER XV
AN EXCITING JOURNEY AND HUNT

Timothy had leaped down into the hole when George had jumped. He now ran ahead of the children, puzzled at their wanting to explore such a cold, dark place. Both Julian and Dick had torches, which threw broad beams before them.

There was not much to be seen. The Secret Way under the old house was narrow and low, so that the children were forced to go in single file, and to stoop almost double. It was a great relief to them when the passage became a little wider, and the room a little higher. It was very tiring to stoop all the time.

"Have you any idea where the Secret Way is going?" Dick asked Julian. "I mean – is it going towards the sea, or away from it?"

"Oh, not towards the sea!" said Julian, who had a very good sense of direction. "As far as I can make out the passage is going towards the common. Look at the walls – they are rather sandy in places, and we know the common has sandy soil. I hope we shan't find that the passage has fallen in anywhere."

They went on and on. The Secret Way was very straight, though occasionally it would round a rocky part in a curve.

"Isn't it dark and cold?" said Anne, shivering. "I wish I had put on a coat. How many miles have we come, Julian?"

"Not even one, silly!" said Julian. "Hallo – look here – the passage has fallen in a bit there!"

Two bright torches shone in front of them and the children saw that the sandy roof had fallen in. Julian kicked at the pile of sandy soil with his foot.

"It's all right," he said. "We can force our way through easily. It isn't much of a fall, and it's mostly sand. I'll do a bit of kicking!"

After some trampling and kicking, the roof-fall no longer blocked the way.

There was now enough room for the children to climb over it, bending their heads low to avoid knocking them against the top of the passage. Julian shone his torch forward, and saw that the way was clear.

"The Secret Way is very wide just here!" he said suddenly, and flashed his torch around to show the others.

"It's been widened out to make a sort of little room," said George. "Look, there's a kind of bench at the back, made out of the rock. I believe it's a resting-place."

George was right. It was very tiring to creep along the narrow passage for so long. The little wide place with its rocky bench made a very good resting-place. The four tired children, cold but excited, huddled together on the funny seat and took a welcome rest. Timmy put his head on George's knee. He was delighted to be with her again.

"Well, come on," said Julian, after a few minutes. "I'm getting awfully cold. I do wonder where this passage comes out!"

"Julian – do you think it could come out at Kirrin Farmhouse?" asked George, suddenly. "You know what Mrs Sanders said – that there was a secret passage leading from the farmhouse somewhere. Well, this may be the one – and it leads to Kirrin Cottage!"

"George, I believe you're right!" said Julian. "Yes – the two houses belonged to your family years ago! And in the old days there were often secret passages joining houses, so it's quite plain this secret way joins them up together! Why didn't I think of that before?"

"I say!" squealed Anne, in a high, excited voice, "I say! I've thought of something too!"

"What?" asked everyone.

"Well – if those two artists have got Uncle's papers, we may be able to get them away before the men can send them off by post, or take them away themselves!" squeaked Anne, so thrilled with her idea that she could hardly get the words out quickly enough. "They're prisoners at the farmhouse because of the snow, just as we were at the cottage."

"*Anne!* You're right!" said Julian.

"Clever girl!" said Dick.

"I *say* – if we *could* get those papers again – how wonderful it would be!" said George. Timmy joined in the general excitement, and jumped up and down in joy. Something had pleased the children, so he was pleased too!

"Come on!" said Julian, taking Anne's hand. "This is thrilling. If George is right, and this Secret Way comes out at Kirrin Farmhouse somewhere, we'll somehow hunt through those men's rooms and find the papers."

"You said that searching people's rooms was a shocking thing to do," said George.

"Well, I didn't know then all I know now," said Julian. "We're doing this for your father – and maybe for our country too, if his secret formula is valuable. We've got to set our wits to work now, to outwit dangerous enemies."

"Do you really think they are dangerous?" asked Anne rather afraid.

"Yes, I should think so," said Julian. "But you needn't worry, Anne, you've got me and Dick and Tim to protect you."

"I can protect her too," said George, indignantly.

"You're fiercer than any boy I know!" said Dick.

"Come on," said Julian, impatiently. "I'm longing to get to the end of this passage."

They all went on again, Anne following behind Julian, and Dick behind George. Timmy ran up and down the line, squeezing by them whenever he wanted to. He thought it was a very peculiar way to spend a morning!

Julian stopped suddenly, after they had gone a good way. "What's up?" asked Dick, from the back. "Not another roof-fall, I hope!"

"No – but I think we've come to the end of the passage!" said Julian, thrilled. The others crowded as close to him as they could. The passage certainly had come to an end. There was a rocky wall in front of them, and set firmly in it were iron staples intended for footholds. These went up the wall and when Julian turned his torch upwards, the children saw that there was a square opening in the roof of the passage.

"We have to climb up this rocky wall now," said Julian, "go through that dark hole there, keep on climbing – and goodness knows where we come out! I'll go first. You wait here, everyone, and I'll come back and tell you what I've seen."
The boy put his torch between his teeth, and then pulled himself up by the iron staples set in the wall. He set his feet on them, and then climbed up through the square dark hole, feeling for the staples as he went.

He went up for a good way. It was almost like going up a chimney shaft, he thought. It was cold and smelled musty.

Suddenly he came to a ledge, and he stepped on to it. He took his torch from his teeth and flashed it around him.

There was a stone wall behind him, at the side of him and stone above him. The black hole up which he had come, yawned by his feet. Julian shone his torch in front of him, and a shock of surprise went through him.

There was no stone wall in front of him, but a big wooden door, made of black oak. A handle was set about waist-high; Julian turned it with trembling fingers. What was he going to see?

The door opened outwards, over the ledge, and it was difficult to get round it without falling back into the hole. Julian managed to open it wide, squeezed round it without

losing his footing, and stepped beyond it, expecting to find himself in a room.

But his hand felt more wood in front of him! He shone his torch round, and found that he was up against what looked like yet another door. Under his searching fingers it suddenly moved sideways, and slid silently away!

And then Julian knew where he was! I'm in the cupboard at Kirrin Farmhouse – the one that has a false back! he thought. The Secret Way comes up behind it! How clever! Little did we know when we played about in this cupboard that not only did it have a sliding back, but that it was the entrance to the Secret Way, hidden behind it!

The cupboard was now full of clothes belonging to the artists. Julian stood and listened. There was no sound of anyone in the room. Should he just take a quick look round, and see if those lost papers were anywhere about?

Then he remembered the other four, waiting patiently below in the cold. He had better go and tell them what had happened. They could all come and help in the search.

He stepped into the space behind the sliding back. The sliding door slipped across again, and Julian was left standing on the narrow ledge, with the old oak door wide open to one side of him. He did not bother to shut it. He felt about his feet, and found the iron staples in the hole below him. Down he went, clinging with his hands and feet, his torch in his teeth again.

"Julian! What a time you've been! Quick, tell us all about it!" cried George.

"It's most terribly thrilling," said Julian. "Absolutely super! Where do you suppose all this leads to? Into the cupboard at Kirrin Farmhouse – the one that's got a false back!"

"Golly!" said Dick.

"I *say!*" said George.

"Did you go into the room?" cried Anne.

"I climbed as far as I could and came to a big oak door," said Julian. "It has a handle this side, so I swung it wide open. Then I saw another wooden door in front of me – at least, I thought it was a door, I didn't know it was just the false back of that cupboard. It was quite easy to slide back and I stepped through, and found myself among a whole lot of clothes hanging in the cupboard! Then I hurried back to tell you."

"Julian! We can hunt for those papers now," said George, eagerly. "Was there anyone in the room?"

"I couldn't hear anyone," said Julian. "Now what I propose is this – we'll all go up, and have a hunt round those two rooms. The men have the room next to the cupboard one too."

"Oh good!" said Dick, thrilled at the thought of such an adventure. "Let's go now. You go first, Ju. Then Anne, then George and then me."

"What about Tim?" asked George.

"He can't climb, silly," said Julian. "He's a simply marvellous dog, but he certainly can't climb, George. We'll have to leave him down here."

"He won't like that," said George.

"Well, we can't carry him up," said Dick. "You won't mind staying here for a bit, will you, Tim, old fellow?"

Tim wagged his tail. But, as he saw the four children mysteriously disappearing

148

up the wall, he put his big tail down at once. What! Going without him? How could they?

He jumped up at the wall, and fell back. He jumped again and whined. George called down in a low voice.

"Be quiet, Tim dear! We shan't be long."

Tim stopped whining. He lay down at the bottom of the wall, his ears well-cocked. This adventure was becoming more and more peculiar!

Soon the children were on the narrow ledge. The old oak door was still wide open. Julian shone his torch and the others saw the false back of the cupboard. Julian put his hands on it and it slid silently sideways. Then the torch shone on coats and dressing-gowns!

The children stood quite still, listening. There was no sound from the room. "I'll open the cupboard door and peep into the room," whispered Julian. "Don't make a sound!"

The boy pushed between the clothes and felt for the outer cupboard door with his hand. He found it, and pushed it slightly. It opened a little and a shaft of daylight came into the cupboard. He peeped cautiously into the room.

There was no one there at all. That was good. "Come on!" he whispered to the others. "The room's empty!"

THE ISLAND OF ADVENTURE

AN EXTRACT

❦ ILLUSTRATED BY ❦
STUART TRESILIAN

The Island of Adventure was the first book to feature Lucy-Ann, Dinah, Jack, Philip and Kiki the parrot. The children are all staying at Craggy-Tops, the cliff-top home of Philip and Dinah's aunt and uncle. Their stay on the wild Cornish coast is spoilt only by the interference of Joe, the sullen odd-job man who works at Craggy-Tops and is constantly spying on the children and trying to stop them exploring the cliffs and caves...

CHAPTER VII
A STRANGE DISCOVERY

If it had not been for Joe, life at Craggy-Tops, once the children had settled down to their daily tasks, would have been very pleasant. There seemed so much to do that was fun — swimming in the sheltered cove, where the water was calm, was simply lovely. Exploring the damp, dark caves in the cliffs was fun. Fishing from the rocks with a line was also very exciting, because quite big fish could be caught that way.

But Joe seemed to spoil everything, with his scowls and continual interference. He always seemed to appear wherever the children were. If they bathed, his sour face appeared round the rocks. If they fished, he came scowling out on the rocks and told them they were wasting their time.

"Oh, leave us alone, Joe," said Philip impatiently. "You act as if you were our keeper! For goodness' sake go and get on with your own work, and leave us to do what we want to do. We're not doing any harm."

"Miss Polly said to me to keep an eye on you all," said Joe sulkily. "She said to me not to let you get into danger, see."

"No, I don't see," said Philip crossly. "All I can see is that you keep on popping up wherever we are and spoiling things for us. Don't keep prying on us. We don't like it."

Lucy-Ann giggled. She thought it was brave of Philip to talk to the big man like that. He certainly was a nuisance. What fun they would have had if he had been jolly and good-tempered! They could have gone fishing and sailing in his boat. They could have fished properly with him. They could have gone out in the car and picnicked.

"But all because he's so daft and bad-tempered we can't do any of those things," said Lucy-Ann. "Why, we might even have tried to sail out to the Isle of Gloom to see if there were many birds there, as Jack so badly wants to do, if only Joe had been nice."

"Well, he's not nice, and we'll never go to Gloom, and if we did get there, I bet there wouldn't be any birds on such a desolate place," said Philip. "Come on — let's explore that big cave we found yesterday."

It really was fun exploring the caves on the shore. Some of them ran very far back into the cliff. Others had holes in their roofs, that led to upper caves. Philip said that in olden times men had used the caves for hiding in, or for storing smuggled goods. But there was nothing to be seen in them now except seaweed and empty shells.

"I wish we had a good torch," said Jack, as his candle was blown out for the sixth time that morning. "I shall soon have no candles left. If only there was a shop round the corner where we could slip along and buy a torch! I asked Joe yesterday to get me one when he went shopping in the car, but he wouldn't."

"Oooh — here's a most enormous starfish!" said Philip, holding his candle down to the floor of the damp cave. "Do look — it's a giant one, I'm sure."

Dinah gave a shriek. She hated creepy-crawly things as much as Philip liked them. "Don't touch it. And don't bring it near me."

But Philip was a tease, and he picked up the great starfish, with its five long fingers, and walked over to Dinah with it. She flew into a furious rage.

"You beast! I told you not to bring it near me. I'll kill it if you do."

"You can't kill starfish," said Philip. "If you cut one in half it grows new fingers, and, hey presto, it is two starfishes instead of one. So there! Have a look at it, Dinah – smell it – feel it."

Philip pushed the great clammy thing near to his sister's face. Really alarmed, Dinah hit out, and gave Philip such a push that he reeled, overbalanced and fell headlong to the floor of the cave. His candle went out. There was a shout from Philip, then a curious slithering noise – and silence.

"Hi, Tufty! Are you all right?" called Jack, and held his candle high. To his enormous astonishment, Philip had completely disappeared. There was the starfish on the seaweedy ground – but no Philip was beside it.

The three children stared in the greatest amazement at the clumps of seaweed hanging from the walls of the cave, spreading over the ground. Wherever had Philip gone?

Dinah was scared. She had certainly meant to give Philip a hard blow – but she hadn't meant him to disappear off the face of the earth. She gave a yell.

"Philip! Are you hiding? Come out, idiot!"

A muffled voice came from somewhere. "Hi! – where am I?"

"That's Tufty's voice," said Jack. "But where is he? He's nowhere in this cave."

The children put their three candles together and looked round the small, low-roofed, seaweedy cave. It smelled very dank and musty. Philip's voice came again from somewhere, sounding rather frightened.

"I say! Where am I?"

Jack advanced cautiously over the slippery seaweed to where Philip had fallen when Dinah had struck him. Then suddenly he seemed to lose his footing, and, to the surprise of the watching girls, he too disappeared, seeming to sink down into the floor of the seaweedy cave.

By the wavering light of their two candles the girls tried to see what had happened to Jack. Then they saw the explanation of the mystery. The fronds of seaweed hid an opening in the floor of the cave, and when the boys had put their weight on to the seaweed covering the hole, they had slipped between the fronds down into some cave below. How strange!

"That's where they went," said Dinah, pointing to a dark space between the seaweed covering that part of the floor. "I hope they haven't broken their legs. However shall we get them out?"

Jack had fallen on top of poor Philip, almost squashing him. Kiki, left behind in the cave above, let out an ear-piercing screech. She hated these dark caves, but always came with Jack. Now he had suddenly gone, and the parrot was alarmed.

"Shut up, Kiki," said Dinah, jumping in fright at the screech.

"Look, Lucy-Ann, there's a hole in the cave floor there, just between that thick seaweed. Walk carefully, or you'll disappear too. Hold up my candle as well as your own and I'll see if I can make out exactly what has happened."

What had happened was really very simple. First Philip had gone down the hole into a cave below, and then Jack had fallen on top of him. Philip was feeling frightened and bruised. He clutched Jack and wouldn't let go.

"What's happened?" he said.

"Hole in the cave floor," said Jack, putting out his hands and feeling round to see how big the cave was they had fallen into. He touched rocky walls on each side of him at once. "I say – this is a mighty small cave. Hi, girls, put the candles over the hole so that we can see something."

A lighted candle now appeared above the boys and they were able to see a little.

"We're not in a cave. We're in a passage," said Jack, astonished. "At least, we're at the beginning of a passage. I wonder where it goes to... right into the cliffs, I suppose."

"Hand us down a candle," called Philip, feeling better now. "Oh, goodness – here's Kiki."

"Can't you shut the door?" said Kiki, in a sharp voice, sitting hard on Jack's shoulder, glad to be with her master again. She began to whistle, and then told herself not to.

"Shut up, Kiki," said Jack. "Look, Philip — there really is a passage leading up there — awfully dark and narrow. And what a smell there is! Dinah, pass that candle down quickly, do!"

Dinah at last managed to hand down a lighted candle. She lay flat on the seaweedy cave floor, and just managed to pass the candle down through the hole. Jack held it up. The dark passage looked mysterious and strange.

"What about exploring it?" said Philip, feeling excited. "It looks as if it ought to go below Craggy-Tops itself. It's a secret passage."

"More likely a short crack in the cliff rocks that leads nowhere at all," said Jack. "Kiki, don't peck my ear so hard. We'll go into the open air soon. Hi, you girls! We think we'll go up this funny passage. Are you coming?"

"No, thanks," said Lucy-Ann at once, who didn't at all like the sound of a seaweedy passage that ran, dark and narrow, through the cliffs. "We'll stay here till you come back. Don't be long. We've only got one candle now. Have you some matches in case your candle goes out?"

"Yes," said Jack, feeling in his pocket. "Well, goodbye for the present. Don't fall down the hole."

The boys left the dark hole under which they stood and began to make their way up the damp passage. The girls could no longer hear their voices or footsteps. They waited patiently in the cave above, lighted by one flickering candle. It was cold and they shivered, glad of their warm jerseys.

The boys were a very long time. The two girls became impatient and then alarmed. What could have happened to them? They peered down the hole between the great fronds of seaweed and listened. Not a sound could be heard.

"Oh dear — do you think we ought to go after them?" said Lucy-Ann desperately. She would be frightened to death going up that dark secret passage, she was sure, and yet if Jack was in need of help she would have no hesitation in jumping down and following him.

"Better go and tell Joe and get him to come and help," said Dinah. "He'd better bring a rope, I should think. The boys would never be able to climb up through the hole back into this cave, without help."

"No, don't let's tell Joe," said Lucy-Ann, who disliked the man thoroughly, and was afraid of him. "We'll wait a bit longer. Maybe the passage was a very long one."

It was — far longer than the boys expected. It twisted and turned as it went through the cliff, going upwards all the time. It was pitch-dark, and the candle did not seem to light it very much. The boys bumped their heads against the roof every now and again, for it was sometimes only shoulder-high.

It grew drier as it went up. Soon there was no seaweedy smell at all, but the air felt stale and musty. It was rather difficult to breathe.

"I believe the air is bad here," panted Philip, as they went on. "I can hardly breathe. Once or twice I thought our candle was going out, Freckles. That would mean the air was very bad. Surely we shall come to the end of this passage soon."

As he spoke, the passage went steeply upwards and was cut into rough steps. It ended abruptly in a rocky wall. The boys were puzzled.

"It's not a real passage, then," said Philip, disappointed. "Just a crack in the cliff rocks, as you said. But these do really look like rough steps, don't they?"

The light of the candle shone down on to the steps. Yes — someone had hewn out those steps at one time — but why?

Jack held the candle above his

head – and gave a shout. "Look! Isn't that a trap-door above our heads? That's where the passage led to – that trap-door! I say – let's get it open if we can."

Sure enough, there was an old wooden trap-door, closing the exit of the passage, above their heads. If only they could lift it! Wherever would they find themselves?

CHAPTER VIII
IN THE CELLARS

"Let's push at it together," said Philip, in excitement. "I'll put the candle down on this ledge."

He stuck the candle firmly into a crack on the ledge. Then he and Jack pushed hard at the trap-door just above their heads. A shower of dust fell down, and Philip blinked his eyes, half blinded. Jack had closed his.

"Blow!" said Philip, rubbing his eyes. "Come on, let's try again. I felt it move."

They tried again, and this time the trap-door suddenly gave way. It lifted a few inches, and then fell back again, setting free another cloud of dust.

"Get a rock or big stone and we'll stand on it," said Jack, red with excitement. "A bit more of a push and we'll get the thing right open."

They found three or four flattish stones, put them in a stout pile, and stood on them. They pushed against the trap-door, and to their delight it lifted right up, and fell backwards with a thud on the floor above, leaving a square opening above the heads of the boys.

"Give me a heave up, Jack," said Philip. He got such a shove that he shot out through the trap-door opening and landed on a rocky floor above. It was dark there and he could see nothing.

"Hand up the candle, Freckles, and then I'll haul you up," said Philip. The candle was handed up, but went out suddenly.

"Blow!" said Philip. "Oh glory, what's that?"

"Kiki, I expect," said Jack. "She's flown up."

Kiki had not made a sound or said a word all through the secret passage. She had been alarmed at the dark strange place, and had clung hard to Jack all the way.

Philip hauled Jack up, and then groped in his pocket for matches to light the candle again. "Where do you suppose we are?" he said. "I simply can't imagine."

"Feels like the other end of the world," said Jack. "Ah — that's better. Now we can see."

He held up the lighted candle and the two boys looked round.

"*I* know where we are," said Philip suddenly. "In one of the cellars at Craggy-Tops. Look — there are boxes of stores over there. Tins of food and stuff."

"So there are," said Jack. "My word, what a fine store your aunt keeps down here! Golly, this is quite an adventure. Do you suppose your aunt and uncle know about the secret passage?"

"I shouldn't think so," said Philip. "Aunt Polly would be sure to have mentioned it to us, I should think. I don't seem to know this part of the cellars very well. Let me see — where is the cellar door now?"

The boys wandered down the cellar, trying to find the way out. They came to a stout wooden door, but, to their surprise, it was locked.

"Blow!" said Philip, annoyed. "Now we shall have to creep all the way back down that passage again. I don't feel like doing that, somehow. Anyway, this isn't the door that leads out of the cellars into the kitchen. You have to go up steps to that one. This must be a door that shuts off one part of the cellars from the other. I don't remember seeing it before."

"Listen — isn't that somebody coming?" said Jack suddenly, his sharp ears hearing footsteps.

"Yes — it's Joe," said Philip, hearing the familiar cough he knew so well. "Let's hide. I'm not going to tell Joe about that passage. We'll keep it to ourselves. Shut the trap-door down quickly, Jack, and then we'll hide behind this archway here. We could slip out quietly when Joe opens the door. Blow out the candle."

They shut the trap-door quietly and then, in the pitch-darkness, hid behind the stone archway near the door. They heard Joe putting a key into the lock. The door swung open, and the man appeared, looking huge in the flickering light of his lantern. He left the door open, and went towards the back of the cellar, where the stores lay.

The boys had on rubber shoes, and could have slipped out without Joe knowing anything at all — but Kiki chose that moment to imitate Joe's hollow cough. It filled the cellar with mournful echoes, and Joe dropped his lantern with a crash. The glass splintered and the light went out. Joe gave a howl of terror and fled out of the door at once, not even pausing to lock it. He brushed against the two boys as he went, and gave another screech of fright, feeling their warm bodies as he passed.

Kiki, thrilled at the result of her coughing imitation, gave an unearthly screech that sent Joe headlong through the other part of the cellars, up the steps and through the cellar door. He almost fell as he appeared in the kitchen, and Aunt Polly jumped in astonishment.

"What's the matter? What has happened?"

"There's things down there!" panted Joe, his face looking as scared as it ever could look.

"Things! What do you mean?" said Aunt Polly severely.

"Things that screech and yell and clutch at me," said Joe, sinking into a chair, and closing his eyes till nothing but the thinnest slits could be seen.

"Nonsense!" said Aunt Polly, stirring a saucepan vigorously. "I don't know why you wanted to go down there anyway. We don't need anything from the cellars this morning. I've plenty of potatoes up here. Pull yourself together, Joe. You'll frighten the children if you behave like this."

The two boys had collapsed into helpless laughter when they had seen poor Joe running in alarm from the cellar, yelling for all he was worth. They clutched each other and laughed till they ached.

"Well, Joe is always trying to frighten us by tales of peculiar 'things' that wander about at night," said Jack, "and now he's been caught by his own silly stories — and been almost frightened out of his wits."

"I say — he's left the key in the door," said Philip, who had now lit his candle again. "Let's take it. Then, if ever we want to use that passage again, we can always get out this way if we want to, by unlocking the door."

He put the big key into his pocket, grinning. Maybe the odd-job man would think it was one of the "things" he was always talking about that had gone off with his key.

The boys went into the part of the cellar they knew. Philip looked with interest at the door through which they had come.

"I never knew there was another cellar beyond this first one," he said, looking round the vast underground room. "How did I never notice that door before, I wonder?"

"Those boxes must have been piled in front of it to hide it," said Jack. There were empty boxes by the door, and now that he thought of it, Philip remembered seeing them in a big pile every time he had gone into the cellar. They had been neatly piled in front of that door. A trick of Joe's, no doubt, to stop the children going into the second cellar, where all those stores were kept. How silly and childish! Well, he couldn't stop them going there now.

"We can go there through the secret passage, or we could go there through the door, because I've got the key now," thought Philip, pleased at the idea of being able to outwit the man if he wanted to.

"I suppose those steps lead up to the kitchen, don't they?" said Jack, pointing to them. "Is it safe to go up, do you think? We don't want anyone to see us, or they'd ask awkward questions."

"I'll slip up to the top, open the door a crack, and listen to see if anyone is about," said Philip. So up he went. But Joe had gone out and his aunt was no longer there, so the big kitchen was empty and silent. The boys were able to slip out, go to the outer door, and run down the cliff-path without anyone seeing them at all.

"The girls will wonder whatever has become of us," said Jack, suddenly remembering Dinah and Lucy-Ann, waiting patiently for them in the cave where the hole was that led into the passage. "Come on – let's give them an awful fright, shall we? They'll be expecting us to come back through the secret passage – they'll never expect us to come back this way."

They made their way down to the rocky shore. They went to the caves they had explored that morning and found the one that had the hole. The two girls were sitting by the hole, anxiously discussing what they ought to do.

"We really *must* go and get help now," said Lucy-Ann. "I'm sure something has happened to the boys. Really I am."

Philip suddenly spotted the giant starfish again, the one that had caused all the trouble. Very silently he picked it up. Without making a sound, he crept over the seaweedy cave floor to poor Dinah. He placed the starfish on her bare arm, where it slithered down in a horrible manner.

Dinah leaped up with a shriek that was even worse than Kiki's loudest one. "Oh – oh – Philip's back again, the beast! Wait till I get hold of you, Philip! I'll pull all your hair out of your head! You hateful boy!"

In one of her furious rages Dinah leaped at Philip, who ran out of the caves and on to the sandy shore in glee. Lucy-Ann threw her arms round Jack. She had been very anxious about him.

"Jack! Oh, Jack, what happened to you? I waited so long. How did you come back this way? Where did the passage lead to?"

Shrieks and yells and shouts from Dinah and Philip made it impossible for Jack to answer, especially as Kiki now joined in the row, screeching like an express train in a tunnel.

There was a fine fight going on between Philip and Dinah. The angry girl had caught her brother, and was hitting out at him for all she was worth.

"I'll teach you to throw starfish at me. You mean pig! You know I hate those things. I'll pull all your hair out."

Philip got free and ran off, leaving a few of his hairs in Dinah's fingers. Dinah turned a furious face to the others.

"He's a beast. I shan't talk to him for days. I wish he wasn't my brother."

"It was only a bit of fun," began Jack, but this made matters worse. Dinah flew into a temper with him too, and looked so fierce that Lucy-Ann was quite alarmed, and thought she would have to defend Jack if Dinah rushed to slap him.

"I won't have anything to do with any of you," stormed Dinah, and walked off angrily.

"Now she won't hear all we've found this morning," said Jack. "What a spitfire she is! Well, we'll have to tell you, Lucy-Ann. We've had a real adventure."

Dinah, walking off in a fury, suddenly remembered that she had not heard the story of the secret passage and where it came out. Forgetting her rage, she turned back at once.

She saw Lucy-Ann and the two boys together. Philip turned his back on her as she came up. But Dinah could be as sudden in her good tempers as she was in her bad ones. She put her arm on Philip's.

"Sorry, Philip," she said. "What happened to you and Jack in that secret passage? I'm longing to know."

So peace was restored again, and soon the two girls were listening in the greatest excitement to all that the boys had to tell.

"It was an adventure, I can tell you," said Jack. So it was — and there were more to come!

THE MYSTERY OF THE SECRET ROOM

AN EXTRACT

∽ ILLUSTRATED BY ∽

J. ABBEY

While hiding in the branches of a tree in the garden of the deserted Milton House, the Five Find-Outers notice that one of the upstairs rooms is fully furnished, while the rest of the house is empty and covered in dust and cobwebs. Fatty (Frederick Algernon Trotteville) decides to investigate the secret room by visiting Milton House in the middle of the night!

CHAPTER XV
THE SECRET ROOM

It was most enjoyable talking over Fatty's plans for the night. All the Find-Outers and Buster gathered round the fire in Pip's playroom, and talked.

"My mother and father will be away for two days," said Fatty. "That's lucky. They won't know if I'm there tonight or not. I shall go down to the summer-house in the grounds of Milton House and make myself comfortable there with a couple of rugs. If I don't hear anything by midnight, I shall get in at the coal-hole."

"Fatty – suppose you're caught?" said Pip.

"Yes – I'd thought of it," said Fatty, considering. "If I'm caught, one of you had better know. I'll tell you what – if I'm caught, I shall throw a note out of the

window of whatever room I am locked up in – I imagine if I'm caught I shall be locked in somewhere – and one of you must scout round the grounds tomorrow morning and look out for the note. See? It will be in invisible writing, of course."

This sounded terribly exciting. Bets looked solemn. "Don't be caught, Fatty. I don't want you to be caught."

"Don't worry. I'm pretty smart," said Fatty. "People would have to be pretty clever to catch me!"

"Well – that's settled, then," said Larry. "You are going down to Milton House tonight in disguise, and you're going to wait till midnight to see if any one comes. If nobody comes, you're going to get down the coal-hole and explore the secret room, to see if you can get any information about the mysterious John Henry Smith. By the way – I do wonder why that window was barred if there were no children in that house."

"Don't know," said Fatty. "But I expect I shall find out."

"If you don't get caught, you'll come back home, go to bed, and meet us in the morning with whatever news you've got," said Larry. "But if you don't turn up, one of us will snoop round the grounds and wait for a letter written in invisible ink. Don't forget to take an orange with you, Fatty, in case you have to write that note."

"Of course I shan't forget," said Fatty. "But as I shan't be caught, you needn't worry – there won't be any letter floating out of a window!"

"Anyway, Fatty, you know how to get out of a locked room if you have to," said Bets.

"Of course!" said Fatty. "I shall be all right, you may be sure."

As Fatty's parents were away, the Find-Outers decided to go down to his house after tea and watch him disguise himself. They all felt excited, though Bets had now got the idea that this mystery was a dangerous one, and she was rather worried.

"Don't be silly," said Fatty. "What danger can there be in it? I shall be all right, I tell you. This is an adventure, and people like me never say no to an adventure."

"You *are* brave, Fatty," said Bets.

"This is nothing!" said Fatty. "I could tell you of a time when I really *was* brave. But I expect I should bore you." He looked round inquiringly.

"Yes, you *would* bore us," said Pip. "Are you going to wear those terrible teeth again, Fatty?"

"You bet!" said Fatty, and slipped them into his mouth. At once his whole appearance changed as he grinned round, the frightful sticking-out teeth making him look completely unlike himself.

Fatty looked fine when the Find-Outers at last left him, taking Buster with them. Fatty had decided that it wouldn't do to leave the little dog behind in the house as he might bark all night long. So he was to spend the night with Larry and Daisy. Bets wanted him, but Pip said that their mother would be sure to ask all kinds of why and wherefore questions if Buster suddenly appeared for the night, and that might lead to something awkward.

So Larry took him home, and Buster, rather surprised, trotted along with him and Daisy, limping every now and again whenever he remembered. He quite thought that Fatty would be along to fetch him from Larry's sooner or later.

Fatty sat up fairly late reading. He was in his French-boy disguise, and looked fine. If the maid had popped her head into his room she would have got a shock. But nobody saw him at all.

At about ten o'clock Fatty slipped out of the house. The moon was almost full, and shone brightly down on the white snow. Fatty's footsteps made no sound at all.

He went down the road, took the way over the hill, and at last walked down Chestnut Lane, keeping well to the hedge, in the black shadows there. He saw nobody. Mr Goon the policeman was not about that night, being busy nursing a very bad cold which had suddenly and most annoyingly seized him. Otherwise he had fully meant to hang about Milton House to see if he could find out any thing that night.

Now he was in bed, sneezing hard and dosing himself with hot lemon and honey, determined to get rid of the cold by the next day, in case those tiresome children got ahead of him in this new mystery.

So there was no one to watch Fatty. He slipped in at the drive gate, kept to the shadows, and made his way round the house, hoping that no one would notice his footprints the next day. He came to the little tumble-down summer-house and went in. He had two thick rugs with him, and put them down on the seat.

He had a look up at the secret room, with its strange bars. Was there any one there yet? Would any one come that night?

It was cold. Fatty went back to the summer-house and cuddled himself up in the rugs. He soon felt warm again. He grew rather sleepy, and kept blinking to keep himself awake. He heard the church clock in the village strike eleven. Then he must have fallen asleep, for the next thing he knew was the clock striking again! This time it struck twelve.

"Golly!" said Fatty. "Midnight! I must have fallen asleep. Well – as nothing has happened, and no one has come, or is likely to come as late as this, I'll just pop down the coal-hole!"

Fatty had put on his oldest clothes. His mother was not as particular as Pip's, but even she would remark on clothes marked with coal-dust. Fatty looked a proper little ruffian as he threw off the rugs and stood listening in the moonlight. He had on the curly wig, he had made his face very pale, he had stuck on dark eyebrows, and, of course, he had the awful teeth. He was certainly enough to startle any one if there had been someone to see him.

He made his way round the hedges of the garden to the kitchen entrance, keeping well in the shadows. He came to the coal-hole. Snow had covered it again, but Fatty knew just about where it was. He cleared the snow away from it, and bent down to pull up the round iron lid.

It needed a jolly good tug, but at last up it came, unexpectedly suddenly, so that Fatty sat down with a bump, and the lid clanged down, making quite a noise.

Fatty held his breath, but nothing happened. He got up cautiously, pushed the lid to one side, and then shone his torch down the dark opening to see how far below the floor was.

Fortunately for him there was a heap of coal just below the hole. He could let himself down on it fairly easily. So down he went, and landed on the coal, which at once gave beneath him, so that he went slithering down the side of the heap.

He picked himself up and switched on his torch. He saw a flight of stone steps leading upwards to a shut door – the kitchen or scullery door, he guessed. He went up slowly, and turned the handle of the door.

It opened into a large scullery, into which the moon shone brightly. It was completely empty. He went into the next room, which was a kitchen. That, too, was empty, but in the dust of the floor Fatty saw the same large footprints that he had seen in the snowy drive the day before.

Perhaps I can see into the secret room! thought the boy, his heart beating fast. It was a strange feeling to be all alone in a deserted house, knowing that people came there secretly for some mysterious reason!

Fatty felt certain there was nobody at all in the house, but all the same he jumped at any moving shadow, and almost leaped out of his skin when a floorboard creaked loudly under his foot.

He looked into room after room. All were completely empty. He explored all the ground floor, the first floor, and the second floor. The secret room was on the

third floor, at the top of the house. Fatty went up the stairs to the last floor, trying to walk as quietly as possible even though he felt so certain that there was nobody else in the house but himself.

He came to the top floor. He looked into the first room he came to. It was empty. He looked into the next one; that was empty too. But the third one was the secret room!

Fatty pushed open the door quietly and slowly. He peeped in. It lay silent and still in the brilliant moonlight – a very comfortable room, large, high-ceilinged like all the rooms, and very well furnished.

Fatty walked round the

room. It had evidently been roughly cleaned and thoroughly dusted not long before. A little pile of tins of meat and fruit stood on a shelf. The kettle on the stove had water in it. A tin of tea was on the table. Books stood on the window-sill, and Fatty turned over the pages of some. They were in a foreign language and he couldn't understand a word.

The sofa had been prepared as a kind of bed, for the cushions were piled at one end, and cosy rugs had been folded there. It was all very strange.

I suppose I'd better get back to the summer-house, thought Fatty. I wish I could find some letters or documents of some sort that would tell me a bit about this strange room. But there don't seem to be any.

He sat down on the sofa and yawned. Then his eye caught sight of a small cupboard in the wall. He wondered what was in it. He got up – but the cupboard was locked. Fatty put his hand into his pocket and brought out a perfectly extraordinary collection of keys. He had secretly been making a hoard of these, as he had learned that most detectives can lock or unlock doors or cupboards. They had odd keys called skeleton keys which could apparently unlock with ease almost anything that needed a key.

But a skeleton key had proved impossible to buy, and, indeed, had led to many awkward questions being put by the shopkeepers whom he had asked for one. So Fatty had been forced to collect any old key he could find, and he now had a very varied collection which weighed down the pocket of his coat considerably. He took them all out.

Most patiently and methodically Fatty tried first one key and then another in the lock of the little cupboard, and to his delight, and also his surprise, one key did manage to unlock the door!

Inside was a small book, a kind of notebook, and entered in it were numbers and names, nothing else at all. It seemed very dull to Fatty.

Perhaps Inspector Jenks may like to have a look at it, he thought, and he pocketed the little book and locked the cupboard door again. We shall soon be reporting this mystery to him, and he may like to have all the bits of evidence we can find.

He sat down on the sofa again. He no longer felt excited, but very sleepy. He looked at his watch. It was a quarter-past one! Gracious, he had been a long time in Milton House!

"I'll just have a bit of a rest on this comfy sofa," said Fatty, and curled himself up. In half a minute he was sound asleep. What a mistake that was!

CHAPTER XVI
A BAD TIME FOR FATTY

Fatty slept soundly. His adventure had tired him. The couch was extremely comfortable, and although there was no warmth in the room, the rugs were thick and cosy. Fatty lay there dreaming of the time when he would be an even more important detective than the famous Sherlock Holmes.

He did not hear the sound of a car about half-past four in the early morning. The wheels slid silently over the snow, and came to a stop outside Milton House.

Fatty did not hear people walking up the drive. Nor did he hear a latch-key being put into the lock of the front door. He heard no voices, no footsteps, but the old empty house suddenly echoed to them.

Fatty slept on peacefully. He was warm and comfortable. He did not even wake up when someone opened the door of the secret room and came in.

Nobody saw him at first. A man crossed to the window and carefully drew the thick curtains across before switching on the light. Not a crack of light could be seen from outside once the window curtains were drawn.

Another man came into the room – and he gave a cry of surprise. "Look here!"

He pointed to the couch, where Fatty still slept as peacefully as Goldilocks had slept in the Little Bear's bed long ago!

The two men stared in the utmost astonishment at Fatty. His curly wig of black hair, his big black eyebrows, and the awful teeth made him a peculiar sight.

"Who is he? And what's he doing here?" said one of the men, amazed and angry. He shook Fatty roughly by the shoulder.

The boy woke up and opened his eyes under the shaggy eyebrows. In a trice he knew where he was, and realised that he had fallen asleep in the secret room – and now he was caught! A little shiver of fear went down his back. The men did not look either friendly or pleased.

"What are you doing here?" said the bigger fellow of the two, a ruddy-faced man with eyes that stuck out like Mr Goon's, and a short black beard. The other man was short, and had a round white face with black button-eyes and the thinnest lips Fatty had ever seen.

The boy sat up and stared at the two men. He really didn't know what to say.

"Haven't you a tongue in your head?" demanded the red-faced man. "What are you doing on our premises?"

Fatty decided to pretend he was French again.

"*Je ne comprends pas*," he said, meaning that he didn't understand.

But unfortunately one of the men spoke French and he rattled off a long and most alarming sentence in French, which Fatty couldn't understand at all. Fatty then decided he wouldn't be French; he would speak the nonsense language that he and the others sometimes spoke together when they wanted to mystify anyone.

"Tibbletooky-fickle-farmery-toppy-swick," he said quite solemnly.

The men looked puzzled. "What language is that?" said the red-faced man to his companion. He shook his head.

"Speak French," he commanded Fatty.

"Spikky-tarly-yondle-fitty-toomar," answered Fatty at once.

"Never heard a language like that before," said the red-faced man. "The boy looks foreign enough. Wonder where he comes from. We'll have to find out how he got here."

He turned to Fatty again, and addressed him first in English, then in French, then in German, and then in a fourth language Fatty had never heard.

"Spikky-tarly-yondle," said Fatty, and waggled his hands about just like his French master at school.

The pale-faced man spoke to his companion. "I believe he's foxing," he said in a low voice that Fatty could not hear. "He's just pretending. I'll soon make him talk his own language. Watch me!"

He suddenly bent over Fatty, took hold of his left arm, dragged it behind him and twisted it. Fatty let out an agonised yell.

"Let go, you beast! You're hurting me!"

"Aha!" said the pale-faced man. "So you *can* talk English, can you? Very interesting. Now — what about talking a little more, and telling us who you are and how you came here."

Fatty nursed his twisted arm, feeling rather alarmed. He was very angry with himself for falling asleep and getting so easily caught. He looked sulkily at the man and said nothing.

"Ah! — he wants a little more coaxing," said the pale-faced man, smiling with his thin lips and showing long yellow teeth. "Shall we twist your other arm, boy?"

He took hold of Fatty's right arm. Fatty decided to talk. He wouldn't give away more than he could help.

"Don't you touch me," he said. "I'm a poor homeless fellow, and I'm doing no harm sleeping here."

"How did you get in?" said the red-faced man.

"Through the coal-hole," said Fatty.

"Ah!" said the man, and the thin-lipped one pursed up his mouth so that his lips completely vanished.

He looked very hard and cruel, Fatty thought.

"Does anyone else know you're here?" said the red-faced man.

"How do I know?" said Fatty. "If anyone had seen me getting down the coal-hole they'd know I was here. But if they didn't see me, how would they know?"

"He is evading the question," said the thin-lipped man. "We can only make him talk properly by giving him much pain. We will do so. A little beating first, I think."

Fatty felt afraid. He was quite sure that this man would go to any lengths to get what he wanted to know. He stared sulkily at him.

Quite suddenly, without any warning, the thin-lipped man dealt Fatty a terrific blow on his right ear. Then, before the boy could recover, he dealt him another blow, this time on his left ear. Fatty gasped. Bright stars danced in front of his eyes, and he blinked.

When the stars went, and the boy could see again, he gazed in fear at the thin-lipped man, who was now smiling a horrible smile.

"I think you will talk now?" he said to Fatty. "I can do other things if you prefer."

Fatty was very frightened now. He felt that he would rather give away the whole mystery than have any more blows. After all, he wouldn't be harming the other Find-Outers, and he knew they would be only too glad for him to save himself from harm or injury. This was just very, very bad luck.

"All right. I'll talk," said Fatty, with a gulp. "There's not much to tell you, though."

"How did you find out about this room?" demanded the red-faced man.

"By accident," said Fatty. "A friend of mine climbed that tree outside, and looked in and saw this room."

"How many know about it?" rapped out the thin-lipped man.

"Only me and the other Find-Outers," said Fatty.

"The other what?" said the man, puzzled.

Fatty explained. The men listened.

"Oh! – so there are five children in this," said the red-faced man. "Any grown-up know about this affair?"

"No," said Fatty. "We — we are rather keen on solving mysteries if we can — and we don't like telling grown-ups in case they interfere. There's only me and the other four in this. Now that I've let you know, you might let me go."

"What! — let you go and have you spread the news around?" said the thin-lipped man scornfully. "It's bad enough to have you interfering and messing up our plans without running the risk of letting you go."

"Well, if you don't, the others will come snooping round to see what's happened to me," said Fatty triumphantly. "I've already arranged for them to come and find out what's happened if I'm not at home this morning."

"I see," said the thin-lipped man. He spoke quickly to the other man in a language Fatty could not follow. The red-faced man nodded. The thin-lipped man turned to Fatty.

"You will write a note to the others to say that you have discovered something wonderful here, and are guarding it, and will they all come to the garden as soon as possible," he said.

"Oh! — and I suppose you think that you can catch them too when they come, and lock them up till you've finished whatever secret business you are on!" said Fatty.

"Exactly," said the man. "We think it would be better to hold you all prisoner here till we have finished our affairs. Then you can tell what you like."

"Well, if you think I shall write a letter that will bring my friends into your hands, you're jolly well mistaken!" said Fatty hotly. "I'm not such a coward as that!"

"Are you not?" said the thin-lipped man, and he looked at Fatty so strangely that the boy trembled. What would this horrible man do to him if he refused to write the note? Fatty didn't dare to think.

He tried to stare back bravely at the man, but it was difficult. Fatty wished desperately he had not gone into this midnight adventure so light-heartedly. He longed for old Buster. But perhaps it was as well that Buster was not there. These men might kick him and misuse him cruelly.

"We shall lock you up," said the thin-lipped man. "We have to go in a little while, but we shall come back soon. You will write this note whilst we are gone. If it is not done by the time we come back, there will be trouble for you, bad trouble — trouble you will not forget all the rest of your life."

Fatty's spirits went up a little when he heard he was to be locked up. He might be able to escape if so! He had a folded newspaper in his pocket. He was sure he could use his trick of getting out of a locked room all right. Then his spirits sank again.

"We will lock you into this so-comfortable room," said the red-faced man. "And we will give you paper and pen and ink. You will write a nice, excited note that will bring all your friends here quickly. You can throw it out of the window."

Fatty knew he could never escape from the secret room. A thick carpet ran right to the door. There was no space beneath the edge of the door to slip a key. None at all. He would be a real prisoner. He could not even escape down the tree because the window was so heavily barred.

The thin-lipped man placed a sheet of notepaper on a table, and laid beside it a pen and a little ink-stand.

"There you are," he said. "You will write this note in your own way and sign it. What is your name?"

"Frederick Trotteville," said Fatty gloomily.

"You are called Freddie, then, are you not?" said the thin-lipped man. "You will sign your letter 'Freddie,' and when your friends come into the garden, I will fling your note from the window – but you will not speak to them."

The red-faced man looked at his watch. "We must go," he said. "It is time. Everything is ready here. We will get the rest of these interfering kids and lock them up till we have finished.

It won't hurt them to starve for a day or two in an empty room!"

They went out of the room. Fatty heard the key turn in the lock. He was a prisoner. He stared gloomily at the shut door. It was his own fault that he was in this fix. But he wasn't going to get the others into it too — no, not even if those men beat him black and blue!

CHAPTER XVII
THE SECRET MESSAGE

Fatty heard the footsteps of the men clattering down the uncarpeted stairs. He heard the front door close quietly. He heard the sound of a car starting up. The men had gone.

He tried the door. It was locked all right. He went to the window. It was pitch-dark outside. He opened the window and felt the bars. They were too close together for him to slip out between them. He was indeed a prisoner.

He went and sat down again, shivering. Fright and the winter's chill made him shake all over. He saw the electric fire and decided to put it on. He might as well be warm, anyway!

He sat down once more and gazed gloomily at the sheet of notepaper. What a bad detective he was, to allow himself to be caught like this! It was terribly careless. The others would never admire him again.

Well, I shan't write that letter, anyway, thought the boy, but he trembled to think what his punishment might be if he didn't.

Then an idea came to him. It was really brilliant. He sat and thought about it for a while. Yes — it would work if only the others were bright enough to catch on to the idea too!

I'll write an invisible letter on this sheet of paper, and I'll write a letter in ink on it as well! thought Fatty. I bet Pip and the others will think of testing it for secret writing. Golly — what an idea this is! To write two letters on one sheet, one seen and the other unseen! I bet the men will never think of that!

He looked at the sheet of paper. It was faintly ruled with lines. He could write his secret letter between the lines and the other letter on the lines! When the others tested it for secret writing, they would then be able to read his real letter easily.

Fatty's hands shook with excitement. He might be able to do something startling now! He must think carefully what to write. The men who used this room were evil, and they used it as a meeting-place for evil reasons. They must be stopped. They were evidently in the middle of some big affair at the moment, and it was up to Fatty to stop them.

He took a rather squashy orange from his pocket. He looked round for a glass. There was one on the shelf. He squeezed his orange into it, then picked up the pen the men had left. The nib was clean and new.

Should he write the visible letter first, or the secret one? Fatty decided on the visible one, because it would be easier then to write the invisible one, as he could see where he had written the first letter.

He began:

Dear Find-Outers, — I have made a wonderful discovery, most awfully exciting. I can't leave here, because I am guarding something — but I want to show you what it is. All of you come as soon as you can, and I will let you in when you knock. — Yours, Freddie.

That seemed all right — just what the man had commanded him to write. But the others would smell a rat as soon as they saw the name "Freddie" at the bottom. He always signed himself Fatty in notes like this.

Then he set to work to write the letter in secret ink — or rather in orange juice.

Dear Find-Outers — he wrote — *Don't take any notice of the visible letter. I'm a prisoner here. There's some very dirty work going on; I don't quite know what. Get hold of Inspector Jenks at once and tell him everything. He'll know what to do. Don't you come near the place, any of you. — Yours ever, Fatty.*

That just took him to the bottom of the sheet. Not a trace of the secret writing was visible; only the few sentences of the inked writing were to be seen. Fatty felt pleased. Now, if only the others guessed there was a secret message and read it, things might be all right.

Inspector Jenks will see to things, thought Fatty, and it was comforting to think of the clever, powerful inspector of police, their very good friend, knowing about this curious affair. Fatty thought of him — his broad cheerful face, his courtesy, his tallness, his shrewdness.

It was now about six o'clock. Fatty yawned. He had had a poor night. He was hungry and tired, but warmer now. He curled himself up on the sofa again and slept.

He was awakened by the men coming into the room again. He sat up, blinking. Daylight now came in through the window.

The thin-lipped man saw the paper on the table and picked it up. He read the letter in silence and then handed it to the other man.

"This is all right," he said. "We'll bag all the silly little idiots, and give them a sharp lesson. Will they all come down to see where you are, boy?"

"I don't know," said Fatty. "No, probably not. Maybe just one or two of them."

"Then they're sure to take the letter to show the others, and bring them back here," said the thin-lipped man. "We'll keep a look-out for them. We'll hide in the garden and catch the lot. Jarvis is downstairs now too. He can help."

They opened some tins and had breakfast. They gave the hungry Fatty a small helping of ham sandwich, and he gobbled it up. They suddenly noticed his glass of yellow juice and one of them picked it up.

"What's this?" he said, smelling it suspiciously. "Where did it come from?"

"It's orange juice," said Fatty, and he drank it up. "I had an orange with me and I squeezed it. I can't help being thirsty, can I?"

He set down the glass. The men evidently thought no more of it but began to talk together in low voices, again using the language that Fatty did not understand. He was very bored. He wondered if one of the others would come soon. As soon as someone found he hadn't got home, surely they would come and look for him! What were the Find-Outers doing?"

They were all wondering how Fatty had got on that night. Bets was worried. She didn't know why, but she really did feel anxious.

"I hope Fatty is all right," she kept saying to Pip. "I do hope he is."

"That's about the twenty-third time you've said that!" said Pip crossly. "Of course he's all right. Probably eating an enormous breakfast this very minute."

Larry and Daisy called in at Pip's soon after breakfast, looking cross.

"We've got to catch the bus and take some things to one of our aunts," said Daisy. "Isn't it a bore — just when we wanted to hear if Fatty had found out anything. You and Bets will have to see if he's home, Pip."

"He may come wandering down, if he's at home," said Pip. "Oh, you've got Buster with you! Well, I'll take him back to Fatty's for you, shall I?"

Pip's mother wouldn't let him go out till about twelve o'clock, as she had made up her mind that he and Bets were to tidy out their cupboards. This was a job Pip hated. It took ages. Grumbling loudly, he began to throw everything out on to the floor.

"Oh, Pip, let's hurry up and finish this job," begged Bets. "I can't wait to find out if Fatty's home all right."

Buster fussed round, sniffing at everything that came out of the cupboards. He was upset and worried. His beloved master hadn't fetched him from Larry's the night before, and here was the morning and nobody had taken him back to Fatty yet. Not only that, but they apparently wouldn't let him go by himself! He was so miserable that he limped even more badly than usual, though his leg was now quite healed.

At last the cupboards were finished and Pip and Bets were told they might go out in the snow. They put on hats and coats, whistled to Buster, and set off to Fatty's.

They slipped in at his garden door and whistled the tune they always used as a signal to one another. There was no reply.

A maid popped her head out into the passage. "Oh!" she said, "I thought it was Master Frederick. He didn't sleep here last night, the naughty boy. I suppose he stayed the night with you or Master Larry — but he ought to have told me. When is he coming back?"

This was a real shock to Pip and Bets. So Fatty hadn't come back from Milton House? What had happened?

"Oh! — he'll be back today I expect," Pip said to the anxious maid. He dragged Bets out into the garden. She was crying.

"Don't be so silly," said Pip. "What's the good of crying before you know what's happened to Fatty?"

"I knew something had happened to him. I knew he was in danger, I did, I did," wept poor Bets. "I want to go down to Milton House and see what's happened."

"Well, you won't," said Pip. "There may be danger. You look after Buster for me. I'll go down myself."

"I'll come too," said Bets bravely, wiping her eyes.

"No, you won't," said Pip firmly. "I'm not going to have you running into danger. You don't like danger, anyway. So you be a good girl and take Buster home with you. I'll be back as soon as I can — and maybe I'll bring Fatty with me, so cheer up."

Still crying, poor Bets went off with the puzzled Buster, who simply could not understand what had happened to Fatty. He seemed to have disappeared into thin air!

Pip was much more worried than he had let Bets see. He couldn't help thinking that something serious must have happened. But what could it be? Fatty would surely never allow himself to be caught. He was far too clever.

Pip went over the hill and down Chestnut Lane. He came to the gate of Milton House. He gazed in cautiously. He could see more footprints, and there were new car-wheel prints.

He went round the hedge, slipped in at a gap, and found himself by the summer-house. Inside were the rugs Fatty had taken to keep himself warm. But there was no Fatty there.

He stepped cautiously into the garden, and one of the men, who was watching, saw him from a window. He had with him the sheet of notepaper on which Fatty had written the two letters.

The man bent down, so that he could not be seen, opened the window a crack at the bottom, gave a loud whistle to attract Pip's attention, and then let the paper float out of the window.

Pip heard the whistle and looked up. To his enormous surprise he saw a sheet of paper floating out of one of the second-storey windows. Perhaps it was a message from Fatty.

The boy ran to where the paper dropped and picked it up. He recognised Fatty's neat hand-writing at once. He read the note through, and his heart began to beat fast.

"Fatty's on to something," he thought. "He's found some stolen jewels or something and he's guarding them. He wants us all to be in it! I'll run back to the others, and bring them back with me. What an adventure! Good old Fatty!"

He scampered off, his face bright. The man watched him go and was satisfied. That young idiot would soon bring the other children down with him, and then they could all be locked up safely before they gave the game away!

Fatty saw Pip too and began to have a few horrid doubts. Were the Find-Outers smart enough to guess there was a secret letter in between the lines of inked writing? Suppose they didn't? He would have led them all into a trap!

A NIGHT ON THUNDER ROCK

~ ILLUSTRATED BY ~

H. M. BROCK

Three children with their own boat camp for the night on a small island called Thunder Rock. In the middle of the night they discover that they are not the only people on the island...

"Daddy, we've got something to ask you," said Robert. "We do hope you'll say 'yes'!"

"Well, I'm not promising till I know what it is," said Daddy, cautiously. "I've been caught that way before!"

"It's something quite simple," said Rita.

"Yes, something you'd love to do yourself," said Fred. "It's this — can we spend a night on Thunder Rock?"

Thunder Rock was a tiny rocky island not far out from the coast. The three children had a small boat of their own, and were used to rowing about by themselves. They had often rowed to Thunder Rock and had a picnic there.

"So now you want to spend a *night* there," said their father. "Well, what does your mother say?"

"She says we must ask *you*," said Robert. "Say 'yes,' Daddy. Only just one night. It would be such fun to camp out there all by ourselves."

"We'd take rugs and things," said Rita. "We'd choose a very fine warm night. It would be heavenly to go off to sleep at night with the waves beating on the rocks round us, and the stars blinking above us."

"And waking up in the morning with the sun, and slipping into the water first thing for a swim," said Fred. "Come on, Dad — say 'yes'."

"Well, what about that old boat of yours?" said his father. "I heard it was leaking. Is it safe?"

"Pretty safe, because we can always bale out the water," said Rita. "We don't mind. Anyway we can all swim. But I don't think the poor old boat will last much longer, Daddy. Are new boats very expensive?"

"Very," said her father. "No hope of getting one, so don't make plans. You'll have to make the leaky old tub do for some time – but mind, if it gets too bad we'll have to scrap it. No good running into danger, and you never know."

"Well – can we go to Thunder Rock for the night?" asked Fred. "You haven't said yet."

His father smiled. "All right – you can go. Take your food with you, and rugs and things. You'll be all right. It *is* fun to camp out on a little island like that. You feel so very much all on your own."

"Oh, *thanks*, Daddy! We never thought you'd say 'yes'!"

In delight the three children rushed off to their mother to tell her. "Well, I do hope you'll all be all right," she said. "You're old enough to look after yourselves now – Robert is fourteen and very strong. Don't get up to any silly tricks though. And be sure that old tub of yours doesn't leak too much."

The children said nothing about their boat. She really was leaking very badly, and needed a lot of baling to keep her from sinking lower and lower! But if only she would last till they had had their night on Thunder Rock!

They made all their plans. Rita fetched a pile of old rugs and old coats. Fred went to ask Cook for a few tins of meat and fruit to take with them, and some ginger-beer. Robert went to get the boat ready. They planned to set off that evening, have a picnic supper, a swim in the sun-warmed water, and then a lovely talk lying on the rugs, looking up to the starry sky.

"It will be gorgeous hearing the waves lapping round all the time," said Robert. "Fancy being all by ourselves like that, too. Nobody to send us here and there, nobody to ask what we're up to, nobody to say we're making too much noise!"

They said goodbye and set off in the boat. Everything had been piled in. Had they forgotten anything? No, they didn't think so. Robert and Fred pulled at the oars and Rita baled hard. "Blow this leak! It's getting worse. I honestly don't think the poor old tub will last much longer."

"Well, Ted, the fisherman, says she's too old to mend," said Robert, pulling hard. "Say when you're tired of baling, Rita, and I'll have a turn and you can row." Gulls cried loudly all round them. The sea was very calm, and only a slight swell lifted the boat now and again. The sun shone from the western sky, and the water gleamed blue and purple and green. Lovely!

They got to Thunder Rock at last. They pulled the boat into a tiny cove, out of reach of the waves. Rita took out the rugs and old coats and spread them on a sandy place between some high rocks.

"We'll be well sheltered here," she said. "And the sand is warm and soft. Won't it be gorgeous sleeping out here? Now what about supper?"

Supper was lovely. Tinned salmon, tinned pineapple, new bread and butter, chocolate and ginger-beer. "Better than any meal on a table!" said Fred. "Now let's have a look round Thunder Rock and then have a swim when our supper's settled a bit."

Thunder Rock was a strange little island. It was nothing but rocks and coves. Nothing grew on it at all, except seaweed. The sea-birds came to it, and liked to stand on the highest rocks, gazing out to sea. They fluttered away a little when the children came near to them, but did not fly right off.

"Lovely things!" said Rita, watching a big gull alight. "I wouldn't mind being a gull – swimming, flying, paddling, gliding, diving – what a nice life!"

They had their swim and then lay on their rugs in the twilight, warm and glowing. They put on pyjamas, and then Fred yawned. "Golly, are you sleepy already?" said Rita. "I'm not. I want to enjoy every minute of this exciting evening. Don't let's go to sleep yet."

"Of course we won't," said Robert, nibbling a bar of chocolate. "The sun's quite gone now. There's not a single bit of pink cloud left in the sky. But it's still very warm."

"The waves sound nice, splashing all round Thunder Rock," said Rita, looking sleepy. They went on talking for a while, and then Fred gave another yawn, a most enormous one this time.

"I really don't believe I can keep awake," he said. "I do want to, but my eyes keep closing. I bet we'll sleep well tonight – with nothing whatever to disturb us except the sound of the sea!"

"All right. We'll say goodnight then," said Rita. "I feel sleepy, too. I'm going to fix my eyes on that bright star over there and see how long I can keep awake. It's so lovely out here all alone on Thunder Rock."

It was not long before they were all asleep. The stars shone in the sky, and the sea splashed quietly on the rocks. There was no other sound to be heard.

But wait a minute – *was* there no other sound? Robert suddenly woke up with a jump. He lay there for a moment, wondering where he was. How odd to see the sky above him instead of the ceiling of his bedroom! Then he remembered — of course — he was on Thunder Rock. Good!

He was just about to go to sleep again when he heard the sound that had awakened him. It was an extra loud splash — and then another and another. Regular splashes.

Robert sat up. It sounded like a boat being rowed along, not far from Thunder Rock!

Then he heard low voices. That made him stiffen to attention even more. A boat near Thunder Rock — and voices in the middle of the night. What did it mean?

Cautiously Robert awoke Fred and whispered in his ear. "Don't make a row. There's a boat being rowed to Thunder Rock. I can hear it — and voices too."

The boys sat and listened. But the boat did not come to Thunder Rock after all. It went right round it and the voices died away. The splash of the oars could no longer be heard.

"The boat's on the landward side of the rock now," whispered Robert. "Let's go round and see if we can spot it. There's only starlight to see by but we might just make it out."

They walked cautiously over the rocks, and round to the other side of the little island. They could see a dark mass some way off — that must be the boat! But who was in it — and why come rowing over the sea at this time of night? Where to? And where from?

"It's all jolly mysterious," said Robert. "Now let's think. Where is that boat heading for?"

"It's going towards the rocky cliffs of the mainland," said Fred. "I should think towards the part that is always washed by the sea — the part we've never been able to explore properly because you can't get round to it."

"There might be caves there," said Robert. "I wonder where the boat came from, though. It seemed to come from out at sea — and yet it was only rowed."

"Do you know — I bet that boat came from some motor launch some way out," said Fred, suddenly. "They wouldn't dare to bring it right in, if they were doing anything they shouldn't, because the motor would be heard. I bet the boat left the launch right out to sea — and was rowed in quietly, with some kind of goods. Probably they've come from France."

"Do you mean *smuggled* goods?" said Robert in sudden excitement. "My word — smugglers!"

"Well, you know there are plenty of smugglers today, now that things are expensive and difficult to get," said Fred. "We've heard Mother talking about it with Daddy, I bet you anything you like we've just heard a boat-load of smugglers passing, with smuggled goods in the boat – and they're heading for the cliffs, where they've either got a hiding-place or friends to take the goods from them!"

Robert whistled. He gazed towards the dark land, which could be faintly seen as a black blur in the starlit night. "Yes. You may be right. Smugglers! I say, what are we going to do about it?"

"Let's go and wake Rita," said Fred. "We can talk about it then, all together. My word, I feel wide awake now, don't you?"

Rita was very excited when she heard the boys' news. "You might have wakened me before," she said indignantly. "Do you suppose the smugglers' boat will come back?"

"Well – yes – I suppose it may," said Robert. "I hadn't thought of that. We'd better keep a look-out."

They all went round to the other side of the little island, and strained their eyes towards the distant cliffs. Then Robert gave an exclamation.

"Look – I'm sure I can see a light – it must be at the bottom of the cliffs, I should think."

They all stared hard, and soon Rita and Fred could see a faint light, too.

"I bet that's where the smugglers are, with their goods!" said Robert.

They sat and watched and talked for a long time. The light disappeared. Then suddenly Robert's sharp ears heard something and he clutched Rita and Fred, making them jump.

"They're coming back! Sh!"

And then there came the sound of oars again, and a murmur of voices. The boat passed in the darkness, a blur against the water. The children hardly dared to breathe.

They began to whisper when the boat was out of hearing.

"They must have put the goods in a cave! Let's go tomorrow and find out!"

"Sh! Listen! I believe I can hear a motor starting up a good way out. I bet the smugglers are off back to France!"

"I wish daylight would come. I want to go off and hunt for the smuggled goods!"

But day did not come. It was still only the middle of the night and the children fell asleep again and could hardly believe, in the morning, that anything had happened in the night.

"But it must have, because we all know about it!" said Rita. "So it can't have been a dream. Let's have breakfast and then go and explore those cliffs. We can row quite near to them."

So after a meal they set off in their leaky old boat. They rowed towards the towering, rocky cliffs, round whose base the sea washed continually.

They came nearer and nearer, and then, when they were afraid of going on the rocks, they rowed round the cliffs, examining every foot of them as carefully as they could.

And they found what they were looking for! They came suddenly to a cleft in the cliff, and guided their boat carefully towards it. A wave took them into the curious crack and they found themselves in an enclosed channel, walled in by steep cliffs, with not much more room than the boat needed for itself.

On one side of the channel was a cave, running into the cliff, quite hidden from the sea outside. "You hold the boat steady by hanging on to this rock, Fred, and I'll have a look into the cave," said Robert. He leaped from the boat on to a rock and then peered into the cave. He gave a yell.

"I say! Stacks of things! Boxes and packages of all kinds. This is where those smugglers put their things. I bet someone on the mainland collects them when it's safe to do so – probably by boat."

He went back to the boat and got in. "I'd like to undo some of those things," he said. "But I suppose I'd better not. It's a matter for the police now."

"Is it really?" said Rita, looking rather scared. "Well, come on, then. Let's get back home."

They shoved the boat down through the cleft of the cliff back to the open sea again. Robert and Fred took the oars. Fred gave a shout of dismay.

"I *say!* You'll have to bale like fury, Rita, the boat's awfully full of water. We'll be swimming soon! Get the baler, quick."

Certainly the boat was leaking worse than ever. Rita began to bale quickly. The boys rowed hard. But the boat was heavy now with water, and it was difficult going. In the end the boys had to stop rowing and help Rita with the baling.

When they had got the boat a good bit lighter, they took the oars again.

"You'll have to buck up," said Rita, anxiously. "It'll fill again directly. It must have sprung another leak. I hope we get back before it fills and sinks!"

The boat began to fill quickly again. The boys rowed hard. Just before they got to shore the boat quietly began to sink beneath them!

They had to get out and wade to shore, carrying what they could of their goods. "That's very bad luck," said Robert, sadly. "I liked that old boat. I'm afraid she's done for now. Come on, let's go home and tell Mother what's happened. Then she can ring up the police."

Mother was amazed at all they had to tell. She was horrified about the boat, and very glad they had got home safely, though they were very wet.

"I can hardly believe this tale of smugglers," she said. "But I suppose I'd better ring up the police. I'll do it now, whilst you go and put on dry things." It wasn't long before an inspector of police was round in his car. He listened with the greatest interest to all that the children told him.

"I expect they've really hit on something," he told their mother. "We know smuggling is going on all round the coast. But it's difficult to trace. I'll get a boat and go round to this cave. Perhaps I could take the children's boat and they could direct me to the place."

"It's sunk," said Fred, sorrowfully. "We haven't got a boat! We feel very upset about it. Ted, the fisherman, will lend you his. We'll come too."

The inspector found that the goods in the cave were most certainly smuggled. "Silk stockings! Bottles of brandy! Perfume of all kinds! My word, this is a haul!" he said in delight. "Well, we'll remove all these goods tonight when nobody is likely to see us, and then we'll set a watch for the smugglers' friends, whoever they are. They are sure to come to fetch the goods soon. And we will also put somebody on Thunder Rock, lying in wait for the smugglers when they come again, as they are sure to do."

It all sounded very exciting indeed. The children wanted to go to Thunder Rock with the watchers, but the inspector said "no." "There may be danger – shooting, for instance," he said. "You're better out of things like that. I'll let you know what happens, never fear!"

He kept his word, and brought them a very exciting story the next week. "We've got the men who receive the goods," he began. "We caught them rowing round to the cave to fetch them. And now we've got the smugglers too! Three of them!"

"Did you catch them in their boat?" asked Rita.

"We followed their boat when it went back to the open sea," said the inspector. "And there, sure enough was a smart little motor launch waiting for them. We got the whole lot – so that spot of smuggling is stopped for a little while at any rate."

"What a good thing we went to spend the night on Thunder Rock!" said Fred. "Jolly bad luck our boat is gone, though."

"Oh, I wouldn't worry about that," said the inspector, in an airy voice. "We want to give you a reward for your help – you'll find it in Ted the fisherman's charge if you care to go and look!"

The children tore down to the beach, and found Ted there, grinning. Beside

his boat lay another one, newly-painted and smart.

"Good morning to you," said Ted. "Come to have a look at your new boat? Smart, isn't she? My word, you're lucky children, aren't you?"

"We are!" said Rita, in delight. "Bags I row her first! Oh, what a beauty. Come on, boys – haul her down the beach. Off we go!"

And off they went, bobbing lightly up and down on the waves. They rowed to Thunder Rock, pulled the boat up on the sand and lay down in the sun.

"Good old Thunder Rock!" said Fred, banging the sand below him with his open hand. "If it hadn't been for you we'd never have got that marvellous – wonderful – super – new boat!"

SMUGGLERS' CAVE

~ ILLUSTRATED BY ~
STANLEY LLOYD

*Ronnie, Susan and George love their rambling old house
and when they learn that it is to be sold, they decide to
hunt for the lost family jewels...*

R onnie, Susie and George were all feeling very sad. Not so much
because they were going back to their boarding-schools in a few days,
but because when they next broke up for the holidays, their lovely
home, Grey Towers, would belong to someone else!

"Why can't we keep it for ourselves?" asked Susie. "Mother, it's been our
home, and Daddy's home, and Grandpa's home, and even Great-Grandpa's home!
Why have we got to leave? It ought to be our home too!"

"Well, dear, we're poor now," said her mother. "We can't afford to keep up a
big place like this, even though it has belonged to us for three hundred years! Our
family used to be rich, you know, in your great-great-grandfather's time. But then
he offended a friend of the king of that day and he was stripped of all his money
and the famous family jewels."

"All of them?" said Ronnie, who had heard this story before. "I thought,
Mother, that Great-Great-Grandpa hid some of his treasure."

"So the tale goes," said Mother. "But I'm afraid I don't believe that now,
Ronnie. It would have been found long ago if it had been hidden. Anyway, dozens
of our family have looked for it and haven't found it."

"I've looked for it too," said George, the eldest. "I've looked everywhere. I
thought there might be a secret panel or something somewhere Mother — that led
to a hidden cupboard — but I never found anything!"

"And all because long ago one of our family offended somebody, we've got to
leave the home we love, and go and live somewhere we'll hate!" said Ronnie.

"I do so love Grey Towers," said Susie. "Mother, I can't bear to think I'll
never come home to it again. I shall go and say goodbye to every single bit of it

186

before I go back to school."

"Yes, we'd better do that," said Ronnie. "We'll go into every room and every corner, so that we'll remember it always. Let's start now. Let's go up to the towers, and look out of the windows, so that we can see all the country round that we know so well."

"Yes. And we'll even go down to the cellars, and say goodbye to those," said George. "Not that I've ever been very fond of them, but I'm not going to miss anything!"

"Well, we'll take Jumpy with us then," said Susie. "There might be rats there and I don't like them. Jumpy can chase them for us. He's a good dog for rats."

They began to say goodbye for the last time to all the places they loved so well – the rounded tower rooms at each end of the house – their own bedrooms, tucked into the roof – their big playroom with its magnificent view of the nearby sea – the long dark landing where they had often hidden to pounce at one another.

"We mustn't leave out anything," said Susie, dolefully. "We'll do the cellars last. Where's Jumpy?"

"Jumpy!" called George, when at last they were ready to go down into the dark cellars. "Jumpy! Come along! We want you to come down and chase RATS! RATS, boy, RATS!"

"And that's about all we shall find down in those old cellars," said Susie, with a shiver. And down the stone steps they went, with Jumpy leaping beside them.

The cellars were deep down under the house. They were dark, and smelled damp and musty. There was no electric light there, so the children had torches. Jumpy didn't mind the dark at all. He rushed here and there, sniffing in every corner for rats.

Old barrels lined the walls. Empty bottles, thick with dust and cobwebs, stood on dark shelves. Wooden crates stood about. It was not a very pleasant place. There were three or four cellars of different sizes. Nothing of any value was kept there now, because Mother said it was too damp to store things. So it wasn't really a very interesting place after all.

"I don't feel I mind saying goodbye to the cellars, really," said Susie, flashing her torch round. "I never liked them much. Ugh, is that a frog?"

"No – a rat! Hey, Jumpy, here's a RAT for you. Rat, quick!" yelled George. Jumpy raced up at once, his tail quivering in delight. The rat shot into the next cellar and Jumpy tore after him. The children followed, flashing their torches.

The rat ran round the cellar looking for a way of escape, but there was none there. It went into the last cellar of all, a place so hung with cobwebs that Susie stopped in dismay, feeling the webby fingers across her face.

"It's horrid here!" she said. "I won't go in!"

Jumpy chased the rat to a corner, where a big barrel stood. Then he scraped and whined loudly, trying to get beneath the barrel.

"The rat's found a way out somehow," said Ronnie, in disgust. "I wonder if it could have gone under this barrel. Help me to overturn it, George. That's right – over she goes! There, Jumpy, is the rat under it?"

No, it wasn't. But there was a dark hole there and Jumpy suddenly fell down it unexpectedly, disappearing with a loud yelp!

"Gracious! What's happened to Jumpy?" said Susie, in alarm. The boys shone their torches on the floor under the barrel they had overturned.

"There's a round hole there! Where *does* it lead to?" said George. "Look, it's had a wooden lid or something over it at one time – but it's rotted away. What a funny thing! Jumpy! Are you all right?"

A doleful wail came up. Jumpy was plainly not at all happy. He was frightened out of his life! The boys shone their torches down the hole. Far down they could see two green eyes gleaming up at them. It was poor Jumpy, looking up in despair.

"We'll get a rope and go down and get Jumpy up," said George. "What a funny pit! What can it be for? We'll go down and see, shall we? Maybe it was just a hiding-place for a smuggler!"

"Yes, that's it," said Ronnie. "We know that smuggling was carried on here ages ago. Fancy us never finding this old hole before. Come on – let's get a rope and rescue poor old Jumpy. What a row he's making!"

Soon the three children had found a rope and were back in the dark cellars. Jumpy was still howling mournfully, and the echoes of his doleful voice filled the cellars and made Susie shiver.

"I don't like it," she said. "Let's rescue Jumpy quickly and get back into the daylight again!"

"I'd better go down on the rope and tie Jumpy to it, and you must haul him up somehow," said George. "Then I'll come up on the rope myself. It's not very far down – only about eight feet I should think."

He let the rope down, after first tying it firmly to an iron hook in the wall. Then down he went, hand over hand to poor Jumpy. The dog was thrilled to see him and barked joyfully.

George stood at the bottom of the hole, and felt for Jumpy's collar. He meant to tie the rope round him in such a way that the others could haul him up without hurting him.

He switched on his torch – and then he gave a loud cry that made the others jump. "I say! It isn't just a hole! There's an opening here – it must lead into a passage! Gracious, how exciting!"

Ronnie and Susie almost fell down the hole in their excitement. What! An opening out of the hole? Where *could* it lead to?

"I'm coming down too!" shouted Ronnie and down he went, almost on top of George. Jumpy, happy now that the children were with him, had pranced out through the opening at the bottom. George shouted up to Susie.

"Wait a bit before you come down. Let me and Ronnie get into the opening, or you'll land on top of us. I'll shout when we're ready."

Susie waited till he shouted. Then down she went on the rope too, hand over

hand, as she had been taught to do at gym.

She saw a small opening at one side of the wall of the hole. She had to bend down to get through it. The two boys were there, waiting, their torches switched on.

"It's a passage!" said Ronnie, excitedly. "See? There it goes, down and down! Shall we explore it?"

"Well, of *course!*" said George. "What do you think! I'll go first. Let me squeeze by you. Gracious, isn't it narrow?"

"Now Jumpy's gone again," said Ronnie. "He must be halfway down the passage by now. JUMPY! Come back, you silly, or you'll get lost."

A distant bark answered him. Jumpy was doing a bit of exploring himself! The children followed, their heads bumping into the rocky roof of the passage every now and again.

"It's leading towards the sea!" cried Ronnie. "It'll come out somewhere on the shore, I bet it will!"

The passage went down and down, sometimes so steep and rocky that the children almost fell. It was all very strange and exciting. Their torches made patches of light in the darkness, and now and again they caught sight of Jumpy's wagging tail some way in front of them.

Ronnie suddenly heard a curious noise. He stopped. "Listen," he said, in alarm. "What's that? Can you hear that strange booming sound? Whatever can it be?"

"I know!" said Susie. "It's the sea! We're coming near the sea. I wonder what part of the beach we shall come out on. Won't anyone walking on the beach be astonished to see us!"

Suddenly the steep little passage came to an end. In front of them the children saw a huge wooden door, studded with nails, fitting roughly into a rocky archway.

"A door!" said George. "Fancy finding a door down here! Is it locked?"

It wasn't locked – but it was bolted. Luckily the bolts were on their side of the door! With Jumpy watching impatiently, George and Ronnie tried their best to push back the heavy bolts. They couldn't — but the screws that held the bolts to the door suddenly gave way, for they were set in wood that had rotted and grown weak with the years. They fell out and the door swung open before them.

They flashed their torches beyond it. They saw a cave there, a surprisingly large one, with a high rocky roof and a smooth sandy floor. Directly opposite was a tiny opening, just big enough for a man to creep through, that looked out on the sea just below! It was a most astonishing sight.

Daylight came in through the hole in the cave-wall. The children switched off their torches and looked round.

"Old trunks! Brass-bound boxes!" cried Ronnie running to where they stood in untidy heaps here and there. "Look Susie, look George! Do you suppose they'll be empty?"

"Of course," said George. He looked round the cave. "This must have been one of the old smugglers' caves," he said. "A jolly well-hidden one too. You can only get into it from the seaward side by that hole there. The smugglers would have to unpack their goods on the moonlit shore, and carry them by hand to that hole, and hand them in to someone ready in this cave."

"But George – how did these boxes and trunks get here?" asked Susie, looking at them. "If they didn't come from the shore – they must have come from our house, Grey Towers, years and years ago!"

"Susie's right! They may have belonged to Grey Towers!" shouted Ronnie, and he flung himself down by one of the boxes. "Quick, let's open them and see what's in them. Oh, quick, quick, quick!"

The children couldn't open the boxes. They must be locked! They were bitterly disappointed. But then, lying half-buried in the sand nearby, George suddenly spied an old bunch of keys!

"We'll try these!" he cried, and was soon busy fitting key after key into one of the trunks. Suddenly one key turned with a grating noise — and George flung open the lid. Packed hurriedly inside, flung in anyhow, were all kinds of jewels! Even now, after all the years of hiding, they gleamed brightly.

"Oh – *look!*" said Susie, in an awed voice, and held up what she felt sure must be an emerald and diamond necklace. "And look at this – it's like a dog-collar made of rubies. And this – and this!"

"It's the old Grey Towers lost treasure!" said George, and he looked very solemn and yet very excited. "The treasure our Great-Great-Grandfather must have hidden when he was in disgrace with the king in those days. And somehow nobody can have known where he hid it, and when he was taken away and imprisoned and killed, the treasure stayed here and was never, never found — because nobody ever knew about that little round hole in the cellar under the big barrel!"

After this long speech all the children sat silent, thoughts spinning round in their heads. "We shan't need to leave our dear old home now! We can stay on at Grey Towers! We can sell all these things and be rich!"

"But will it be treasure-trove? Will the queen have to have it?" asked Susie, suddenly.

"Of course not. It's our family's riches, even though they've been lost for years!" said George. "My word — what *will* Mother say?"

"Look what's in *this* box — old gold pieces!" said Ronnie, unlocking another treasure-hoard. "What a lovely sound they make when I run my hand through them! I say — let's fill our pockets with this money, and dress ourselves up in all the shining jewels, and go and find Daddy and Mother! We'll make them stare all right!"

This seemed a lovely trick to play, and a fine way to show off their great find. Quickly the children decked themselves out in heavy necklaces, bracelets, brooches, pins, and sparkling belts. They filled their pockets with the money, and took some in their hands to fling down before their parents!

"Let's put that collar of rubies on Jumpy," cried George, and, giggling with excitement, they did so. Jumpy was astonished by such a heavy collar, but he didn't seem to mind.

Then off they went up the secret passage to the cellars, shouting and laughing in delight. "Here comes the old lost treasure! Here comes the old lost treasure!"

And you should have seen their parents' faces when they saw three dirty, dusty, gleaming children arriving with a ruby-collared dog, flinging gold pieces about, and shouting at the tops of their voices.

"We shan't leave Grey Towers after all, we shan't, we shan't!"

And, of course, they didn't!

THE VALLEY OF ADVENTURE

AN EXTRACT

❧ ILLUSTRATED BY ❧
STUART TRESILIAN

Jack, Lucy-Ann, Dinah and Philip are at the airport with their friend Bill Smugs, who is about to take them on a trip in his private aeroplane. The children get into the wrong plane, not realising their mistake until two men hurry on board, firing shots behind them. The plane takes off and the children hide while they think of a plan. When the plane lands, they find themselves in a desolate valley in a land far from England. Discovering the men's food store, the boys take some tins, while the girls make a camp in a nearby small cave...

CHAPTER XI
THE CAVE OF ECHOES

It was very early in the afternoon. The boys knew they would have plenty of time to go to the bush where their tins were hidden and fetch them to the cave. Perhaps between them they could carry one sack.

"We'd better go now," said Jack. "We'll have to keep a sharp look-out for those men, because they were going to have a jolly good look round, and we don't want them to spot us. Now, you're sure you girls will be all right?"

"Quite," said Dinah lazily. She felt glad she was not going to go all the way back to that bush and then drag a heavy sack to the cave. She lay back on the

194

moss. It was so very very soft, and springy too.

Jack slung his binoculars round him. They might be useful in trying to spot any men from far off. He and Philip slid through the green fronds of fern. Jack called back to the girls, raising his voice high.

"If you *should* happen to spot anyone near here, remember to untie the string that ties back those ferns *at once*, see?" he said. "Then they will swing back and the cave will be completely hidden. Lucy-Ann, see that Kiki doesn't follow us."

Lucy-Ann had Kiki on her shoulder, where Jack had just put her. She put her hand round the bird's ankles and held her. Kiki knew then that she was not supposed to go with Jack and Philip and she gave a dismal squawk.

"What a pity, what a pity!" she said gloomily, and raised up her crest fiercely. But Lucy-Ann would not let her go. She held her until Jack and Philip were out of sight. Then she lowered her hand and Kiki flew off her shoulder and out of the cave. She perched on a rock looking for Jack.

"Down the well," she said grumpily. "Blackbirds down the well."

"No, blackbirds in a pie," said Lucy. "What a bird you are for getting things mixed up, Kiki!"

"Poor Kiki!" said Kiki, and cracked her beak loudly. "Poor Kiki!"

She flew back into the cave. Dinah was fast asleep, stretched out on the green moss, her mouth open. Kiki flew over and put her head on one side, looking at Dinah's open mouth. Then she plucked up a bit of moss with her curved beak.

"Kiki! Don't you dare to put that into Dinah's mouth!" cried Lucy-Ann, knowing Kiki's mischievous ways. "You're a bad bird!"

"Wipe your feet," said Kiki crossly, and flew to the back of the cave. Lucy-Ann turned over on her tummy and watched her. She didn't trust Kiki in this mood.

The sun poured into the cave. It felt airless in there. Lucy-Ann thought it would be a good idea to untie the fronds and let them swing together, to keep out the sun. So she pulled the bit of string that Jack had shown her and at once the ferny curtain descended, and the cave was lost in a dim green twilight, rather exciting to be in.

Dinah didn't wake. Lucy-Ann lay on her tummy again, thinking of all that had happened. The noise of the waterfall came in, rather muffled now, for the curtains of fronds were very thick.

"Kiki," said Lucy-Ann. "Kiki, where are you?"

There was no answer from Kiki. Lucy-Ann tried to make out where the parrot was. She must be sulking because Philip and Jack hadn't taken her with them. Silly old Kiki!

"Kiki! Come over here!" said Lucy-Ann. "Come and talk to me. I'll teach you 'Three little kittens have lost their mittens'."

Still there was no answer from Kiki, not even a squawk. Lucy-Ann wondered why. Even if Kiki sulked she would usually talk back if anyone spoke to her.

She peered towards the back of the cave. No Kiki there. She looked at the ledge on which their goods were neatly arranged. No Kiki there.

Well, where was she, then? She hadn't flown out between the fern-fronds, that was certain. She must be here somewhere in the cave!

On the rocky ledge was a torch. Lucy-Ann felt for it and took it into her hand. She switched it on and flashed it round the cave. Kiki was nowhere to be seen. She was not even perched up anywhere in the low roof of the cave. How very mysterious!

Lucy-Ann now felt quite alarmed. She awoke Dinah, who sat up, rubbing her eyes, cross to be awakened.

"What's the matter?" she said. "I was having such a lovely snooze."

"I can't find Kiki," said Lucy-Ann. "I've looked everywhere."

"Don't be silly. She's gone out of the cave after Jack, I expect," said Dinah, even crosser. She lay down again and yawned. Lucy-Ann shook her.

"You're not to go to sleep again, Dinah. I tell you, Kiki was here a little while ago — at the back of the cave — and now she's gone. Absolutely vanished."

"Well, let her — she'll come back all right," said Dinah. "Leave me alone, Lucy-Ann."

She shut her eyes. Lucy-Ann didn't like to say any more. Dinah could be so fierce when she was cross. The little girl sighed and wished the boys were back. What *had* happened to Kiki?

She got up and walked across the moss to the back of the cave. The rock was folded in on itself there, and there was plenty of space behind one of the folds. Lucy-Ann looked cautiously into the dark space, expecting to see Kiki hiding there, ready to cry "Boo" at her, as she sometimes most annoyingly did.

But Kiki wasn't there. Lucy-Ann flashed her torch up and down the little hidden corner, and suddenly her torch came to a stop, focused on one place.

"Why — there's a hole there!" said Lucy-Ann in surprise. "That's where Kiki must have gone!"

She clambered up to the hole, which was about shoulder-high. It was just big enough for her to squeeze through. She expected to drop down into another cave the other side, but she didn't. The hole went upwards slightly, a round, narrow tunnel. Lucy-Ann felt sure Kiki must have disappeared into this peculiar, dark little tunnel.

"Kiki!" she yelled, and flashed her torch in front of her. "Where are you, idiot? Come back!"

No sound from Kiki. Lucy-Ann squeezed herself right into the round tunnel, wondering how long it was. It was almost as round as a pipe. Maybe water had forced its way through at one time, but now it was quite dry. Lucy-Ann could not hear any sound of the waterfall once she went into the tunnel, though she listened hard. It was very quiet there.

"KIKI!" she yelled. "KIKI!"

Dinah heard the yell in her dreams and awoke with a jump. She sat up crossly again. But this time Lucy-Ann was not in the cave with her. Now it was Dinah's turn to feel scared. She remembered that Lucy-Ann had said that Kiki had suddenly disappeared. Now it seemed as if Lucy-Ann had too. The fronds of fern were hanging over the entrance. Lucy-Ann would not have been pushed out through them without telling Dinah she was going out.

Dinah examined the cave well. No Lucy-Ann. Oh, goodness, now what had happened to her and Kiki?

She heard another yell, sounding rather muffled and distant. She went to the back of the cave and discovered the hidden space. She fetched another torch from the ledge and shone it up and down. She stared in amazement when she saw two shoes sticking out of a round hole about as high as her shoulder.

She tugged at Lucy-Ann's ankles and yelled at her.

"Lucy-Ann! What do you think you're doing? Where are you going? What's up that hole?"

197

Lucy-Ann yelled back. "I don't know, Dinah. I found it by accident. I think Kiki must have gone up it. Shall I go up and see if I can find her? You come too."

"All right," called Dinah. "Go on up."

Lucy-Ann wriggled further up the narrow pipe-like tunnel. It suddenly widened out and, by the light of her torch, she saw below her another cave — but a vast one this time.

She managed to get out of the hole, and had a look round at the cave. It was more like an underground hall. Its roof was very high indeed. From somewhere in its dim vastness came a mournful voice.

"What a pity, what a pity!"

"Kiki! So you are here!" cried Lucy-Ann, and then listened in astonishment to the echo that sounded immediately. "Here, here, here, are here, are here!" cried the echoes, repeating themselves in a weird and strange manner.

"Hurry up, Dinah!" called Lucy-Ann, not liking the echoes at all.

"Up, Dinah, Dinah, Dinah!" called the echoes at once. Kiki flew over to Lucy-Ann, frightened. So many voices! Whatever could they all be?

"Poor Kiki!" said the parrot, in a fright. "Poor Kiki!"

"Kiki, Kiki, Kiki!" called the echoes. The parrot shivered and gazed all round, trying to see who called her. She suddenly gave a loud and defiant squawk.

At once a score of squawks sounded all round, as if the cave was filled with hundreds of parrots. Kiki was simply astounded. Could there be so many birds there that she couldn't see?

Dinah crawled out of the hole and stood by Lucy-Ann. "What an enormous place!" she said.

"Place!" shouted the echoes.

"Everything we say is repeated," said Lucy-Ann. "It's weird."

"Weird, it's weird," said the echoes.

"Well, let's whisper, then," said Dinah, whispering herself. The cave was at once filled with mysterious whispers, which scared the girls even more than the repeated shouts they had heard. They clutched one another. Then Dinah recovered herself.

"It's only the echoes," she said. "You often get them in enormous caves like this. I wonder if anyone has ever been here before."

"Never, I should think," said Lucy-Ann, flashing her torch all round. "Fancy! We may be treading in a place that no one else has ever trodden in before!"

"Let's explore the cave a bit," said Dinah. "Not that there seems much to see, but we might as well do something whilst we're waiting for the boys."

So they walked slowly round the great dark cave, their footsteps repeated a hundred times by the echoes. Once, when Dinah sneezed, the girls were really frightened by the enormous explosive noises that came from all round them. The echoes certainly enjoyed themselves then.

"Oh, don't sneeze again, Dinah," begged Lucy-Ann. "It's really

awful to hear the echoes sneezing. Worse than hearing them squawk like Kiki."

They had gone almost all the way round the cave when they came to a passage leading out of it - a high, narrow passage, between two walls of rocks.

"Look at that!" said Dinah, surprised. "A passage! Do you suppose it leads anywhere?"

"It might," said Lucy-Ann, and her eyes gleamed. "Don't forget, Dinah, that those men are after treasure. We don't know what kind — but it's just possible it might be hidden somewhere in these mountains."

"Let's follow the passage, then," said Dinah. "Kiki! Come along. We don't want to leave you behind."

Kiki flew to her shoulder. In silence the two girls entered the narrow, rocky passage, their torches gleaming in front of them. What were they going to find?

CHAPTER XII

BEHIND THE WATERFALL

The passage was a very winding one. It led a little downwards and the floor was very uneven to the feet. The girls tripped and stumbled very often. Once the roof came down so low that they had to crawl under it. But it grew high again almost at once.

After a while they heard a noise. They couldn't imagine what it was. It was a deep and continuous roar that never stopped even for a second.

"What's that?" said Dinah. "Are we getting into the heart of the mountain, do you think, Lucy-Ann? That's not the roar of a mighty fire, is it? What can it be? What is there that could make that noise in the middle of a mountain?"

"I don't know," said Lucy-Ann, and immediately wanted to go back. A fire in the heart of a mountain, a fire that roared like that? She didn't in the least want to see it. She felt hot and breathless at the thought.

But Dinah wasn't going back now that they had come so far.

"What, go back before we've found out where this passage goes to?" she said. "Of course not! The boys would laugh like anything when we told them. We don't often get the chance of discovering something before they do. Why, we might even happen on the treasure, whatever it is, Lucy-Ann."

Lucy-Ann felt that she didn't care at all about the treasure. All she wanted was to get back to the safety of the cave she knew, the cave with the green fern-curtains.

"Well, you go back, then," said Dinah unkindly. "I'm going on. Baby!"

It was more frightening to think of going back to the cave of echoes by herself than to go on with Dinah. So poor Lucy-Ann chose unwillingly to go on. With that strange muffled roar in her ears she pressed on down the winding passage, keeping close to Dinah.

The roar became louder.

And then the girls knew what it was. It was the waterfall, of course! How stupid of them not to think of that! But it sounded so different there in the mountain.

"We're *not* going into the heart of the mountain after all," said Dinah. "We're coming out near the waterfall. I wonder where."

They got a tremendous surprise when they did see daylight. The passage suddenly took one last turn and took them into subdued daylight that flickered and shone round them in a curious way. A draught of cold air met them, and something wetted their hair.

"Lucy-Ann! We've come out on to a flat ledge just *behind* the waterfall!" cried Dinah in astonishment. "Look, there's the great mass of falling water just in front of us! Oh, the colours in it! Can you hear me? The water is making such a noise."

Overwhelmed by surprise and by the noise, Lucy-Ann stood and stared. The water made a great rushing curtain between them and the open air. It poured down, shining and exultant, never stopping. The power behind it awed the two girls. They felt very small and feeble when they watched that great volume of water pouring down a few feet in front of them.

It was amazing to be able to stand on a ledge just behind the waterfall and yet not be affected by it in any way except to feel the fine spray misting the air. The ledge was very wide, and ran the whole width of the fall. There was a rock about a foot high at one end of the ledge and the girls sat down on it to watch the amazing sight in front of them.

"What will the boys say?" wondered Dinah. "Let's stay here till we see them coming back. If we sit on this rock, just at the edge of the waterfall, we can wave to them. They will be so astonished to see us here. There's no way of getting to this ledge from above or below, only from behind, from the passage we found."

"Yes. We'll surprise the boys," said Lucy-Ann, no longer frightened. "Look, we can see our cave up there! At least, we can see the giant fern whose fronds are hiding it. We shall easily be able to see the boys when they come back."

Kiki was very quiet indeed. She had been surprised to come out behind the great wall of water. She sat on a ledge and watched it, blinking every now and again.

"I hope she won't be silly enough to try and fly through the waterfall," said Lucy-Ann anxiously. "She would be taken down with it and dashed to pieces. I know she would."

"She won't do anything so silly," said Dinah. "She's wise enough to know what would happen if she tried something like that. She may fly out round the edge of the waterfall, though.

Still, there shouldn't be much danger for her in that."

The girls sat there for a long time, feeling that they would never get tired of watching the turbulence of the waterfall. After a long time, Lucy-Ann gave a cry and caught Dinah's arm.

"Look – is that the boys coming? Yes, it is. They've got a sack between them. Good! Now we shall have plenty of food."

They watched the two boys labouring up the rocks that led to the cave. It was no good waving to them yet. Then suddenly Dinah

stiffened with horror.

"What's the matter?" said Lucy-Ann in alarm, seeing Dinah's face.

"Look — someone is following the boys!" said Dinah. "See — it's one of the men! And there's the other one too! Oh, my goodness, I don't believe either Philip or Jack know it! They'll watch where they go and our hiding-place will be found! JACK! PHILIP! OH, JACK, LOOK OUT!"

She went to the very edge of the waterfall, and, holding on to a fern growing there, she leaned out beyond it, yelling and waving, quite forgetting that the men could see and hear her as well as the boys.

But alas, Jack and Philip, engrossed in the task of getting the heavy sack up the rocks, neither saw nor heard Dinah — but the men suddenly caught sight of her and stared in the utmost astonishment. They could not make out if she was girl, boy, man or woman, for the edges of the waterfall continually moved and shifted. All they could make out was that there was definitely someone dancing about and waving behind the great fall.

"Look!" said one man to the other. "Just look at that! See — behind the water! That's where they're hiding. My word, what a place! How do they get there?"

The men stared open-mouthed at the waterfall, their eyes searching for a way up to it that would lead to the ledge where the excited figure stood waving.

Meantime, Jack and Philip, quite unaware of the following men, or of Dinah either, had reached the curtain of fern. Philip pushed the ferns aside, and Jack hauled the sack up through them, panting painfully, for it was heavy.

At last the sack lay on the floor of moss. The boys flung themselves down, their hearts thumping with the labour of climbing up steeply to the cave, dragging such a heavy sack. At first they did not even notice that the girls were not there.

Not far off, some way below, stood the two men, completely bewildered. In watching Dinah behind the waterfall, they had just missed seeing Jack and Philip creep through the ferns into their cave. So, when they turned from gazing at the waterfall, they found that the boys they had so warily followed had utterly disappeared.

"Where have they gone?" demanded Juan. "They were on that rock there when we saw them last."

"Yes. Then I caught sight of that person waving down there, and took my eyes off them for a minute — and now they've gone," growled Pepi. "Well, there's no doubt where they've gone. They've taken some path that leads to that waterfall.

They hid behind it – and a clever place it is, too. Who would think of anyone hiding just behind a great curtain of water like that? Well, we know where to find them. We'll make our way to the water and climb up to that ledge. We'll soon hunt the rats out."

They began to climb down, hoping to find a way that would lead them to the ledge behind the waterfall. It was difficult and dangerous going, on the slippery rocks.

In the cave the boys soon recovered. They sat up, and looked round for the girls.

"Hallo – where are Lucy-Ann and Dinah?" said Jack in astonishment. "They promised to stay here till we got back. Surely to goodness they haven't gone wandering about anywhere? They'll get lost, sure as anything!"

They were not in the cave. That was absolutely certain. The boys did not see the hole in the fold of rock at the back. They were extremely puzzled. Jack parted the ferns and looked out.

To his enormous astonishment he at once saw the two men clambering about on rocks near the waterfall. His eyes nearly dropped out of his head.

"Look there!" he said to Philip, closing the fronds a little, fearful of being seen. "Those two men! Golly, they might have seen us getting in here! How did they get here? We saw them safely by the plane, on our way to the bush!"

Dinah had now disappeared behind the waterfall. She could not make up her mind whether or not the men had seen the boys climbing in through the fern to their cave. In any case, she thought she ought to warn them of the men's appearance. She felt sure that neither Jack nor Philip knew they were there.

"Come on, Lucy-Ann," she said urgently. "We must get back to the boys. Oh, goodness, look at those men! I believe they are going to try and get over here now. They must have spotted me waving. Do come quickly, Lucy-Ann."

Shivering with excitement, Lucy-Ann followed Dinah along the dark, winding passage that led back to the cave of echoes. Dinah went as quickly as she could, flashing her torch in front of her. Both girls forgot all about Kiki. The parrot was left sitting alone behind the waterfall, spray misting her feathers, watching the clambering men with interested eyes. She had not heard the girls going off.

Dinah and Lucy-Ann came out into the cave of echoes at last. Dinah stopped and considered.

"Now, where exactly was that hole we came through?" she said.

"Came through, through, through," called the echoes mockingly.

"Oh be *quiet!*" cried Dinah to the echoes.

"QUIET, QUIET, QUIET!" yelled back the irritating voices. Dinah flashed her torch here and there and, by a very lucky chance, she found the hole. In a trice she was in it, crawling along, with Lucy-Ann close behind her. Lucy-Ann had an awful feeling that somebody was going to clutch her feet from behind and she almost bumped into Dinah's shoes in her efforts to scramble down the hole as quickly as possible.

Jack and Philip were peeping through the ferns watching the men, when the girls dropped out of the hole at the back of the cave, came round the fold of rock and flung themselves on the boys. They almost jumped out of their skin.

Philip hit out, thinking that the enemies were upon them. Dinah got a stinging box on the ear, and yelled. She immediately hit out at Philip and the two rolled on the floor.

"Don't, oh, don't!" wailed Lucy-Ann, almost in tears. "Philip, Jack, it's us! It's us!"

Philip shook off Dinah and sat up. Jack stared in amazement. "But where did you come from?" he demanded. "Golly, you gave us an awful scare, I can tell you, jumping out like that! Where have you been?"

"There's a hole back there we went into," explained Dinah, giving Philip an angry look. "I say, do you two boys know that those men were following you? They were not very far behind you. We were scared stiff they would see you climbing up here."

"Were they *following* us?" said Jack. "Golly, I didn't know that. Peep out between those fronds, you girls, and see them hunting for us down there."

NUMBER SIXTY-TWO

John Hollins considers himself to be something of a detective — he's always on the lookout for a mystery to solve!

Ever since John had solved the mystery of Melling Cottage he had been on the look-out for another. But mysteries didn't seem to come along very often — and some mysteries turned out not to be mysteries after all!

There was the time when he had seen a man and a woman quarrelling in a garden, and suddenly the man flashed out a knife... but when John yelled out that he was going for the police, it turned out that the two were only rehearsing their parts in a play.

John had felt very foolish over that. And another time he had reported a mysterious sack on the other side of a hedge, apparently full of stolen goods. But it was only a sack of potatoes left there by the farmer for his brother to fetch as he passed by on his way to market.

I'd better be careful next time, thought John to himself. I won't report anything unless I'm absolutely sure about it.

Now one afternoon he went by himself to Oaktree Wood. There was a big tree there he liked to climb. It was an easy one, and he could get almost to the top. From the top he could see a very long way indeed.

It was like being in a ship, because the wind swayed the tree, big as it was, and the movement was like a boat going over waves. John liked it. If he shut his eyes he felt as if he were right out at sea.

So this afternoon up the tree he went. He was soon at the top, looking out over the countryside, which lay smiling in the summer sunshine.

John had a book with him. He opened it, settled himself comfortably on a branch and began to read. Sometimes he looked out from his high perch, and saw the lorries, buses and cars going along the roads.

He saw a car stop and pull off the road on to the grass verge. A man got out and disappeared. John waited idly for him to come back, but he didn't. Surely he hadn't gone for a picnic all by himself? John went on reading his book, occasionally glancing up to see if the car was still there.

After half an hour the car was still pulled up, empty. John began to wonder about it. Then he suddenly heard the crack of a twig in the wood below, as if someone had trodden on one and broken it.

There's somebody coming through the wood, thought John, and glanced down through the leaves. But the tree was too thick for him to see anything below on the ground.

He heard a match struck. Somebody was lighting a cigarette. Perhaps he was waiting for someone? John heard a slight cough down below. The man was under the tree. Another twig cracked.

Then there came the sound of someone making his way through the bushes, and a low voice said, "That you, Lou?"

"Yes," said the man under the tree. "Number sixty-two, tomorrow."

"Okay," said the other voice and its owner made his way back through the bushes again. That was all. Not another word was said. The man under the tree went off, and in about ten minutes' time John saw him come out of the wood and get into the car.

John strained his eyes to see the number of the car. He could make out the first two letters – ST, and the last figure, which was 0, but that was all. He wrote it down in his notebook.

"*Car number ST…0,*" he wrote. "*Red in colour. Sports saloon. Can't see make.*"

John often wrote things of this kind down but as a rule they were all wasted. Still, you never knew. Things might come in useful sometime. He began to think about the strange message the man under the tree had given to the other, who was, apparently, already hidden in the wood.

"Number sixty-two, tomorrow."

What did it mean? What was Number sixty-two? And why tomorrow? John frowned, and puzzled over it. Should he report what he had seen and heard? No, better not. It might be nothing again.

Perhaps number sixty-two is a house somewhere they mean to burgle, thought John, suddenly. Number sixty-two. Where is there a number sixty-two? It must be a fairly long street if there are over sixty houses in it. I'll go and do a little exploring.

Before he slid cautiously down the tree, he listened to see if anyone might be about – the man hiding in the wood for instance. But he could hear nothing, so down he went, as quietly as he could. Once on the ground he sped through the trees as if he were a rabbit with a dog after him!

He went to the village. There must be a number sixty-two somewhere. What was the longest road? Yes, Summers Avenue must be. He went along it, looking for sixty-two.

"Forty-one, forty-three, forty-five – oh, these are the odd numbers. I want the evens." He crossed the road and came to the evens.

"Forty-two, forty-four, forty-six – blow, there are only two more. Forty-eight – fifty. There's no sixty-two."

He went down another street but there were even fewer houses there. That was no good. Then he went to Limmers Street, which was a terrace of small houses. Ah, there was a sixty-two – good! John looked hard at it.

Nobody would want to rob a tiny house like that, surely! The curtains were dirty and ragged. Two or three equally dirty and ragged children were playing on the doorstep. No, this couldn't be the sixty-two. That was quite certain.

Well, there's only the High Street left then, thought John, and went there.

However, he felt that sixty-two could hardly be the one meant by the man, for it was the police station! It had no number, of course, but as it stood between shops labelled sixty and sixty-four, it was clear that it must be sixty-two, if it had a number at all!

"I can't understand it," said John, puzzled. "There are only two sixty-twos — and one's a rundown little house and the other's the police station. Perhaps the sixty-two doesn't mean the number of a house at all."

Then he wondered if by any chance the number might be a telephone number. No — the man wouldn't have said "sixty-two" then, he would have said "six-two" because that was how telephone numbers were given. People said "one-o" not "ten," they said "seven-three" not "seventy-three" and the man would certainly have said "six-two" not "sixty-two."

So telephone numbers were ruled out as well. Then what in the world could "sixty-two" mean?

Should John go to the police now, and tell them what he had heard? No, he still didn't want to, because it just might mean nothing, and he would be laughed at.

He turned to go home. As he went he saw a man running by in white singlet and shorts. Then after a while another came. They were practicing running for races. John stared at them idly. Then he stiffened. Each man had a number on, in big black figures! The first man's number was 14. The next man's was 34. Then came a third man, padding along — he was 53.

John looked after the runners. Could the number 62 belong to one of these runners? Was it a *man*, number sixty-two, that that fellow was talking of? If so, *why*?

He went on towards his home, thinking hard. Daddy was at home. Perhaps he would be able to tell him about the runners, and their big race.

Yes, his father knew all about it. He had been a fine runner in his time, and he told John that there was to be a ten mile race the next day, on a certain route, and that so far as he knew almost a hundred competitors were entered for it.

"Then there may be a number sixty-two?" asked John.

"Yes, of course. But why do you ask that?" said his father.

"Oh — I was thinking of something," said John. "Daddy, is there a list of the competitors up anywhere? I'd like to have a look and see if I know any of them, if so."

"Yes. If you go along to the athletic club room, you are sure to see a list there," said his father. "I didn't know you were so interested in running!"

John smiled and went off. He found the athletic club room and peeped in. The secretary was there. "What do you want, youngster?" he asked.

"Could I just look at the list of runners?" said John. "For the ten-mile race tomorrow?"

"Yes, it's over there," said the secretary, and pointed with his pen. "They start at Beamers End, each running two minutes after the last. And they end at Longfields club room."

"Er – do they run past Oaktree Wood?" asked John. The secretary nodded. John began to look down the list of names. He came to number sixty-two.

"62. Laurie Baxter." Who was Laurie Baxter? He looked at the address. "16, Renfrew Street." That was a poor street in the next town.

"Laurie Baxter, 16, Renfrew Street." Now why in the world should anyone want to kidnap Laurie Baxter running in a ten-mile race?

"Who will win, do you think?" asked John. "Laurie Baxter?"

"Good gracious, no," said the secretary. "He'll be about halfway. He's not much good."

"Oh well – thank you very much," said John and went out. Now, was he right or wasn't he, in thinking that Laurie Baxter was the number sixty-two that the man in the wood was telling the other fellow about, for some reason or another? And was he right in thinking that the fellow in hiding was going to lie in wait for Laurie Baxter? If only he knew!

He couldn't possibly go to the police and say "I think that Laurie Baxter, in tomorrow's race, will probably disappear halfway through, and not turn up at the end because somebody in Oaktree is lying in wait for him!" It sounded too silly for words – and it might not be true. It was only what John *thought*, not what he knew.

He wondered what to do. Then he decided that he, too, would hide at the edge of Oaktree Wood, just before the race, and he would see if anything happened. He could always give the alarm if an attack was made on number 62.

So, the next afternoon, feeling rather excited, John made his way to Oaktree Wood. He chose a tree that overlooked the stretch of road that ran by the wood, down which the runners would go, and he climbed it, making sure that there was nobody to see him.

Then he sat on a branch and waited. After a long long time the first runner appeared. He was number 7. Apparently they were not running in their right order, but just anyhow, each starting off two minutes after the last.

Then number 16 appeared, and after him number 43. Then came 1 and 8 and 17, each some time after the other. Would 62 never come?

Then came one that looked like 62 but when he got nearer John saw that he was 63. Blow! Three or four more came — and then, surely, surely this was 62.

It was! He was a weedy youth, not a very good runner, with thin shoulders and skinny legs. He came along the road to a curve. And then things happened.

Somebody shot out from the hedge, clamped strong arms round Laurie and dragged him swiftly back into the undergrowth. His hand was over Laurie's mouth.

John gasped. It was all so sudden. He caught a glimpse of a second man, and then Laurie was bundled away so quickly that except for a swishing of branches as the men forced their way into the undergrowth, there was nothing to be seen or heard.

John shinned down the tree quickly. He ran after the men, but they had disappeared. Then, in the distance, he heard the sound of a car being started up. Oh, so the men had a car hidden somewhere in a glade, had they? If only he could see it and take its number!

But by the time he got to the little clearing, the car was moving away, and all that John could see was that it was red. Red! Then probably it was the same car he had seen the man in the day before. He had got the two first letters and the last number of the car, but that was all. Blow!

The car came to a road in the wood and soon the sound of its engine died away in the distance. John sat down on an old tree trunk to think. Now he wished he had gone to the police, and reported what he had thought might happen. It had happened. He didn't know why, or what the men were after – but the thing was, Laurie Baxter had been attacked and taken away in a car. He'd better go to the police and tell them about that!

So off he went. He marched into the station and asked to speak to the sergeant, who was a friend of his uncle's. Then he told him what he knew

"Please, sir, Laurie Baxter, number 62 of the ten-mile runners, was attacked and taken off in a car, just as he was running beside Oaktree Wood," said John. "I saw it happen. I was up in a tree, waiting for it to happen, as a matter of fact."

"*Waiting* for it to happen!" said the sergeant, surprised. "What do you mean? How did you know it would happen?"

John told him everything – how he had overheard the number 62 in the wood, said by the man from the car – how he had examined all houses that might be the sixty-two meant – and then how he had thought it must be the number 62 of the runners.

"And it was," said John. "I wonder why Laurie Baxter was attacked, though."

"I don't," said the sergeant, grimly. "I have an idea that he was in a burglary committed three weeks ago, and that he got off with most of the goods and sold them – whilst the others got nothing! They were scared in the middle of the robbery, and two of them fled, but Laurie apparently didn't. He waited, then when all was quiet, he took the goods and made off. I reckon the other fellows are wild with him, and want to know what he's done with their share!"

"Oh," said John. "But why didn't you arrest Laurie then, if you knew all this?"

"We questioned him, and put a watch on him," said the sergeant, "but we thought if we let him go free the others might make contact with him – and then we'd pull in the whole

lot. But now it looks as if we've lost them all."

"Well, sir – I managed to get the first two letters and the last number of their car," said John, eagerly. "Look – ST…0. The car was red, sir, and was a sports saloon."

"Good boy!" said the sergeant, and took John's notebook. "This will help tremendously. We can stop all cars of this description."

Then a radio call at once went out to police patrols. "Calling all cars, calling all cars. Please watch for a red car, make unknown, sports saloon type, first two letters ST, last number 0. Three men inside. Hold for questioning. Over."

"Can I stay here and see if anything happens, please?" asked John, excited.

"Right," said the sergeant. "Seeing that you've brought us so much information, you can wait – I might want to ask you more questions, mightn't I?"

So John waited. He had a cup of tea with the sergeant and felt very important. Many telephone calls came in, but nothing exciting, until at last there came the one the sergeant wanted. He turned to John.

"They've got them! The car was caught at Reading. The whole number is STA 120. It's a Humber, sports saloon, red. Three men inside, one of them Laurie Baxter. Now we'll get going!"

They did. Laurie was so angry with his companions for attacking and kidnapping him that he gave the whole show away. He told where the rest of the unsold stolen goods were, and related his companions' share in the various robberies they had committed together.

"So now," finished the sergeant, smiling at the thrilled boy in front of him, "they'll all spend a nice quiet little time thinking over their sins in prison. They'll commit no more robberies for a while – thanks to you, Detective John!"

And Detective John went proudly home. He'd solved another problem. Now – what would the next one be?

THE CASE OF THE FIVE DOGS

John Hollins solves another mystery when he helps his friends prove that their dogs are not responsible for worrying sheep.

One day, when John was sitting reading in his garden, he heard his name called. He looked up and saw the face of a little girl peeping over the wall.

"Hallo, Meg – what do you want?" asked John.

"Oh John – can we come in for a minute? There's Colin here and George, and me and Katie. We want to talk to you."

"Come on over the wall then," said John, surprised. They all clambered over. Meg and Katie were ten, George and Colin were about twelve. With them were their dogs.

"What's up?" asked John. "I say, keep your dogs in order, won't you? Dad's just planted out some new things in the beds."

The boys and girls settled down on the grass, each holding the collar of their own dog. "You see, John, we know you're an awfully good detective," said George. "So we thought you might help us. Something awful has happened."

"What?" asked John, feeling rather important at being called an awfully good detective.

"This morning some of Farmer Warner's sheep were chased by dogs," said George. "One fell in the stream and broke its leg."

"And the farmer went to the police and he said it was our dogs that did it," said Katie, almost in tears. "He said one of his sheep was killed the other day by dogs, and he saw an Aberdeen like my Jock, a terrier like George's Sandy, a Sealyham like Meg's and a spaniel like Colin's in the road outside the field. So now he says it was our dogs that killed his sheep last week, and ours that chased them today."

214

"And perhaps they'll be shot," said Colin, gloomily. "Or else our fathers will be fined. But we know it wasn't our dogs."

"We want you to help us," said George. "You've got to prove that it was somebody else's dog, not ours, see? You're a clever enough detective for that, aren't you?"

"Well – I don't know," said John. "This isn't quite like any case I've had before. To begin with – some dog must have killed that sheep. If we could prove that first, we'd be halfway to saving your dogs. But we don't know what dog did it."

"Yes, we do," said Colin at once. "It was the log-man's dog – you know, the man who comes all round the district selling logs. He's got a horrible black dog, big and fierce and ugly."

"Oh, yes, I know it, said John. "It's the only dog I'm really scared of. It looks so fierce and it growls like anything if anyone goes near it. I always think it looks as bad-tempered as its master."

"Yes, that's the one," said Meg.

"But how do you know it's the dog that killed the sheep?" asked John. "Did you see it?"

"No, but we know someone who did," said George. "You know, there's a gypsy caravan near that field, and there are some children living there. One's called Julie, and we sometimes speak to her. She told us she saw the big black dog chase the sheep and kill it."

"Well then – that's easy! She's only got to tell the police that!" said John.

"She won't. She's afraid of the police. She says if we try to make her tell, she'll say she doesn't know anything," said Colin. "She says her father would beat her black and blue if she told anything to the police. He's so scared of policemen."

"I told the policeman who came about my dog that I knew it was the big black one belonging to the log-man," said George. "But when he came again he said the log-man said he wasn't in the district that evening, so it couldn't have been his dog, because it never leaves him."

"And now it's *our* dogs that are bearing the blame for everything!" said Meg, fiercely, putting her arms round her

Sealyham. "Why, Scamp doesn't even chase *cats*! I'm not going to have him shot for something that isn't his fault."

"So you see, John, you *must* do something!" said Katie. "We could only think of coming to you. Will you help us?"

"Yes, of course," said John, who was very fond of dogs. "But it's going to be difficult to make a man own up to his dog killing a sheep, if he's already said that neither he nor his dog were here that evening. Have you asked if anyone else saw him or his dog that evening near Farmer Warner's sheep field?"

"Yes, we've asked *everyone*," said Colin. "But nobody did. You know, there was a big meeting on the green that night, and simply everyone was there. There might not have been a single person anywhere near the field when the sheep was killed — except Julie, and she won't tell."

"She ought to tell," said Meg. "That dog once bit their baby. It's still got the scar. Julie showed it to me."

"It's an awful dog," said George. "It'll end up killing somebody. John, can you do something?"

"Well, I'll try," said John. "But somehow I just don't know how to begin. First — what day was the sheep killed?"

"Last Friday," said Colin. "I was on the green with the others. We were listening to the speaker, and I was watching an aeroplane doing stunts in the sky. It wrote 'Moon' against the blue, and we all laughed, because it was Mr Moon who was speaking at the meeting. It was a jolly good advertisement for him. He wants everyone to vote for him, doesn't he?"

"Fancy hiring an aeroplane to write your name in the sky!" said Meg. "I wish one would write mine. I'd feel very important."

"Well, let's get back to our subject," said John. "The sheep was killed on Friday. Julie says she saw the log-man's black dog kill it. The log-man says he wasn't here and neither was his dog. Where does he say he was, I wonder?"

"He swears he was fifteen miles away," said Colin. "Out on his bicycle, he says. He'd sold all his logs that day, and went to speak to a man at Five-Mile-Hill about timber, but he wasn't there. Anyway, the log-man swears he was miles and miles away from here. He says his dog loped along beside his bike all the way. So there you are!"

"Did Julie see the log-man as well as his black dog, on Friday when the dog killed the sheep?" said John.

"No. But she said she heard his peculiar whistle, when he whistled to the dog to come to him," said Colin. "You know his whistle? It's awfully loud and shrill. He puts two fingers in his mouth when he does it. Julie can do it too. But I can't."

"Well – it looks as if the dog and the man were there on Friday then, when everyone else was on the green listening to Mr Moon," said John. "But how in the world can we prove it?"

"The log-man is coming again tomorrow," said Meg, suddenly. "It's his day for our village. Couldn't you talk to him, John?"

"Well..." said John, and stopped. He didn't like the log-man, and he didn't think the log-man would like him, either. And he certainly didn't like the log-man's dog. It gave him a horrid feeling when the big black creature sniffed round his ankles. He felt as if at any moment it might take a bite out of his leg.

"Oh, please, please do," said Meg. "We'll come and be with you, if you like. But we'd better leave our dogs at home, or that awful black dog will gobble them up!"

"Yes, for goodness' sake don't bring your dogs," said John, picturing a free fight between them and the black dog going on all round him. "All right. I'll think of something to say to him. You can all be with me and listen to what he says."

The log-man always went to the village inn, when he was near, and brought out a drink for himself. He sat down on the log bench beside the green in the evening sunshine, and ate bread and jam and drank his beer. His dog always lay at his feet.

"He'll be there about six o'clock," said John. "I often see him there then. We'll be playing about, and I'll go up and try to draw him into conversation. You can all listen hard. But don't mention the word 'dogs' or he'll be on his guard."

"Right," said Colin. "He doesn't know any of us. Now mind, everybody – leave your dogs at home so that they can't get out."

John was a bit worried about this new problem. It wasn't like his others at all. He didn't see how to tackle it, no matter how hard he puzzled about it. He lay in bed that night and pondered over it.

Julie had seen the dog killing the sheep and had heard the log-man whistling to him that Friday evening. Therefore he must have been there. But he said he was miles and miles away. Everyone else, unfortunately, seemed to have been on the green, listening to Mr Moon, and looking at his name being written in the sky. It was fortunate for the log-man that nobody was anywhere near Farmer Warner's field that evening!

After a long while John made a plan. He didn't think it was very good – but it just might work. He'd see.

So, the next evening, about six o'clock, he, Meg, Katie, Colin and George went to the green, near the Rose and Crown Inn. They began to play a game with a bat and ball. No dog was near. All had been left safely at home.

"Here's the log-man now," said John, in a low voice. "See, there's his cart. He's driving his old brown horse, and that awful black dog is sitting up beside him just as he always does."

The cart drew up outside the inn. The man got down and went inside. He came out with a tankard and went to sit in the evening sunshine on a wooden bench beside the green. He pulled a packet of sandwiches out of his pocket.

"We'll give him a minute or two, then I'll go up and ask if he knows the time," said John, and threw the ball to Colin. All the children kept an eye on the black dog. He lay beside his master, but they felt that at any moment he might go after their ball.

In a little while John went up to the log-man, followed by the others. "Could you please tell me the time?" he asked.

"Look at the church clock," said the log-man, in a surly voice. Blow! John had forgotten that the church clock could be seen from the green.

"Oh, yes, of course – thanks," he said. "A quarter-past six," he said to the others. Then he looked at the black dog.

"Fine big dog you've got," he said, politely. "I bet he eats a lot. Can he catch rabbits?"

The log-man looked at him. "My dog don't chase nothing," he said. "He don't chase even a sparrow. He just keeps alongside of me."

"But surely he would chase a cat?" said Colin, joining in. "All dogs chase cats."

"Well, this one don't," said the log-man. "He don't chase nothing."

The dog looked at them out of bloodshot eyes and growled.

"He won't bite, will he?" said Meg, retreating hastily.

"Never bit anyone in his life," said the log-man. "Best-tempered dog I ever had."

The dog growled again and showed yellow teeth. None of the children liked him at all.

"Is he afraid of anything?" asked John. "You know – afraid of guns or noises or anything like that? Some dogs are."

"No. He ain't afraid of nothing," said the log-man.

"I knew a dog once that was scared stiff of aeroplanes," said John.

"Mine don't mind nothing," said the log-man and took a long drink.

"I think I can hear an aeroplane now," said John. "Oh no – it's a car. I say – have you heard of those aeroplanes that can write in the sky? I wish I could see one!"

"You did see one – don't you remember – it wrote 'moon' in the sky," said Colin, astonished at John's forgetfulness.

"No – surely it wrote 'sun'," said John. "Wait a bit – yes – I'm remembering – it wrote 'sun', didn't it?"

"Gah – it wrote 'moon', of course," said the log-man, munching hard. "Can't you read, then? It wrote 'moon' plain as anything. That's a wonderful thing that is, to write in smoke in the sky."

"Let's see – it was a white aeroplane, wasn't it?" said John, as if he was trying hard to remember. But everyone put him right.

"No, it was one of those silvery-grey ones, it was, really!"

John appealed to the log-man. "It wasn't, was it? It was white."

"You're wrong," said the log-man, and took another sandwich. "It was grey. Saw it as clear as could be. *And* the markings too – L.G.O. they were, whatever they might mean. My eyes are as good as yourn any day."

He got up, emptied the dregs from his tankard on to the grass and went into the inn. He came out again, followed by his dog, and climbed up to his cart. Without so much as a wave he drove off.

The children crowded round John. Only Colin had seen how his little plan had worked. The others hadn't.

"John – how very, very clever of you – to lead the conversation round to aeroplanes like that – and to make him say he'd seen that one writing 'moon' in the sky, and to make him describe it too!"

"Well – but what's so clever about all that?" said Meg.

"Can't you see, silly? That plane came over on Friday evening, and *only* Friday evening – and the log-man said he was miles away! Well, how could he have seen that aeroplane writing in the sky, if he wasn't here?"

There was a silence. John and Colin looked triumphantly round. "There you are!" said John. "He's admitted he was here – and we've got five witnesses. Come on, we'll go to the police station."

And off they all went. John's friend the sergeant was there, and he took them into his room, looking amused. He listened to their whole story without interrupting once. Then he made a few notes.

"Very interesting," he said, "very, very interesting. And very smart work too, Detective John. We will follow this up and ask the log-man how he managed to see this aeroplane doing its tricks when he was fifteen miles away."

The children next went to Julie. They told her what had happened. "Suppose the log-man admits he and his dog were here, will you say what you saw?" asked Colin. "You must, you know – because you'll be a proper witness then."

Julie looked scared. "Will I get into trouble if I don't say?" she asked.

"Yes, awful trouble!" said John, hard-heartedly. "Oh, Julie – surely you will speak up for our dogs – you wouldn't want them to be shot, would you, instead of a wicked dog that has killed a sheep and already bitten your baby?"

"Well, all right then," said Julie. So when a policeman called, Julie told him all she had seen, and, armed with this, and the other information the children had given him, the sergeant went off to interview the log-man.

He came back again in his car, and saw the children gathered together on the green, waiting for him. This time they had their dogs with them.

He stopped his car. The children crowded round him. "Well, he's confessed," said the sergeant. "He was in the district, his dog was with him, it did go for the sheep, and then he whistled it off. He says he didn't know a sheep was killed at the time, and was too afraid to confess when he did hear. I don't know about that. Anyway, what do you think that dog did?"

"What?" asked the children. The sergeant showed them a bandaged leg.

"Took a nip out of me!" he said. "Silly thing to do, wasn't it? He's going to be punished for all his misdeeds, you may be sure – and your dogs can now go home without a stain on their character – thanks to good old Detective John!"

"Woof," said the dogs at once. "Woof!" And they tried to lick John as if they did honestly understand what he had done for them. He really is a very good detective, isn't he?

FIVE GO OFF TO CAMP

AN EXTRACT

~ ILLUSTRATED BY ~
EILEEN SOPER

*The Five are camping out on the moors with one of
the boys' teachers, Mr Luffy. They are just waking up
to a bright, sunny morning...*

CHAPTER III
ANNE'S VOLCANO

Julian awoke first in the morning. He heard a strange and lonely sound floating overhead. "Coor-lie! Coor-lie!"

He sat up and wondered where he was and who was calling. Of course! He was in his tent with Dick – they were camping on the moors. And that wild cry overhead came from a curlew, the bird of the moorlands.

He yawned and lay down again. It was early in the morning. The sun put its warm fingers in at his tent opening, and he felt the warmth on his sleeping-bag. He felt lazy and snug and contented. He also felt hungry, which was a nuisance. He glanced at his watch.

Half-past six. He really was too warm and comfortable to get up yet. He put out his hand to see if there was any chocolate left from the night before, and found a little piece. He put in into his mouth and lay there contentedly, listening to more curlews, and watching the sun climb a little higher.

He fell asleep again, and was awakened by Timmy busily licking his face. He sat up with a start. The girls were peering in at his tent, grinning. They were

223

fully dressed already.

"Wake up, lazy!" said Anne. "We sent Timmy in to get you up. It's half-past seven. We've been up for ages."

"It's a simply heavenly morning," said George. "Going to be a frightfully hot day. Do get up. We're going to find the stream and wash in it. It seems silly to lug heavy buckets of water to and fro for washing, if the stream's nearby."

Dick awoke too. He and Julian decided to go and take a bathe in the stream. They wandered out into the sunny morning, feeling very happy and very hungry. The girls were just coming back from the stream.

"It's over there," said Anne, pointing. "Timmy, go with them and show them. It's a lovely little brown stream, awfully cold, and it's got ferns along its banks. We've left the bucket there. Bring it back full, will you?"

"What do you want us to do that for, if you've already washed?" asked Dick.

"We want water for washing up the dishes," said Anne. "I suddenly remembered we'd need water for that. I say, do you think we ought to wake up Mr Luffy? There's no sign of him yet."

"No, let him sleep," said Julian. "He's probably tired out with driving the car so slowly! We can easily save him some breakfast. What are we going to have?"

"We've unpacked some bacon rashers and tomatoes," said Anne, who loved cooking. "How do you light the stove, Julian?"

"George knows," said Julian. "I say, did we pack a frying-pan?"

"Yes. I packed it myself," said Anne. "Do go and bathe if you're going to. Breakfast will be ready before you are!"

Timmy gravely trotted off with the boys and showed them the stream. Julian and Dick at once lay down in the clear brown bed, and kicked wildly. Timmy leaped in too, and there were yells and shrieks.

"Well – I should think we've woken up old Luffy now!" said Dick, rubbing himself down with a rough towel. "How lovely and cold that was. The trouble is it's made me feel twice as hungry!"

"Doesn't that frying bacon smell good?" said Julian, sniffing the air. They walked back to the girls. There was still no sign of Mr Luffy. He must indeed sleep very soundly!

They sat down in the heather and began their breakfast. Anne had fried big rounds of bread in the fat, and the boys told her she was the best cook in the world. She was very pleased.

"I shall look after the food side for you," she said. "But George must help with the preparing of the meals and washing-up. See, George?"

George didn't see. She hated doing all the things that Anne loved to do, such as making beds and washing-up. She looked sulky.

"Look at old George! Why bother about the washing-up when there's Timmy only too pleased to use his tongue to wash every plate?" said Dick.

Everyone laughed, even George. "All right," she said, "I'll help of course. Only let's use as few plates as possible, then there won't be much washing-up. Is there any more fried bread, Anne?"

"No. But there are some biscuits in that tin," said Anne. "I say, boys, who's going to go to the farm each day for milk and things? I expect they can let us have bread, too, and fruit."

"Oh, one or other of us will go," said Dick. "Anne, hadn't you better fry something for old Luffy now? I'll go and wake him. Half the day will be gone if he doesn't get up now."

"I'll go and make a noise like an earwig outside his tent," said Julian, getting up. "He might not wake with all our yells and shouts, but he'd certainly wake at the call of a friendly earwig!"

He went down to the tent. He cleared his throat and called politely: "Are you awake yet, sir?"

There was no answer. Julian called again. Then, puzzled, he went to the tent opening. The flap was closed. He pulled it aside and looked in.

The tent was empty! There was nobody there at all.

"What's up, Ju?" called Dick.

"He's not here," said Julian. "Where can he be?"

There was silence. For a panic-stricken moment Anne thought one of their strange adventures was beginning. Then Dick called out again: "Is his bug-tin gone? You know, the tin box with straps that he takes with him when he goes insect-hunting? And what about his clothes?"

Julian inspected the inside of the tent again. "Okay!" he called, much to everyone's relief. "His clothes are gone, and so has his bug-tin. He must have slipped out early before we were awake. I bet he's forgotten all about us and breakfast and everything!"

"That would be just like him," said Dick. "Well, we're not his keepers. He can do as the likes! If he doesn't want breakfast, he needn't have any. He'll come back when he's finished his hunting, I suppose."

"Anne! Can you get on with the doings if Dick and I go to the farmhouse and see what food they've got?" asked Julian. "The time's getting on, and if we're going for a walk or anything today, we don't want to start too late."

"Right," said Anne. "You go too, George. I can manage everything nicely, now that the boys have brought me a bucketful of water. Take Timmy. He wants a walk."

George was only too pleased to get out of the washing-up. She and the boys, with Timmy trotting in front, set off to the farmhouse. Anne got on with her jobs, humming softly to herself in the sunshine. She soon finished them, and then looked to see if the others were coming back. There was no sign of them, or of Mr Luffy either.

"I'll go for a walk on my own," thought Anne. "I'll follow that little stream uphill and see where it begins. That would be fun. I can't possibly lose my way if I keep by the water."

She set off in the sunshine and came to the little brown stream that gurgled down the hill. She scrambled through the heather beside it, following its course uphill. She liked all the little green ferns and the cushions of velvety moss that edged it. She tasted the water – it was cold and sweet and clean.

Feeling very happy all by herself, Anne walked on and on. She came at last to a big mound of a hill-top. The little stream began there, halfway up the mound. It came gurgling out of the heathery hillside, edged with moss, and made its chattering way far down the hill.

"So that's where you begin, is it?" said Anne. She flung herself down on the heather, hot with her climb. It was nice there, with the sun on her face, and the sound of the trickling water nearby.

She lay listening to the humming bees and the water. And then she heard another sound. She took no notice of it at all at first.

Then she sat up, frightened. "The noise is underground! Deep, deep underground! It rumbles and roars. Oh, what is going to happen? Is there going to be an earthquake?"

The rumbling seemed to come nearer and nearer. Anne didn't even dare to get up and run. She sat there and trembled.

Then there came an unearthly shriek, and not far off a most astonishing thing happened. A great cloud of white smoke came right out of the ground and hung in the air before the wind blew it away. Anne was simply horrified. It was so sudden, so very unexpected on this quiet hillside. The rumbling noise went on for a while and then gradually faded away.

Anne leaped to her feet in a panic. She fled down the hill, screaming loudly: "It's a volcano! Help! Help! I've been sitting on a volcano. It's going to burst, it's sending out smoke. Help, help, it's a VOLCANO!"

She tore down the hillside, caught her foot on a tuft of heather and went rolling over and over, sobbing. She came to rest at last, and then heard an anxious voice calling:

"Who's that? What's the matter?"

It was Mr Luffy's

voice. Anne screamed to him in relief. "Mr Luffy! Come and save me! There's a volcano here!"

There was such terror in her voice that Mr Luffy came racing to her at once. He sat down beside the trembling girl and put his arm round her.

"Whatever's the matter?" he said. "What's frightened you?"

Anne told him again. "Up there – do you see? That's a volcano, Mr Luffy. It trembled and rumbled and then it shot up clouds of smoke. Oh quick, before it sends out red hot cinders!"

"Now, now!" said Mr Luffy, and to Anne's surprise and relief he actually laughed. "Do you mean to tell me you don't know what that was?"

"No, I don't," said Anne.

"Well," said Mr Luffy, "under this big moor run two or three long tunnels to take trains from one valley to another. Didn't you know? They make the rumbling noise you heard, and the sudden smoke you saw was the smoke sent up by a train below. There are big ventholes here and there in the moor for the smoke to escape from."

"Oh, good gracious me!" said Anne, going rather red. "I didn't even *know* there were trains under here. What an extraordinary thing! I really did think I was sitting on a volcano, Mr Luffy. You won't tell the others will you? They would laugh at me dreadfully."

"I won't say a word," said Mr Luffy. "And now I think we'll go back. Have you had breakfast? I'm terribly hungry. I went out early after a rather rare butterfly I saw flying by my tent."

"We've had breakfast *ages* ago," said Anne. "But if you'd like to come back with me now I'll cook you some bacon, Mr Luffy. And some tomatoes and fried bread."

"Aha! It sounds good," said Mr Luffy. "Now – not a word about volcanoes. That's our secret."

And off they went to the tents, where the others were wondering what in the world had become of Anne. Little did they know she had been "sitting on a volcano"!

228

THE RILLOBY FAIR MYSTERY

AN EXTRACT

∽ ILLUSTRATED BY ∽
GILBERT DUNLOP

Roger, Diana, Snubby and Barney believe that there is a connection between the fair where Barney works and a series of robberies in which priceless manuscripts are stolen from locked rooms. Great-uncle Robert, an expert on old manuscripts, is staying with them for a few weeks. Snubby, who is always playing jokes on people, tells Great-uncle Robert that "The Green Hand Gang" is responsible for the robberies. When the fair moves to Rilloby, the children discover that Marloes Castle has a wonderful collection of old manuscripts. They decide to keep watch on the castle each night in the hope of catching robbers attempting a break-in...

CHAPTER XXI
MIDNIGHT AT THE CASTLE

Snubby could hardly contain himself all day. He whistled and sang and was altogether so noisy and restless that Great-uncle Robert nearly went mad. Wherever he was he could hear Snubby making a noise. What was the matter with that boy?

The evening came at last. To Mrs Lynton's surprise, Snubby didn't seem to be hungry for his dinner. Nor did Diana. Roger ate solidly as usual. He wasn't so excitable as the other two.

229

"Do you feel quite well, Snubby?" asked Mrs Lynton anxiously when he refused a second helping. "And you too, Diana?"

"I'm all right," said Snubby, and Mrs Lynton, looking at his bright red cheeks and shining eyes, had no more doubts about his health.

"I suppose you've been stuffing yourself up with sweets and ice-creams again," she said. "Well, I shall think twice about getting you a nice supper if you do that."

They all went to bed at the usual time but they didn't undress. Roger fell asleep and had to be woken at half-past ten.

"Are Mother and Dad in bed yet?" whispered Roger.

"Yes. They went early, thank goodness. There isn't a light anywhere except in Great-uncle's room," said Diana. "He's reading in bed, I expect."

They crept downstairs, warning each other to look out for Snoek. But Snoek was away on business of her own that night. Loony crept down with them, his tail-stump wagging. What was up?

They went into the moonlit garden, and out of the gate. Then they made off across the fields to Marloes Castle. There was a short-cut to it which didn't take very long.

They came to the big iron gates, and then disappeared into the hedge on the other side. Diana gave a sudden little scream.

"Shut up, idiot!" said Roger fiercely in a low tone. Diana pulled away from him, shaking.

"There's somebody there already!" she whispered, "Oh, Roger!"

So there was. But it was only Barney and Miranda, who had got there first, and happened to choose just the bit of hedge that Diana had pushed herself into! Barney came out grinning.

"Sorry I scared you, Diana. You scared me too. You were all so quiet I didn't hear you. I got an awful fright when you pushed against me in the hedge."

"Have you seen anything or anyone?" asked Roger.

"Not a thing," said Barney. "Come on. We'll choose a place to get over the wall. I've got a rough rope-ladder and a few thick sacks. Carry the sacks, Roger and Snubby, and I'll take the rope."

With Miranda on his shoulder, and Loony at his heels, Barney led the way, keeping to the shadows of the hedge. They came at last to a place where the wall curved round, and the spikes did not seem to be quite so thick.

"This'll do," said Barney in a low voice. "Snubby, will Loony growl if he hears anyone, and warn us?"

"Yes, of course," said Snubby. "Loony, do you hear? You're on guard. On guard!"

"Woof," said Loony, understanding at once, and he sat down, ears, eyes and nose all on guard together.

The four of them got busy. Barney threw the rope-ladder up deftly to the spikes. The first time it slithered back again. The second time the spikes held one of the rungs. Barney pulled. It was quite tight. Up he went like a cat, his feet treading the wooden rungs lightly. "Chuck up the sacks," he whispered down. Roger and Snubby threw them up one by one.

Barney put them in a neat pile over a dozen or so of the sharp, pointed spikes. Then, sitting on the sacks, he pulled at the rope-ladder till he had got a lot of loose slack up – enough to let half the ladder down the other side into the grounds!

That's jolly clever! thought Roger admiringly. A ladder up to the top – and a ladder down the other side – and a pile of sacks in the middle to protect him against the spikes! I should never have

thought of all that.

"Come on up," whispered Barney.

Diana went up first. Barney helped her over and she sat on the sacks beside him. He then helped her down the other side. Then came Roger. Then Snubby, hauling up Loony with great difficulty, helped by Barney.

"No good leaving him outside the wall," gasped Snubby. "He'd bark the place down. Gosh, Loony, you're an awful lump. Whoa there – you're falling! I say, he's gone down the other side at top speed. He'll break his legs!"

There was a thud and a yelp. Diana called up softly. "It's all right. He's not hurt. He's like Snoek, always falls on his feet!"

Barney pulled up the ladder so that no one could climb up it from the road. The place he had chosen to climb over the wall was in deep shadow, and nobody could see the pile of sacks on the spikes from the road. Barney slipped down and joined the others.

"Where shall we hide?" whispered Roger, excited.

Barney stood a moment or two to get his bearings. "There are the barred windows up there," he whispered. "Let's make our way to that clump of trees. We can watch the windows easily from there."

They crept from tree to tree and shrub to shrub until they were under the clump that Barney had decided on. From there they could easily see the barred windows. Now, if any thief were going to enter from outside, they couldn't possibly help seeing him!

They found a dry place under a bush and huddled together, parting the branches to keep a good look-out on the windows. From somewhere not far off a church clock began to strike. It chimed first – and then the deep clanging sounds came through the moonlit night.

"One, two, three," counted Snubby under his breath. "It's going to strike twelve. It's midnight! We must watch out. Lie down, Loony. Not a whimper from you! On guard, old fellow. On guard!"

There wasn't a sound anywhere. Then a nightingale began to sing. But it didn't sing for long – just tried out its notes and stopped. Not for a week or two would it sing all night long.

Not even an owl hooted. The children watched the moon move slowly along the sky, and waited patiently. Loony listened with both his ears. Diana always thought he would be able to hear much better if his ear-holes were not covered up by such long, drooping ears. But, drooping ears or not, he still heard twice as well as they did.

The church clock chimed the quarter and then the half-hour. Snubby yawned. Diana felt cold. Miranda cuddled inside Barney's shirt and went to sleep. The clock chimed the three-quarters. Still there was no sound. There was not even a tiny breeze blowing that night, and no mouse or rat or rabbit was to be seen or heard.

"I say – I don't think the thief's coming tonight," whispered Barney. "It's long past midnight. This can't be the night. We'd better go."

Nobody minded! They were cold and tired. The excitement had fizzled out and they all thought longingly of nice warm beds. Loony gave a sigh of relief when he felt them on the move once more.

"Come on, then," said Diana thankfully. "We've had enough for tonight. We'll try again tomorrow."

They made their way to the wall, still keeping well in the shadows, just in case anyone was about.

Over the wall they went and down the other side. Barney sat on the sacks beside the rope, unhitched it from the spikes, and threw it down to Roger.

"Have to leave the sacks here and hope no one notices them," he said, taking a flying leap to the ground. He landed on hands and knees and rolled over, quite unhurt. He sat up.

"Don't you think the sacks will be noticed by anyone coming down the lane? " asked Diana anxiously.

"No. This bit of the wall is well hidden by trees, and unless anyone is actually walking just below, looking up, I don't think they'd be noticed," said Barney. "We'll stuff the rope-ladder under this bush. Save us carrying it to and fro."

They were silent and disappointed as they went off down the lane. They said goodnight at the fork, and Barney went one way and they another, taking the short-cut across the fields.

"Better luck next time," said Roger to Diana rather gloomily, when he said goodnight. "Gosh, I'm sleepy."

They all overslept the next morning, of course, and Mr Lynton told them wrathfully that they would have to go to bed an hour earlier that night.

But alas, when the evening came, Barney, Roger and Diana were all feeling ill! Diana and the two boys had gone over to see Barney at Rilloby Fair, and Roger had bought some sausage sandwiches. Snubby refused them, and bought himself some tomato sandwiches, of which he was very fond.

As he was the only one who didn't feel very sick that night, everyone felt that the sausage sandwiches must be to blame! Barney put Young-Un in charge of the hoopla stall and staggered off to the caravan he shared with somebody else, feeling really ill. Roger and Diana got home somehow, and promptly collapsed in the hall, groaning.

Snubby rushed to tell Mrs Lynton. "It's the sausage sandwiches," he explained. "There must have been something wrong with them. They feel awfully sick."

They were, poor things. Mrs Lynton got them into bed and dosed them well. Snubby looked in on them and was quite shocked to see them looking so green.

"Oh, I say – what about tonight?" he asked in a loud whisper. "Will you be able to go and watch?"

Roger groaned. "Of course not. I don't feel as if I shall ever be able to get up again."

Diana didn't even answer when he asked her. She felt really ill. Snubby tiptoed out with a most surprised Loony, and fell over Snoek on the stairs.

"Oh, Snubby – *don't* do that," said Mrs Lynton crossly, looking out of the lounge door. "Can't you possibly be quiet when people are feeling ill?"

"Well, I like *that!*" said Snubby indignantly. "How did I know Snoek was lying in wait for me? It's Snoek you want to nag at, not me."

"Now, Snubby, don't you talk to me like that," began Mrs Lynton, advancing on him. But Snubby fled.

What about tonight? *Somebody* ought to watch, surely? All right – Snubby would watch all alone!

CHAPTER XXII
A NIGHT OUT FOR SNUBBY

Snubby went to bed very early, for two reasons. One was that Mrs Lynton was worried about the other two, and was inclined to be very cross with Snubby. He thought it best to get out of her way. The other was that he had quite made up his mind to go and watch in the castle grounds by himself that night, and he wanted to get a little sleep before he went.

So he popped off to bed immediately after supper and took an alarm clock with him, set for quarter-past eleven. He put it under his pillow, wrapped in a scarf so that it would be heard only by him. He hoped Roger wouldn't hear it.

Roger was sound asleep, exhausted by his bouts of sickness. Snubby didn't undress. He just got into bed and shut his eyes. Immediately he was asleep, and slept peacefully till the alarm went off. Loony, who was on his bed, leaped up in fright, barking.

"Shut up, you silly, crazy idiot!" said Snubby fiercely, and Loony shut up. Snubby lay and listened for a moment, after he had shut off the alarm. Had anyone heard?

Apparently not. Roger muttered something in his sleep, but that was all. Nobody else seemed to be stirring. Good! Snubby got cautiously out of bed, and felt for his clothes, remembered with agreeable surprise that he was fully dressed, and got his coat out of the cupboard. He had been cold the night before, and Snubby didn't like feeling cold!

"Come on, Loony – and if you fall over Snoek on the stairs I'll drown you," Snubby threatened. They got downstairs safely, and were soon running over the fields, Loony surprised but pleased at this second unusual excursion.

They came to the castle walls as the church clock struck the three-quarters. A quarter to midnight, thought Snubby, feeling feverishly about in the bush for the rope-ladder. Blow it – where's the ladder? Is this the right bush?

It wasn't. Loony knew the right bush and dragged out the ladder for Snubby. Then followed an agonising five minutes with Snubby trying to throw the ladder up to the spikes.

It wasn't as easy as it had looked when Barney did it. Snubby grew extremely hot and agitated.

"Go up and stick, you beast of a ladder!" he muttered. And miraculously, the ladder did stick on a spike or two, and held.

Up went Snubby joyfully, pleased to find that the ladder was fairly close to the pile of sacks that Barney had left on the spikes. He lifted them off and pulled them to the rope-ladder. Soon he was sitting on them, the spikes beneath him blunted by the sacking. He hauled up the ladder in the way that Barney had done, and soon half was on one side of the wall and half on the other. Snubby felt really proud of himself.

As he climbed down the other side, into the ground, the church clock struck midnight. "Dong, dong, dong," it began. A whine reached Snubby, and he stopped short.

"Blow! I've forgotten Loony. I don't see how I'm going to get him up without help tonight. He'll have to stay on the other side. I'll put him on guard."

He climbed up to the top again, and whispered to Loony. "It's all right, old fellow. I shan't be long. You're on guard, see? On guard."

Loony settled down with a whimper. All right, he would be on guard – but he thought it was very mean of Snubby to go off without him.

Snubby crept over to the clump of trees where he and the others had stood the night before. It was a moonlight night again – but with much more cloud about. There were periods of brilliant light and then periods of darkness when the moon went behind clouds. Snubby settled down under a bush and waited.

He felt extremely pleased with himself. He had been the only one sensible enough not to take the sausage sandwiches. He had actually got over the wall by himself – and he didn't feel a scrap scared. Not a scrap. He hadn't even got Loony with him and he felt as brave as a lion. Yes, Snubby felt very pleased with himself indeed, ready for anything that might happen.

The moon went in. Everywhere became dark – and in the darkness Snubby thought he heard a little noise. He didn't know if it was near him or not. He listened, and thought he heard another small noise. No, it wasn't near him – it was over by the castle, he thought. He waited impatiently for the moon to come out again.

When it came out Snubby got a terrific shock. A black shadow seemed to be climbing up the side of the castle walls! Up it went, and up, lithe and confident. Snubby strained his eyes. Who was it? It was too far away to see. Was it Tonnerre? No, surely it wasn't nearly big enough for him – but the moonlight played tricks with your eyes.

It looked as if the black figure was climbing up a pipe, leaping on to window-sills, climbing up again – and now scrambling up ivy. This was the thief all right! No doubt about that!

But how was he going to get through the barred windows? Snubby held his breath to see. The bars were so close together. Oh, *blow* the moon – it had gone behind a cloud again.

When it came sailing out once more there was no sign of the climbing figure. It had vanished. Snubby suddenly began to feel very scared indeed. His hair gradually rose up from his head with a horrid prickly sensation. Shivers went down his spine. He longed for Loony.

His eyes began to play tricks with him. Was that a figure standing at the bottom of the castle walls, far below the barred windows? Or was it a shadow? Was that a figure halfway up the walls? No, no, that was the outline of a small window. Was that a figure up on the roof by the chimney? No, no, of course not, it was a shadow, just the shadow of the chimney. And was that a...?

Snubby groaned and shut his eyes. He was scared stiff. Why had he come? Why had he thought he was so brave? He daren't look anywhere because he thought he saw sinister figures creeping, climbing, running. Oh, Loony, Loony, if only you weren't on the other side of the wall!

There was a noise near him. Somebody was panting not far off. Snubby turned quite cold with fear. He stayed absolutely still, hoping that whoever or whatever it was would go away.

But it didn't. It came nearer and nearer. There was the crack of twigs, the rustle of dead leaves under the bushes.

Snubby nearly died of fright.

And then, worse than ever, something stuck itself into his back and snuffled there. Snubby was absolutely petrified. WHAT was it?

A tiny whimper came to him, and Snubby felt so relieved that he could have wept. It was LOONY!

He got the spaniel's head in his hands and let the delighted Loony lick his face till it was wet all over. "Loony!" he whispered. "It's really you! How did you get here? You couldn't climb that ladder! Oh, Loony, I was never so glad to see you in all my life!"

Loony was simply delighted at his welcome. Having been left on guard, he had been afraid that Snubby would be very angry to see him. But it was all right. Snubby was pleased, very very pleased. It didn't matter that Loony had left the place he had to guard, had found a convenient hole by the wall, and had enlarged it to go underneath it with terrific squeezings and struggling.

Everything was all right. He had found his master, and what a welcome he had got!

Snubby recovered completely from his fright. He sat with his arm round Loony and squeezed him, telling him in whispers what he had seen. Then he stiffened again as Loony growled softly, his hackles rising at the back of his neck.

"What is it? What's the matter? Is it the thief coming back?" whispered Snubby. But it was quite impossible to see anything because the moon was now behind a very big cloud indeed. Loony went on growling softly. Snubby didn't dare to move. He thought he heard noises from the direction of the castle and longed for the moon to come out again.

It came out for a fleeting instant and Snubby thought he saw a black figure descending the walls again, but he couldn't be sure. Anyway he was sure of one thing – he wasn't going to move from his hiding-place for a very long while! He didn't want to bump up against that terrifying robber.

He cuddled up to Loony, and put his head on the dog's warm, silky-coated body. Loony licked him lovingly.

Most surprisingly, Snubby went to sleep. When he awoke he couldn't at first think where he was. Then with a twinge of fright, he remembered. Good gracious – how long had he been asleep? He waited till the church clock struck again, and found with relief that he hadn't slept for more than half an hour. How *could* he have gone to sleep like that? Anyway it should be safe to go home again now. Surely the thief would have gone long since. My word, what a tale he had to tell the others!

Feeling a good deal braver with Loony at his heels, Snubby pushed his way cautiously out of the bush. The moon came out and lit up the castle brilliantly. Nothing was to be seen of any climbing, creeping figure. With a sigh of relief, Snubby made his way to the wall.

Somehow he missed his way and wandered too far to the left, towards the iron gates. And then he got a really dreadful shock!

He came through a little copse of trees and found himself looking into a small dell – and from the dell many pairs of gleaming eyes looked up at him! He could see small, shadowy bodies behind – but it was the eyes that frightened him. The moon sent its beams into the little dell and picked out the glassy, staring eyes that seemed to watch Snubby warily.

Loony growled and then barked, his hackles rising again. He backed away and began to whimper. Then Snubby knew that poor Loony too was scared, and he turned and fled. How he ran, stumbling through bushes and shrubs, tearing his coat, scratching his legs, away, away from those gleaming eyes that waited for him in the dell.

How he found the ladder he never knew. He climbed up it, pulled it up behind him, loosened it from the spikes and sent it down to the ground. He left the sacks and flung himself to the ground. He wasn't as clever as Barney at this kind of thing, and fell far too heavily, twisting one ankle and bruising and grazing his knees badly.

Loony ran to find his hole. He squeezed through with difficulty and raced up to Snubby. Snubby was trembling, almost in tears. He flung his arms round Loony's neck.

"Keep with me, Loony. Let's go home. There's something strange about and I don't like it. Keep near me."

Loony had every intention of doing so. He wasn't feeling too happy himself. He kept as close to Snubby's feet as he could, almost tripping him up at times. The two of them took the short-cut across the fields and got home at last.

Roger was sound asleep. So was Diana. Snubby longed to wake them up and tell them everything, but he hadn't the heart to. They had both been so very, very sick.

But he woke them up early in the morning and told them! He shook Roger and woke up Diana. He made Roger go into Diana's room, and then he told them both.

"I had an adventure last night," he said. "You'll never believe it!"

OFF WITH THE ADVENTUROUS FOUR AGAIN

∾ ILLUSTRATED BY ∾

BEATTIE

The Adventurous Four — Andy, Jill, Mary and Tom — are exploring the small, rocky islands around the coast near where Andy lives. They land on one of the islands to eat their picnic and soon find themselves in the middle of an adventure!

CHAPTER I
WHICH ISLAND SHALL WE CHOOSE?

A fisher-boy stood by his red-sailed fishing-boat. He screwed up his eyes in the sun, and watched a little house not far off. Would those three children never come?

He sat down on the edge of his fine little fishing-boat. It was called the *Andy*, and that was the boy's name, too. Andy was tall and brown and his eyes shone like the blue sea behind him. He drummed his bare heels impatiently on the side of the boat.

Then he heard a yell and saw three children racing out of the little house he had been watching. "Here they are at last!" he said, and stood up, waving.

Tom came first, a wiry boy of twelve, with flaming red hair. Then came the twins, his sisters Mary and Jill, their long golden plaits flying behind them. They flung themselves on Andy and almost knocked him over.

"Now, now," he said, fending them off. "You're late. I almost set off without you."

"Sorry, Andy – but Mother made us finish some jobs," said Jill. "Anyway, we've got all the day, haven't we? And it doesn't even matter what time we get back tonight because Mother's going to spend the night with a friend – and there's only deaf old Jeanie at home. She says she's not going to wait up for us! We can creep in any time we like. So hurrah for a day on the sea!"

"Got plenty of food, Andy?" asked Tom anxiously. "Any sausages?"

"Ay, there's a tin for you," said Andy, grinning. "What a one you are for sausages, Tom. Look down in the cabin and see if you think there's enough food to last you!"

Tom squinted down into the tiny cabin. Yes, there seemed plenty to eat and drink. Good.

"Help me up with the sail," called Andy. "There's a strong breeze this morning. We'll scud along at a fine pace."

Once on the sea, the two boys put up the sail. Andy took the tiller. The wind filled the little red sail and the boat fled along like a live thing.

"This is what I like," said Jill, contentedly, letting her hand drag in the cool, clear water. "The look of the sea, the smell of the sea, and the feel of the sea. Lovely!"

"I think every single boy and girl ought to have a boat," announced Mary. "A boat to row and to sail. There's nothing like it! Oh, Andy – aren't you lucky to have a boat of your very own like this? Ooooh – what a lot of spray! I'm drenched!"

The boat had cut into a sudden wave and a shower of salty spray had fallen over the twins. They shook their golden heads. "Lovely!" said Mary. "Do it again, Andy!"

"Where are we going?" asked Tom. "Have you made up your mind yet, Andy? You said you'd take us to one of the little islands round about."

"I've not made up my mind!" said Andy, his brown hand on the tiller.

"I thought maybe we'd just cruise round a few, and you could pick one you fancied. We could have a picnic there."

"One with birds, please," said Jill.

"Yes. With *tame* birds," said Mary, "tame enough to let us go right up to them."

Andy laughed. "Right! You can pick one with tame birds then. But don't blame me if you get pecked."

The boat sped on over the water. The sea was a cornflower blue in the distance, but round the boat it was a lovely emerald green, and it glittered as they cut through it. "The land is getting farther and farther away," said Jill. "It's almost as if the coast was going away from us, not us away from the coast! What a good thing there's a stiff breeze."

"Yes. We'd be cooked if there wasn't," said Tom. "Andy, did you catch a lot of fish this week? Was your father pleased?"

"He was fine and pleased," said Andy. "If he hadn't been I'd not have been given this day off. Like to take a turn at the tiller, Tom? She's going beautifully this morning — seems as if she's enjoying the trip as much as we are!"

Jill patted the little boat. "Of course she's enjoying it," she said. "That's what's so nice about a boat. She comes alive on the sea, and enjoys everything, too.

I'd like to be a boat and rush along like this, bouncing and bobbing over the waves."

"Yes – and it must be nice at night to make your bed on the waters and hear the little plash-plash-plash against your sides," said Mary. "And lovely to feel your sail billow out and pull you along!"

The land was now so far away that it was impossible to see even the high church tower. The coast lay like a blue, undulating line on the horizon. The *Andy* had certainly gone at top speed with the wind!

"Let's look out for the islands now," said Andy. "We'll be seeing them soon."

"I suppose we'll be the only people on any of them," said Tom. "That's what I like. I don't like crowds. I like to be with a few people I like and go adventuring. That's the life for me!"

"Well, you seem to enjoy school all right," said Jill, lazily. "Whenever we come down for your Sports Day you're always right in the very middle of a yelling, pushing crowd of boys – I don't see you huddled away in a corner with just one or two."

"Oh, well – school's different," said Tom. "It's nice being in a crowd then. Ah – I see the first island!"

Everyone looked where Tom pointed. It was so small and so far away that at first the girls couldn't see it, though Andy's sharp, long-sighted eyes had actually seen it even before Tom had.

"Yes, that's an island," said Jill. "What sort is it, Andy?"

"No good to us," said Andy. "Just a half-mile or so of bare rock. Even the birds don't like it much. The waves sweep it from end to end in a storm."

"Golly! I'd like to be on it in a storm, and feel the waves sweeping round my feet," said Tom.

"You wouldn't! They'd sweep round your neck!" said Andy, drily. "Look – we're coming near it now. It's not much of an island."

The *Andy* swooped nearer. "No," said Tom, "it's a poor sort of island – all seaweedy. I can't see even a bird. We pass this one by! On, Andy, on!"

They left the rocky little island behind, and another one loomed up, with yet another to the right. "This is fun," said Jill, standing up and taking hold of the mast. "Andy, do you know every one of these little islands scattered on the sea here?"

"Oh no," said Andy. "There are too many – about fifty or sixty, I should think. All too small or too bleak to live on, besides being too far from the

mainland for comfort. I know some of them and I've landed on a good few. Now, you watch carefully as we cruise by and see if there's one to your liking – tame birds and all!"

They sailed by island after island. Some were flattish, some had towering rocks, some were bare and some were covered with wiry grass and pink sea-thrift. Most of them were very small and some were joined to each other by long ridges of rock.

"There's one with birds!" cried Jill, pointing. "Look! And it seems a nice kind of island, with plenty of grass and cushions of thrift. Sail round it, Andy."

Andy took the tiller from Tom and the boat made a tour round the little island. At one part Andy thought he wouldn't get round, because a ridge of rock ran right out on to the next island. But his sharp eyes caught sight of a little channel where the rocky ridge appeared to break or dip down. He cautiously sailed the *Andy* up and peered down. The water was deep and clear – so on went the *Andy* through the narrow little channel between the rocky ridges.

"Well – I think this is the island for us," said Tom. "It looks well-grown with grass, and there are plenty of birds about – especially on that high cliff on the west side of the island. Let's land here, Andy."

Andy looked about for a cove to send the boat into. He saw exactly what he wanted – a sloping sandy cove where waves ran up and back. He waited for a big wave and then rode in on it. He leaped out as the wave ran back, and held the boat. He flung the rope round a convenient rock.

They all sprang out. The wet sand felt cool to their hot feet. They pulled the boat up a little way, but she was too heavy to pull up far.

"Now – shall we explore first – or watch the birds – or have a meal?" said Jill. "I bet I know what Tom will say. He'll want his sausages! That means we'll have to make a fire to cook them."

"No," said Tom. "It's too hot for sausages. We'll open a tin of ham and have it with the new bread Jeanie gave us. Andy, let's get out enough food and carry it with us now, and go to find a good place to have it in."

They chose out the food they wanted – a tin of ham, the bread, two crisp lettuces in a wet cloth, a bag of red tomatoes, and a basket of ripe plums.

"That's what I call a jolly nice meal," said Tom, pleased. "What about the drinks? I could drink a bathful of lemonade!"

"Well, find the bath first," said Jill. "I've got the drinks – a bottle of orangeade and a bottle of water to go with it. Or perhaps I'd better bring two bottles of water – if you're all as thirsty as I am you'll need them!"

They set off, carrying the food. Tom suddenly stopped. "Blow! We've left behind the tin-opener as usual. Why do we *always* forget it?"

"I've got it," said Andy. "Come on. What about going up to the top of that cliff there? There are plenty of birds on the rocky ledges to watch. We'll get a fine breeze there, too."

"And a wonderful view!" said Jill.

"And cushions of pink thrift to sit on!" said Mary. "It's so nice of it to grow in tufts like this. I like the little pink flowers, too. I say – isn't the sea *blue!*"

It certainly was – and when they were all sitting on cushions of thrift, high up on the cliff, it seemed unbelievably blue. The breeze blew strongly and kept them nice and cool.

"This is fine," said Tom, opening the tin of ham. "Nobody near us for miles and miles and miles. No trippers. No horrible litter. Just us and the birds and the sea."

"A very, very peaceful day," said Jill. But she spoke too soon. It wasn't going to be *quite* such a peaceful day as she thought!

CHAPTER 11
'HADN'T WE BETTER LOOK OUT?'

The picnic lasted quite a long time. Tom said it was a pity to leave any of the ham, so they didn't. The tomatoes were so nice and juicy that they went far too quickly, and Tom said he'd like some more.

"All right. Have as many as you like," said Jill. "But you'll have to go and get them. You've just finished the last one."

Tom was too lazy to get up and go back to the boat. So he delved into the basket of plums instead. Jill hastily removed it after a bit.

"There ought to be quite a nice lot of plum trees springing up on this island next year," said Tom, spitting out his sixth stone. "People coming here will be most astonished. I say – look at that gull. It's coming right up to us. Well, you wanted tame birds, Jill. Here's one for you."

The gull was a young one. It was quite unafraid, and had probably never even seen a human being before. It was very inquisitive indeed. The children watched it, wonderingly.

It walked right up to Tom, put its head on one side and stared at him solemnly. Tom put his head on one side and stared back. The twins laughed.

The gull then stared at Tom's bare feet, lunged at his big toe and gave it an enormous peck. Tom gave a tremendous yell, and rolled away quickly. He sat up and rubbed his bruised toe, glaring at the surprised gull.

"What did you do that for? Don't you know a toe when you see one? You're too tame for my liking. Go away and be wild!"

The gull listened, and then walked over to Andy, who held out a bit of bread to it. It pecked at it, swallowed greedily and looked round for more. It walked right over Andy's legs and made for Tom again.

The twins roared. Andy made a noise like a gull calling, and the bird looked even more surprised. It opened its great wings and flapped them, giving an answering call.

"My word – what a wind!" said Tom. "Hey, gull, you almost blew my hair off then. Can't you go and flap yourself a bit farther off? Oh, my, he's coming for me again."

The gull caused them a great deal of amusement. It was so very friendly and so very inquisitive. It pecked at the ribbons on the girls' plaits, it stood on Jill's foot, it even tried to sit on Tom's head but he wouldn't let it. It pecked a plum out of the basket and swallowed it whole, stone and all.

"Here! That's enough!" said Tom, in a hurry, snatching the basket up. "You've had the plum I'd got my eye on. Don't you know they're bad for gulls?"

"My word – here come a few of his friends," said Andy, amused. Sure enough three or four more gulls were walking up to join their friend. Tom stood up.

"I feel it's time to go," he said. "I shan't have a toe left to stand on, soon!"

But the gulls were scared when he suddenly stood up, and with a great sweep of wings they flew back to their rocky ledge on the cliff, where they sat together, looking out to sea. Tom sat down again.

The picnic was soon finished, and all the orangeade was drunk.

"Have to take the bags and tin and bottles back to the boat," said Jill, sleepily. "Who's going to?"

"Oh, let's sit here in peace for a while," said Mary. "I could do with a nap. But first I'm going to climb up to the top of that little rocky hill and see how many islands I can see from there. I should be able to see all round the island then."

She got up and climbed the rocky hill. It went up almost to a point, and Mary sat right at the very top, enjoying the strong breeze and the hot sun.

Islands to the left, islands to the right, islands all round! How exciting they looked! How odd that nobody lived there. They were empty except for the birds. Not even a rabbit lived on the little rocky islands. Mary gazed at the next island to theirs – the one almost joined to it by the ridge of rock through which was the channel where their boat had sailed. It looked an island much like theirs, but far rougher and hillier.

And then Mary stared. She could see something. But what was it? Something white was flying and fluttering in the air. Not smoke. It didn't look like smoke. It looked almost like tiny white birds. She called to Jill.

"Jill – have you got the glasses? Bring them here, will you? I want to look through them at something puzzling on the next island."

Jill brought them. Mary set them to her eyes and stared through them. Now she would be able to see what the white things were.

"How very strange!" she said. "They look exactly like bits of paper – letters or something! They can't be, though. No trippers ever come to these islands. Look through the glasses, Jill, and see what you think!"

Jill focused the glasses on the white things. She nodded. "Yes – it's paper of some kind, flying in the breeze. How peculiar. Who would come here with paper and let it loose on an island? It's just nonsense."

By now the boys were interested, too, and they came up. Each in turn looked through the glasses, and all of them agreed that for some reason or other papers *were* flying about on the next island.

"But whose papers – and how did they get there – and why?" said Tom, puzzled.

"Dropped by an aeroplane?" suggested Jill.

"What! Dropped on a lonely island like that? What for?" said Tom, scornfully. "Or do you mean by accident?"

"Well – I suppose it *might* have been by accident," said Jill.

"These islands are off the route of any aeroplane," said Andy. "You'll not see one here from one year's end to another. Those papers could only have been brought by boat."

"Well – I suppose we must just put them down to trippers!" said Mary. "How disgusting! Why bring a load of newspapers – or whatever they are – and leave them there to fly about?"

"It's a bit peculiar," said Andy. "Well, come on, we can't stay here all day looking at papers flying about. Let's take our own litter back to the boat. And then what shall we do? Explore this island? Make friends with any more gulls?"

"Oh, no – not that," said Tom, hastily. "I can hardly walk as it is, my big toe is so bruised. No – let's do a spot of exploring."

"I'd like to go and see what those papers are, flying about the next island," said Jill, unexpectedly.

"Well – that's not a bad idea," said Tom. "Not at all a bad idea. The thing is – how do we get there? By boat? It would be a bit of a fag to get the *Andy* and sail off again."

"Well – couldn't we walk along that ridge of rocks and swim across the little channel we went through, and then climb up the opposite ridge of rocks and walk to the next island that way?" asked Jill.

"Oh, yes! We meant to have a bathe, anyway!" said Mary, pleased. "Let's go back to the boat with our bottles and things, change into our bathing-suits, and go off to the next island for the afternoon. We can easily swim across that little channel. It will make an exciting swim."

Everyone thought this a very good idea. They went back to the *Andy* with their litter, and changed into bathing-things. "Lovely!" said Jill. "It's far too hot to wear clothes today. I wonder we didn't come out in bathing-suits, anyway!"

The tide was in a little, but the Andy was quite safe. The children stowed away their litter, and put the bottles and the basket into the cabin. Tom got some bars of chocolate and put them into a waterproof bag round his neck.

"Just in case we get hungry before we get back," he explained. "You never know!"

"Well, after that enormous meal I don't feel as if I shall be hungry for about two days," said Jill. "I shan't want any of your chocolate!"

They set off. They soon came to where the rocky ridge stretched out from their own island. They walked lightly along it in their bare feet. They soon found that it was better to walk on the lower part, which was occasionally washed by the waves, than on the upper part, which was burned hot by the sun and scorched their feet.

It was fairly easy to cross the ridge, though sometimes they had to clamber round on hands and knees in case they slipped. They came to where the rocks dipped right down into the sea, making the little channelway. They climbed down to where the ridge reached the water and looked into the channel.

"Can't see any bottom at all," said Tom, peering down. "Looks as if the rocks break off. Well, in we go, and swim across. It looks gorgeous!"

They dived in one after another. They could all swim like fish, of course, and even the girls were very strong swimmers. They swam swiftly across the gleaming channel, enjoying the cool water on their bodies. They didn't want to climb out when they got to the other side, it was so lovely in the water.

So they swam about for a bit, splashing one another, and clutching at legs, and swimming under the water with their eyes open, watching for anything exciting down below. But there was nothing to see, not even a fish, and at last they pulled themselves up on the rocks opposite.

"Well! I'm still hot!" said Jill. "Wasn't that lovely?"

"Heavenly," said Mary. "I'm not hot, though. I'd like to climb up the ridge and go on to the next island."

"Well, come on, then," said Andy. "I'd like to go, too."

They clambered along that ridge and came to the next island. It was not as green as theirs, though cushions of sea-pinks grew here and there, and tufts of wiry grass sprang up where there was any earth.

"Now – whereabouts did we see that paper flying?" said Jill, stopping. "Oh look – that's a bit, I'm sure! Yes, it is – look, blowing over there."

They ran to the piece of paper. It flapped along like a live thing. Tom pounced on it and picked it up. The others crowded round him.

"It's a kind of document," said Tom. "It's got all kinds of weird numbers and things on it – and look, where it's torn, there's a bit of a plan or something. What can it be?"

"I don't know," said Jill. "But – it looks sort of *important* to me! Let's go and pick up some of the other papers. They must be somewhere about. This is really very peculiar. Tom – you don't suppose there's anyone here, do you? Hadn't we better look out?"

CHAPTER III
THERE'S SOMETHING
VERY PECULIAR!

For the first time the four children felt that there might be someone else on the islands besides themselves! It wasn't really a very nice thought. Where was the boat that anyone else might have come in? There was no sign of one. It might, of course, be hidden away in some cove they couldn't see.

On the other hand, someone might have come and gone — leaving behind a mass of papers to blow about. But how very strange, if so!

"Let's find some more papers," said Jill, and they went forward, keeping a look-out. It wasn't long before they came on four or five more, flapping about in the breeze. They were much the same as the first one they had picked up, except that one was on blue paper instead of cream.

"More figures — more plans," said Tom, looking at them. "And such tiny writing I can hardly read it — and if I could read it all I'd not understand it! Andy, what *are* these papers?"

"I don't know much about these things," said the fisher-boy, slowly, "but it seems to me they're plans of some kind. I don't know what of. Maybe a building, maybe a liner, maybe a submarine — I don't know. But why they're blowing about here beats me! If they're stolen — and I think they may be — why scatter them over

250

an island! Why not use them, copy them perhaps – and then burn them? Or at least keep them in some safe place? It's very strange."

"Who do they belong to, anyway?" said Jill, looking all round as if she expected the owner to appear. "*Someone* must have brought them here. Where's he gone?"

"Goodness knows," said Andy. "But I tell you what I think – I think we should collect all we see and take them back to the *Andy* with us. If they're important it would be the right thing to do – and if they're not – well, it won't matter."

"Yes. That's a good idea," said Jill, and she picked up a few more. She straightened them out, folded them neatly, and put them together. The others began to do the same.

Then Tom gave an exclamation. "I say! Come and look here!"

He was behind a rock. The others ran to him at once. They saw him bending over what looked like a suitcase. It was open, and from it came the papers that flew about everywhere! Even as they looked, the wind tugged at another in the case, and sent it high into the air. Mary caught it. It was a blue one, and had another lot of figures and diagrams on it.

"A suitcase!" said Andy, amazed. "Full of papers. Who put it there? And why has it been left open?"

"More and more mysterious," said Jill. She looked carefully at the suitcase. It was not a very good one – it was made of imitation leather and had cheap locks. She suddenly saw that one end of it was badly dented.

"Look," she said. "See the dent – it's had a fall – been dropped from a height, I should think. Goodness, do you suppose an aeroplane *has* dropped it?"

"No! It would have been bashed to pieces," said Tom. He looked at the dented end of the case, and then glanced upwards. They were in a rocky spot, open to the wind and sun except behind them where a tall cliff rose up, towering high.

"I bet it's fallen from somewhere on this rocky wall," said Tom. "If it did, whichever end it fell on would be dented by the rock it hit – the case would burst open its clasps – and the papers would fly out one by one in the wind. *That's* the solution, I think."

"Yes. But it doesn't solve the question of who owns the case, how it got here, and why it fell off the cliff," said Andy, soberly. "I rather think there must be people on this island."

"I hope not," said Jill. "I don't feel as if I should like them very much."

251

They looked up at the rocky cliff above them. About two-thirds of the way up a dark place showed. Was it a cave of some sort?

"I'll go up and see," said Andy, and began to clamber up at once. The others watched him in silence. Andy came to the cave and looked in at the entrance. Then he made a sign to the others to be silent, and very quietly he clambered back.

"Two men there," he whispered. "Sound asleep. On the ledge of the cave's entrance there is another case – but it seems only to have clothes in. There's a picnic basket, too. Who in the world are they? And how did they get here and why?"

"I can't think," said Tom, puzzled. "Unless – unless they've stolen all these plans and documents, got a boat in the night, came here, and are waiting for someone to fetch the case – waiting to hand everything over for payment."

"You may be right," said Andy. "Anyway, I think we should pick up all the papers we can see, stuff them into the case and take it away with us. There's *something* very peculiar about the whole thing. We'd better be quick, though. Those men may wake up at any minute."

The four children began to stuff the papers into the case as fast as they could. But, before they could finish picking up every one, they heard the sound of voices from the cave above.

"Quick!" said Tom, shutting the case in a hurry. "We'd better take this and go. They'll be out in a minute. If we keep behind this hill we can get down to the ridge of rocks without being seen."

They set off as quietly as they could, Andy and Tom carrying the suitcase between them. It wasn't really very heavy because it only held papers. They hurried as much as possible and came to the rocky ridge.

"Get to the other side, then if the men come out of the cave and look round they won't see us," said Andy. So down they clambered to the east side of the ridge and kept out of sight as they made their way to the channel between the rocks.

But there they had a setback. How were they going to get the suitcase across the channel without soaking the papers inside and probably destroying them? That was a puzzle! They couldn't risk wetting the papers – they might be quite priceless.

"Look here – I've got an idea," said Andy at last. "Let's hide the suitcase somewhere here. Then I'll swim across by myself, go along the ridge on the other side, make my way to the *Andy*, and push her off on the water. I'll sail her here, to the channel, and you can all get into her as I pass – and chuck the suitcase down on deck. It won't hurt it – and if it bursts open again, well, we must just see that

252

the wind doesn't get the papers!"

"Jolly good idea," said Tom. "You go off now, Andy, and get the boat. We'll hide the suitcase somewhere near — and wait for you."

Andy slid into the water, and they watched him swim swiftly across the little channel. He clambered out on the other side, waved to them, and then went across the rocks to the mainland. He disappeared, and the others sat down and looked at one another.

"Suppose those men go looking for the suitcase and find *us*?" said Jill, fearfully. "What do we say?"

"We just say we're picnicking here for the day," said Tom. "And we'll say we're being picked up by somebody later on. That's perfectly true — but the men may think that a boat has dropped us here for the day and will fetch us this evening."

"I see — so they won't guess we've already *got* a boat here and are going off in it — with the papers!" said Jill. "I do wish we hadn't got to stick on *this* island, because of the suitcase. I'd feel much safer on the other one!"

"So would I," said Mary. "I don't know why we didn't go with Andy — except that I don't want to leave Tom on his own."

"I wouldn't have minded," said Tom. "Look out — I can hear the men. They sound pretty angry!"

Sure enough, the two men appeared in the distance, and the children cowered down behind a rock. "We haven't hidden the suitcase yet. We *are* idiots!" whispered Tom. He pulled it nearer to him, and looked round desperately for a hiding-place.

"Look — there's a hole under this rock," whispered Jill. "It would just about take the case. Shove it under, and I'll pull off some seaweed and drape it over the hole to hide the case!"

Tom pushed the case into the hole quickly, and the girls pulled seaweed from the rocks around and began to drape it so that the hole and the suitcase were well-hidden.

Jill sat with her legs dangling over it, and her heart began to beat quickly as she heard the voices of the men coming nearer.

"They've seen us!" said Tom. "They'll yell in a minute."

He was right. The men suddenly caught sight of them and stopped in astonishment. "Hey! You children! What in the world are you doing here?" shouted one of the men.

"Hallo! We're here picnicking for the day!" yelled Tom, waving as if he were pleased to see them. "Are you? This is a nice island, isn't it?"

The two men came right up. They looked wary and suspicious. "Look here," said the other man, who had a beard and looked rather fierce, "look here – we've lost a suitcase. Have you seen one?"

"A suitcase! What a funny thing to lose on an island like this!" said Jill, with a laugh. "I expect it's blown out to sea – with the papers!"

"What papers?" snapped the first man. "Did you see any?"

"Oh, yes – they were blowing about all over the place," said Mary. "Heaps of them. I expect there are plenty scattered over the island still. They can't *all* have blown out to sea!"

"How did the case get open? And where is it now?" said the bearded man, to his friend. He turned to the children again. "How did you get here? By boat?"

"Oh yes, of course," said Tom. "But we've got to wait till we're picked up again."

"I see. I suppose the boat dropped you here this morning, and will pick you up this evening," said the first man.

"When are *you* going?" asked Jill, innocently. "Is a boat coming to pick you up, too? Did you come to watch the birds or something?"

"Er – yes, yes – we're bird-watchers," said the bearded man, hurriedly. "We – er – we had a suitcase full of papers about birds – notes, you know – and we're upset to find our case gone, and the papers, too. We'll have to look over the island and pick up all we can. Er – what part of the island is your boat coming to call for you?"

"Look – there's a paper!" cried Tom, anxious to get away from the subject of boats. The men turned and saw a piece in the distance. One ran to get it. The other joined him and they looked at it, nodding. They talked together for a while, and then came back to the children, looking stern.

"Now look here," said the bearded man, "we're not satisfied with what you've told us. We think you've got that suitcase somewhere – and what is more we think you may have a boat in some cove or other. Tell us the truth and we'll let you go – if not, well, we'll find your boat, scuttle her, and leave you here on this deserted island by yourselves!"

"All right," said Tom, boldly, "if you think we're thieves, and aren't telling the truth, you look for the suitcase and hunt in every cove of this island for our boat!"

"We will!" said the bearded man, getting angry. He turned to his friend. "Stay here and watch these kids," he said. "I'm going all over the island to see if I can find where they've put the case – and I'm going to look for their boat, too. That'll be the end of it if I find it!"

"I'll watch the kids," said the other man grimly, and he sat down nearby. Tom winked at the two frightened girls. The men didn't for one moment dream that their boat was on the *next* island, not on this one – nor did they dream that the suitcase was at that moment under Jill's dangling legs! But, oh dear – how Tom hoped that Andy didn't come *too* soon with the boat!

CHAPTER IV
QUITE A NICE LITTLE OUTING, WASN'T IT?

The bearded man went off to look for the suitcase and the boat. On the way the children saw him bend down to pick up one or two more papers. We must have missed those, they thought. Blow!

Tom got up and clambered up and down the rocks. Mary joined him. But Jill sat still, feeling that if she didn't sit on the seaweed that dangled down over the hidden suitcase, it might slip and expose it! That would be dreadful.

"By the way," said Tom, going up to the man who was watching them, "you said you were bird-watchers, didn't you? Have you seen that lovely Cormorpetrel? And did you notice all the Kittygillies? Lovely, aren't they?"

The girls knew that Tom was making up these bird-names but the man didn't. He nodded surlily. "Yes, lovely birds."

"Where did you say your boat was?" asked Tom, beginning to enjoy himself. "Or did somebody drop you here? And is somebody coming to fetch you? If not we could give you a lift home ourselves."

The man scowled. "Keep your mouth shut," he said. "I'm not talking to silly kids like you. You tell me where you boat is and I'll tell you where mine is!"

"Can't tell you that if I'm to keep my mouth shut!" said Tom. "Anyway, your friend will soon tell you if he finds our boat."

It seemed a long time till the bearded man came back. He must have walked over the tiny island two or three times, hunting here and there, and he had also walked all round the beaches and examined every little inlet to see if he could find a boat. When at last he came towards them once more the children saw that he had picked up quite a few papers.

He shook his head as he came up to the first man. "No boat," he said. "I've looked in every cove. They told the truth — their boat is nowhere on this island — they must be going to be picked up tonight. I haven't found the suitcase, though."

"Perhaps one of those big gulls carried it off," said Jill, innocently, pointing to where an enormous gull glided with widespread wings over their heads.

"Pah!" said the man. "Well, let me tell you this, you kids — if you've taken that suitcase of ours, we shall know it — because we shall be on the watch for your boat to come tonight — and if we see you going down to it with a suitcase, you'll be very VERY sorry. Fred, go up to that hill-top there and sit down. You can see all round the island from there and you'd see a boat coming in miles away. The mainland is over there — keep a strict watch in that direction and all round too."

The other man nodded. He got up and walked to the hill the bearded man pointed out. It was in the middle of the island and was very high. He sat himself down on the top. The bearded man gave the three children one of his best scowls, and went off, apparently to look for more blown-about papers.

"He won't find many more," whispered Tom. "We picked up practically all there were! Gosh — if only he knew that Jill is sitting practically on top of his precious suitcase!"

"Don't!" said Jill. "I felt as if he must see it through my legs and the seaweed every time he looked in my direction."

"What do we do now?" asked Mary. "Wait for Andy? That man up on the hill will spot the red sail as soon as Andy comes round."

"If only we could tell Andy not to put it up!" said Tom. "If he *rowed* round he might not be seen. Those rocks would hide him, and I don't think that fellow up there can see right down to where we are, I'm pretty sure he can't see the channel."

"Andy's a jolly long time," said Mary. "I feel rather worried about him. Surely he should be here by now?"

"Yes, he should," said Tom. "I'm just wondering if he's found that he can't shove the boat off. It might have sunk down into the sand or something. Anyway, the tide was coming in so he might be able to get it on the water then. We can only wait. Oh, I say! I've just thought of something!"

"What?" said the two girls, eagerly.

"This," said Tom, producing the waterproof bag he had brought. "The chocolate! You could do with it now, I bet! Or do you still feel you can't eat anything, Jill?"

"I feel *frightfully* hungry," said Jill. "Thank goodness you brought the chocolate. I expect it's all squishy and smells of oilskin, but I shan't mind!"

It *was* squishy, and it *did* smell of oilskin, but certainly no one minded. They ate it all except for a piece they kept for Andy.

"I wonder what the time is," said Jill at last. "The sun's going down. I do wish Andy would come. I suppose you could slip into the water, swim across the channel and go and find Andy, couldn't you, Tom? He might have had an accident, or something."

Tom considered. "No. I don't think I'd better do that. If that fellow up there saw me, I would give the game away properly. He'd guess our boat was on the next island if he spotted me swimming across. But I'll go when it's a bit darker."

"Let's play catch or something," said Mary. "I'm getting a bit cold in my bathing-things. It'll warm us up!"

So they played rather a dangerous game of catch on the rocks. Still, it warmed them up. By the time they were tired of it the sun was just disappearing.

"Now it will soon get dark," said Jill. "Hallo! Here's Mr Beard again!"

So it was. He came up to the children. "It looks as if your boat isn't coming for you," he said. "What do you suppose has happened? Weren't they going to pick you up in daylight?"

"I can't imagine *what's* happened!" said Tom, truthfully. "What about *your* boat? Is it coming at night? A motor boat, perhaps?"

The bearded man didn't answer. He joined the other man on the hill, and they talked earnestly together.

Tom suddenly gave the girls a nudge. "Look! Our boat! The sail isn't up, thank goodness! Andy's rowing."

"They won't see him now – it's getting too dark," said Jill. "What about the suitcase? Do we get it out now?"

"No. Not till the boat is exactly in the middle of the channel. Then we'll drag out the case and drop it, plonk, on the deck," said Tom. "I'll do that. You two girls go down to the lowest rock now, ready to dive in and swim to the boat."

Jill and Mary went obediently down to the lowest rocks and waited, trembling with excitement. They could just make out the two men sitting on the high, rocky hill. Andy and the boat came nearer and nearer. How the children hoped he would not hail them!

He didn't. He rowed carefully into the channel and at once spotted the two girls. They dived in cleanly and swam the few strokes to the boat.

And at that moment one of the men gave a loud shout. "What's that? Look – it's a boat – a rowing boat, too! Where did it come from? Quick, those children will be away in it. Stop it – we must stop it!"

Andy pulled the two girls into the boat, and then worked it as near to the rocks as he could without danger. He could see Tom dragging out the suitcase from under the seaweedy rock.

"Quick!" he called. "They're coming! Quick, Tom!"

Poor Tom was being as quick as ever he could – but the suitcase had swollen a little with the damp under the rock, and was now jammed fast. He tugged and tugged, hearing the shouts and the running footsteps coming nearer and nearer. *Blow!* Would this suitcase never come out?

It came out with such a rush that Tom fell down the rock below and almost rolled right down into the water. He clutched at a handful of seaweed and saved himself. The suitcase slid on top of him. He rolled over, got up, snatched at the handle and went as quickly as he dared over the slippery rocks.

A big stone came whizzing near his head. He ducked. Goodness! Those fellows were throwing bits of rock and stones at him! Another stone hit the suitcase, and then one glanced off his ankle, making him wince.

"Chuck it, heave it in!" shouted Andy. "I'm just here – I'm near enough for you to jump in, too. Come on, Tom!"

Tom saw the boat just below him. He heaved the suitcase up and threw it down to the boat. It almost knocked Andy over. The girls pulled it quickly to one side and waited for Tom to jump it, too.

But he missed his footing and fell between the boat and the rocks. He spluttered and gasped and grabbed at the side of the boat. Andy caught hold of him and hauled him in. A large piece of rock bounced on deck and the girls screamed.

Andy seized the oars and rowed for dear life. The men clambered swiftly down the rocks and came to the channel. But the boat had slid out of it now and was making for the open sea.

"Come on – we'll swim after it!" yelled the bearded man. "We can catch it!"

Both men dived in and began a terrific side-crawl, making headway at once.

"The sail! Put up the sail!" shouted Andy, rowing frantically. "Tom, Jill, Mary – put up the sail!"

The three worked desperately at the ropes. The sail unfolded. It went up – it shook out, and the wind immediately filled it! Andy shipped the oars and picked up the bit of rock from the deck. He looked so fierce that the girls felt alarmed. What was he going to do?

The bearded man had caught up with the boat! He was a wonderful swimmer, and he was now clinging to the side trying to haul himself up, panting hard.

Andy raised the rock. "Take your hands off my boat or I'll make you!" he shouted. "Take them off!"

The man took one look at the rock that he himself had thrown at Tom, and sank back into the sea. He wasn't going to have his hands struck by that heavy rock! The children watched him treading water, panting, glaring at them as if he would like to drown them all!

The sail was billowing out and the *Andy* was surging along well now, with Andy at the tiller. The man was soon lost to sight. So were the two islands! It was getting really dark now, and Andy would have to go carefully, or they would find themselves sailing the seas till morning!

"Phew!" said Tom, flopping down on the deck. "What an excitement! I nearly had a fit when I fell into the water instead of stepping on deck! Andy, why were you so long?"

"Well, first I couldn't get the boat off the sand," said Andy. "And I thought I'd go up to that cliff-top where we had our picnic and see if I could signal to you that I'd be a bit of time coming. So up I went – and I spotted the men talking to you, so I guessed I'd better wait till it was getting dark before I brought the boat round. That's why I didn't put up the sail, of course. I didn't want it to be seen."

"Clever old Andy!" said Jill, hugging him. "We got worried about you. I bet those men are kicking themselves now. They know we've got their precious suitcase and most of the papers – and we're off home with them."

"Yes, and I bet they hope the boat that is coming to get them will be along tonight!" said Mary. "Or else they'll be taken off in a police-boat!"

"We'd better telephone the police as soon as we get back," said Tom. "I'd love to know what these papers are that we've got!"

Andy took them all back safely. He steered by the stars he knew so well, and by the time the moon was up the Andy was nosing along the little jetty. She was soon tied up, and the four children left her to bob peacefully there. Tom carried the suitcase home, and then rang up the police. Jeanie was in bed and fast asleep! What she was missing!

It proved to be quite an exciting night. The papers in the suitcase were, as the children had thought, all stolen.

"Hush-hush plans for something I mustn't even mention!" said the big superintendent, shovelling them back quickly into the case. "I don't know who this case belongs to but we'll borrow it for the time being. My word – half the police in the kingdom have been looking for these papers!"

"Are they so very valuable?" said Tom. "Would it have been a terrible loss if they hadn't been found?"

"Oh, we've got copies," said the superintendent, snapping the suitcase shut. "But the point is – we don't want anyone else to have them; especially the fellows you got them from. They were probably waiting for a fast motor launch to pick them up, and were going to hand them over to someone in the know and get a vast sum for them."

"Shall you fetch the men yourself?" said Jill.

"No," said the superintendent, grinning. "I guess they'll be dealt with all right by the fellows who come for the plans. We shan't hear any more of *them* – they'll run half round the world to get away from the fury of the people who come for the plans and find they aren't there! Well – thanks for your good work. Quite a nice little outing, wasn't it?"

"Fine," said Andy. "Best picnic we've ever had! I could do with a few more like that, sir!"

"So could we!" said the others, and went to the door to see Andy and the superintendent off.

"Goodnight!" called everyone, and Jeanie upstairs woke up with a jump.

"Those children!" she said, sleepily. "What *ever* have they been up to now?"

SECRET SEVEN ON THE TRAIL

AN EXTRACT

∾ ILLUSTRATED BY ∾
GEORGE BROOK

Jack's sister, Susie, fools the Secret Seven (Jack, Peter, Janet, Barbara, George, Colin and Pam) into thinking that she is on the track of an adventure. So when Jack and George overhear Susie and her friend Jeff talking about a visit to Tigger's Barn, they decide to follow them. But Susie and Jeff hide, leaving Jack and George to go to the barn alone - where they really do find a mystery!

CHAPTER VII
AT TIGGER'S BARN

Jack and George had no idea at all that they had left Jeff and Susie behind them in the hall. They imagined that the two were well in front of them, hurrying to Tigger's Barn! They hurried too, but, rather to their surprise, they did not see any children in front, however much they strained their eyes in the moonlit night.

"Well, all I can say is they must have taken bicycles," said George, at last. "They *couldn't* have gone so quickly. Has Susie got a bike, Jack?"

"Oh yes, and I bet she's lent Jeff mine," said Jack, crossly. "They'll be at Tigger's Barn ages before us. I hope the meeting of those men isn't over before we get there. I don't want Susie and Jeff to hear everything without us hearing it too!"

Tigger's Barn was about a mile away. It was up on a lonely hill, hemmed in by trees. Once it had been part of a farmhouse, which had been burned down one night. Tigger's Barn was now only a tumble-down shell of a house, used by tramps who needed shelter, by jackdaws who nested in the one remaining enormous chimney, and by a big tawny owl who used it to sleep in during the daytime.

Children had played in it until they had been forbidden to in case the old walls gave way. Jack and George had once explored it with Peter, but an old tramp had risen up from a corner and shouted at them so loudly that they had fled away.

The two boys trudged on. They came to the hill and walked up the narrow lane that led to Tigger's Barn. Still there was no sign of Jeff or Susie. Well, if they had taken bicycles, they would certainly be at Tigger's Barn by now!

They came to the old building at last. It stood there in the rather dim moonlight, looking forlorn and bony, with part of its roof missing, and its one great chimney sticking up into the night sky.

"Here we are," whispered Jack. "Walk quietly, because we don't want to let Jeff and Susie know we're here, or those men either, if they've come already! But everything is very quiet. I don't think the men are here."

They kept in the shadow of a great yew hedge, and made their way on tiptoe to the back of the house. There was a front door and a back door, and both were locked, but as no window had glass in, it was easy enough for anyone to get inside the tumble-down place if they wanted to.

Jack clambered in through a downstairs window. A scuttling noise startled him, and he clutched George and made him jump.

"Don't grab me like that," complained George, in a whisper. "It was only a rat hurrying away. You nearly made me yell when you grabbed me so suddenly."

"Sh!" said Jack. "What's that?"

They listened. Something was moving high up in the great chimney that towered from the hearth in the broken-down room they were in.

"Maybe it's the owl," said George, at last. "Yes, listen to it hooting."

A quavering hoot came to their ears. But it didn't really sound as if it came from the chimney. It seemed to come from outside the house, in the overgrown garden. Then an answering hoot came, but it didn't sound at all like an owl.

"Jack," whispered George, his mouth close to Jack's ear, "that's not an owl. It's men signalling to one another. They *are* meeting here! But where are Susie and Jeff?"

"I don't know. Hidden safely somewhere, I expect," said Jack, suddenly feeling a bit shaky at the knees. "We'd better hide too. Those men will be here in half a minute."

"There's a good hiding-place over there in the hearth," whispered George. "We can stand there in the darkness, right under the big chimney. Come on, quick. I'm sure I can hear footsteps outside."

The two boys ran silently to the hearth. Tramps had made fires there from time to time, and a heap of ashes half-filled the hearth. The boys stood ankle-deep in them, hardly daring to breathe.

Then a torch suddenly shone out, and raked the room with its beam. Jack and George pressed close together, hoping they did not show in the great hearth. They heard the sound of someone climbing in through the same window they had come in by. Then a voice spoke to someone outside.

"Come on in. Nobody's here. Larry hasn't come yet. Give him the signal, Zeb, in case he's waiting about for it now."

Somebody gave a quavering hoot again. "Ooooo-oo-oo! Ooooo, ooo-oo-oo!"

An answering call came from some way away, and after about half a minute another man climbed in. Now there were three.

The two boys held their breath. Good gracious! They were right in the middle of something very strange! Why were these men meeting at this tumble-down place? Who were they and what were they doing?

Where were Susie and Jeff, too? Were they listening and watching as well?

"Come into the next room," said the man who had first spoken. "There are boxes there to sit on, and a light won't shine out there as much as it does from this room. Come on, Larry – here, Zeb, shine your torch in front."

264

CHAPTER VIII
AN UNCOMFORTABLE TIME

The two boys were half-glad, half-sorry that the men had gone into another room. Glad because they were no longer afraid of being found, but sorry because it was now impossible to hear clearly what the men were saying.

They could hear a murmur from the next room.

Jack nudged George. "I'm going to creep across the floor and go to the door. Perhaps I can hear what they are saying then," he whispered.

"No, don't," said George, in alarm. "We'll be discovered. You're sure to make a noise!"

"I've got rubber-soled shoes on. I shan't make a sound," whispered back Jack. "You stay here, George. I do wonder where Susie and Jeff are. I hope I don't bump into them anywhere."

Jack made his way very quietly to the doorway that led to the next room. There was a broken door still hanging there, and he could peep through the crack. He saw the three men in the room beyond, sitting on old boxes, intently studying a map of some kind, and talking in low voices.

If only he could hear what they said! He tried to see what the men were like, but it was too dark. He could only hear their voices, one a polished voice speaking clearly and firmly, and the other two rough and unpleasant.

Jack hadn't the slightest idea what they were talking about. Loading and unloading. Six-two or maybe seven-ten. Points, points, points. There mustn't be a moon. Darkness, fog, mist. Points. Fog. Six-two, but it might go as long as seven-twenty. And again, points points, points.

What in the world could they be discussing? It was maddening to hear odd words like this that made no sense. Jack strained his ears to try and make out more, but it was no use, he couldn't. He decided to edge a little nearer.

He leaned against something that gave way behind him. It was a cupboard door! Before he could stop himself Jack fell inside, landing with a soft thud. The door closed on him with a little click. He sat there, alarmed and astonished, not daring to move.

"What was that?" said one of the men.

They all listened, and at that moment a big rat ran silently round the room, keeping to the wall. One of the men picked it out in the light of his torch. "Rats," he said. "This place is alive with them. That's what we heard."

"I'm not sure," said the man with the clear voice. "Switch off that light, Zeb. Sit quietly for a bit and listen."

The light was switched off. The men sat in utter silence, listening. Another rat scuttered over the floor.

Jack sat absolutely still in the cupboard, fearful that the men might come to find out who had made a noise. George stood in the hearth of the next room, wondering what had happened. There was such dead silence now, and darkness too!

The owl awoke in the chimney above him, and stirred once more. Night-time! It must go hunting. It gave one soft hoot and dropped down the chimney to make its way out through the bare window.

It was as startled to find George standing at the bottom of the chimney as George was startled to feel the owl brushing his cheek. It flew silently out of the window, a big moving shadow in the dimness.

George couldn't bear it. He must get out of this chimney-place, he must! Something else might fall down on him and touch his face softly. Where was Jack? How mean of him to go off and leave him with things that lived in chimneys! And Jack had the torch with him too. George would have given anything to flick on the light of a torch.

He crept out of the hearth, and stood in the middle of the floor, wondering what to do. What *was* Jack doing? He had said he was going to the doorway that led to the next room, to see if he could hear what the men said. But were the men there now? There wasn't a sound to be heard.

Perhaps they have slipped out of another window and gone, thought poor George. If so why doesn't Jack come back? It's horrid of him. I can't bear this much longer!

He moved over to the doorway, putting out his hands to feel if Jack was there. No, he wasn't. The next room was in black darkness, and he couldn't see a thing there. There was also complete silence. Where *was* everyone?

George felt his legs giving way at the knees. This horrible old tumble-down place! Why ever had he listened to Jack and come here with him? He was sure that Jeff and Susie hadn't been stupid enough to come here at night.

He didn't dare to call out. Perhaps Jack was somewhere nearby, scared too. What about the Secret Seven password? What was it now? Cheeky Charlie!

If I whisper Cheeky Charlie, Jack will know it's me, he thought. It's our password. He'll know it's me, and he'll answer.

So he stood at the doorway and whispered: "Cheeky Charlie! Cheeky Charlie!"

No answer. He tried again, a little louder this time, "Cheeky Charlie!"

And then a torch snapped on, and caught him directly in its beam. A voice spoke to him harshly.

"What's all this? What do you know about Charlie? Come right into the room, boy, and answer my question."

CHAPTER IX
VERY PECULIAR

George was extremely astonished. Why, the men were still there! Then where was Jack? What had happened to him? He stood there in the beam of the torch, gaping.

"Come on in," said the voice, impatiently. "We heard you saying "Cheeky Charlie". Have you got a message from him?"

George gaped still more. A message from him? From Cheeky Charlie? Why, that was only a password! Just the name of a dog! What did the man mean?

"*Will* you come into the room," said the man, again. "What's the matter with you, boy? Are you scared? We shan't eat a messenger from Charlie."

George went slowly into the room, his mind suddenly working at top speed. A messenger from Charlie. Could there be someone called Charlie, Cheeky Charlie? Did these men think he had come from him? How very extraordinary!

"There won't be no message from Charlie," said the man called Zeb. "Why should there be? He's waiting for news from *us*, isn't he? Here, boy — did Charlie send you to ask for news?"

George could do nothing but nod his head. He didn't want to have to explain anything at all. These men appeared to think he had come to find them to get news for someone called Charlie. Perhaps if he let them give him the message, they would let him go without any further questions.

"Can't think why Charlie uses such a dumb kid to send out," grumbled Zeb. "Got a pencil, Larry? I'll scribble a message."

"A kid that can't open his mouth and speak a word is just the right messenger for us," said the man with the clear voice. "Tell Charlie what we've decided, Zeb. Don't forget that he's to mark the tarpaulin with white lines at one corner."

Zeb scribbled something in a notebook by the light of a torch. He tore out the page and folded it over. "Here you are," he said to George. "Take this to Charlie, and don't you go calling him Cheeky Charlie, see? Little boys that are rude get their ears boxed! His friends can call him what they like, but not you."

"Oh, leave the kid alone," said Larry. "Where's Charlie now, kid? At Dalling's or at Hammond's?"

George didn't know what to answer. "Dalling's," he said at last, not knowing in the least what it meant.

Larry tossed him fifty pence. "Clear off!" he said. "You're scared stiff of this place, aren't you? Want me to take you down the hill?"

This was the last thing that poor George wanted. He shook his head.

The men got up. "Well, if you want company, we're all going now. If not, buzz off."

George buzzed off, but not very far. He went back again into the other room, thankful to see that the moon had come out again, and had lit it enough for him to make his way quickly to the window. He clambered out awkwardly, because his legs were shaking and were not easy to manage.

He made for a thick bush and flung himself into the middle. If those men really were going, he could wait till they were gone. Then he could go back and find Jack. *What* had happened to Jack? He seemed to have disappeared completely.

The men went cautiously out of Tigger's Barn, keeping their voices low. The owl flew over their heads, giving a sudden hoot that startled them. Then George heard them laugh. Their footsteps went quietly down the hill.

He heaved a sigh of relief. Then he scrambled out of the bush and went back into the house. He stood debating what to do. Should he try the password again? It had had surprising results last time, so perhaps this time it would be better just to call Jack's name.

But before he could do so, a voice came out of the doorway that led to the further room.

"Cheeky Charlie!" it said, in a piercing whisper.

George stood stock still, and didn't answer. Was it Jack saying that password? Or was it somebody else who knew the real Cheeky Charlie, whoever he might be?

Then a light flashed on and caught him in its beam. But this time, thank goodness, it was Jack's torch, and Jack himself gave an exclamation of relief.

"It *is* you, George! Why in the world didn't you answer when I said the password? You must have known it was me."

"Oh, Jack! Where were you? I've had an awful time!" said George. "You shouldn't have gone off and left me like that. Where have you been?"

"I was listening to those men, and fell into this cupboard," said Jack. "It shut on me, and I couldn't hear another word. I didn't dare to move in case those men came to look for me. But at last I opened the door, and when I couldn't hear anything, I wondered where *you* were! So I whispered the password."

"Oh, I see," said George, thankfully. "So you didn't hear what happened to *me*? The men discovered me – and…"

"*Discovered* you! What did they do?" said Jack, in the greatest astonishment.

"It's really very peculiar," said George. "You see, *I* whispered the password too, hoping *you* would hear it. But the *men* heard me whispering "Cheeky Charlie", and they called me in and asked me if I was a messenger from him."

Jack didn't follow this, and it took George a little time to explain to him that the three men seemed really to think that someone they knew, who actually was called Cheeky Charlie, was using George as a messenger!

"And they gave *me* a message for him," said George. "In a note. I've got it in my pocket."

"No! Have you really!" said Jack, suddenly excited. "Gosh, this is thrilling. We might be in the middle of an adventure again. Let's see the note."

"No. Let's go home and then read it," said George. "I want to get out of this tumble-down old place, I don't like it a bit. Something came down the chimney on me, and I nearly had a fit. Come on, Jack, I want to go."

"Yes, but wait," said Jack, suddenly remembering. "What about Susie and Jeff? They must be somewhere here too. We ought to look for them."

"We'll have to find out how they knew there was to be a meeting here tonight," said George. "Let's call them, Jack. Honestly, there's nobody else here now. *I'm* going to call them anyway!"

So he shouted loudly: "Jeff! Susie! Come on out, wherever you are!"

His voice echoed through the old house, but nobody stirred, nobody answered.

"I'll go through the place with the torch," said Jack, and the two boys went bravely into each broken-down, bare room, flashing the light all round.

There was no one to be seen. Jack suddenly felt anxious. Susie was his sister. What had happened to her?

"George, we must go back home as quickly as we can, and tell Mother that Susie's disappeared," he said. "And Jeff has too. Come on quick! Something may have happened to them."

They went back to Jack's house as quickly as they could. As they ran to the front gate, Jack saw his mother coming back from her meeting. He rushed to her.

"Mother! Susie's missing! She's gone! Oh, Mother, she went to Tigger's Barn, and now she isn't there!"

His mother looked at him in alarm. She opened the front door quickly and went in, followed by the two boys.

"Now tell me quickly," she said. "What do you mean? Why did Susie go out? When —"

A door was flung open upstairs and a merry voice called out: "Hallo, Mother! And don't scold us because it's so late; we've been waiting for Jack and George to come back."

"Why, that's Susie," said her mother, in surprise. "What did you mean, Jack, about Susie disappearing? What a silly joke!"

Sure enough, there were Susie and Jeff upstairs, with the whole floor laid out with railway lines!

Jack stared at Susie in surprise and indignation. Hadn't she gone out, then? She grinned at him wickedly.

"Serves you right!" she said rudely. "Who came spying on our Famous Five meeting? Who heard all sorts of things and believed them? Who's been all the way to Tigger's Barn in the dark? Who's a silly-billy, who's a——"

Jack rushed at her in a rage. She dodged behind her mother, laughing.

"Now, Jack, now!" said his mother. "Stop that, please. What has been happening? Susie, go to bed. Jeff, clear up your lines. It's time for you to go. Your mother will be telephoning to ask why you are not home. Jack! Did you hear what I said? Leave Susie alone."

Jeff went to take up his lines, and George helped him. Both boys were scared of Jack's mother when she was cross. Susie ran to her room and slammed the door.

"She's a wicked girl," raged Jack, "she – she – she——"

"Go and turn on the bath-water," said his mother, sharply. "You can both go without your supper now. I *will not* have this behaviour."

George and Jeff disappeared out of the house as quickly as they could, carrying the boxes of railway things. George completely forgot what he had in his pocket – a pencilled note to someone called Cheeky Charlie, which he hadn't even read! Well, well, well!

THE RUBADUB MYSTERY

AN EXTRACT

❧ ILLUSTRATED BY ❧
GILBERT DUNLOP

Roger, Diana, Snubby and his dog, Loony, together with a friend of the family called Miss Pepper, are staying at Rubadub Inn, on the coast close to a secret submarine base. Barney and his monkey, Miranda, are also staying at the inn, along with other guests. One evening the children all go along to the show on the pier where Snubby is planning to enter the Children's Competition…

CHAPTER XV

Iris stepped forward.

"Now comes the end of our programme and perhaps the best part," she said with her engaging smile. "The Children's Competition. As usual we have two prizes of five pounds, one for the cleverest boy, and one for the cleverest girl."

A jingling noise from the Funny Man proclaimed that the money was ready and waiting. "Can I go in for it, please, Miss?" said the Funny Man pathetically. "I'm not nearly as rich as all these children here. I can sing 'Three Blind Mice' well, I can, really."

Iris went on with her little speech. "We don't mind what you do — sing, dance, recite, play our piano, tell us a funny story — or even do a bit of conjuring that will put Mr Marvel into the shade. Now come along — who will be first?"

Two small girls and a boy pushed their way eagerly to the stage. Another girl followed, and two more boys. Roger gave Snubby a nudge. "Go on! Do your stuff too, Snubby."

But Snubby was unaccountably overcome with nerves, and he glowered at Roger. "I'm not going to make a fool of myself, so shut up."

The children proved very ordinary indeed. Two of the girls played the piano, thumping hard and strong. One boy sang a comic song, of which nobody could hear a single word.

Another small girl did a competent little step dance, but was obviously so conceited that nobody clapped very much except her fond and admiring mama, who must nearly have worn the skin off her hands.

Then a boy about Snubby's age gave a recitation at top speed so that nobody could follow it at all. He then retired from the platform, also at top speed, quite overcome by his effort.

The third boy refused to perform after all. He stood up on the platform the picture of misery.

"I've forgot me words," he kept saying. "I've forgot me words. Mum, what's me words?"

Mum had apparently forgotten them, too, so the small boy left the platform in tears.

"Now now, children!" said Iris reprovingly. "I'm *sure* there's somebody else who can try for the five pounds. We do badly want another boy."

"Let *me* try, Miss, do let *me* try," urged the Funny Man, putting on a little-boy voice. "I can do things lovely! Oh yes, I can! I'm top of my form, I am, for singing and whistling." He pursed up his mouth to whistle, but hard as he blew, no sound came. So he produced a big whistle from his pocket and blew on that, making Iris jump violently. Everyone laughed, he was so idiotic.

"One more boy!" urged Iris. "Just one. Then we shall have had three girls performing and three boys."

The Funny Man came to stand beside Iris. He looked straight at Snubby. Then he pointed at him. "Look, Iris," he said, "there's the World's Wonder down there. See him? Chap with red hair, turned-up nose and freckles! Finest banjo player the world has ever seen. Pays a hundred pounds for each of his banjos. Whew!"

Everyone craned their necks to look at Snubby. He went scarlet to the roots of his red hair. "Come on, son!" cried the Funny Man. "Shy are you? Not you! Come on up and play us your banjo. Tell us your tune and the pianist will accompany you."

"Go on, Snubby," said Roger. "You've got to, now. Those other boys were frightful."

Snubby went up to the platform, half annoyed, half pleased at the Funny Man's patter. He stood facing the audience. The Funny Man solemnly placed a chair beside him. "To put your leg up on," he informed him. "That's a heavy banjo you have there. Rest it on your leg, mate. Now – what's your tune?"

Snubby suddenly entered into the fun of it. He laughed. "I'll play you 'What's the time when it's twelve o'clock'," he announced, and put his leg up on the chair. The song he had chosen was very popular just then, a silly jigging tune that was admirable for the banjo. The pianist nodded. He knew the tune well.

"I must just tune up," said Snubby, and he solemnly tuned up the strings of his imaginary banjo, making twanging noises as if he really were screwing the wires to their correct pitch. People began to laugh.

"Right. Ready?" said Snubby to the pianist. "Not too loud, please. Tune all through, the chorus twice."

He brought his hand down on imaginary strings and made a startling twanging noise. Then off he went, twanging away with his right hand, making a most remarkable banjo-like noise that followed the tune absolutely correctly. Snubby could make his noises very loudly, and the pianist did not drown him at all, but followed him perfectly. They made an excellent pair.

"Twang-a-twang-twang-twang, twang-a-twang-twang," went Snubby, and ended off with what sounded like a marvellous chord. He put down his leg and bowed solemnly.

He got more applause than any other member of the show had been given, even more than Mr Marvel! He looked such an odd, cheeky, amusing fellow with his red hair and wide grin. Everyone yelled for more.

"One more – can you manage it?" asked the Funny Man, delighted. "Any other instrument?"

"I've happened to bring my zither," said Snubby solemnly, and put down his imaginary banjo and took up his imaginary zither. "I'll have to sit down for this, please."

He sat down, and once more he and the pianist gave an extraordinary performance together. Snubby reproduced the harp-like sounds of a zither perfectly, and instead of a jiggy song, he chose a romantic tune, "If I could only give you the moon". He didn't sing it, of course, but made the sound of a zither playing the tune. It was most remarkable. Everyone listened intently, Miss Pepper feeling more surprised than she had ever felt in her life.

Fancy *Snubby*, the crazy, idiotic *Snubby* holding a big audience like this with just a little make-believe! Roger and Diana felt swollen up with pride to think they had such a clever cousin!

The tune ended. The Funny Man bowed to Snubby. "Quite a maestro!" he said, and Snubby wondered whether he was being rude or complimentary. He had never heard the word before. But the Funny Man was delighted with him. He turned to the audience. "And now to give out the prizes," he said. "We award the girl's prize to little Lorna Jones for her step dancing."

There was very slight applause. Certainly Lorna had been good, but nobody had liked the little show-off.

"The boy's prize goes – of course – to our young friend here, for..."

But the rest of his words were drowned in claps and stamps and cheers. Evidently everyone approved of that award. Snubby, redder than ever, bowed, and took the five pounds. What an evening! Whoever would have thought that his crazy habit of strumming imaginary musical instruments would have brought Snubby such tumultuous applause?

CHAPTER XVI
WHAT HAPPENED IN THE NIGHT

Snubby walked home in a whirl of excitement. "Now don't let all this go to your head," said Roger, afraid that Snubby might become quite unbearable. "After all, you can't *really* play the banjo or the zither – and you can only pick out 'chopsticks' on the piano. You're no musician, really."

"And for goodness' sake don't play banjos and things all over the hotel," begged Diana. "They won't like it a bit if you do."

Snubby took not the slightest notice. "I've been wondering if I could do an organ," he said. "Or a drum."

"*No*, Snubby," said Miss Pepper firmly. "Oh dear, here comes Miss Twitt. Hurry!"

But Miss Twitt was determined to pile praises on Snubby. "The little wonder!" she said, as she hurried up to them. "What a little marvel! The clever little boy. He's a born player, isn't he, Miss Pepper?"

"Well – I wouldn't say *that*," said Miss Pepper. "He can't play a note, actually."

"Fancy that! It just shows how wonderful he is to make people think he *can* play!" prattled Miss Twitt. "I *quite* thought it was a real banjo, you know. He really *ought* to join the pierrots, oughtn't he? Everyone would come to hear him!"

Miss Pepper glanced at Snubby and was horrified to see a pleased and fatuous smile on his face. He was drinking it all in!

"Snubby's little tricks are quite all right to amuse his friends at school," she said firmly. "But that's really all they are. It's silly to think them anything else, Miss Twitt."

Fortunately they had now reached the inn. "I want a drink," announced Snubby. "All that twang-a-twanging has made me thirsty. Can I have a lemonade, Miss Pepper – two if you like? Oh, I say – wait a bit, though – I'd forgotten my five pounds. Drinks all round, please! What'll you have, Miss Pepper? Miss Twitt? Orangeade? Lemonade? Or go a splash and have ginger-beer?"

Diana began to giggle. Snubby really could be very funny. Miss Pepper ordered the drinks and then sent all three children, and a very sleepy Loony, up to bed.

"It's late," she said. "Very late. Take your orangeade with you. No, Snubby, I don't care if you have five pounds or ten pounds, you can't have more than one orangeade. No, Loony can't have one either. Water is quite good enough for him."

Snubby went off sorrowfully. He had hoped to stay downstairs until Iris, Mr Marvel and the Funny Man came back, and also Professor James, who had still not returned. Praise from them would be worth a hundred times more than fulsome words from Miss Twitt.

Snubby was too excited to go to sleep that night. Roger snored gently and peacefully while Snubby tossed and turned, his mind full of wonderful plans. He would practise more and more imaginary instruments to play. He would appear on platforms in great halls. He would broadcast – perhaps he wouldn't, though, because people might think he was *really* playing a banjo or zither or guitar – they wouldn't be able to *see* that he hadn't really got one.

Well, what about television, then? That would be the thing. And what about a drum? He was sure he could make that big BOOM-BOOM noise. He began to practise it very softly. Then he couldn't resist doing a very loud BOOM!

And then a most frightening thing happened. As soon as Snubby had delivered his BOOM, another BOOM came – a terrific one, muffled and very frightening. The inn shook. Snubby sat up in bed, scared.

Bombs! he thought. No – can't be. Of course – it's an explosion in the Submarine Bay. Some experiment like the one we heard the other day.

He thought for a moment. But wait a minute – this is the middle of the night – about half-past two, I should think. They wouldn't experiment then, and wake everyone up.

The noise hadn't, however, awakened Roger, who was in his deepest sleep. It hadn't awakened Diana either. Miss Pepper had heard it, and had sat up, listening. But as there was no more sound she had lain down again.

Snubby felt restless. He couldn't possibly lie down and go to sleep tonight. A thought flashed into his head. He would go up that little stairway that led to the

skylight, open it, and peer out. He *might* be able to see something through that cleft in the cliff — something down in the Submarine Bay!

He slipped out of bed and went to the door. He opened it and went out on to the dark landing. Nobody seemed to be stirring. Perhaps they hadn't heard the noise then.

Snubby stole to the little door that shut off the steep staircase. He opened it quietly. Yes — there was the staircase — he could feel it with his foot though he couldn't see it. He went up cautiously. It was a clear night and Snubby could see stars shining through the little square of glass set in the middle of the trap-door that opened on to the roof.

He opened it, pushing it back carefully, so as not to make a sound. He looked out.

Gosh! Something *had* happened down in the Submarine Bay. Snubby could see quite clearly through the cleft in the cliff. Far away, on the other side of it, was the bay, and something was burning there, on the water. Searchlights were playing here and there. Snubby held his breath. Something had happened. Some awful accident, perhaps. He wished he could see more.

"Perhaps if I climb right out of the trap-door I can find a bit higher place to see from," he thought. "It would be quite easy."

He climbed to the topmost stair and found it simple to get out on the roof, which, just there, was flat. Snubby looked round. There was a rise in the roof just to the right of him, where a set of chimneys rose up together. He could sit on the little rise, beside a chimney.

He made his way cautiously across to the rise in the roof, and crawled up it on hands and knees. Now he was by a chimney. But the wind swept him that side, so he crawled round in between two chimneys where he was well protected. One chimney was warm — good!

But to his disappointment he couldn't see much more of the bay than he had seen before, although he was now a little higher. Searchlights were still criss-crossing, and the flames of whatever was burning were still as high. Perhaps a submarine had exploded and was on fire.

Snubby cuddled up to the warm chimney, feeling daring to be out on the roof in the middle of the night. He suddenly sniffed the air.

He could smell something. What was it? Cigarette smoke! Couldn't be! No one else was up on the roof in the middle of the night — smoking a cigarette too!

He craned his neck round the chimney, and saw, in the distance, a tiny glow, the red, burning end of somebody's cigarette. Someone else had heard the explosion then and had come to see what could be seen.

He soon saw that the glowing end was just where the trap-door opened on to the roof. Somebody must be standing on the stairs there, looking out and smoking. Snubby was just about to give a low call to tell them that he, too, was there, and had heard everything, when he stopped himself.

No. He'd get into a frightful row for being out on the roof at night. If Miss Pepper heard of it she would be furious. There wouldn't be any second helpings for the rest of the holidays! Silence was best. But *who* was it there? Snubby screwed up his eyes, but he could only make out a blob of a head with the glowing end of the cigarette in front.

After a while the smoker finished his cigarette and threw it down the roof. Snubby heard the soft creak of the stairs. Somebody was going down them – but that somebody had shut down the trap-door first! Snubby's heart missed a beat or two. He could imagine himself sitting out on the roof all night – falling asleep – rolling down the roof – oh, how simply horrible!

He crept across to the trap-door. As he got there, a light sprang up in the window of a room some distance away. Snubby stopped. Who was in there? Probably whoever it was, was the smoker of a few minutes before – he must have returned to his room and switched on his light. Snubby decided to see who it was.

He crawled to another position, and found that he could look right across the roof into the lighted room. The curtains were drawn across, but there was a space of about a foot left in the middle.

"Gosh! It's old Professor James!" said Snubby. "What a good thing I didn't let him know I was up here. He'd have told Mrs Glump and Miss Pepper and got me into an awful row!"

He tried the trap-door with a trembling hand. Had the Professor slipped the catch into place, so that it could not be opened?

With an enormous sigh of relief Snubby found that he *could* open it. Thank goodness! He swung it back, and then clambered on to the narrow wooden stairway. He closed the trap-door quietly and then climbed down the stairs. He opened the door at the bottom, went on to the landing and back to his room. Roger was still fast asleep.

Just as he was about to shut his door he saw a line of light under a door nearby. It was Mr Marvel's door. So he had heard the explosion too. Snubby debated whether to go in and have a chat about it – surely Mr Marvel would welcome him now that he had given such a fine performance in the show!

He decided against it, however. Mr Marvel wasn't quite the person to enjoy a midnight chat. He might start to do a bit more unpleasant magic on Snubby!

CHAPTER XVII
THE NEXT DAY

In the morning the whole inn was agog with the news of the explosion in the night. So were the papers.

GREAT EXPLOSION IN HUSH-HUSH BAY, said the headlines. WAS IT SABOTAGE? ARE OUR SECRETS SAFE? INHABITANTS OF SURROUNDING TOWNS ALMOST HURLED FROM THEIR BEDS.

"What a lie!" said Snubby. "The bed just shook, that's all. And you didn't even wake, Roger. I did!"

"Did you?" said Roger. "Was it really a big explosion?"

"Terrific," said Snubby. "Tremendous. Louder than thunder. I got out of bed and went up that stairway to look out of the trap-door – and I saw something burning like anything. And searchlights going like mad over the bay."

"Sh! Miss Pepper will hear you," said Diana. "She'd be furious if she thought you went wandering about at night – especially up to the roof."

"She didn't hear," said Snubby. He glanced round. Old Professor James was nearby reading a newspaper. He was deaf so he wouldn't have heard either. Mr Marvel and the Funny Man were also near – they would have heard, but probably they didn't know about the staircase anyway.

"I did something else too," said Snubby, lowering his voice. "I got out on the roof and sat beside a jolly warm chimney. Somebody else came up the staircase and looked out too. The old Professor, I think. Fancy him hearing the explosion and not you, Roger!"

"I expect the vibration woke him, not the noise," said Diana. "I say – it's pretty serious, isn't it? One of our newest submarines blown up to the surface – and then burned to nothing! I do wish you'd woken me up, Snubby!"

"You'd have hated seeing it," said Snubby. "Is it sabotage, do you think? I mean – would it be possible for any one to get into the bay and do a thing like that to damage us? I should have thought things were much too strict and closely guarded."

"It was probably an accident," said Roger. "You can't have successful experiments without accidents. Look at the things that happen in the lab at school!"

"Oh well — we *plan* some of those," said Snubby. "A bit of well-planned trickery! All the same — I'd like to know if it *was* an accident. I don't want to think of people somewhere around planning to blow up more submarines — especially while we're staying here."

"Why? Are you afraid of being mixed up in another mystery?" asked Roger with a grin.

"*Afraid!*" said Snubby with scorn. "I *like* mysteries. I dote on them. But this isn't a mystery, it seems to me. I bet it's an accident."

Whether it was or not they didn't learn from any of the papers that morning or evening. The press seemed to shut down on the incident, which annoyed the children very much.

That afternoon was wet. The rain poured down and the children looked gloomy.

"It's a glumpish afternoon," said Snubby. "What shall we do? Shall I practise my banjo?"

"Not unless you go up on the roof or somewhere far away," said Roger. Snubby had produced his imaginary banjo, zither, guitar and harp at different times that day, and Roger and Diana were getting a little tired of the remarkable twanging, zizzing, buzzing sounds produced by Snubby.

"Let's go up that little stairway and see if the poor old submarine is still burning," said Snubby. "I promise I won't take any musical instruments with me!"

They ran upstairs to their landing and went to the little door that enclosed the staircase. Snubby turned the handle. But the door wouldn't open!

"What's the matter with it? Is it stuck?" he said, and pulled violently. All that happened was that the handle came completely off in his hand and he sat down heavily on a startled Loony.

"Ass! You *would* do that!" said Roger.

"Things always come off in my hand," complained Snubby. "Now what shall we do?"

"You'll have to go and own up to Mrs Glump," said Diana. "Go on, Snubby. If you were brave enough to get out and sit on the roof last night, surely you're brave enough to confess to Mrs Glump."

So Snubby had to go and find Mrs Glump. She was in a peculiar little den, adding up rows and rows of figures, and didn't look at all pleased to see Snubby. He explained what had happened.

"But why did you pull at the handle so violently?" asked Mrs Glump, resting her face on her four or five chins, and looking most majestic. Snubby wished he had a few chins he could look majestic with too. He felt very small beside Mrs Glump, and she made him feel like a naughty little boy.

"Well, I pulled hard because the door stuck," said Snubby. "It's locked, I think."

"Locked! But the key would be in the lock anyway," said Mrs Glump.

"There wasn't a key. I looked," said Snubby. "I'm sure it's locked, Mrs Glump. I thought you must have locked it. I'm sorry about the handle. I've still got two pounds left out of the five I won at the end-of-pier show yesterday. Would that pay for a new handle?"

"I expect so," said Mrs Glump. "But I'm sure Danny has an old one he could fix on quickly. Go and ask him. And I hear I must congratulate you on winning the prize yesterday. Let me see – you played the banjo, didn't you?"

"Not a real one. My imaginary one. Paid a hundred pounds for it!" said Snubby with a grin, and immediately began to play a jigging, strident tune, twang-twanging in a most lifelike manner.

Mrs Glump began to laugh. She had a very curious laugh. It seemed to begin somewhere deep down and then rumbled all the way past her magnificent chins, and came out as a very hearty affair indeed.

Snubby stopped, bowed and grinned. "You're a caution," said Mrs Glump. "Get on with you! Go and find Danny about the handle. And don't shut my door too violently in case the whole door comes off in your hand."

Snubby went out, pleasantly surprised. She wasn't really glumpish at all! He made his way to the kitchen to find Danny. He was polishing some horse-brasses one by one and making a very good job of it.

"Hallo, Danny. Can I help you? I collect horse-brasses too," said the cheerful Snubby. "I say, did you hear about me winning five pounds at the show last night?"

Danny listened and nodded. "You," he said. "You win. Good boy."

"My word, you *are* a chatterbox today," said Snubby, rubbing vigorously at a brass.

"What you do?" asked Danny earnestly.

"This," said Snubby, and played his imaginary banjo again. To his enormous surprise, Danny also picked up an imaginary banjo and began to twang it, making a most peculiar noise as he did so, almost as good as Snubby's!

"Here — what's all this?" said a voice, and the face of the young waiter poked round the door. "Some band performing here?"

Danny fled at once, out into the backyard. He sat down, blinking his eyes, confused. Years and years ago he had had a real banjo and he could play it. But when he had fallen from the rope, during a wire-walking act, he had hurt his head — and after that Danny was different. Poor Danny!

He sat till his mind cleared a little. He began to smile. Yes — he remembered his old banjo — and the tunes he played. He twanged imaginary strings again.

Snubby came into the yard to find him. "Oh, there you are, Danny. I say, I forgot to tell you what I wanted you for. Have you got a spare door-handle? I've somehow pulled off the handle of the door that shuts in that little stairway leading to the roof."

"Roof," said Danny. He stared at Snubby and then suddenly leaned forward. He whispered loudly in his ear. "Mind bad men up there! Bad men!"

Snubby drew back, startled. Danny smiled and nodded at him. Then his face grew solemn again. "Bad, bad, bad," he whispered again. "Danny see. Danny watch. Danny follow. Bad!"

Snubby looked at Danny doubtfully. Poor old fellow — what peculiar imaginings had he got now? He couldn't imagine Danny watching people and stalking them! Snubby decided to humour him.

"Snubby see. Snubby watch. Snubby follow," he said, equally solemnly. "Gosh, we sound like Red Indians or something. Danny, where's an old door-handle? Let's find one and go in. I'm not too keen on sitting out here in the rain — twang-a-twang-twang-twang, zizz-a-zizz-ziz-ziz. Ker-plonk! There — I knew a string would bust if I played out in the rain. See that?"

He held out his imaginary banjo, and Danny laughed delightedly. It was the first time Snubby had heard him laugh. It was a ripple, just like a very young child's. Snubby patted Danny on the back.

"That's right. Laugh your troubles away! Have you got a door-handle, for the third time of asking?"

Danny had. He produced one from a shed and went upstairs. He was clever with his fingers and had soon fixed it on the door. He gave it a pull.

"Locked," said Snubby. "And the key's gone. Who did that? And why? I tell you, Danny, there were mysterious goings on up here last night!"

"Indeed? And what were they?" said a voice.

Snubby jumped and turned round. Mr Marvel the conjurer was standing outside his door. Snubby thought furiously. No – he wasn't going to give anything away and get himself into trouble.

"Oh, nothing," he said airily. "I was just putting the wind up old Danny. I say, sir – that was a wizard act you put on last night. How did you guess those articles – and the initials on the back of the watch? Beats me!"

"That's *my* secret," said Mr Marvel. "Did you hear the explosion last night?"

"Yes. I jolly well did," said Snubby. "Did you?"

"No, I didn't," said Mr Marvel, which surprised Snubby very much. Hadn't he seen a line of light under Mr Marvel's door when he, Snubby, had come down from the roof to go to bed again?

"I saw a light under your door though," blurted out Snubby, and could have kicked himself.

"Indeed? And what were *you* doing out on the landing at that time of night?" said Mr Marvel at once.

"Just peeped out to see if anyone was awake after the explosion," said Snubby. "I say, sir – you *were* clever at the show last night!"

But Mr Marvel was gone. Snubby was left staring at a closing door. He made a face at it. All right – *be* snorty, Mr Marvel! You *were* awake last night! Snubby shook a furious fist, marched into his own room, and slammed the door!

FIVE GO DOWN TO THE SEA

AN EXTRACT

~ ILLUSTRATED BY ~
EILEEN SOPER

The Famous Five are staying with Mr and Mrs Penruthlan at Tremannon Farm in Cornwall, where they meet Yan, whose great-grandad works as a shepherd on the farm. It is the first Sunday morning of their holiday, and they are all out in the farmyard.

CHAPTER V
YAN – AND HIS GRANDAD

The next day was Sunday. It made no difference to the time that the two Penruthlans got up, however. As Mrs Penruthlan said, the cows and horses, hens and ducks didn't approve of late Sunday breakfasts! They wanted attending to at exactly the same time each day!

"Will you be going to church?" asked Mrs Penruthlan. "It's a beautiful walk across the fields to Tremannon Church, and you'd like Parson. He's a good man, he is."

"Yes, we're all going," said Julian. "We can tie Timmy up outside. He's used to that. And we thought we'd go up and see your old shepherd this afternoon, Mrs Penruthlan, and see what tales he has to tell."

"Yan will show you the way," said the farmer's wife, bustling off to her cooking. "I'll get you a fine Sunday lunch. Do you like fresh fruit salad with cream?"

"You bet!" said everyone at once.

"Can't we help you to do something?" said Anne. "I've just seen all the peas you're going to shell. Piles of them! And don't you want help with those redcurrants? I love getting the currants off their stalks with a fork!"

"Well, you'll have a few odd minutes before you go to church, I expect," said Mrs Penruthlan, looking pleased. "It *would* be a bit of help today. But the boys needn't help."

"I like that!" said George, indignantly. "How unfair! Why shouldn't they, just because they're boys?"

"Don't fly off the handle, George," grinned Dick. "We're going to help, don't worry. We like podding peas too! You're not going to have all the treats!"

Dick had a very neat way of turning the tables on George when he saw her flying into a tantrum. She smiled unwillingly. She was always jealous of the boys because she so badly wanted to be one herself, and wasn't! She hitched up her shorts, and went to get a pan of peas to shell.

Soon the noise of the popping of pods was to be heard, a very pleasant noise, Anne thought. The four of them sat on the big kitchen step, out in the sun, with Timmy sitting beside them, watching with interest. He didn't stay with them long though.

Up came his four friends, the little Scottie trotting valiantly behind, trying to keep up with the longer legs of the others. "Woof!" said the biggest collie. Timmy wagged his tail politely, but didn't stir.

"Woof!" said the collie again, and pranced around invitingly.

"Timmy! He says 'Will you come and play?'," said George. "Aren't you going? You aren't the least help with shelling peas, and you keep breathing down my neck."

Timmy gave George a flying lick and leaped off the step joyfully. He pounced on the Scottie, rolled him over, and then took on all three collies at once. They were big, strong dogs, but no match for Timmy!

"Look at him," said George, proudly. "He can manage the whole lot single-handed."

"Single-footed!" said Dick. "He's faster than even that biggest collie and stronger than the whole lot. Good old Tim. He's come in jolly useful in some of our adventures!"

"I've no doubt he will again," said Julian. "I'd rather have one Timmy than two police dogs."

"I should think his ears are burning, the way we're talking about him!" said Anne. "Oh, sorry, Dick, that pod popped unexpectedly!"

"That's the second lot of peas you've shot all over me," said Dick, scrabbling inside his shirt. "I *must* just find one that went down my neck, or I shall be fidgeting all through church."

"You always do," said Anne. "Look — isn't that Yan?"

It was! He came sidling up, looking as dirty as ever, and gave them a quick smile that once more entirely changed his sullen little face. He held out his hand, palm upwards, and said something.

"What's he saying?" said Dick. "Oh, he's asking for a sweet."

"Don't give him one," said Julian, quickly. "Don't turn him into a little beggar. Make him *work* for a sweet this time. Yan, if you want a sweet, you can help pod these peas."

Mrs Penruthlan appeared at once. "But see he washes those filthy hands first," she commanded, and disappeared again. Yan looked at his hands, then put them under his armpits.

"Go and wash them," said Julian. But Yan shook his head, and sat down a little way away from them.

"All right. Don't wash your hands. Don't shell the peas. Don't have a sweet," said George.

Yan scowled at George. He didn't seem to like her any more than she liked him. He waited till someone split a pod, and a few peas shot out on the ground instead of into the dish. Then he darted at them, picked them up and ate them. He was as quick as a cat.

"My grandad says come and see him," announced Yan. "I'll take you."

"Right," said Julian. "We'll come this afternoon. We'll get Mrs Penruthlan to pack us up a basket, and we'll have a tea in the hills. You can share it if you wash your hands and face."

"I shouldn't think he's ever washed himself in his life," said George. "Oh, here's Timmy come back. I *will* not have him fawn round that dirty little boy. Here, Timmy!"

But Timmy darted to Yan with the greatest delight and pawed at him to come and have a game. They began to roll over and over like two puppies.

"If you're going to church, you'd better get ready," said Mrs Penruthlan, appearing again, this time with arms floured up to the elbow. "My, what a lot of peas you've done for me!"

"I wish I had time to do the reducurrants," said Anne. "We've practically finished the peas, anyway, Mrs Penruthlan. We've done thousands, I should think!"

"Ah, Mr Penruthlan is very fond of peas," said the farmer's wife. "He can eat a whole tureen at one sitting."

She disappeared again. The children went to get ready for church, and then off they went. It certainly was a lovely walk over the fields, with honeysuckle trailing everywhere!

The church was small and old and lovely. Yan went with them, trailing behind, right to the church door. When he saw George tying Timmy up to a railing, he sat down beside him and looked pleased. George didn't look pleased, however. Now Timmy and Yan would play about together all the time she was in church! How annoying!

The church was cool and dark, except for three lovely stained-glass windows through which the sun poured, its brilliance dimmed by the colours of the glass. "Parson" was as nice as Mrs Penruthlan had said, a simple friendly person whose words were listened to by everyone, from an old, old woman bent almost double in a corner to a solemn-eyed five-year-old clutching her mother's hand.

It was dazzling to come out into the sun again from the cool dimness of the church. Timmy barked a welcome. Yan was still there, sitting with his arm round Timmy's neck. He gave them his sudden smile, and untied Timmy, who promptly went mad and tore out of the churchyard at sixty miles an hour. He always did that when he had been tied up.

"Come and see Grandad," said Yan to Dick, and pulled at his arm.

"This afternoon," said Dick. "You can show us the way. Come after lunch."

So, after the children had had a lunch of cold boiled beef and carrots, with a dumpling each, and lashings of peas and new potatoes, followed by a truly magnificent fruit salad and cream, Yan appeared at the door to take them to see his grandad.

"Did you see the amount of peas that Mr Penruthlan got through?" said Anne, in awe. "I should think he really *did* manage a tureen all to himself. I wish he'd say something besides 'Ah' and 'Ock' and the other peculiar sounds he makes. Conversation is awfully difficult with him."

"Is Yan taking you up to Grandad?" called Mrs Penruthlan. "I'll put a few cakes in the basket for him, too, then, and for Grandad."

"*Don't* make us up a big tea," begged Dick. "We only want a snack, just to keep us going till high tea."

But all the same the basket was quite heavy when Mrs Penruthlan had finished packing it!

It was a long walk over the fields to the shepherd's hut. Yan led the way proudly. They crossed the fields and climbed stiles, walked up narrow cart-paths, and at last came to a cone-shaped hill on which sheep grazed peacefully. Half-grown lambs, wearing their woolly coats, unlike the shorn sheep, gambolled here and there – then remembered that they were nearly grown up, and walked sedately.

The old shepherd was sitting outside his hut, smoking a clay pipe. He wasn't very big, and he seemed shrivelled up, like an apple stored too long. But there was still sweetness in him, and the children liked him at once. He had Yan's sudden smile which lit up eyes that were still as blue as the summer sky above.

His face had a thousand wrinkles that creased and ran into one another when he smiled. His shaggy eyebrows, curly beard and hair were all grey, as grey as the woolly coats of the sheep he had lived with all his life.

"You're welcome," he said, in his slow Cornish voice. "Yan told me about you."

"We've brought our tea to share with you," said Dick. "We'll have it later on. Is it true that your father was one of the Wreckers in the old days?"

The old fellow nodded his head. Julian got out a bag of boiled sweets, and offered them to the old man. He took one eagerly. Yan edged up at once and was given one too.

Judging by the crunching that went on old Grandad still had plenty of teeth! When the sweet had gone, he began to talk. He talked slowly and simply, almost as Yan might have done, and sometimes paused to find a word he wanted.

Living with sheep all his life doesn't make for easy talking, thought Julian, interested in this old man with the wise, keen eyes. He must be much more at home with sheep than with human beings.

Grandad certainly had some interesting things to tell them, dreadful things, Anne thought.

"You've seen the rocks down on Tremannon coast," began Grandad. "Wicked rocks they are, hungry for ships and men. Many a ship has been wrecked on purpose! Ay, you can look disbelieving-like, but it's true."

"How did they get wrecked on purpose?" asked Dick. "Were they lured here by a false light, or something?"

The old man lowered his voice as if he was afraid of being overheard.

"Way back up the coast, more than a hundred years ago, there was a light set to guide the ships that sail round here," said Grandad. "They were to sail towards that light, and then hug the coast and avoid the rocks that stood out to sea. They were safe then. But, on wild nights, a light was set two miles farther down the coast, to bemuse lost ships, and drag them to the rocks round Tremannon coves."

"How wicked!" said Anne and George together. "How *could* men do that?"

"It's amazing what men will do," said Grandad, nodding his head. "Take my old dad now – a kind man he was and went to church, and took me with him. But he was the one that set the false light burning every time, and sent men to watch the ship coming in on the rocks – crashing over them and breaking into pieces."

"Did you – did you ever see a ship crashing to its death?" asked Dick, imagining the groaning of the sailing ships, and the groaning of the men flung into the raging sea.

"Ay, I did," said Grandad, his eyes taking on a very faraway look. "I was sent to the cove with the men, and had to hold a lantern to bemuse the ship again when she came to the rocks. Poor thing, she groaned like a live thing when she ran into those wicked rocks, and split into pieces. And the next day I went to the cove to help get the goods that were scattered all around the cove. There were lots drowned that night, and —"

"Don't tell us about that," said Dick, feeling sick. "Where did they flash the false light from? From these hills, or from the cliff somewhere?"

"I'll show you where my dad flashed it from," said Grandad, and he got up slowly. "There's only one place on these hills where you could see the light flashing. The Wreckers had to find somewhere well hidden, so that their wicked light couldn't be seen from inland, or the police would stop it, but it could be seen plainly by any ship on the sea near this coast!"

He took them round his hill, and then pointed towards the coast. Set between two hills there the roof of a house could just be seen, and from it rose a tower. It could only be seen from that one spot! Dick took a few steps to each side of it, and at once the house disappeared behind one or other of the hills on each side of it.

"I was the only one who ever knew the false light could be seen from inland," said Grandad, pointing with his pipe-stem towards the far-off square tower. "I was watching lambs one night up here, and I saw the light flashing. "And I heard there was a ship wrecked down in Tremannon cove that night so I reckoned it was the Wreckers at work."

"Did you often see the light flashing over there, when you watched the sheep?" asked George.

"Oh yes, many a time," said the shepherd. "And always on wild, stormy

nights, when ships were labouring along, and in trouble, looking for some light to guide them into shore. Then a light would flare out over there, and I'd say to myself, 'Now may the good God help those sailors tonight, for it's sure that nobody else will'! "

"How horrible!" said George, quite appalled at such wickedness. "You must be glad that you never see that false light shining there on stormy nights now!"

Grandad looked at George, and his eyes were scared and strange. He lowered his voice and spoke to George as if she were a boy.

"Young man," he said, "that light still flares on dark and stormy nights. The place is a ruin, and jackdaws build in the tower. But three times this year I've seen that light again! Come a stormy night it'll flare again! I know it in my bones, I know it in my bones!"

CHAPTER VI
A STRANGE TALE

The four children shivered suddenly in the hot sun, as they listened to the shepherd's strange words. Were they true? Did the Wreckers' light still flash in the old tower on wild and stormy nights? But why should it? Surely no Wreckers any longer did their dreadful work on this lonely, rocky coast?

Dick voiced the thoughts of the others. "But surely there are no wrecks on this coast now? Isn't there a good lighthouse farther up, to warn ships to keep right out to sea?"

Grandad nodded his grey head. "Yes. There's a lighthouse, and there's not been a wreck along this coast for more years than I can remember. But I tell you that light flares up just as it used to do. I see it with my own eyes, and there's nothing wrong with them yet!"

"I've seen it too," put in Yan, suddenly.

Grandad looked at Yan, annoyed. "You hold your tongue," he commanded. "You've never seen the light. You sleep like a babe at night."

"I've seen it," said Yan, obstinately, and moved out of Grandad's way quickly as the old man raised his hand to cuff the small boy.

Dick changed the subject. "Grandad, do you know anything about the Wreckers' Way?" he asked. "Is it a secret way to get down to the coves from inland? Was it used by the Wreckers?"

Grandad frowned. "That's a secret," he said shortly. "My dad showed it to me, and I swore I would never tell. We all had to swear and promise that."

"But Yan here said that you taught the way to him," said Dick, puzzled.

Yan promptly removed himself from the company and disappeared round a clump of bushes. His old great-grandad glared round at the disappearing boy.

"Yan! That boy! He doesn't know anything about the Wreckers' Way. It's lost and forgotten by every man living. I'm the last one left who knows of it. Yan! He's dreaming! Maybe he's heard tell of an old Wreckers' Way, but that's all."

"Oh!" said Dick, disappointed. He had hoped that Grandad would tell them the old way, and then they could go and explore it. Perhaps they could go and search for it, anyhow! It would be fun to do that.

Julian came back to the question of the light flashing from the old tower by the coast. He was puzzled. "Who could possibly flash that light?" he said to Grandad. "You say the place is a ruin. Are you sure it wasn't lightning you saw? You said it came on a wild and stormy night."

"It wasn't lightning," said the old man shortly. "I first saw that light near ninety years ago, and I tell you I saw it again three times this year, same place, same light, same weather! And if you told me it wasn't flashed by mortal hands, I'd believe you."

There was a silence after this extraordinary statement. Anne looked over towards the far-off tower that showed just between the two distant hills. How strange that this spot where they were standing was the only place from which the tower could be seen from inland. The Wreckers had been clever to choose a spot like that to flash a light from. No one but old Grandad up on the hills could possibly have seen the light and guessed what was going on, no one but the callous Wreckers themselves.

Grandad delved deep into more memories stored in his mind. He poured them out, tales of the old days, strange unbelievable stories. One was about an old woman who was said to be a witch. The things she did!

The four stared at the old shepherd, marvelling to think they were, in a way, linked with the witches, the Wreckers and the killers of long-ago days, through this old, old man.

Yan appeared again as soon as Julian opened the tea-basket. They had now gone back to the hut, and sat outside in the sunshine, surrounded by nibbling sheep. One or two of the half-grown lambs came up, looking hot in their unshorn woolly coats. They nosed round the old shepherd, and he rubbed their woolly noses.

"These are lambs I fed from a bottle," he explained. "They always remember. Go away now, Woolly. Cake's wasted on you."

Yan wolfed quite half the tea. He gave Anne a quick grin of pure pleasure, showing both his dimples at once. She smiled back. She liked this funny little boy now, and felt sorry for him. She was sure that his old Grandad didn't give him enough to eat!

The church bells began to ring, and the sun was now sliding down the sky. "We must go," said Julian, reluctantly. "It's quite a long walk back. Thanks for a most interesting afternoon, Grandad. I expect you'll be glad to be rid of us now, and smoke your pipe in peace with your sheep around you."

"Ay, I will," said Grandad, truthfully. "I'm one for my own company, and I like to think my own thoughts. Long thoughts they are, too, going back nearly a hundred years. If I want to talk, I talk to my sheep. It's rare and wonderful how they listen."

The children laughed, but Grandad was quite solemn, and meant every word he said. They packed up the basket, and said goodbye to the old man.

"Well, what do you think he meant when he talked about the light still flashing in the old tower?" said Dick, as they went over the hills back to the farm. "What an extraordinary thing to say. Was it true, do you suppose?"

"There's only one way to find out!" said George, her eyes dancing. "Wait for a wild and stormy night and go and see!"

"But what about our agreement?" said Julian, solemnly. "If anything exciting seems about to happen we turn our backs on it. That's what we decided. Don't you remember?"

"Pooh!" said George.

"We ought to keep the agreement," said Anne, doubtfully. She knew quite well that the others didn't think so!

"Look! Who are all these people?" said Dick, suddenly. They were just climbing over a stile to cross a lane to another field.

They sat on the stile and stared. Some carts were going by, open wagons, their canvas tops folded down. They were the most old-fashioned carts the children had ever seen, not in the least like travellers' caravans.

Ten or eleven people were with the wagons, dressed in the clothes of other days! Some rode in the wagons and some walked. Some were middle-aged, some were young, but they all looked cheerful and bright.

The children stared. After Grandad's tales of long ago these old-time folk seemed just right! For a few moments Anne felt herself back in Grandad's time, when he was a boy. He must have seen people dressed like these!

"Who are they?" she said, wonderingly. And then the children saw red lettering painted on the biggest cart: THE BARNIES.

"Oh! It's the Barnies! Don't you remember Mrs Penruthlan telling us about them?" said Anne. "The strolling players, who play to the country folk around, in the barns. What fun!"

The Barnies waved to the watching children. One man, dressed in velvet and lace, with a sword at his side, and a wig of curly hair, threw a leaflet or two to them. They read them with interest.

The Barnies are coming!
They will sing, they will dance, they will fiddle.
They will perform plays of all kinds.
Edith Wells, the nightingale singer.
Bonnie Carter, the old-time dancer.
Janie Coster and her fiddle.
John Walters, finest tenor in the world.
George Roth — he'll make you laugh!
And Others.
We also present Clopper, the Funniest Horse in the World!
The Barnies are coming!

"This'll be fun!" said George, pleased. She called out to the passing wagons: "Will you be playing at Tremannon Farm?"

"Oh, yes!" called a man with bright, merry eyes. "We always play there. You staying there?"

"Yes," said George. "We'll look out for you all. Where are you going now?"

"To Poltelly Farm for the night," called the man. "We'll be at Tremannon soon."

The wagons passed, and the cheerful, oddly-dressed players went out of sight. "Good," said Dick. "Their show may not be first-rate, but it's sure to be funny. They looked a merry lot."

"All but the man driving the front cart. Did you see him?" said Anne. "He looked pretty grim, I thought."

Nobody else had noticed him. "He was probably the owner of the Barnies," said Dick. "And has got all the organisation on his shoulders. Well, come on. Where's Timmy?"

They looked round for him, and George frowned. Yan had followed them as usual, and Timmy was playing with him. Bother Yan! Was he going to trail them all day and everyday?

They went back to the peaceful farmhouse. Hens were still clucking around and ducks were quacking. A horse stamped somewhere near by, and the grunting of pigs came on the air. It all looked quite perfect.

Footsteps came through the farmyard, and Mr Penruthlan came by. He grunted at them and went into a barn.

Anne spoke in almost a whisper. "I can imagine *him* living in the olden days

296

and being a Wrecker. I can really!"

"Yes! I know what you mean," said Dick. "He's so fierce-looking and determined. What's the word I want? *Ruthless!* I'm sure he would have made a good Wrecker!"

"Do you suppose there *are* any Wreckers now, and that light really is flashed to make ships go on the rocks?" said George.

"Well, I shouldn't have thought there were any Wreckers in this country, anyway," said Dick. "I can't imagine that such a thing would be tolerated for an instant. But if that light is flashed, what is it flashed for?"

"Old Grandad said there hadn't been any wrecks on this coast for ages," said Julian. "I think really that the old man is wandering a bit in his mind about that light!"

"But Yan said he had seen it, too," said Anne.

"I'm not sure that Yan's as truthful as he might be!" said Julian.

"Why did Grandad say that the light isn't flashed by mortal hands now?" asked George. "It must be! I can't imagine any other hands working it! He surely doesn't think that his father is still doing it?"

There was a pause. "We could easily find out if we popped over to that tower and had a look at it," said Dick.

There was another pause. "I thought we said we wouldn't go poking about in anything mysterious," said Anne.

"This isn't really mysterious," argued Dick. "It's just a story an old man remembers, and I really can't believe that that light still flashes on a wild, stormy night. Grandad must have seen lightning or something. Why don't we settle the matter for good and all and go and explore the old house with the tower?"

"I should like to," said George firmly. "I never was keen on this 'Keep away from anything unusual' idea we suddenly had. We've got Timmy with us — we can't possibly come to any harm!"

"All right," said Anne, with a sigh. "I give up. We'll go if you want to."

"Good old Anne," said Dick, giving her a friendly slap on the back. "But *you* needn't come, you know. Why don't you stay behind and hear our story when we come back?"

"Certainly *not*," said Anne, quite cross. "I may not want to go as much as you do, but I'm not going to be left out of anything, so don't think it!"

"All right. It's settled then," said Julian. "We take our opportunity and go as soon as we can. Tomorrow, perhaps."

Mrs Penruthlan came to the door and called them. "Your high tea is ready. You must be hungry. Come along indoors."

The sun suddenly went in. Julian looked up at the sky in surprise. "My word, look at those black clouds!" he said. "There's a storm coming! Well, I thought there might be, it's been so terribly hot all day!"

"A storm!" said George. "That light flashes on wild and stormy nights! Oh, Julian, do you think it will flash tonight? Can't we — *can't* we go and see?"

CHAPTER VII
OUT IN THE NIGHT

Before the children had finished their high tea, the big kitchen-sitting-room was quite dark. Thunder clouds had moved up from the west, gathering together silently, frowning and sinister. Then, from far off, came the first rumble of thunder.

The little Scottie came and cowered against Mrs Penruthlan's skirts. He hated storms. The farmer's wife comforted him, and her big husband gave a little unexpected snort of laughter. He said something that sounded like "oose".

"He's *not* as timid as a mouse," said his wife, who was really marvellous at interpreting her husband's peculiar noises. "He just doesn't like the thunder. He never did. He can sleep with us in our room tonight."

There were a few more sounds from Mr Penruthlan to which his wife listened anxiously. "Very well, if you have to get up and see to Jenny the horse in the night, I'll see Benny doesn't bark the house down," she said. She turned to the children. "Don't worry if you hear him barking," she said. "It will only be Mr Penruthlan stirring."

The thunder crashed and rumbled again, this time a little nearer, and then lightning flashed. Then down came the rain. How it poured! It rattled and clattered on the roof in enormous drops, and then settled down into a steady downpour.

The four children got out their cards and played games by the light of the oil lamp. There was no electricity at Tremannon. Timmy sat with his head on George's knee. He didn't mind the thunder but he didn't particularly like it.

"Well, I think we'd better go to bed," said Julian at last. He knew that the Penruthlans liked to go to bed early because they got up so early, and as they did not go upstairs until after the children did, Julian saw to it that they, too, went early.

They said goodnight and went up to their bare little rooms. The windows were still open and the small curtains drawn back, so that the hills, lit now and again by lightning, showed up clearly. The children went and stood there, watching. They all loved a storm, especially Dick. There was something powerful and most majestic about this kind of storm, sweeping over hills and sea, rumbling all round, and tearing the sky in half with flashes of lightning.

"Julian, is it possible to go up to that place the shepherd showed us and see if the light flashes tonight?" said George. "You only laughed when I asked you before."

"Well, I laugh again!" said Julian. "Of course not! We'd be drenched, and I

don't fancy being out in this lightning on those exposed hills, either."

"All right," said George. "Anyway, I don't feel quite such an urge to go now that it's so pitch- dark."

"Just as well," said Julian. "Come on, Dick, let's go to bed."

The storm went on for some time, rumbling all round the hills again, as if it were going round in a circle.

The girls fell asleep, but the boys tossed about, feeling hot and sticky.

"Dick," said Julian, suddenly, "let's get up and go out. It's stopped raining. Let's go and see if that light is flashing tonight. It should be just the night for it, according to old Grandad."

"Right," said Dick, and sat up, feeling for his clothes. "I simply can't go to sleep, even though I felt really sleepy when I undressed."

They pulled on as few clothes as possible, for the night was still thundery and hot. Julian took his torch and Dick hunted for his.

"Got it," he said at last. "Are you ready? Come on, then. Let's tiptoe past the Penruthlans' door, or we may wake that Scottie dog! He's sleeping there tonight, don't forget."

They tiptoed along the passage, past the Penruthlans' door and down the stairs. One stair creaked rather alarmingly, and they stopped in dismay, wondering if Ben the Scottie would break out into a storm of barking.

But he didn't. Good! Down they went again, switching on their torches to see the way. They came to the bottom of the stairs. "Shall we go out by the front door or back door, Ju?" whispered Dick.

"Back," said Julian. "The front door's so heavy to open. Come on."

So they went down the passage to the back door that led out from the kitchen. It was locked and bolted, but the two boys opened it without too much noise.

They stepped out into the night. The rain had now stopped, but the sky was still dark and overclouded. The thunder rumbled away in the distance. A wind had got up and blew coolly against the boys' faces.

"Nice cool breeze," whispered Dick. "Now – do we go through the farmyard? Is that the shortest way to the stile we have to climb over into that first field?"

"Yes, I think so," said Julian. They made their way across the silent farmyard, where, in the daytime, such a lot of noise went on, clucking, quacking, grunting, clip-clopping, and shouting!

Now it was dark and deserted. They passed the barns and the stables. A little "hrrrrrumphing" came from one of the stables. "That's Jenny, the horse that's not well," said Julian, stopping. "Let's just have a look at her and see if she's all right. She was lying down feeling very sorry for herself when I saw her last."

They flashed their torch over the top half of the stable door, which was pulled back to let in air. They looked in with interest.

Jenny was no longer lying down. She was standing up, munching something. Goodness, she must be quite all right again! She whinnied to the two boys.

They left her and went on. They came to the stile and climbed over. The rain began drizzling again, and if the boys had not had their torches with them they would not have been able to see a step in front of them, it was so dark.

"I say, Ju – did you hear that?" said Dick, stopping suddenly.

"No. What?" said Julian, listening.

"Well, it sounded like a cough," said Dick.

300

"One of the sheep," suggested Julian. "I heard one old sheep coughing just like Uncle Quentin does sometimes, sort of hollow and mournful."

"No. It wasn't a sheep," said Dick. "Anyway, there aren't any in this field."

"You imagined it," said Julian. "I bet there's nobody idiotic enough to be out on a night like this, except ourselves!"

They went on cautiously over the field. The thunder began again, a little nearer. Then came a flash, and again the thunder. Dick stopped dead once more and clutched Julian's arm.

"There's somebody a good way in front of us, the lightning just lit him up for half a second. He was climbing over that stile, the one we're making for. Who do you suppose it is on a night like this?"

"He's apparently going the same way that we are," said Julian. "Well, I suppose if we saw *him* he's quite likely to have seen *us!*"

"Not unless he was looking backwards," said Dick. "Come on, let's see where he's going."

They went on cautiously towards the stile. They came to it and climbed over. And then a hand suddenly clutched hold of Dick's shoulder!

He jumped almost out of his skin! The hand gripped him so hard and so fiercely that Dick shouted in pain and tried to wriggle away from the powerful grip.

Julian felt a hand lunge at him, too, but dodged and pressed himself into the hedge. He switched off his torch at once and stood quite still, his heart thumping.

"Let me go!" shouted Dick, wriggling like an eel. His shirt was almost torn off his back in his struggles. He kicked out at the man's ankles and for one moment his captor loosened his grasp. That was enough for Dick. He ripped himself away and left his shirt in the man's hand!

He ran up the lane into which the stile had led and flung himself under a bush in the darkness, panting. He heard his captor coming along, muttering, and Dick pressed himself farther into the bush. A torchlight swept the ground near him, but missed him.

Dick waited till the footsteps had gone and then crawled out. He went quietly down the lane. "Julian!" he whispered, and jumped as a voice answered almost in his ear, just above his head!

"I'm here. Are you all right?"

Dick looked up into the darkness of a tree, but could see nothing. "I've dropped my torch somewhere," he said. "Where are you, Ju? Up in the tree?"

A hand groped out and felt his head. "Here I am, on the first branch," said Julian, "I hid in the hedge first and then climbed up here. I daren't put on my torch in case that fellow's anywhere around and sees it."

"He's gone up the lane," said Dick. "My word, he nearly wrenched my shoulder off. Half my shirt's gone! Who was he? Did you see?"

"No. I didn't," said Julian, clambering down. "Let's find your torch before we go home. It's too good to lose. It must be by that stile."

They went to look. Julian still didn't like to put on his torch, so that it was more a question of feeling for Dick's torch, not looking! Dick suddenly trod on it and picked it up thankfully.

"Listen, there's that fellow coming back again, I'm sure!" said Dick. "I heard the same dry little cough! What shall we do?"

"Well, I don't now feel like going up to the shepherd's hill to see if that light is flashing from the tower," said Julian. "I vote we hide and follow this chap to see where he goes. I don't think anyone who is wandering out tonight can be up to any good."

"Yes. Good idea," said Dick. "Squash into the hedge again. Blow, there are nettles here! Just my luck."

The footsteps came nearer, and the cough came again. "I seem to know that cough," whispered Dick.

"Sh!" said Julian.

The man came up to the stile, and they heard him climbing over it. After a short time both boys followed cautiously. They couldn't hear the man's footsteps across the grass, but the sky had cleared a little and they could just make out a moving shadow ahead of them.

They followed him at a distance, holding their breath whenever they kicked against a stone or cracked a twig beneath their feet. Now and again they heard the cough.

"He's making for the farm," whispered Julian. He could just see the outline of the big barns against the sky. "Do you think he's one of the labourers? They live in cottages round about."

The man came to the farmyard and walked through it, trying to make as little sound as possible. The boys followed. He went round the barns and into the little garden that Mrs Penruthlan tended herself. Still the boys followed.

Round to the front door went the man, and the boys held their breath. Was he going to burgle the farmhouse? They tiptoed nearer. There came the sound of a soft click, and then of bolts being shot home! After that there was silence.

"He's gone in," said Julian in amazement.

"Don't you know who it was? Can't you guess now?" said Dick. "We both ought to have known when we heard that cough! It was Mr Penruthlan! No wonder he almost dislocated my shoulder with his strong hand!"

"*Mr Penruthlan* — gosh, yes, you're right," said Julian, astonished, almost forgetting to speak in a whisper. "We didn't notice that the front door was undone because we went out the back way. So it was him we followed. How silly! But what was he doing out on the hills? He didn't go to see the horse, she wasn't ill."

"Perhaps he likes a walk at night," suggested Dick. "Come on, let's go in ourselves. I feel a bit chilly with practically no shirt on!"

They crept round to the back door. It was still open, thank goodness! They went inside, bolted and locked it, and tiptoed upstairs. They heaved sighs of relief when they were safely in their room again.

"Switch on your torch, Julian, and see if my shoulder is bruised," said Dick. "It feels jolly painful."

Julian flashed his torch on Dick's shoulder. He gave a low whistle. "My word, you've got a wonderful bruise all down your right shoulder. He must have given you an awful wrench."

"He did," said poor Dick. "Well, I can't say we had a very successful time. We followed our host through the night, got caught by him, and then followed him all the way back here. Not very clever!"

"Well, never mind, I bet no light flashed in that tower," said Julian, getting into bed. "We haven't lost much by not going all the way to see!"

GOOD WORK, SECRET SEVEN

AN EXTRACT

◗ ILLUSTRATED BY ◖
BRUNO KAY

*Peter and Janet, two members of the Secret Seven, have been visiting
a friend, when their father arrives in his car to take them home.
That's when their adventure begins!*

CHAPTER VI
A SUDDEN ADVENTURE

They ran down the path and climbed into the car at the back. It was quite
dark, and Daddy's headlights shed broad beams over the road.

"Good children," he said. "I only had to wait half a minute." He
put in the clutch and pressed down the accelerator; the car slid off
down the road.

"I've just got to call at the station for some parcels," said Daddy. "I'll leave
the car in the yard with you in it. I shan't be a minute."

They came to the station, and Daddy backed the car out of the way at one
end of the station yard. He jumped out and disappeared into the lit entrance of
the station.

Peter and Janet lay back on the seat, beginning to feel that they *might* have
over-eaten! Janet felt sleepy and shut her eyes. Peter began to think about the
evening before, and Susie's clever trick.

He suddenly heard hurried footsteps, and thought it must be his father back
again. The door was quickly opened and a man got in. Then the opposite door was

opened and another other man sat down in the seat beside the driver's.

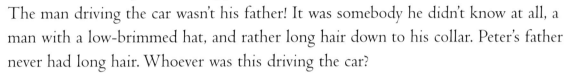

Peter thought his father had brought a friend with him to give him a lift, and he wondered who it was. It was dark in the station yard, and he couldn't see the other man's face at all. Then the headlights went on, and the car moved quickly out of the yard.

Peter got a really terrible shock as soon as the car passed a lamppost. The man driving the car wasn't his father! It was somebody he didn't know at all, a man with a low-brimmed hat, and rather long hair down to his collar. Peter's father never had long hair. Whoever was this driving the car?

The boy sat quite still. He looked at the other man when they went by a lamppost again. No, that wasn't his father either! It was a man he had never seen before. His head was bare and the hair was very short, quite different from his companion's.

A little cold feeling crept round Peter's heart. Who were these men? Were they stealing his father's car? What was he to do?

Janet stirred a little. Peter leaned over to her and put his lips right to her ear.

"Janet!" he whispered. "Are you awake? Listen to me. I think Daddy's car is being stolen by two men, and they don't know we're at the back. Slip quietly down to the floor, so that if they happen to turn round they won't see us. Quick now, for goodness' sake!"

CHAPTER VII
SOMETHING TO WORK ON

Janet was awake now, very much awake! She took one scared look at the heads of the two men in front, suddenly outlined by a street lamp, and slid quickly down to the floor. She began to tremble.

Peter slipped down beside her. "Don't be frightened. I'll look after you.

So long as the men don't know we're here, we're all right."

"But where are they taking us?" whispered Janet, glad that the rattling of the car drowned her voice.

"I've no idea. They've gone down the main street, and now they're in a part of the town I don't know," whispered Peter. "Hallo, they're stopping. Keep down, Janet, and don't make a sound!"

The driver stopped the car and peered out of the open window. "You're all right here," he said to his companion. "No one's about. Get in touch with Q8061 at once. Tell him Sid's place, five o'clock any evening. I'll be there."

"Right," said the other man and opened his door cautiously. Then he shut it again, and ducked his head down.

"What's up? Someone coming?" said the driver.

"No. I think I've dropped something," said the other man, in a muffled voice. He appeared to be groping over the floor. "I'm sure I heard something drop."

"For goodness' sake! Clear out now while the going's good!" said the driver impatiently. "The police will be on the look-out for this car in a few minutes. I'm going to Sid's, and I don't know anything at all about you, see? Not a thing!"

The other man muttered something and opened his door again. He slid out into the dark road. The driver got out on his side; both doors were left open, as the men did not want to make the slightest noise that might call attention to them.

Peter sat up cautiously. He could not see or hear anything of the two men. The darkness had swallowed them completely. In this road the lampposts were few and far between, and the driver had been careful to stop in the darkest spot he could find. He had switched headlights and sidelights off as soon as he had stopped.

Peter reached over to the front of the car and switched them on. He didn't want anything to run into his father's car and smash it. He wished he could drive, but he couldn't, and anyway, he was much too young to have a licence. What should he do now?

Janet sat up, too, still trembling. "Where are we?" she said. "Have those men gone?"

"Yes. It's all right, Janet; I don't think they're coming back," said Peter. "Well, I wonder who they were and why they wanted to come here in the car? Talk about an adventure! We were moaning last night because there wasn't even the smell of one, and now here's one, right out of the blue!"

"Well, I don't much like an adventure in the dark," said Janet. "What are we going to do?"

"We must get in touch with Daddy," said Peter. "He must still be waiting at the station, unless he's gone home! But we haven't been more than a few minutes. I think I'll try to find a telephone box and telephone the station to see if Daddy is still there."

"I'm not going to wait in the car by myself," said Janet, at once. "Oh dear, I wish we had Scamper with us. I should feel much better then."

"The men wouldn't have taken the car if Scamper had been with us," said Peter, getting out. "He would have barked, and they would have run off to someone else's car. Come on, Janet, get out. I'll lock the doors in case there is anyone else who might take a fancy to Daddy's car!"

He locked all the doors, Janet holding his torch for him so that he could see what he was doing. Then they went down the street to see if they could find a telephone box anywhere.

They were lucky. One was at the corner of the very road where they were! Peter slipped inside and dialled the railway station.

"Station here," said a voice at the other end.

"This is Peter, of Old Mill House," said Peter. "Is my father at the station still, by any chance?"

"Yes, he is," said the voice. "He's just collecting some parcels. Do you want to speak to him? Right, I'll ask him to come to the phone."

Half a minute later Peter heard his father's voice. "Yes? Who is it? *You*, Peter!

But – but aren't you still in the car, in the station yard? Where are you?"

Peter explained everything as clearly as he could, and his father listened to his tale in amazement. "Well! Two car thieves going off with my car and not guessing you and Janet were in it. Where are you?"

"Janet's just asked somebody," said Peter. "We're in Jackson Street, not far from the Broadway. Can you get here, Dad, and fetch the car? We'll wait."

"Yes. I'll get a taxi here in the yard," said his father. "Well, of all the things to happen!"

Janet and Peter went back to the car. Now that they knew their father would be along in a few minutes they no longer felt scared. Instead they began to feel rather pleased and important.

"We'll have to call a Secret Seven meeting about this *at once*," said Peter. "The police will be on to it, I expect, and *we'll* work on it too. What will Susie do *now*? Who cares about her silly tricks? Nobody at all!"

CHAPTER VIII
ANOTHER MEETING

In a short time a taxi drew up beside the car and the children's father jumped out.

"Here we are!" called Janet, as her father paid the taxi-man.

He ran over, and got into the driver's seat. "Well! Little did I think my car had been driven away while I was in the station," he said. "Are you sure you're all right?"

"Oh yes," said Peter. "We were half asleep at the back; the men didn't even spot us. They got in and drove straight to this place, then got out. They hardly said a word to one another."

"Oh. Well, I suppose they weren't really car thieves," said his father. "Just a couple of young idiots who wanted to drive somewhere instead of walk. I shan't bother to inform the police. We'd never catch the fellows, and it would be a waste of everyone's time. I've got the car back; that's all that matters."

The two children felt a little flat to have their extraordinary adventure disposed of in this way.

"But aren't you *really* going to tell the police?" asked Peter, quite disappointed.

"The men may be real crooks."

"They probably are. But I'm not going to waste *my* time on them," said his father. "They'll be caught for something sooner or later! It's a good thing you had the sense to keep quiet in the back of the car!"

Their mother was a good deal more interested in the affair than Daddy, yet even she thought it was just a silly prank on the part of two young men. But it was different when Peter telephoned Jack and told him what happened. Jack was absolutely thrilled.

"Gosh! Really! I wish I'd been with you!" he shouted in excitement, clutching the telephone hard. "Let's have a meeting about it. Tomorrow afternoon at three o'clock? We've all got a half-term holiday tomorrow, haven't we? We'll tell the others at school there's a meeting on. I'll... Sh. Sh!"

"What are you shushing about?" asked Peter. "Oh, is that awful Susie about? All right, not a word more. See you tomorrow."

Next afternoon, at three o'clock, all the Secret Seven were down in the shed, Scamper with them too, running from one to another excitedly. He could feel that something important was afoot!

The oil-stove was already lit and the shed was nice and warm. Curtains were drawn across the windows in case anyone should peer in. Nobody had had time to bring things to eat, but fortunately George had had a present of a large bag of humbugs from his grandmother. He handed them round.

"I say, how super," said Jack. "Your granny does buy such *enormous* humbugs. They last for ages. Now we shall all be comfortable for the rest of the afternoon, with one of these in our cheeks."

They sat round on boxes or on old rugs, each with their cheeks bulging with a peppermint humbug. Scamper didn't like them, which was lucky. The children made him sit by the door and listen in case anyone came prying, that awful Susie, for instance, or one of her silly friends!

Peter related the whole event, and everyone listened, thrilled.

"And do you mean to say your father isn't going to the police?" said Colin. "Well, that leaves the field free for us. Come along, Secret Seven, here's something right up our street!"

"It's very exciting," said Pam. "But what exactly are we going to work on? I mean, what is there to find out? I wouldn't even know where to *begin*!"

"Well, I'll tell you what I think," said Peter, carefully moving his humbug to the other cheek. "I think those men are up to something. I don't know what, but I think we ought to find out something about them."

"But how can we?" asked Pam. "I don't like the sound of them, anyway."

"Well, if you don't want to be in on this, there's nothing to stop you from walking out," said Peter, getting cross with Pam. "The door's over there."

Pam changed her mind in a hurry. "Oh no, I *want* to be in on this; of course I do. You tell us what to do, Peter."

"Well we don't *know* very much," said Peter. "Excuse me, all of you, but I'm going to take my humbug out for a minute or two, while I talk. There, that's better. No, Scamper, don't sniff at it; you don't *like* humbugs!"

With his sweet safely on a clean piece of paper beside him, Peter addressed the meeting.

"We haven't really much to go on, as I said," he began. "But we have a *few* clues. One is 'Sid's Place'. We ought to try and find where that is and watch it, to see if either of the men go there. Then we could shadow them. We'd have to watch it at five o'clock each day."

"Go on," said George.

"Then there's Q8061," said Peter. "That might be a telephone number. We could find out about that."

"That's silly!" said Pam. "It doesn't look a bit like a telephone number!"

Four Enid Blyton adventure stories: 'The Adventure of the Secret Necklace' (first published in 1954), 'The Mystery of the Missing Necklace' (first published in 1947), 'The Rubadub Mystery' (first published in 1952) and 'The Mystery of the Strange Messages' (first published in 1957).

Stuart Tresilian illustrated all of the 'Adventure' series. He painted this jacket for the book when it was reprinted in 1960.

'The Famous Five Special' contained three full-length Famous Five stories. It was published in 1959 and the jacket, by Eileen Soper, depicts some of the characters the Five meet in their adventures.

'The Secret of the Old Mill', published in 1948, was the very first story to feature the Secret Seven. The illustrations were by Eileen Soper, who illustrated the Famous Five books.

'The Secret Seven', originally published in 1949, was the first book in the Secret Seven series. The jacket was painted by George Brook, who illustrated the first four Secret Seven adventures.

'Five on a Treasure Island' was first published in 1942. The illustration on the left shows the jacket used on early editions of the book. In 1951 Eileen Soper painted a new jacket for the book, which is shown on the right.

Peter took no notice of Pam. "One man had a low-brimmed hat and long hair down to his collar," he said. "And I *think* there was something wrong with one hand — it looked as if the tip of the middle finger was missing. I only *just* caught sight of it in the light of a lamppost, but I'm fairly sure."

"And the other man had very short hair," said Janet, suddenly. "I did notice that. Oh, and Peter, do you remember that he said he thought he'd dropped something? Do you think he had? We never looked to see! He didn't find whatever it was."

"Gosh, yes. I forgot all about that," said Peter. "That's most important. We'll all go and look in the car at once. Bring your torches, please, Secret Seven!"

CHAPTER IX
THE SEVEN GET GOING

Scamper darted out into the garden with the Seven. Jack looked about to see if Susie or any of her friends were in hiding, but as Scamper didn't run barking at any bush, he felt sure that Susie must be somewhere else! They all went to the garage. Peter hoped that the car would be there. It was! The children opened the doors and looked inside.

"It's no good us looking in the back," said Peter. "The men were in front."

He felt about everywhere, and shone his torch into every corner of the front of the car. The garage was rather dark, although it was only half-past three in the afternoon.

"Nothing!" he said disappointed.

"Let *me* see," said Janet. "I once dropped a pencil and couldn't find it, and it was down between the two front seats!"

She slid her fingers in between the two seats and felt about. She gave a cry and pulled something out. It was a spectacle case. She held it up in triumph.

"Look! That's it. He dropped his spectacle case!"

"But he didn't wear glasses," said Peter.

"He could have reading glasses, couldn't he?" said Janet. "Like Granny?"

She opened the case. It was empty. She gave another little squeal.

"Look, it's got his name inside! What do you think of *that*? And his telephone number! *Now* we're on to something!"

The Secret Seven crowded round to look. Janet pointed to a little label inside. On it neatly written was a name and number. "Briggs. Renning 2150."

"Renning – that's not far away!" said Peter. "We can look up the name in the telephone directory and see his address. Gosh, what a find!"

Everyone was thrilled. Jack was just about to shut the door of the car when he suddenly remembered that no one had looked under the left-hand front seat, where the man who had dropped something had sat. He took a little stick from a bundle of garden bamboos standing in a nearby corner and poked under the seat with it, and out rolled a button!

"Look!" said Jack, holding it up.

Peter gave it a glance.

"Oh that's off my father's mac," he said. "It must have been there for ages."

He put it into his pocket, and they all went back to the shed, feeling very excited.

"Well, first we find out Mr Briggs's address. Then we all ride over to see him," said Peter. "We'll make him admit he dropped it in the car, and then I'll pounce like anything and say, 'And what were you doing in my father's car?'. I'm sure the police would be interested if we could actually tell them the name and address of the man who went off in Dad's car like that, and probably they would make him give the name of the other man too!"

This long speech made Peter quite out of breath. The others gazed at him in admiration. It all sounded very bold.

"All right. What about now, this very minute, if we can find his address in Renning?" said Jack. "Nothing like striking while the iron's hot. We could have tea in that little tea-shop in Renning. They have wonderful macaroons. I ate five last time I was there."

"Then somebody else must have paid the bill," said Colin. "Yes, do let's go now. It *would* be fun, but you can do the talking, Peter!"

"Have you all got your bikes?" said Peter. "Good. Let's just go in and take a look at the telephone directory, and get the address. Mr Briggs, we're coming after you!"

The telephone directory was very helpful. Mr H.E.J. Briggs lived at Little Hill, Rayne Road, Renning. Telephone number 2150. Peter copied it down carefully.

"Got enough money for tea, everyone?" he asked.

Colin had only a penny or two, so Peter offered to lend him some. Now they were all ready to set off.

Peter told his mother they were going out to tea, and away they went, riding carefully in single line down the main road, as they had been taught to do.

Renning was about three miles away, and it didn't really take them long to get there.

"Shall we have tea first?" asked George, looking longingly at the tea-shop they were passing.

"No. Work first, pleasure afterwards," said Peter, who was always very strict about things like that. They cycled on to Raynes Road.

It was only a little lane, set with pretty little cottages. Little Hill was at one end, a nice little place with a colourful garden.

"Well it doesn't *look* like the home of a crook," said Jack. "But you never know. See, there's someone in the garden, Peter. Come on, do your job. Let's see how you handle things of this sort. Make him admit he dropped that spectacle case in your father's car!"

"Right!" said Peter, and went in boldly at the garden gate. "Er – good afternoon. Are you Mr Briggs?"

CHAPTER X
PETER FEELS HOT ALL OVER

As soon as Peter saw the man closely, he knew at once that he wasn't either of the men in the car. For one thing, this man had a big round head, and a face to match, and both the other men had had rather narrow heads, as far as he had been able to see.

The man looked a little surprised. "No," he said. "I'm not Mr Briggs. I'm just a friend staying with him. Do you want him? I'll call him."

Peter began to feel a little uncomfortable. Somehow this pretty garden and trim little cottage didn't seem the kind of place those men would live in!

"Henry! Henry, there's someone asking for you!" called the man.

Peter saw that the other Secret Seven members were watching eagerly. Would "Henry" prove to be one of the men they were hunting for?

A man came strolling out, someone with trim, short hair and a narrow head. Yes, he *might* be the man who had sat in the left-hand seat of the car, except that he didn't in the least look as if he could possibly take someone else's car!

Still you never know! thought Peter.

The man looked inquiringly at him. "What do you want?" he said.

"Er – is your name Mr H. E. J. Briggs, sir?" asked Peter, politely.

"It is," said the man looking amused. "Why?"

"Er – well, have you by any chance lost a spectacle case?" asked Peter.

All the rest of the Seven outside the garden held their breath. What would he say?

"Yes. I *have* lost one," said the man surprised. "Have you found it? Where was it?"

"It was in the front of a car," answered Peter, watching him closely.

Now if the man was one of the car thieves, he would surely look embarrassed, or deny it. He would know that it was the case he had dropped the night before and would be afraid of saying "Yes, I dropped it there."

"What an extraordinary thing!" said the man. "Whose car? You sound rather *mysterious*. Losing a spectacle case is quite an ordinary thing to do, you know!"

"It was dropped in my father's car last night," said Peter, still watching the man.

"Oh no, it wasn't," said Mr Briggs at once. "I've lost this case for about a week. It can't be mine. I wasn't in anyone's car last night."

"It is the man we want, I bet it is!" said Pam in a low voice to Janet. "He's telling fibs!"

"The case has your name in it," said Peter, "so we know it's yours. And it *was* in my father's car last night."

"Who is your father?" said the man, sounding puzzled. "I can't quite follow

what you're getting at. And where's the case?"

"My father lives at Old Mill House," began Peter, "and he's…"

"Good gracious! He's not Jack, my farmer friend, surely?" said Mr Briggs. "That explains everything! He very kindly gave me a lift one day last week, and I must have dropped my spectacle case in his car then. I hunted for it everywhere when I got back home. Never thought of the car, of course! Well, well, so you've brought it back?"

"Oh, are you the man my father speaks of as Harry?" said Peter, taken aback. "Gosh! Well I suppose you *did* drop your case, then, and not last night, as I thought. Here it is. It's got your name and telephone number in it. That's how we knew it was yours."

He held it out, and the man took it, smiling. "Thanks," he said, "and now perhaps you'll tell me what all the mystery was about, and why you insisted I had dropped it last night, and why you looked at me as if I were somebody Very Suspicious Indeed."

Peter heard the others giggling, and he went red. He really didn't know *what* to say!

"Well," he said, "you see, two men took my father's car last night, and when we looked in it today we found this case, and we thought perhaps it belonged to one of the men."

Mr Briggs laughed. "I see, doing a little detective work. Well, it's very disappointing for you, but I don't happen to be a car thief. Look, here's fifty pence for bringing back my case. Buy some chocolate and share it with those interested friends of yours watching over the hedge."

"Oh no, thank you," said Peter, backing away. "I don't want anything. I'm only too glad to bring your case back. Goodbye!"

He went quickly out of the garden, most relieved to get away from the amused eyes of Mr Briggs. Goodness, what a mistake! He got on his bicycle and rode swiftly away, the other six following.

They all stopped outside the tea-shop.

"Whew!" said Peter, wiping his forehead. "I DID feel awful when I found out he was a friend of my father's! Dad is always talking about a man called Harry, but I didn't know his surname before."

"We thought we were so clever, but we weren't this time," said Colin. "Bother! The spectacle case was nothing to do with those two men in the car, but perhaps the button is?"

"Perhaps," said Peter. "But I'm not tackling anyone wearing macs with buttons that match the one we found, unless I'm jolly certain he's one of those men! I feel hot all over when I think of Mr Briggs. Suppose he goes and tells my father all about this?"

"Never mind," said Jack, grinning. "It was great fun watching you. Let's have tea. Look, they've got macaroons today."

In they went and had a wonderful tea. And now, what next? Think hard, Secret Seven, and make some exciting plans!

THE ADVENTURE OF THE SECRET NECKLACE

AN EXTRACT

❧ ILLUSTRATED BY ❧
ISABEL VEEVERS

Bob and Mary are staying with their granny and their cousin Ralph. Granny tells them the story of a valuable necklace that had been in their family for generations before being lost. Bob and Mary decide to hunt for the necklace and find a clue that the fifth book on the fifth shelf in the library will help them to discover a secret room. As Ralph, who is a bit of a bully, has been trying to prevent them from finding the necklace, they decide to explore the library on their own in the middle of the night...

CHAPTER XI
IN THE MIDDLE OF THE NIGHT

Granny had some friends to see her that night. They stayed late, and it was difficult for the children to keep awake. In the end they took it in turns to keep awake for half an hour, sleeping soundly in between.

At last Bob, who was the one awake, heard the cars leaving the front door, and heard Granny coming upstairs. Click – click – click! That was the electric lights being turned off. Now, except for a light on the landing outside, and in Granny's room, the house was in darkness.

Bob woke up Mary. "The visitors have gone," he whispered. "And Granny has come up to bed. Let's put on our slippers and dressing-gowns and go down. Granny won't hear us or see us now she's in her bedroom."

Mary leaped out of her bed, wide awake with excitement. She switched on her torch, and put on her slippers and dressing-gown. "My fingers are shaking!" she whispered to Bob. "Oh Bob – isn't this thrilling?"

They went down the stairs very cautiously, and came into the big hall. The moon shone in through the window there, and lit up every corner. Mary was glad. She didn't like pitch-black shadows!

They went into the study. The moon shone through the windows there too, and showed them the ladder still up by the big bookcase. They went to it.

"Now – the fifth book on the fifth shelf, counting from the left," said Bob. He went up the ladder, and then came down again. "I can reach the fifth shelf easily, without using the ladder!" he said, and pushed it aside.

He took out the fifth book from the left of the fifth shelf and gave it to Mary. Then he began to feel about at the back of the gap where the book had stood. Mary stood watching him, trembling in excitement, trying to shine her torch where it would best help Bob.

He gave a little cry. "Mary! There's something here – a sort of knob. I'm twisting it – no, it won't twist. I'll pull it – oh it's moved!"

There was a noise as he pulled the knob, and then another noise – a creaking, groaning noise. The bookcase suddenly seemed to push against Bob, and he stepped back surprised.

The whole case was moving slowly out from the wall, leaving a small space behind it of about a foot. The knob worked some lever that pushed the bookcase forward in a most ingenious way! Mary stared, holding her breath. How strange!

"The secret door will be behind the bookcase!" said Bob, forgetting to whisper in his excitement. "I'll squeeze behind and see if I can find it."

He squeezed himself behind, shining his torch on the wooden panelling. Mary heard him take a sudden breath. "Yes! it *is* here, Mary! The old, old secret door! It must be years and years since anyone went through it."

"Can you open it?" asked Mary, her voice trembling. "Oh Bob!"

Bob was feeling all over the small door, which appeared to be cut out of the panelling. His fingers came to a little hole and he poked his first finger through it. It touched something, and there was a click as if a latch had fallen.

The door swung open suddenly and silently in front of Bob. A little dark passage was behind, and Bob shone his torch into it. "Mary! Come on! I've got the door open and it leads into the secret passage. Let's see where it goes. Come on!"

Mary squeezed herself behind the bookcase to the open door. It was no higher than her head. Bob was already in the passage, and he held out his hand to her.

"Come on. It goes upwards here, in steep steps, behind the panelling. Hold my hand."

It was dark and musty in the passage, and in one or two places they had to bend their heads because the roof was so low. It seemed to be a secret way behind the panelled walls of the study – but as the steps went on and on upwards Bob guessed they must now be behind the walls of some room upstairs.

The passage suddenly turned to the left, and then instead of going upwards ran level. It came to a sudden end at another door – a sturdy one this time, studded with big nails. It had a handle on the outside in the shape of a big iron ring, and Bob turned it.

The door opened into a tiny room, so tiny that it could only hold a wooden stool, a little wooden table, and a narrow bench on which there was an old, rotten blanket.

A wooden bowl stood on the table, and a tumbler made of thick glass. They could see nothing else inside the room at all.

"This is an old hidey-hole," said Bob, almost too thrilled to speak. "I wonder how many people have hidden here from their enemies, at one time or another? Look, there's even an old blanket left here by the last person."

"There's no sign of the necklace," said Mary, shining her torch round the tiny room. "But look, Bob — what's that — in the wall there?"

"A cupboard — a very rough one," said Bob. "Not much more than a hole in the wall. Give me the stool, Mary. I'll stand on it and shine my torch inside!"

He stood on the stool, and peered into the hole, holding his torch to light him. He gave a cry and almost fell off the stool.

"Quick! Get up and look, Mary! Oh, *quick!*"

CHAPTER XII
THE HIDEY-HOLE

Mary pushed Bob off the stool and stood on it herself, her heart beating fast in excitement. She shone her torch into the hole. At once something sparkled brilliantly, and flashed in the torchlight! "Bob! Is it the necklace?" she cried. "Oh *Bob!*"

"You can be the one to take it out," said Bob. "Be careful of it now — remember it may be worth thousands of pounds!"

Half fearfully Mary put in her hand. She took hold of the sparkling mass, and gave a squeal.

"There are *lots* of things — not only a necklace. A bracelet — and rings — and brooches — oh, they're *beautiful*, Bob!"

"Hand them out to me one by one," said Bob. "Carefully now. Oh Mary — what*ever* will Granny say?"

Mary handed Bob the things — a bracelet that shone like fire with red rubies — another one that glittered with diamonds — rings with stones of all sizes and shapes — brooches — and last of all the magnificent emerald and diamond necklace that the twins had seen round the necks of the five women in the portraits! Yes — there was no doubt of it — this was the long-lost necklace!

Bob put everything in his dressing-gown pocket. It was the only place he could put them in. They felt quite heavy there!

"Now let's go and wake Granny!" he said, as Mary got off the stool. He shone his torch on the door, which had closed behind them. "Come on, Mary. I wonder what Ralph will say when he knows we've got the jewellery!"

"I don't care *what* he says!" said Mary. "He didn't deserve to share in our adventure because of his meanness in reading us out the wrong directions!"

Bob was trying to open the door. "It's funny – there's no handle this side," he said. "I wonder how it opens?"

He pushed it, but it wouldn't move. He pulled it and shook it, but it didn't open. He kicked it, but it stayed firmly shut.

Mary suddenly felt frightened. "I say, Bob – wouldn't it be dreadful if we couldn't get it open? Would we have to stay here for ever?"

"Don't be so silly! Somebody would find the bookcase was moved, and would explore and discover the secret door, and come up the passage and find us," said Bob.

"But I don't want to be here all night!" wailed Mary. "I don't like it – and my torch is getting very weak. I hope yours is all right. I don't want to be here all in the dark."

"I shall look after you," said Bob, firmly. "You know that brothers always look after their sisters. Just think of all the lovely treasures we've got tonight, Mary. What about putting everything on? That will help you to pass the time."

Mary thought that was a very good idea, and soon she was gleaming brightly

as she put on brooches, bracelets, rings and necklace! The rings were too large so she had to close her hands to keep them from falling off.

"You look wonderful!" said Bob, shining his torch on Mary. "Like a princess!"

Suddenly they heard a noise, and Mary clutched at Bob. "What was that?" she whispered. "Did you hear it?"

The noise came again. A kind of shuffling noise — was it somebody coming up the passage? Who could it be? Surely nobody lived in this little secret room?

The twins stood absolutely still, hardly daring to breathe — and then they heard a familiar voice!

"Hey! Bob! Mary! Are you here?"

"Ralph!" yelled the twins, feeling extremely glad to hear his voice. "Yes, we're here — but we can't open the door from this side. Open it from your side, will you?"

Ralph turned the handle outside and the door opened! He looked in, shining his torch. When he saw Mary, sparkling and glittering in the beam of his torch, his mouth fell open in surprise. He could hardly say a word.

"Oh!" he said at last. "So you found the necklace then! You *might* have waited for me, Bob."

"I like *that!*" said Bob. "You weren't going to wait for *us*, were you? You've got up in the middle of the night to come and explore all by yourself, haven't you? And you found that we were before you!"

"No. No, Bob, you're wrong," said Ralph earnestly. "I couldn't go to sleep tonight, because I was worried that you thought I was so mean — you thought I'd given you wrong directions on purpose…"

"Well, didn't you?" demanded Bob.

"No," said Ralph. "No, I didn't. You see — I'm not good at reading. I can't read at all to myself, really, unless it's very very easy — but I was ashamed to tell you I couldn't read those words in the old book — and I just said what I thought, and it was wrong, of course."

There was silence for a minute. "I see," said Bob at last. "So you didn't even read that book after tea yesterday — the one you seemed to finish so quickly. You do tell dreadful stories, Ralph."

"I know. The thing is — I'm so big that people expect me to know an awful lot and I don't," said Ralph. "So I pretend, you see. And I was sorry tonight and I came to your room to tell you — but you were gone!"

322

"So you followed us," said Mary. "Well, I'm very glad you did, Ralph, or we'd have been here all night. I'm sorry we called you mean. We really and truly thought you read out wrong directions on purpose to stop us finding the door."

"I'm sorry too," said Bob, and solemnly held out his hand. The boys shook hands.

"I missed the adventure," said Ralph, sorrowfully.

"Never mind – you came in at the end of it," said Mary. "Now – let's go and wake Granny!"

CHAPTER XIII
THE END OF THE ADVENTURE

The three children left the tiny hidey-hole behind them, and went in single file down the secret passage. They came at last to the little secret door that led into the study, behind the bookcase.

The moon still shone through the windows and Mary's jewellery sparkled even more brilliantly. The boys thought she looked lovely!

They went quietly up the stairs to Granny's bedroom, and knocked on the door.

"Who's there?" said Granny's voice, sleepily.

"It's us – the twins and Ralph," said Bob.

"What's the matter? Is one of you ill?" called Granny. "Come in – the door isn't locked."

They heard a click as Granny put on her light. They opened the door and went in, still in their slippers and dressing-gowns.

Granny looked at them anxiously, thinking that one of them at least must be ill. She suddenly saw all the glittering jewellery that Mary had on.

"Mary! What have you got on? Where did you get all that?" she began. Then she saw the necklace. "Mary – that necklace! Good gracious, am I dreaming, or is that the lost necklace? I *must* be dreaming!"

"You're not, Granny," said Mary, coming close to the bed. "It *is* the lost necklace – look, it's the same one that is painted in all those portraits – the big green emeralds and everything!"

"My dear child!" said Granny, in wonder, and put out her hand to touch the

sparkling stones. "But these rings — and brooches — where *did* you find them? Sit on my bed and tell me. I can't wait to hear!"

So the three of them cuddled into Granny's soft eiderdown, and told their strange story — all about the plans in the old book — the mention of the passage and the directions for finding the secret door — and the hidey-hole where, most unexpectedly, they had found the jewellery in the little cubby-hole in the wall.

"I just can't believe it!" Granny kept saying. "I just can't. To think it was there, in a place that every single person had forgotten through all these years! And all these other treasures too. How I wish I knew the story of why they were hidden there — some thief, I suppose, stole them and put them in the safest place he knew — and then couldn't get to them again!"

"Will they be yours, all these things, Granny?" asked Mary.

"The necklace certainly will, because it belongs to the family," said Granny, "and I expect the other things will too. Look, this ruby ring is the one painted on the finger of the third woman in the gallery of pictures!"

So it was. Mary remembered it quite well. She took off all the sparkling jewellery carefully and handed it to Granny.

"That was a real adventure, wasn't it, Granny?" she said.

"It certainly was. Did you enjoy it too, Ralph?" asked Granny.

"Yes," said Ralph, hoping that the twins wouldn't tell that he had only come in at the last. They didn't say a word. They were very sorry that Ralph *hadn't* shared all the adventure now. They felt much more kindly towards him, now they knew why he boasted and told such silly stories.

"You must go back to bed," said Granny, at last. "We'll talk about it all again

324

tomorrow. It's too exciting for words!"

Everyone in the house was thrilled to hear about the midnight adventure. Cookie, who had been called by Mrs Hughes, the housekeeper, early next morning to see the bookcase out of its place, just couldn't believe it all.

"Well, well — it isn't often we have an adventure like this happening in Tall Chimneys!" she said. "I'll have to make a special cake to celebrate it!"

So she did — and she actually made a beautiful necklace all round the cake, in white and green icing. It really was clever of her.

"Well, you will find the rest of your stay here rather dull, I'm afraid, after all this excitement," said Granny, when they sat down to their lunch in the middle of the day.

"No, we shan't," said Mary. "We're going to have a jolly good time with Ralph — aren't we, Bob? We're going to teach him to swim, and to row — and lots of other things!"

Ralph beamed. "Yes. I shan't need to show off and pretend then. Don't you worry, Granny — we're going to have a *grand* time here — and I expect I'll be a lot nicer than I've been before."

"That's good news," said Granny. "You haven't always been nice, but I shall expect great things of you now."

They did have a grand time together, and Ralph learned a whole lot of things he didn't know before. The twins began to like him very much indeed.

Before they left Tall Chimneys, they all had a surprise. Granny said she wanted to give them goodbye presents.

"This is for you, Mary," she said, and gave the little girl a small sparkling brooch that had been in the lost jewellery. "I've had it cleaned and altered — and now it is just right for a little girl like you to wear at a party."

She turned to the boys. "And I've sold a little of the jewellery I didn't want to keep," she said, "and I have bought these watches, one for each of you — just to remind you of the adventure you had at Granny's!"

She gave them two splendid watches, and they put them on proudly. What would the boys at school say when they saw *those*?

"Thank you, Granny!" said the children, and hugged her. "We've had a simply lovely time — and we never never *will* forget our Adventure of the Secret Necklace."

∾

SECRET SEVEN WIN THROUGH

AN EXTRACT

∾ ILLUSTRATED BY ∾
BRUNO KAY

The Secret Seven have found a cave in a nearby quarry and use it as a meeting-place while their shed is being repaired. But someone else is using the cave — and the Seven want to find out who it is...

CHAPTER VI
JACK IS VERY PUZZLED

The cave was a great success. On rainy days it was a wonderful place to lie in and read, or play games. Each of the seven burrowed into the sand and made his or her own bed or hole. Each had a cushion for their head. The shelves were always kept stacked with papers and magazines, and with food and drink.

"We couldn't have found a better place," said Colin. "Jack, does Susie ever bother about where you disappear to for hours on end?"

"Goodness, yes," said Jack. "She keeps on and on about it. She knows our old shed is no longer a meeting-place, because she went to have a look at it. I have to be awfully careful not to let her follow me when I come here. Yesterday I turned round and there she was, keeping to the bushes beside the road, hoping I wouldn't see her."

"What did you do?" asked Pam.

"I turned a corner and went off to the sweet shop instead of coming here," said Jack. "I do hope she won't find our cave."

"Let's go into the quarry and play hide-and-seek," said Janet, getting up. "The sun's out again, and I'm longing to stretch my legs."

So off they all went. Jack was chosen to shut his eyes and count a hundred before he began looking. The cave was to be Home. Jack stood by a tree at the other side of the quarry, counting nice and slowly. When he had counted a hundred, he looked round. Could be see anyone behind a bush, or lying in the lush grass nearby?

No — not one of the others was to be seen. He moved cautiously round his tree, keeping his eyes open for a sudden movement somewhere.

He glanced towards the cave, which he could just see between a gap in the broom bushes that hid it so well. Then he stared. Someone was slipping into the cave! Who was it? He just couldn't see.

That's not fair, thought Jack. They haven't given me a chance to find them. Well, I'll soon find out which of the seven it is, and tell them what I think of them!

He saw a patch of blue nearby and recognised Pam's dress behind a bush. He rushed at her, but she escaped and ran squealing to the cave.

Then he found Barbara, Janet, and Scamper together, crouching behind a great hummock of sand. He ran to catch them and fell headlong over a tuft of grass. They rushed away, the girls squealing and Scamper barking.

He nearly caught Colin behind a tree, but Colin was too quick for him. "Let's see — that only leaves one more," said Jack to himself. "The first one I saw going into the cave — then the three girls — then Colin — myself — and so there's just one more. It's Peter or George."

He hunted here and there, and then suddenly fell over two giggling boys. It was Peter and George, half-buried in the soft sand. Jack grabbed at Peter and caught him, but George escaped to the cave.

"I'm caught all right!" said Peter, grinning. "I'll be 'He' next. Let's call out to everyone in the cave."

"Wait a minute," said Jack, looking puzzled. "There's something I don't understand. Let's go up to the cave."

Peter went with him to the cave, where the other five were waiting.

"What don't you understand?" asked Peter.

"Well, listen — first I saw someone slipping into the cave immediately after I'd finished counting," said Jack, "which wasn't really fair. Then I found Pam, then Janet and Barbara, then Colin, then you and George, Peter."

327

"Well – what's puzzling you?" asked Peter.

"Just this – that makes *eight* of us, not counting Scamper," said Jack. "And what I want to know is, who was the eighth?"

They all counted. Yes, Jack was right. That made eight, not seven. Everyone said at once that they hadn't slipped into the cave before Jack discovered them.

"Well, who was that first person then, if it wasn't any of us?" said Jack, really puzzled. "I tell you I saw somebody go into the cave before I discovered any of you. Who was it?"

Everyone began to look round uneasily. Peter pulled the green curtain back as far as he could, and the sunshine filled the cave, except for the dark places at the back.

"There's nobody here," said Pam. "Oh, Jack, do you suppose it could have been Susie?"

"I don't know. I only just saw *somebody*, but I haven't any idea who it was," said Jack. "And look here, surely that somebody must still be in here! I found Pam almost immediately, and she rushed off to the cave. You didn't see anyone here did you, Pam?"

"Of course not," said Pam. "If I'd seen Susie I would have been furious with her!"

Peter took down a torch from the shelf of rock nearby and switched it on. He flashed it towards the dark corners at the end of the cave. "Come forth!" he

said, in a hollow voice. "Come forth, O wicked intruder!"

But nobody came. The far corners of the cave, now lit brilliantly by the torch, were quite empty.

"It's odd," said Jack, frowning. "Very odd. Give me the torch, Peter. I'll go and see if there's any corner or hole at the end of the cave that we haven't noticed."

"Well, there isn't," said Peter, giving him the torch. "Janet and I had a good look when we first found the cave!"

All the same, Jack went to the far end and had a very good look round, flashing the torch everywhere. There seemed to be nowhere that anyone could hide.

He came back, still looking puzzled. "Cheer up," said Peter. "You must have imagined someone, Jack. Anyway, would anyone come to that cave while we were all of us here, in plain view?"

"But that's just what we were not," said Jack. "We were playing hide-and-seek, and there wasn't a sound, and all of us, except me, were well hidden. Anybody coming here just then would not have heard or seen anything of us. They would have thought the place deserted."

"Yes. I see what you mean," said Peter. "All the same, there's nobody here. So cheer up, Jack, and let's go on with the game. My turn to find you all. Go and hide!"

CHAPTER VII
A REAL MYSTERY

Nobody said any more about Jack's idea that someone had slipped into the cave. Jack began to think he really must have imagined it. Perhaps it was a shadow from a cloud or something? They all played the game of hide-and-seek again and again, and nobody saw mysterious people slipping into the cave any more!

"It's time to tidy up and go home," said Peter, at last. "What a mess we seem to make when we've been in the cave for even a short time!"

The girls shook up the cushions, and the boys gathered up the rubbish and put it into a bag to take home. Then Janet put the rest of the food back on the shelves, and tidied up Colin's set of "Five" books.

"There!" she said. "Everything tidy! If our mothers came and looked in they would be most astonished."

They all laughed. They went out of the cave, and Peter pulled the green curtain carefully across. Then off they went home.

"Same time tomorrow!" called Peter, when they all said goodbye to him and Janet and Scamper at his front gate.

"No! You've forgotten – we're all going to bike over to Penton and see the circus come through," said Colin. "We're meeting at eleven at my house."

"Oh, yes, how could I forget!" said Peter. "We'll go to the cave after lunch tomorrow afternoon."

Next day they had a good morning, watching the long circus procession passing through the little town of Penton. Then they biked back for their lunches, and, at various times, set off to the cave.

Pam and Barbara arrived first, Pam, very pleased because her granny had given her a tin of peppermints for the Secret Seven to enjoy.

"I'll put them beside the other tins," she said. "Hallo – look, Barbara, there's a tin on the floor of the cave. Who do you suppose knocked that down? We're the first here today!"

"Perhaps it overbalanced," said Barbara.

"And gosh, look – we left a whole bar of chocolate, a very big one, just *here*," said Pam. "I put it there myself. That's gone!"

"It's probably somewhere else," said Barbara. Then she herself noticed something. "Gosh, look – three of our cushions are missing! Has somebody been here?"

"It's Susie," said Pam frowning. "That's who it is. She didn't come with us to Penton today, so she must have come here instead! She has followed Jack sometime or other, and found out our meeting-place. Bother Susie!"

"Here are the others," said Barbara. "Let's tell them."

They heard the password murmured outside the cave - "Easter-egg" — then the curtain was pushed aside and in came Colin and George.

"Susie's been here!" said Pam angrily. "Look, there are cushions missing, and our big bar of chocolate is gone, and a tin was on the ground."

"And look, those currant buns we were saving for today are nearly all gone!" said Barbara, opening a tin. "Would you believe it!"

Soon Peter, Janet, and Jack arrived and were also told the news. "But it needn't have been Susie," said Peter, trying to be fair, though he felt perfectly certain it was. "It could quite well have been a tramp."

"He'd have taken lots more things," said Pam. "And what would he want with cushions! We might meet him down a lane carrying them, and we'd know he was the thief at once. No tramp would be as silly as that."

"That's true," said Peter. "Well, Jack, you'll have to find out if it's Susie."

"All right," said Jack, looking troubled. "I'll go now. But somehow I don't think it is Susie, you know. I can't help remembering that person, whoever it was, that I saw slipping into the cave yesterday."

Jack went off to find Susie. The others each took a peppermint from the tin that Pam offered them, and settled down to read. Colin finished his book and went to get another. He gave an exclamation.

"One of my 'Famous Five' books has gone! Has anyone borrowed it? It's *Five go down to the sea*."

Nobody had. "I know it's not Jack," said Colin. "He's just finished reading it. Well, if that's Susie again I'll have something to say to her!"

Jack came back in about an hour. "Easter-egg" he said, outside the cave, and Peter called him in.

"Well," he said, throwing himself down on the sandy floor. "I've had an awful time. Susie says she's never been *near* our new meeting-place, she says she doesn't even know where it is! She flew into such a temper when I accused her of coming and taking things, that Mother heard her, and came to see what was the matter."

"Oh, bother!" said Peter. "You might have kept your mother out of this. What happened next?"

"Mother made me tell where our meeting-place is," said poor Jack, looking really miserable. "I couldn't help it, Peter, really I couldn't. She *made* me."

There was silence. Everyone knew that it was wrong, and also quite impossible, to refuse to tell mothers anything they wanted to know. But to give away their wonderful new meeting-place! How truly shocking.

"Was Susie there when you told?" asked Peter.

"Yes," said Jack. "She was, and she said she was jolly well coming to find the cave and make a real mess of it! I don't think she did come here this morning. She was with Jeff all the time in the garden. Mother said so."

"Well then, who did?" said Peter, puzzled. "It's a strange thief who comes and takes three *cushions!*"

There was a silence. Pam glanced round the cave fearfully. Who was it who came here? Jack had seen someone yesterday, and now the someone had come again today. WHO was it?

"Now that Susie knows about our cave, I think that someone must be here on guard whenever we're not here," said Peter. "I mean — we can't let Susie come and mess everything up. I can quite see that if it wasn't her who came and took the things this morning, she must be really furious with us for thinking it was."

"I wouldn't be surprised if she brought Jeff with her and turned the whole place upside down now," said Jack gloomily. "You don't know Susie like I do."

"Well, let's make things jolly unpleasant for them if they do come," said George. "Let's balance a jug of water on that ledge over the green curtain. As soon as the curtain is moved, the jug will overbalance and pour water all over them."

Pam giggled. "Yes. Let's do that!"

"And let's do what my cousin once did to someone he didn't like," said Colin. "He got a reel of cotton and wound it all over and across the entrance to our summer-house — and he dipped it in honey first! Then when this awful boy walked into the summer-house, he walked right through the sticky threads and thought that an enormous spider's web had caught him!"

"How horrible!" said Pam, shuddering. "To have sticky thread all over you like that!"

"Susie would hate it," said Barbara. "She loathes getting caught in spider thread. But who's got cotton or honey? Nobody here!"

"I can run indoors and get a reel of silk from my work-box," said Janet, "and there's some honey in a jar in our kitchen, I know. But aren't we being rather horrid to Susie?"

"No, Susie will only get caught in our tricks if she finds the cave and comes to turn it upside down," said Pam. "It will be her own fault if she gets caught. Nobody else's."

"It's no good being soft-hearted with Susie," said Jack gloomily. "Actually, sometimes I think she's cleverer than any of us!"

Janet ran off to get the honey and the reel of silk. Barbara complained because her cushion was gone and she now had nothing to rest her head on.

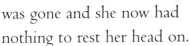

"I suppose whoever took our cushions did it for some kind of silly joke," she said. "And probably threw them into the bushes somewhere."

"I'll go and look," said Colin, and got up. But the cushions were nowhere to be seen, and he soon came back. Janet came with him, having got the reel and the honey.

"We'll get the tricks ready when we go home to tea," said Peter. "I'll slip up after tea to make sure that no one's been into the cave, and I'll come last thing at night too."

Just before they left they arranged the booby-traps. Janet ran the grey silk thread through the sticky honey, and the boys wound it back and forth across the entrance to the cave, twisting it round the plants that lined the edges of the cave entrance from top to bottom.

"There!" said Peter, at last. "No one can get in without getting covered with thin, sticky threads! And what a shock they'll get too, when they draw back the curtain and get swamped with water from that jug! I've balanced it very carefully, so that at the slightest pulling back of the green curtain the water will pour out!"

Everyone giggled and wished they could be there to see the booby-traps catch any intruder. "I hope Jeff comes with Susie, I can't bear him," said Jack. "And shan't I laugh if Susie comes back sticky and wet! Come on, let's go."

After tea Peter went up to the cave to examine the booby-traps. They were still there! The jug of water, half-hidden by leaves, was still in place, and he could see the grey, sticky threads gleaming behind the green curtain.

"Susie and Jeff haven't been yet," he told Janet, when he got back. "I'll slip up again just before it gets dark and have another look."

So up he went once more to the cave, but again the booby-traps were still there, untouched. Susie won't come now, he thought. I'll be up here before nine o'clock tomorrow morning and watch out for her in case she comes then!

CHAPTER VIII
SCAMPER IS A HELP

Jack came to see Peter just before nine next day. "I came to tell you that Susie's not been near the cave," he told Peter. "I kept an eye on her all yesterday evening and this morning. She's gone off to her music lesson now, so we're safe till twelve o'clock anyhow."

"Right," said Peter. "Well, help me with the few jobs I have to do, and then we'll go up with Janet and Scamper. We'll try to get there just before the others come."

So at five to ten, Peter, Janet, Scamper, and Jack made their way to the quarry and then up to the cave.

They looked up to where the jug was so carefully balanced on a ledge, and grinned.

"I'll get it," said Jack, and climbed up to remove it.

"We'll have to break these threads ourselves," said Janet. "What a waste of booby-traps, wasn't it? Ooh, be careful, you'll get honey all over you!"

They broke the threads as carefully as possible, so as not to get themselves sticky, and went into the cave. And then they stood there in astonishment, gazing round as if they could not believe their eyes!

The tins were all opened — and emptied! Some were flung on the floor. Two more of the cushions had gone. A bottle of orangeade had disappeared, and so had a bottle of water. The tin of peppermints had completely vanished, and also some more books. A torch that Colin had left on a shelf had gone too.

"But — but — how could anyone get *in*?" stammered Peter, utterly astonished. "Our booby-traps were still there — those threads were quite unbroken. Nobody could have come in, and yet look at this. I don't like it. There's something very strange going on in this cave – and I just don't – like – it!"

The three children felt scared. It was quite clear that *no one* had gone into the cave, because the sticky silk threads would certainly have been broken. But how could their belongings have been taken, and their tins emptied, if no one had been in the cave?

"You know," said Jack, looking all round him fearfully, "you know, Peter, I was quite certain I saw somebody slipping into the cave that time we played hide-and-seek. You kept saying I must have imagined it, but I didn't."

"Well, certainly *somebody's* about, somebody who likes eating and drinking," said Peter. "And if he didn't get into our cave from the *outside*, he must know a way in from the *inside!*"

"But that's silly too," said Janet. "We know there's no way into the cave from the inside. We've had a jolly good look."

"Scamper seems very interested in the cave this morning," said Jack. "Look at him sniffing and nosing round."

Scamper certainly was interested. He ran here and there excitedly, giving little barks and whimpers, as if to say, "I could tell you such a lot if only I could speak!"

He ran over to the place where he had buried his bone, dug it up, and carefully took it to another corner and buried it there. Peter laughed.

"He's afraid our visitor might find his bone – see how deep he's burying it this time! Hey, Scamper, you're sending sand all over us!"

Janet looked round at the untidy cave with its empty tins and scattered books. Tears came into her eyes. "I made it all so nice," she said. "And we had such a lot of good food here. Who is this horrible visitor who comes when we're not here and steals like this? Where does he come from? How does he get here if he doesn't come in at the entrance?"

"Let's look all round the cave again, very, very carefully to see if there's another entrance somewhere," said Jack. "There might be a small hole that someone could wriggle through, covered with sand."

They looked thoroughly, Scamper sniffing too. But no, no matter how Scamper sniffed all round and about, or how the children dug here and there to find a hole under the rocky walls, nothing was found that would help to solve the mystery.

"And a very strange mystery it is too," said Peter. "I said I didn't like it, and I don't. I vote we clear up this cave and find another meeting-place. It's going to be no fun if we keep having our things stolen and messed about by some unknown visitor."

"Yes. *I* don't feel as if I want to be here any more either," said Janet. "It's a shame. It's such a good place. Well, the others will be along soon, so let's just clear up a bit, and we'll tell them when they come."

It wasn't long before the others came, all four of them, chattering and laughing as they walked through the old quarry.

As soon as they arrived at the cave, Peter told them what had happened. They stared at his grave face and listened in astonishment to what he told them.

"It's very odd," said George. "I don't understand it. Taking food — and cushions — and books! It sounds like someone hiding somewhere and needing food, and something soft to lie on."

"If one or two of us hid here in the cave tonight, we might see whoever it is that comes," said Colin.

There was a silence. Nobody liked the idea at all. This mysterious visitor didn't sound a very nice person to lie in wait for.

"Well," said Peter at last, "I'm no coward, but considering that there really isn't any place in this cave that we could hide in without being seen almost at once, I don't see much point in your suggestion, Colin. I mean the intruder, whoever he is, would probably see *us* before we spotted him. Anyway, I don't like the sound of him."

"Nor do I," said Jack. "I vote we clear out of here and have another meeting-place. What's the sense of bringing stuff here and having it taken as soon as our back's turned?"

They began to clear up the cave. It was really very sad. Scamper watched them in surprise. Why were they looking so miserable? Why were they packing up everything? Well, he'd certainly better get his bone then! He couldn't leave that behind if everyone was leaving the cave!

He ran over to the corner where he had buried it. His sharp nose sniffed something else not far off on a low ledge of rock. Did it belong to the children? It didn't really smell like any of them. Scamper could always tell what shoe or glove belonged to any of the Seven just by sniffing it!

Scamper sniffed at this thing on the ledge, and then picked it up in his mouth. Perhaps it did belong to one of the children after all. He ran with it to Peter and dropped it at his feet with a little bark.

"Hallo, Scamper, what is it?" said Peter. He bent down and picked up a small, dirty notebook with a frayed elastic band round it. "Anyone own this?" he asked, holding it up.

Nobody did. Jack came up, excited.

"Peter! It might have been dropped by our strange visitor! Look inside!"

Peter slipped off the elastic band and opened the little notebook. His eyes suddenly shone. "Yes!" he said, in a low voice. "It *does* belong to our visitor — and here's his name — look. Wow, this is a find! He dropped it when he came raiding our cave last night!"

They all crowded round him in excitement. Peter's finger pointed to a name scribbled at the front of the notebook.

"Albert Tanner," he said. "He's our mysterious visitor. Albert Tanner! Who can he be? Well, we'll find out *somehow!*"

JUST A SPOT OF BOTHER!

The Five Find-Outers and their dog, Buster,
uncover the beginnings of an adventure after Buster
chases a cat on to the roof of an empty house. Can
they solve the mystery ahead of their rival, Mr Goon,
the village policeman?

CHAPTER I
MR GOON IS A NUISANCE

"Let's go down to Fatty's house and see if he'll come for a walk," said Larry to Daisy. "It's a gorgeous day – much too good to spend indoors!"

"All right," said Daisy, putting down her book. "Shall we get Pip and Bets too?"

"We'll call for them on the way," said Larry, and went to find his mother. "Mother – we're going for a walk. We'll be back for lunch."

They went to Pip's house and found him and Bets cleaning out the garden shed. "We're off to Fatty's," said Larry. "Things seem a bit boring today – perhaps Fatty will liven them up! Something usually happens when he's around."

"Oh, good – we'll come too!" said Bets. "I'm tired of this dirty old shed. Mother told us to clean it out, but we can easily finish it when we come back. Do I look too dirty to come out for a walk?"

"You do rather," said Daisy, and brushed down her dress. The dust flew out in a cloud! "There – that's better. There's a black mark on your cheek, too. Got a hanky? Here, use mine."

They set off together, the four of them, and soon arrived at Fatty's house. They whistled, but there was no reply.

"Must be down in his shed," said Larry, and they made their way down to the bottom of the garden, where Fatty's shed was hidden among the close-growing shrubs and trees. Buster the Scottie was in the shed with Fatty, and he barked loudly and joyfully as he heard their footsteps.

"Wuff! Wuff-wuff-wuff!"

Fatty opened the door, grinning. "Hallo! I thought it must be you four, judging by Buster's delighted yaps. What's up? Anything exciting?"

"Not a thing, Fatty," said Larry. "These holidays are pretty boring. It's a super day – what about a walk? We can take old Buster too; he looks as if he wants some of his fat taken off!"

"Wuff," said Buster, quite agreeing. He was always ready for a walk!

"Well, let's go then," said Fatty, shutting his shed door and locking it. "I feel bored, too. Nothing exciting has happened these hols, and we've only a week left. I haven't even seen our enemy!"

"Who? Oh, that fat policeman, Mr Goon!" said Bets. "He's been *very* busy, Mother says, going round and warning people about their dogs."

"Their *dogs*? Why, what's the matter with our dogs, all of a sudden?" said Fatty, surprised. "Buster, do you hear that? You'd better be careful!"

"Well, the farmers have been complaining that dogs are chasing their sheep, and worrying the lambs," said Bets. "So Goon's been warning everyone not to let their dogs wander."

"Well, Buster's far too scared of big old mother sheep to chase them," said Fatty. "He tried it once, and the sheep ran after him, baaing like mad. I never saw Buster run so fast in my life!"

They went down the road, Buster running in front, his tail wagging fast. A large figure in dark blue suddenly swung round the corner on a bicycle, ringing the bell violently. Buster gave a joyful bark, and leaped at the front wheel.

"Clear orf, you!" said a familiar voice, and a foot kicked out at Buster. The bicycle wobbled, and Fatty called to Buster.

"Heel, Buster! Heel, I say! Sorry, Mr Goon. You came round the corner so quickly that you startled old Buster."

"That pest of a dog!" said the big policeman, and jumped off his bicycle. "I was just coming to warn you to keep him locked up. The farmers are complaining of dogs worrying their sheep – and I warn you, if I see a loose dog I'm going to have a few words with the owner!"

"Buster's not loose, he's with *us*," said Fatty. "Anyway, he doesn't wander about by himself."

"You just put him on a lead," commanded Mr Goon.

"I haven't one with me," said Fatty, and walked on with the others. Buster ran back and growled, and Goon hastily mounted his bicycle again, kicking out at the little dog. That was too much for Buster and he sprang at Goon's ankles in delight. The big policeman rode a few feet down the road, still kicking out at Buster, and didn't see a small van coming out of the drive of a house. Fatty gave a loud yell.

"Look out! Mind that van!"

The van braked suddenly, and Goon fell off his bicycle in fright. Buster leaped on him in delight, and Fatty had to rush to pull him off. The van drove round Goon and went off in a hurry. Goon was much too angry with Buster to take any notice of it!

Bets picked Buster up and ran down the road with him, scared that Goon might arrest him and take him away! The others helped poor Goon to his feet, and Fatty dusted him down well.

"That van almost ran over you," he said, trying to distract Goon's anger from Buster to the van. "Coming out of the drive at top speed like that! Not even slowing down or hooting! Might have killed you, Mr Goon! Did you take his number?"

"No. No, I didn't," said Goon, putting his helmet straight. "Where's that dog? I'll – I'll…"

But the others walked on quickly, and left Goon to mount his bicycle again, muttering angrily to himself. It was only when Fatty and the others had turned the corner that something struck Fatty as strange, and he stopped.

"I say – what was that van doing coming out of that drive? The people belonging to the house there are all away – and the house is locked up!"

"Oh, well – it was probably some delivery van – they wouldn't be able to make anyone hear, anyway," said Pip. "Come on, for goodness' sake, or Goon will catch us up!"

CHAPTER 11
COME ON, PUSS!

The five children dodged down a little side-turning, and waited till they saw Goon sailing by, purple in the face.

"Thank goodness he's gone," said Bets, who was scared of the big, loud-voiced policeman. "Let's go down this lane, then we shan't meet him again."

"Right," said Fatty. "It leads down to the river. We'll walk along by the water."

So down to the river they went, and sauntered by the rippling water, which was very blue that sunny morning. Buster ran along happily until he came to the boat-house, and then went to find his friend, Tom the boatman.

"Hallo, Buster," said Tom. "Where's your master? Oh, there you are, Master Frederick – do you want a boat this morning?"

"Well – it might be fun to pull across the river and go to the primrose woods on the other side," said Fatty. "I bet there are millions there this lovely spring day."

"Well, you can take the *Saucy Belle*," said Tom. The five children got in with Buster, who at once ran to the prow, and stood there like a small figurehead. He loved a boat!

They rowed across the river, and landed on the opposite side. They tied up the boat and then made their way to the woods upon the hill. On the way up they passed a big empty house, called River-View, with a "To Be Sold" notice-board beside the gate.

"I say – look at all the daffodils in the front garden here," said Daisy, standing at the gate. "Did you ever see such a sight!"

"Let's go down the path and look at them," said Bets. "My word – if this house was in a town, people would be sure to pick these daffies if they saw the house was empty and to be sold!"

But no one had touched the hundreds of yellow, dancing daffodils, and the five children stood and admired them. Buster couldn't think why they stood and stared at such boring things as flowers! He ran off to explore the garden by himself. He disturbed a cat asleep on a window-sill in the sun, and it yowled in fright when it saw Buster barking below the sill.

Buster leaped at it, and the cat sprang right over his head, and ran to a tree. It was up it in a trice, Buster barking madly at the foot, clawing at the trunk in excitement.

The five children ran to see what was the matter. "Buster! You know you're forbidden to chase cats!" cried Bets. "Oh, look, Fatty, the poor thing's gone right up to the top of the tree!"

"Well – I hope to goodness it can get down," said Fatty. "Let's go – and perhaps it will come down by itself when it sees that we've gone and have taken Buster with us."

So they all trooped out of the front gate, taking one last look at the hundreds of yellow daffodils lining the drive under the trees. Bets turned to watch for the cat to come down the tree, but she couldn't see a sign of it.

"Can we come and see if it's still up the tree, on our way back?" she asked Fatty. "It wasn't a very big cat – not much more than a kitten. It might not know how to climb down a great tree like that."

"Yes. We'll come back and have a look, Bets," said Fatty, smiling. "Buster's a fathead. He knows quite well that he can't catch cats or rabbits, but he always *will* chase them! Come on – we'll go primrosing in the woods now."

There were millions of primroses in the woods on the hill, and the five of them gathered enormous bunches to take home. Then they turned to go back to the river.

"Don't forget, we must look up the tree to see if the cat is still there," said Bets, and Fatty nodded. They went in at the drive gates of the big, empty house again, past the "To Be Sold" notice, and walked by the daffodils. They came to the big tree up which the cat had gone.

They all peered up it, Buster too. "Not a sign of the cat," said Fatty. "It must have come down, Bets. Come on — we'd better go."

But just as they turned to go a sound reached their ears. "Mee-ow! Mee-ow!"

"That's the cat!" said Daisy. "Where is it? That was a frightened miaow, I know it was."

They looked up the tree once more — and then, quite suddenly, Pip caught sight of the cat.

"Look! There it is! Up on the roof of the house, by that chimney!" he said.

"See where that tree-branch reaches out to the roof? It must have run along that, and jumped on to the roof. Now it's scared and can't get down."

"I'd better go up and get it," said Fatty, at once. But Larry leaped up to the lowest bough, and swung himself into the tree before anyone else. He was a fine climber, and was soon at the top. He called coaxingly to the cat.

"Puss! Come on, Puss! Come here to me and I'll take you down. Puss, puss!"
"Mee-ow," said the cat, and didn't move. It sat on the roof beside a skylight, near to a chimney, and looked as if it meant to stay there all day!

Larry slid along the branch to the roof, and Bets held her breath as she saw him climb from the branch to the tiled roof itself.

"Be careful, Larry, old thing," called Fatty, worried. But Larry was used to climbing, and was not at all afraid. He was on the roof now, climbing slowly towards the cat. "Puss!" he said. "Come on, then!" He was now beside the skylight, and the cat only three feet away. He stretched out his arm — and the cat, scared, leaped down the roof, ran to the tree-branch, and half-climbed, half-fell down the tree! It leaped on to a wall and disappeared.

But Larry didn't come down! He sat beside the skylight, peering down into the attic below, looking astonished.

"What's up, Larry? Come on down!" called Fatty impatiently. "Do buck up!"

CHAPTER III
CARPETS! HOW PECULIAR!

Larry gave a shout. "All right! I'm coming! Blow that cat — making me climb all the way up like this. It simply shot down the tree, didn't it?"

He slid down the roof and climbed quickly down the tree. Daisy and Bets were most relieved to see him standing safely beside them. "I was awfully afraid for you," said Bets. "You looked so high up on that roof."

"I saw something a bit strange when I looked down through the skylight there, into a sort of attic below," said Larry. "It was full of rolls of carpets! Do you suppose the people forgot to take them with them?"

"*Carpets!*" said Fatty, astonished. "What do you mean? Wasn't there any old furniture there as well — or boxes — the sort of rubbish you find in an attic?"

"No, *nothing* but carpets," said Larry. "Good-looking ones, too — the kind they call Persian carpets. My granny has one in her hall, and she says it's very valuable."

"I expect the people who are selling the house have stored them there till they sell it," said Daisy. "It would save them storage fees. It costs a lot to pay storage on valuable things, you know."

"Well – if they take long to sell the house, the moths will certainly get at the carpets!" said Larry. "Fatty, do you think we'd better tell the estate agents about those carpets? I mean – if they have been left behind by mistake, when the people left the house, it would be a shame for them to be ruined by moths."

"Right. We'll call at the estate agent's this afternoon," said Fatty. "We shan't have time now. We'll have to buck up, because we're all pretty late. Buster, it's *your* fault! Chasing a cat like that!"

"Woof," said Buster, mournfully, afraid that Fatty was cross with him. They hurried down to to the boat, and rowed across the river at top speed. Soon they were running home, all but Fatty completely forgetting about the curious sight that Larry had seen through the skylight.

Fatty thought about it as he ate his lunch, sitting opposite his mother.

"Whatever are you thinking about so deeply?" asked his mother at last, tired of sitting in silence.

"Persian carpets," said Fatty.

"Good gracious! But why think so deeply about *them*?" asked his mother, astonished.

"They're very valuable, aren't they?" said Fatty. "They oughtn't to be left in an empty house, ought they?"

"Of course not," said his mother, even more astonished. "Nobody in their senses would do such a thing. Moths could completely ruin them in no time. What carpets are you thinking of?"

"Oh – just some that Larry was telling me about," said Fatty hastily, afraid that his mother would ask him questions he would find awkward to answer.

"Dear me – I didn't know Larry was so interested in carpets," said his mother. "What carpets are these?"

Fatty changed the subject. "That reminds me," he said. "Have you an old bit of carpet I could have to put down in my shed, Mother?"

His mother at once forgot about Fatty's interest in Persian carpets, and for the rest of the meal talked at great length about the old rugs she could spare. Fatty was most astonished to hear of so many!

After the meal he remembered that he and the others were to go to the estate agent's to find out about the house on the hill across the river. Once he could discover who the owners were he could write to them – or telephone – and solve the mystery of the carpets. But probably it wasn't a mystery at all!

He was just going to get his bicycle when Buster began barking loudly, as someone came cycling in at the front gate. "It's Goon!" said Fatty, surprised. "Now what does he want? Surely he hasn't come about Buster's behaviour this morning. Blow him!"

He went out to meet Goon, anxious that his mother should not hear the big policeman complaining. Goon dismounted from his bicycle and roared at Buster.

"Now you clear orf, you pest of a dog! You wait till I catch *you* after the sheep! That'll be the end of you!"

Fatty felt angry. Why did Goon always have to shout and make himself so unpleasant? He called Buster to him, and make him sit down at his feet.

"What is it now, Mr Goon?" he said, coldly. "Please don't shout. My mother may be having a rest."

"I've a good mind to send you in a bill for having my suit cleaned," said Mr. Goon. "Look what I did when that dog made me fall off my bike this morning." He showed Fatty a dirty mark all down his coat-sleeve.

"It was that van driving out so suddenly that made you fall," said Fatty. "Not Buster."

"Yes – and I want to ask you something about that too," said Goon, still blustering. "Did you notice the car's number?"

"No. Did you?" asked Fatty. "I saw the name on the side though. But what's all the fuss about? What's wrong with the van? Do you want to prosecute the driver for rushing out of the gate like that?"

"Ha – so you saw the name on the van, did you?" said Mr Goon. "You just tell me what it was, then!"

"You tell me why, first," said Fatty.

"Well, I want to arrest that driver," said Goon importantly. "He and his pal went to that house, knowing its owners are away, forced the door – and went off with all the carpets! And what's more, it's the third time they've done such a thing! So you tell me the name on that van, see?"

Fatty gave a sudden laugh. "It was the baker's van," he said. "I'm afraid you're on the wrong track, Mr Goon. Our baker wouldn't steal carpets. Carpets! Well, that's very, very interesting!"

347

CHAPTER IV
A NICE BIT OF DETECTIVE WORK

The big policeman stared at Fatty in disbelief. "It wasn't the baker's van!" he said. "That wasn't the baker driving it. I saw the driver, and it wasn't the baker!"

"I agree with you," said Fatty. "The thief probably just took the van. I expect he borrows a different one each time he steals carpets, when he hears that people are away for the day, or longer!"

"Yesterday, he went to Lady Burnet's," said Goon. "She'd left two maids there – and the driver told them he was from the cleaner's and had come to take the carpets for cleaning – and they let him have them! He used the *cleaner's* van that time – took it from in front of the shop, bold as you please – and it was found down by the river! Empty!"

Fatty was thinking very, very fast. Should he tell Goon what he knew, or not? Should he tell him of the carpets hidden in the attic of the house across the river? Perhaps he had better…

But he changed his mind when he heard the policeman's next words. "If that dog of yours hadn't gone for me this morning, I'd have been able to challenge the driver of that van, and arrest him, and get back the carpets, and…" he began.

"You wouldn't," said Fatty. "You didn't even know that the van had been borrowed by the thief."

"I'd have guessed it all, if that dog of yours hadn't gone for me!" said Goon. "That dog's as bad as you are, always interfering with the law!"

"That's enough, Mr Goon," said Fatty. "I might have told you a few useful things if you'd been polite – but as it is, I'll get in touch with Superintendent Jenks as soon as I can, to put him on to the carpet thief. I know where the carpets are – and I *think* I know how to get hold of the thief. Good afternoon, Mr Goon!"

And with that Fatty turned his back, and walked down to his shed with Buster pattering at his heels. Mr Goon stared after him in rage.

"I don't believe a word of it!" he shouted. "Not a word! Why, you didn't even know about the carpets till I told you!"

Fatty didn't answer. He was wondering whether to get hold of his friend, the superintendent of police, at once. No – perhaps not. He would look pretty foolish if those carpets that Larry had seen up in that attic were not the stolen ones! He would do as he had planned and go to see the estate agent. He rode off on his bicycle within the next ten minutes, and met the others as he had arranged.

"Daisy, you come with me into the agent's," he said. "I'm not going to ask for the keys or anything – only for the address of the people who want to sell the house."

So in they went, and Fatty said "Good afternoon" politely to the young girl there, sitting at a desk. "Could you please tell me the address of the people who want to sell River-View up on the hill over the river?" he asked.

"Oh, I'm sorry," she said. "But someone is buying it, I think. They have had the keys for a week, and they telephoned today to say they would like them for one more day, as they had *almost* made up their minds to buy the place. So it's not much use my giving you the address of the owners."

"Thank you," said Fatty, and walked out with Daisy, thinking very hard. "They've already had the keys for a week!" he said, "and want them for one more day. That means they are probably going to clear out those carpets tonight. What a nerve they've got! Borrowing other people's vans – walking into houses when they know the owners are away, and taking all the carpets – and then storing them up where no one would ever *dream* of looking for them – in an empty house that's up for sale, and to which they've even got the keys!"

"How do they get the carpets there?" asked Daisy. "Would they go across the river by boat – or take them by car over the bridge?"

"That's a point!" said Fatty, thinking about it. "Not by the bridge, I think, in case the borrowed vans were seen. So that only leaves the river. They must have a boat somewhere in a creek – a covered punt, probably – and punt across at night. Look, shall we take a stroll by the river and see if we can spot some likely boat?"

Everyone agreed that it would be a very good idea, so away by the river they all went, Buster too. It wasn't long before they found what they were looking for!

"Look – there's a house-boat!" said Pip, pointing down to a little hidden creek. "And a small boat beside it! Do you think the thieves would choose a house-boat for stuffing the stolen carpets into, and then use the little row-boat at night to ferry them all across?"

"Yes – I believe you're right, Pip!" said Fatty. "If you *are* right, then we ought to find some carpets in this house-boat, waiting for tonight's removal by boat!"

They slid down into the creek, and tried to peer in at the windows of the house-boat. It was called *Rockabye*, and was a very small one. Its windows had curtains pulled tightly across. Not a thing could be seen inside the boat, which, of course, was strongly padlocked.

"No go," said Pip, disappointed. "Can't see a thing!"

"Wait a bit!" said Larry suddenly. "Look — what do you reckon this is?"

He was pointing down to the railings that ran round the house-boat's small deck. Everyone looked, and Daisy gave a little cry. "Carpet threads! They must have dragged the carpets over the railings, and one got caught on that nail, and left that little tuft of threads. That *proves* we're right!"

They climbed up to the river-bank again, excited. Pip pointed to the field behind. "Car-wheel marks!" he said. "Look, they must have come down that lane, through that gate, and over the field to the river. It's so deserted here that it would be a hundred to one chance if anyone saw them!"

"We'd better get on to the superintendent at once," said Fatty, delighted. "Come on — we'll rush back home, and I'll phone. My word — this is just about the quickest mystery we've ever solved!"

CHAPTER V
QUITE A LOT HAPPENS!

The five, with Buster at their heels, just as excited as they were, cycled back quickly to the town. Fatty went to telephone from the post-office — but to his bitter disappointment the superintendent was not in.

"He won't be back till tonight, sir," said the clerk who answered. "If it's anything important I suggest that you report it to Mr Goon."

That idea didn't appeal to Fatty and the others at all. They debated what to do. "There's not much time to be lost," said Fatty, considering the matter. "I believe the thieves will probably clear off after stealing this last lot of carpets. They said they wanted the keys only till tomorrow, you remember! They'll take today's haul of carpets out of that house-boat tonight and ferry them across the river in that little row-boat, collect the whole lot out of that attic Larry saw, and probably load them into a removal van — another 'borrowed' one — and that will be the last anyone ever hears of them!"

"Well, we certainly can't stop them by ourselves," said Larry soberly. "We'll simply *have* to tell Goon."

So, very much against their will, the five of them cycled down to the police station after tea that evening, with Buster running beside them. Goon was extremely surprised to see them.

"What do you want?" he said roughly. "Come to tell me a cock-and-bull story again about where the stolen carpets are? Well, I warn you, you won't bamboozle *me!*"

"We don't want to bamboozle you," said Fatty, in the polite voice that irritated the policeman so much. "We've come to put our cards on the table. We know where the stolen carpets are — we know how they're taken there — and we know that unless you go there this evening, you'll probably be too late!"

"I'm surprised you don't tell all this to the superintendent instead of me," said Goon, suspiciously. "It's not like you to come to *me!* I'll take a pinch of salt with all you say, see?"

"Very well," said Fatty, annoyed. "Here is our information. Take it or leave it. The last lot of carpets are hidden in the house-boat called *Rockabye*, away up the river. They will be rowed across the water tonight, and taken up the hill to a house called River-View. There are dozens more stolen carpets there, probably all valuable, stuffed into the attic. They will probably all be removed tonight, or at the latest, tomorrow."

"I don't believe a word of it!" said Goon. "Not a word! Nobody could know all that! You want to send me on a wild-goose chase, just like you've done before! AND I happen to know something that proves you're wrong!"

"What's that?" asked Fatty, surprised.

"*There's nobody living at River-View,*" said Goon, triumphantly. "You chose the wrong house to send me to, Mr Clever — an empty one. Now just you clear out, all of you — and I'll be reporting this silly nonsense to the superintendent tonight. My word, you'll get a proper ticking-off, you see if you don't."

Bets looked scared. Fatty hustled them all out, afraid that he was going to lose his temper. Well — he had done his best. Now he must wait and telephone to the superintendent later on, and hope that it would not be too late!

But Mr Goon managed to get in first, and the superintendent listened to him in amazement. "But why should that boy, Frederick, pull your leg?" he asked Goon. "It seems to me there may be something in his tale. I'll ring him myself."

And he did — and listened with very much interest to what Fatty had to say! "Goon didn't believe a word, sir," said Fatty. "But I'm sure we're right! Can you send some men up to River-View before it's too late? I wouldn't be surprised if they're going to remove everything tonight."

"I'll send my men up there, don't you worry," promised the superintendent. "But you keep out of it tonight, Frederick."

Fatty grinned and put back the receiver. *He* wasn't going to keep out of it – or Larry or Pip either! He wouldn't let the girls go, but he and the others would.

And so, about eight o'clock that night, when it was getting dark, the three boys rowed across the river, and then made their way up to River-View. Aha! What was this in the drive, close to the side door? A small removal van! Fatty pushed Larry and Pip into the bushes, and hoped that the superintendent's men would come in time.

To his horror, a strong hand gripped his arm from out of the bush behind him. Fatty froze into stillness. Were the thieves hiding there, then?

A voice hissed in his ear. "I told you to keep out of it!"

Gosh! It was the superintendent himself, waiting in hiding with six other men! Fatty grinned in delight. And now, who on earth was this, coming down the drive, clomping along on heavy feet?

"It's Goon!" whispered Larry in his ear. "He thought he'd better come along, after all, to make sure you were wrong, Fatty! Hallo – now what's happening?"

Plenty seemed to happen all at once! Three men suddenly appeared at the side door, carrying bundles of carpets, standing in the light of a lamp in the passage behind them. Goon challenged them with a shout.

"Hey, you! What are you doing?"

In a trice the men had dropped their bundles, and leaped at Goon. He went down with a yell, and was promptly heaved into the removal van, with carpets loaded on top of him. Fatty could hear his smothered, furious shouts. A chuckle came from behind him. It was the superintendent, highly amused.

"Goon has found out that you spoke the truth to him, Frederick," he whispered. "Now, keep back here in the bushes, please. We're going out after the men!"

He blew his whistle sharply, and Fatty jumped. Then, in a crowd, the superintendent and his men bore swiftly down on the amazed thieves. There were shouts and blows – but it was all over very quickly indeed – far too quickly for the three boys! In no time at all, the three men were locked inside their own removal van, and driven swiftly away to the police station. The superintendent clapped Fatty on the back.

"A neat little job, Frederick, wasn't it?" he said. "Thanks to you! Another hour and we'd have been too late. Can I give you a lift home? Our police car is under some trees, a little way down the road."

"Well – perhaps you'd better take poor Mr Goon instead," said Fatty, generously. "He can't feel too good after being shoved into that van and having carpets thrown all over him. He's sitting down on the gravel path over there, groaning like anything."

"His feelings are hurt more than his body," said the superintendent, hard-heartedly. "If he really didn't believe what you so kindly told him, he shouldn't have come along here tonight. Well – perhaps I'd better give him a lift. Goon – get up. We'll take you back in our car."

"No, thanks, sir," said Goon, staggering up. He had no wish to talk to the superintendent just then. Why, oh why, hadn't he believed the fat boy when he had told him that very peculiar-sounding story? "I've got this house to go through and lock up, sir," he said, "and then I must get in touch with the owners. There's plenty to do! You take those boys instead."

So, very gleefully, Fatty, Larry and Pip rode proudly back in the big black police car. "Another mystery solved, eh, Frederick?" said the superintendent.

"Oh, this really wasn't much of a mystery, sir," said Fatty, modestly. "Let's call it just a spot of bother!"

THE FIVE FIND-OUTERS AND DOG TACKLE THE MYSTERY SNEAK THIEF

ILLUSTRATED BY
DEREK EYLES

Mr Goon believes that Willy Jones the window-cleaner is responsible for a series of burglaries in Peterswood. Fatty and his friends are sure that Willy is innocent, and set out to find the real culprit...

"What are you going to do this morning, Frederick?" said Mrs Trotteville, getting up from the breakfast-table. "Because if you've nothing to do I thought you might perhaps clean out the hen-house."

"Oh, I shall be very busy, Mother!" said Fatty at once. "I've a meeting with the others, round at Larry's and I can't possibly let them down."

"What you really mean is that you *detest* cleaning out the hen-house," said his father, putting down his newspaper. "Well, you know that cleaning it out is one of your holiday jobs — so if you don't want to take it on, just give me ten pounds of your pocket-money, and I'll get the odd-job man to do it."

"I say, Dad — that's a bit steep, isn't it?" said Fatty, shocked. "Ten pounds! Whew! I've only about twelve pounds left to last me till I go back to school. All right. I'll do the hen-house, but give me till this evening — I've promised to meet the others, I really have."

"Ah! Some great mystery to solve, I suppose!" said his father, getting up. "All right – you can leave the hen-house till this evening. If it's not done then, I get Jake to do it – and you do the paying!"

"Well, actually, we *have* got a mystery on hand," said Fatty. "I expect you've heard about it, Mother. There's a sneak-thief going round, taking all sorts of things – anything he can find – jewellery, clocks, silver, money. And we think that possibly we might track him. You know he went to that big house on the hill and took a gold cigarette box, and silver ash trays, and he took the maid's purse – she had left it on the window-sill – and several other things that were lying around."

"Well, I hope he doesn't come here!" said Mrs Trotteville. "He'd find a wonderful lot of things strewn about all over the place – your pullover, for instance, and your watch, and your new cricket-bat – can you tell me why you left that in the larder, Frederick?"

"Oh, gosh – so that's where it is!" said Fatty, surprised. "Now how on earth did it get there?"

"I imagine you left it there when you went to see if Cook had made any new jam-tarts," said his mother. "Well, it's still there if you want it! Now, Frederick remember that hen-house, please, and get on with the job – it's got to be done by this evening."

Fatty groaned. Those hens! Those messy, smelly hens! How in the world did they manage to lay such nice clean eggs? He went out of the room with his dog Buster at his heels, and collected his bat from the larder, while Cook stood suspiciously in the doorway and watched him with sharp eyes.

"Good thing I didn't chop that bat up for firewood!" she said, as he sauntered out of the kitchen. "You just keep out of my larder, see?"

"I can't, while you make such delicious pies and tarts and..." began Fatty, and slid out of the kitchen door just in time to escape a swipe from the large wooden spoon that Cook was using.

He put his bat safely in the hall-cupboard, and then cycled round to Larry's, Buster galloping along behind. The others were already there, sitting solemnly in the meeting-shed. There were four of them – Larry, Daisy, Pip and Bets. Buster was delighted to see them and leaped up and down round them.

"Hallo!" said Fatty. "Sorry I'm late. Buster, sit down and behave yourself."

"Oh, let him lick me if he wants to," said little Bets, hugging the Scottie. "Fatty, we've more news!"

"What! About that sneak-thief, do you mean?" asked Fatty, eagerly.

"Yes," said Larry. "He went to the house next door yesterday evening, when everyone except the old lady was out. She was asleep in her room, and—"

"Did she see him? What was he like?" asked Fatty, at once.

"The poor old lady is blind," said Daisy. "She woke up and heard him, though, and called out to know who it was!"

"He didn't answer, of course," said Larry. "But she said she heard him cough once or twice. He took her lovely little silver clock, and she heard him knock over something which broke."

"What broke?" asked Fatty. "Was it something he was stealing?"

"Might have been – but I should hardly think so – the old lady said it was a bottle of her best violet scent!" said Pip. "She smelled it at once, of course! The thief took a mackintosh belonging to the old lady's son, and some jewellery too."

"Hm – his usual thefts," said Fatty. "Except for the mackintosh, of course. He might have taken that because he wanted big pockets that he could put all the stolen goods into."

"Or maybe because it was pouring with rain last night," said Bets. "It rained like anything – don't you remember?"

"Yes. Yes, you're probably right. Bets," said Fatty. "Has old Goon, the village policeman, been down to investigate yet?"

At that very moment Buster began to bark fiercely, and raced out of the shed at top speed, his hackles rising.

"Buster! Come here! Gosh. I suppose it's old Goon arriving now. Buster can smell him a mile away!" said Fatty, getting up and going down the path to the gate. "Yes – it is Goon! Good morning, Mr Goon — come to find some clues?"

The fat policeman was out of breath, for he had cycled at top speed from the police station. He scowled at Fatty. "You keep out of this!" he said, wheeling his bicycle in at the next-door gate. "You're too late anyway – I reckon I know the thief, and I don't want any help from you, thank you very much!"

As the policeman wheeled his bicycle up to the front door of the next house. Fatty looked round at the others, who were just behind him. "Goon must have polished up his brains a bit," he said, surprised. "Did you hear what he said? He knows who the thief is!"

"We'll wait till he comes out and then go and talk to the next-door gardener," said Larry. "He's a great friend of mine."

So, as soon as Goon came out from the house and disappeared on his bicycle, the five and Buster went quietly through a hole in the hedge to find the gardener.

He was digging in the vegetable beds, and judging by the way he thrust his fork in and out, he was very angry indeed.

"That Goon!" he was muttering. "Him and his clues! I'll clue him!"

"Hallo, Toms," said Larry. "What's upset you?"

"It's that there bobby!" said Toms, digging his fork into the earth so deeply that he had to tug it to get it out again. "Says he knows the thief who came last night – the one who's been stealing all round the houses. Well, he's wrong! He's daft to think it's Willy Jones – he wouldn't do a thing like that!"

"Who's Willy Jones?" asked Fatty, at once.

"What – don't you know Willy Jones the old window-cleaner?" said Toms, in surprise. "He's a friend of mine, he is – a nice old fellow!"

"Oh, yes – of course I know him!" said Fatty. "He's our window-cleaner too! Toms, Mr Goon can't really think it's Willy! Why should he?"

"Well, Willy goes all round the houses, you see – and he has a ladder, and he can peep into windows upstairs and downstairs!" said Toms. "And he can see what silver is about, or jewellery lying around, or money. So Mr Goon reckons it's Willy, seeing that Willy happens to have been cleaning windows at every single house that has been robbed!"

"Is that true?" said Larry. "Has Willy really cleaned windows at every house that has been robbed? You don't mean that he actually climbs off his ladder into rooms, and takes things, do you?"

"Of course not!" said Toms, in scorn. "Willy would never do a thing like that! No, Goon thinks that Willy spots the things as he cleans the windows, and then goes and breaks into the house later on, at night, see? And takes what he spotted earlier on."

"Was Willy cleaning windows here yesterday?" asked Daisy.

"Yes – that's what set Goon on to him today," said Toms, with a frown. "First thing he asks is – "Did you have your windows cleaned yesterday, ma'am?" And when Mrs Lakes says "Yes, we did," Goon looks down his nose at once, and says, "Ha! Just what I thought!" And that's another black mark for poor old Willy, see?"

"It is a bit strange that every house visited by Willy should be robbed the same day – or night," said Fatty, thoughtfully. "That's a bit of a puzzle, I must say. I mean – it's rather a strange coincidence, isn't it?"

"I don't know what a coin – coin – er, well, whatever you said just now, is," said Toms, digging his fork furiously into the ground. "All I know is that old Willy wouldn't rob a sparrow of a bit of bread."

"What about fingerprints?" said Fatty. "Haven't any been found in the houses that the thief visits?"

"Not a one," said Toms, in disgust. "And for why? Because the real thief wears gloves, of course. And I tell you this, old Willy never had a pair of gloves in his life! And I tell you something else, too — if that Goon arrests Willy, I'll go and break the police station down and free him!"

The five children left the angry gardener and went up to the house. Mrs Lakes saw them from the window and beckoned to them.

"Have you been talking to Toms?" she said. "I suppose he told you about the trouble here. My poor old blind mother is very upset to hear that Willy the window-cleaner is the thief."

"Yes, we heard," said Fatty, politely. "We're so sorry that your mother had such a fright, Mrs Lakes. Where is she?"

"In the study," said Mrs Lakes. "Go and talk to her, if you like. She has recovered from her fright now. Come on in."

So the five of them, with Buster at their heels, went into the study. The old lady was very willing to tell them everything — but alas, it was very little more than they already knew.

"I couldn't see him," she said. "But I heard him. I heard him cough, and I heard him knock over my bottle of violet scent, and break it. But he didn't say a single word! Not one. He took my dear little silver clock, too — it's worth a mint of money. It not only tells the time — it shows the date of the month, and the year as well, and rings loudly at any hour I set it for."

"Had you set the alarm for any special time?" asked Fatty.

"Oh, I always set it for seven o'clock," said the old lady. "I like to wake up then, you know. But I hadn't wound it up last night, so it wouldn't have gone off at seven this morning."

Bets gave a little laugh. "So if the thief happens to wind it up, it will go off at seven o'clock this evening!" she said. "What a shock he will get!"

"I hope he will!" said the old lady. "The old window-cleaner is the thief, you know — that's what that clever policeman. Mr Goon, told us. He's going after him this morning."

"Poor old Willy," said Bets. "Fatty — can't you do something? You're sure it's not Willy — well, can't you find out who it is?"

"That's easier said than done, Bets," said Fatty. "This thief is a wily fellow — never leaves a clue behind him, it seems. Well, thank you, Mrs Lakes, we hope you'll soon get over the shock. Goodbye."

They went back to Larry's shed, and talked. "We've only three real clues," said Fatty, dolefully. "One is that the man has a cough. The second is that he might smell of violet scent, if he spilt any on his clothes when he broke the bottle — and the third is that he may be wearing Mr Lakes' old mack. Though I don't really think he'd do that, he'd be spotted too easily!"

"Well — we'll have to spend the day looking for a man with a cough, smelling of violet scent and wearing an old mackintosh," said Pip. "What a hope!"

"It's impossible!" said Larry. "In fact, it's silly. We can't go round listening for people to cough and sniffing them to see if they smell of violets!"

"All right — you think of something better, then," said Fatty. "Buster — put on your thinking-cap, too!"

"Wuff!" said Buster, helpfully, and sat with his head on one side as if he were thinking deeply. Then he scratched himself vigorously, yawned, and lay down to sleep.

"You're no help at all, Buster!" said Fatty. "Well, the only thing we can do is to separate, and walk about all over the town, and see if we can smell anyone with the scent of violets on them! *And* with a cough! Come on — we can at least try! Meet here in an hour's time, and I'll bring some biscuits and lemonade. I bet we'll all be pretty hungry and thirsty by then."

"Wuff," said Buster, approving of the word "biscuits" at once. They all stood up, brushed the floor dust off themselves and set off. They parted at the front gate, Buster going with Fatty.

"Well — good luck!" said Fatty, and jumped on his bicycle. Buster ran beside him as usual. "Just tell me if you suddenly smell violets, Buster," said Fatty, "and I'll leap off at once! Talk about looking for a needle in a haystack — this is even worse than that!"

As Fatty passed the police station, he saw the policeman standing on the steps. He jumped off his bicycle, and shouted to him. "Caught the thief yet, Mr Goon?"

"You clear orf," said the fat policeman. "I'm getting hold of Willy the window-cleaner this morning, and asking him a few straight questions, so don't you go poking your nose into this here business, see."

"I'm looking for a smell," said Fatty, riding off again.

"Just a smell, Mr Goon. And when I find the smell I'll bring it along to the police station!"

"Gah!" said Mr Goon, in disgust, and stared after Fatty angrily. That boy! What did he mean, looking for a *smell*?

Fatty took his bicycle home and then for nearly an hour he and Buster walked round the town sniffing at the people they passed, and taking special notice of men with old mackintoshes or bad coughs. They smelled a large number of different smells and they saw a number of people in old mackintoshes and they heard a lot of people coughing — but none of them smelled of violets at all.

Before long it was time to meet the others so Fatty went home and got the biscuits and lemonade and put them in his bicycle basket to take to the others as he had promised. "Well, any luck?" he asked, as he sat down in Larry's shed once more and passed round the biscuits and lemonade.

"I followed a man with an awful cough," said Larry. "But when I got near him, he smelled of onions, not violets, so he wasn't any good as a suspect."

"And I followed a girl who seemed to smell of violets or something," said Daisy. "I thought perhaps the thief might turn out to be a girl after all, not a man! Maybe she just dressed up like a man when she went out stealing."

"Quite an idea," said Fatty. "After all, nobody's ever seen him. What happened?"

"She met another girl, and told her she'd just had a hair shampoo," said Daisy, dolefully. "A honeysuckle shampoo, whatever that may be. No wonder she smelled strong! So that wasn't any good either."

"Bad luck, Daisy," said Fatty. "Pip? Did you find anything helpful?"

"Not a thing," said Pip. "There must be something wrong with my nose. I didn't smell a single smell."

"Bets?" said Fatty.

"Well, Fatty," said Bets, earnestly, "I didn't smell any smell either — but I did hear something which I thought might be important."

"What?" asked Fatty.

"Well, I was standing by the bus-stop, smelling everyone who jumped off the buses, when I heard one girl say to another: 'Pooh — did you smell that man beside me in the bus? He might have been a bunch of violets!' And the other girl said

360

'Well, it seemed to me as if someone had poured a whole bottle of scent over him!' "

Everyone looked suddenly excited. Fatty clapped Bets on the shoulder. "Ah! This looks as if we're getting somewhere. Go on, Bets. That man may be the thief! What did you do then?"

"Well, the bus had gone on by this time, so I couldn't jump on it and do a little smelling out myself, so I asked the girls about the man. I said "Did this smelly man have a cough?" and they said "Yes, he did.' "

"It's our man, then!" said Larry, excited.

"And I said 'What was he like?' and they said he had on a dark suit…"

"Oh – not an old mac?" said Larry, disappointed.

"Well, if he'd had on the old mac, the violet smell wouldn't have been so noticeable," said Fatty. "The mac would have choked it, so to speak. Besides, it isn't raining. Anything else, Bets?"

"Yes, there's one thing more," said Bets. "The girls said the man asked for a ticket to Birch Corner – the road at the bottom of your garden, Fatty – not the road you live in, but the one that runs parallel!"

"Well!" exclaimed Fatty. "Don't tell me the fellow is going to rob our house – or a neighbour's! I wonder which houses old Willy the window-cleaner is going to today – it's probably one of those that the thief will rob tonight – or maybe today, if he finds one with nobody at home! He seems to follow in Willy's footsteps, so to speak, so that poor old Willy is suspected of the thefts."

"Let's scout round and see if we can find Willy," said Pip. "He'll soon tell us if he's been to any houses round that way today!"

So Larry and Daisy fetched their bikes, and Pip and Bets ran to get theirs, and soon they were all riding to Fatty's road with Fatty leading, and Buster panting along behind.

"There's old Willy!" shouted Pip, as they saw the old man in front of them, riding his bicycle, and carrying his ladder skillfully on his shoulder. "Let's follow him and see where he's going."

Willy went down Fatty's road, took a right-angled turn and rode down to the street that lay parallel to Fatty's. Here the back gardens of the two roads lay back to back. Willy cycled to a house standing about halfway down the road, and leaped off his bicycle.

"Hey, Willy!" yelled Fatty. "How are you? Been doing a lot of work this morning?"

"Ah — it's you, Master Frederick," said Willy, who looked distinctly gloomy. "No — that policeman's been after me, asking me daft questions. Anyone'd think I'd been robbing houses! Messing up my morning! I haven't been able to clean any windows at all. I'm just going to do this house here — Birch-Trees, it's called — and then I'm going home. That policeman has made me feel right upset."

"Oh. So this is the only house whose windows you'll be cleaning today," said Fatty. "Bad luck, Willy. But keep your spirits up! We know you're not the thief."

"That's all very well," grumbled Willy. "What I wants to know is, who *is* the thief? I don't want no fingers pointed at me, what's never even robbed a dog of his bone!"

"Wuff-wuff!" said Buster, quite approving of this. He wagged his tail furiously and licked Willy's hand.

Willy went down the path to the house with his ladder, and the children trooped off to Fatty's shed, and sat down to talk. "If the thief is going to rob a house today, then it's sure to be the one that Willy's cleaning now, the one backing on to your garden, Fatty," said Larry, solemnly. "Can't we go round to Birch-Trees and warn the people to keep a look-out today — or tonight?"

"Yes, let's do that," said Fatty. "Good idea. Come on!" So off they went, and were soon in the road where Birch-Trees was. But someone was there before them — Mr Goon, leaning on his bicycle, earnestly watching Willy cleaning the windows!

"Well — if he's on guard, Birch-Trees should be all right," said Fatty. "Gosh — I must fly! I'll be late! See you all tomorrow at ten!"

Fatty lazed that afternoon, reading a book. His mother came to look for him. "Fatty, whatever have you been doing all morning? You haven't touched that hen-house — and you know what your father said!"

"I'll do it after tea," said Fatty. "I promise, Mother, I will really."

"It will be getting dark then," said his mother. "Remember, Frederick — you'll lose ten pounds of your pocket-money if it's not done!"

Fatty groaned, but after tea he went down to the hen-house, and began the job. He cleaned the floor thoroughly, sluicing it down, and then sweeping it. He cleaned up the yard too, picking up all the old cabbage stalks and the bits and pieces.

"Now I'll do the nesting-boxes," he thought. "And I'll leave the underneath of the shed till last. Gosh, look at the mess of old sacks and boxes that have been chucked there! Phew! I'll have to go and get myself a drink of lemonade or something – all this hard work is making me jolly thirsty!"

He went back to the house and poured himself a long drink of lemonade – and then another. "Now I feel better, Buster!" he said. "Come on, lazy-bones – come along and help me. But don't bark, because the hens will have gone to roost on their perches, or on the nesting-boxes, and you'll disturb them!"

He and Buster once more went down to the hen-house, and Fatty opened its big wooden door. Then he stood still, looking astonished. What in the world was this peculiar smell coming from the hen-house?

"Buster," said Fatty, in an amazed voice. "Buster – do you know what the shed smells of now – VIOLETS! Smell it! Now why on earth should a hen-house suddenly smell of violets?"

"Wuff!" said Buster, puzzled too. He sniffed here and there excitedly, whining a little. Then he put his head on one side and looked up at Fatty.

"Yes, I know what you're saying – just what I'm thinking!" said Fatty. "You think that the thief who stole those things at Mrs Lakes' yesterday, has been here! But why? He wouldn't want to steal eggs, surely?"

Buster seemed uneasy. He ran here and he ran there, he growled, he whined, he looked everywhere, as if there was somebody he couldn't see. The hens grew restless and the three on the nesting-boxes fluttered off and joined the others on the perches. Buster ran to one of the nests and sniffed there, scraping with his paw. Then he ran back to Fatty and then back to the nesting-box, whining with excitement. Fatty went over to him.

He stared in amazement. Something had been hidden under the heap of straw in the nest! Buster had scraped at it and dislodged something. Something that glittered and shone!

"A brooch! A diamond brooch!" said Fatty, in astonishment. "Quick, Buster, look in the other nesting-boxes. We may find something there!"

They certainly did! Under every heap of straw was hidden some piece of jewellery! "And I think I know whose they are!" said Fatty, in delight. "They all belong to the people at Birch-Trees! I've seen the girl there wearing this gorgeous necklace! Whew, Buster – we're on to something!"

Buster barked excitedly, as Fatty pocketed all the jewellery. "You know what's happened, Buster?" said Fatty. "The thief went to Birch-Trees sometime after old Willy had left, and Goon had gone home – and stole all this, so that once more poor old Willy would be blamed. But maybe Goon came back on watch and scared him, so he had to find somewhere nearby to hide the things – and and he slipped down the back garden of Birch-Trees and into our garden – and found the nesting-boxes in the hen-house. And, Buster, he'll be back again to fetch these things tonight. I bet he's hiding somewhere near this very minute, waiting for darkness to come, so that he can slip in without being seen."

Buster was very excited – but he still seemed uneasy, running here and there, and sniffing. "I suppose you can't understand that violet scent, can you, old thing?" said Fatty. "Now listen – you stay here on guard, while I go up and tell my father what we've found, and get him to telephone Goon. Ha! What a shock it's going to be for poor old Goon, when he hear's we've found the stolen things!"

Soon Fatty's father and mother were listening in amazement to his tale, and his father at once rang up Mr Goon. The policeman was astounded. "Ha – Willy again, of course," he said. "He was cleaning windows at Birch-Trees today. I was watching him. I'll be along at once, sir."

In ten minutes' time the hen-yard seemed full of people – Fatty's parents, Fatty, Mr Goon, and the people from Birch-Trees, who had just come home after an afternoon out.

"The thief must have known we were going out!" they said. "He stole any amount of our things! Where is he? Has he gone? Well, he'll surely come back for the things he hid so carefully, in the nesting-boxes!"

"I feel as if he must be hiding somewhere not far off, said Fatty, puzzled. "Buster seems so uneasy. But where on earth can he be? There isn't anywhere to hide!"

And then suddenly something made them all jump, as they stood there in the darkening yard – a loud, shrill noise, a ringing noise that went on and on and on!

"A clock – a clock with its alarm ringing!" said Fatty. "It must be the old lady's clock – the one the thief stole from the Lakes' house yesterday! It was set to ring at seven!"

"But where does the noise come from?" asked Fatty's father, looking all round the yard. "There's nobody here – and no shed to hide in!"

But Buster knew where the noise came from! He raced across to a large bin that held corn for the chickens and scraped at it, barking wildly. "Ha!" said Mr Goon, majestically, and strode across to the bin. He wrenched off the lid, and looked inside – and there, in the remains of the corn, was a small man, huddled up inside the bin!

"So *you're* the thief – not Willy!" said Mr Goon, in astonishment. "*You,*
Skinny Tim! Get out of this bin at once and come along with me."

"I can't. I'm stuck," said Skinny Tim. "I'd have got out before, if I could,
when I heard you coming. I'm stuck, I tell you. Ooooh, the cramp I've got! I'll
never be able to stand up straight again!"

"Serve you right!" said Mr Goon, fiercely. "Making us think it was Willy the
window-cleaner taking those things! My, how you smell! Violets and corn don't
mix! Come on now – out you come."

"I'd have been all right if this here silly clock in my pocket hadn't given the
game away!" said Skinny Tim, groaning as he was hauled out of the bin. "How was
I to know it was an alarm clock – and all set for seven too! My luck's properly out
today!"

He was taken away by Mr Goon, so stiff that he was hardly able to walk.
Buster danced round him in delight, trying to nip his ankles. The man was wearing
the old mackintosh that he had taken from the Lakes, so, as Fatty said,
"Everything fitted beautifully…mac, clock – and scent of violets! Yes, and a cough,
too – just listen to him. I bet he coughed when he was in that bin, and old Buster
heard him!"

"Wuff, wuff," said Buster, agreeing.

Fatty watched Skinny Tim being hauled away down the garden path. "We'll
go and telephone the others," he said to Buster. "Then I'd better come down here
again and quieten those hens. They'll never lay eggs in the morning if they don't
get to roost! What a good thing that Skinny Tim hid his stolen goods in their
nesting-boxes, on the very day I had to clean out the hen-house! What a bit of
luck!"

The hens agreed loudly. "Cluck-cluck, what-luck, cluck-cluck, what-luck!"
they said. Yes, Fatty – it was a bit of luck-cluck-cluck!

A HAPPY ENDING
A POEM

I found a ship upon the sea,

All ready waiting there for me,

So in I jumped and off we sped,

To gleaming waters far ahead.

But soon a wind came moaning by

And clouds filled all the sunny sky,

The sea was speckled with the rain,

And my ship rolled and rolled again.

The waves crashed grandly on the deck,

The sails dripped rain-drops down my neck,

Then straight ahead, I spied a rock,

And braced myself to meet the shock—

Crash! we struck, and there we stayed,

While rain and storm around us played;

The ship at once began to fill,

And down and down we sank – until

I yelled in fear and clutched the side,

Half-drowning in the racing tide,

And just as mast and rigging broke,

I found myself in bed – and WOKE!

AFTERWORD
A POEM

It's goodbye now – the book is done,

You've read the stories one by one,

You've guessed the villains (were you right?)

And slept on Thunder Rock all night!

And in the Smugglers' Cave you found

Treasure lying all around.

You solved with young Detective John

the problems he was working on.

You visited, at dead of night,

A lonely house, and got a fright!

There isn't room to write of all

The fine adventures, big and small,

For see, the book is really done

With all its stories and its fun,

So now goodbye, and let me say

I hope we'll meet again some day!

A MEMOIR OF ENID BLYTON

❧ BY HER DAUGHTER ❧
GILLIAN BAVERSTOCK

One of my clearest childhood memories is of my mother sitting writing a new book, while I rushed home to read the latest pages. All the stories in this treasury were part of my childhood, but the book I loved best was *The Secret Island* which, with *The Treasure Hunters*, *The Secret of Spiggy Holes* and *Five on a Treasure Island*, was written before I was ten and were each read hot off the typewriter!

Soon after a family holiday in Dorset, my mother started *Five on a Treasure Island* and much of the Dorset countryside is reflected in that book. Before she wrote *The Island of Adventure*, she stayed in Cornwall and the description of the towering cliffs and thundering waves is very different from that of the Dorset coast in the Famous Five books.

Later, my sister and I helped to correct proofs of the books, earning a penny for every mistake. We laughed aloud over the Barney stories, especially *The Rubadub Mystery*, and Snubby, and his dog Loonie, based on our own black spaniel, are two of the funniest characters in any book.

The Mystery books are also very amusing, especially Fatty with his disguises and ventriloquism. These books are set in Buckinghamshire near the River Thames, where my mother lived from 1929 to 1938, and she was familiar with the places mentioned, though Peterswood does not exist.

The Secret Seven were real children who had their own secret society and asked my mother to write a story about them. She had only intended to write a single book, but so many readers begged for another that she wrote the whole Secret Seven series. Soon Enid Blyton's great-grandchildren will read them, while the original seven children will tell their grandchildren proudly about their own secret society fifty years ago!

370

ENID BLYTON

1897 – 1968

ACKNOWLEDGEMENTS

We gratefully acknowledge permission to reproduce copyright
material from the following books:

The Secret Island (text)
The Treasure Hunters (text and illustrations)
The Secret of Spiggy Holes (text)
The Secret of Cliff Castle (illustrations)
Smuggler Ben (illustrations)
The Rilloby Fair Mystery (text and illustrations)
Off with the Adventurous Four Again (text)
The Rubadub Mystery (text and illustrations)
reproduced by permission of HarperCollins Publishers Ltd

The Island of Adventure (text and illustrations)
The Valley of Adventure (text, illustrations and dustjacket)
reproduced by permission of Macmillan Children's Books

A Night on Thunder Rock (text)
Smugglers' Cave (text)
Number Sixty-two (text)
The Case of the Five Dogs (text)
reproduced by permission of Award Publications Limited

The Mystery of the Secret Room (illustrations)
Just a Spot of Bother! (illustrations)
The Mystery of the Strange Messages (dustjacket)
reproduced by permission of Egmont Children's Books Limited

The Adventure of the Secret Necklace (illustrations and dustjacket)
reproduced by permission of The Lutterworth Press

Thanks also to Norman Wright for providing photographic reference
and original material, and to Alison Still for her text design.

While every effort has been made to obtain permission, there may still
be cases in which we have failed to trace a copyright holder. The publisher
will be happy to correct any omission in future printings.

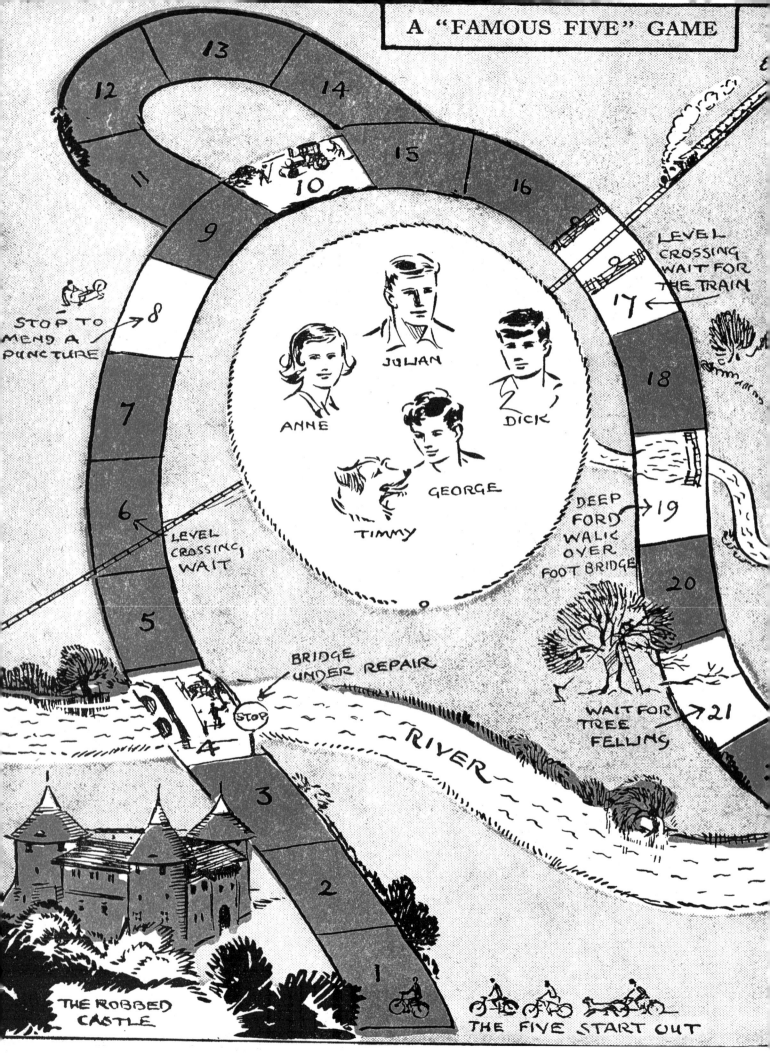

A "FAMOUS FIVE" GAME